Phantom

Susan Kay

Phantom

Delacorte Press

Published by
Delacorte Press
Bantam Doubleday Dell Publishing Group, Inc.
666 Fifth Avenue
New York, New York 10103

Library of Congress Cataloging in Publication Data
Kay, Susan.
Phantom / Susan Kay.
p.   cm.
ISBN 0-385-30296-7
I. Title.
PR6061.A937P48   1991
823'.914—dc20   90-40256   CIP

Manufactured in the United States of America

April 1991

10 9 8 7 6 5 4 3 2 1

For Norman and Judy, who believed.

ACKNOWLEDGMENT

I would like to thank Judy Burns Jacobson for unearthing vital research material on the building of the Paris Opera House; and for giving so generously of her time and insight during the production of this book.

None of us can choose where we will love. . . .
—Erik

Madeleine
1831-1840

I t was a breech birth; and so, right up to the very last moment of innocent ignorance, I remained aware of the midwife's boisterous, bawdy encouragement.

"Just the head now, my dear . . . almost there . . . your son is almost born. But now we must take great care. Do exactly what I say—do you hear me, madame?—exactly!"

I nodded and drew a panting breath, clinging to the towel that had been hung on the wooden bedstead behind my head. The candlelight threw huge shadows up to the ceiling, strange, leering shapes that were oddly threatening to me in the mindless delirium of pain. In that last, lonely moment of thrusting anguish it seemed to me that there was no one left alive in the world but me; that I would be shut up for all eternity in this bleak prison of pain.

There was a great bursting, tearing sensation and then peace . . . and silence; the breathless hush of stunned disbelief. I opened my eyes to see the midwife's face—rosy with exertion only moments before—slowly draining of color; and my housemaid, Simonette, backing away from the bed, with one hand pressed against her mouth.

I remember thinking: *It must be dead.* But sensing even in that confused split second before I knew the truth that it was worse than that . . . much worse.

Struggling to sit up against the damp pillow, I looked down at the bloody sheets beneath me and saw what they had seen.

I did not scream; none of us screamed. Not even when we saw it make a feeble movement and we realized that it wasn't dead. The sight of the thing that lay upon the sheet was so unbelievable that it denied all power of movement to the vocal cords. We only stared, the three of us, as though we expected our combined dumbstruck horror to melt this harrowing abomination back into the realm of nightmare where it surely belonged.

The midwife was the first to recover from her paralysis, swooping forward to cut the cord with a hand that shook so badly, she could hardly hold the scissors.

"God have mercy!" she muttered, crossing herself instinctively. "Christ have mercy!"

I watched with numb detached calm as she rolled the creature in a shawl and dropped it into the cradle that lay beside the bed.

"Run and fetch Father Mansart," she told Simonette in a trembling voice. "Tell him he had better come here at once."

Simonette wrenched open the door and fled down the unlit staircase without a backward glance at me. She was the last servant to live under my roof. I never saw her again after that terrible night, for she never came back even to collect her belongings from the attic bedroom. When Father Mansart came, he came alone.

The midwife was waiting for him at the door. She had done all that her duty required of her and now she was impatient to be gone and forget the part she had played in this bad dream; impatient enough, I observed detachedly, to have overlooked the matter of payment.

"Where's the girl?" she demanded with immediate displeasure. "The maid, Father . . . is she not with you?"

Father Mansart shook his graying head.

"The little mademoiselle refused to accompany me here. She was quite out of her senses with fright and I could not persuade her otherwise."

"Well . . . that doesn't surprise me," said the midwife darkly. "Did she tell you that the child is a monster? In all my years I've never known anything like this . . . and I've seen some sights, as you well know, Father. But it doesn't look very strong, I suppose that's a mercy. . . ."

I listened incredulously. They were talking as though I weren't there, as though this dreadful thing had rendered me some kind of deaf and mindless idiot who had forfeited all right to human dignity.

Like the creature in the cradle I had become an object of horrified discussion; I was no longer a *person.* . . .

The midwife shrugged herself into her shawl and picked up her basket.

"I daresay it'll die. They usually do, thank God. And it's not made a cry, that's always a good hopeful sign. . . . No doubt it'll be gone by morning. But at any rate it's none of my business now, I've done my part. If you'll excuse me, Father, I must be getting along. I promised to look in on another confinement. Madame Lescot—her third, you know. . . ."

The midwife's voice trailed away as she disappeared out into the darkness on the landing. Father Mansart closed the door behind her, put his lantern down on the chest of drawers, and laid his wet cloak across a chair to dry.

He had a comfortable, well-lived-in face, tanned and leathery from walking in all weathers; I suppose he must have been about fifty. I knew that he had seen many terrible things in the course of his long ministry; nevertheless I saw him recoil involuntarily with shock when he looked into the cradle. One hand tightened on the crucifix around his neck while the other hastily made the sign of the cross. He knelt in prayer for a moment before coming to stand by the side of my bed.

"My dear child!" he said compassionately. "Do not be deceived into believing that the Lord has abandoned you. Such tragedies as this are beyond all mortal understanding, but I ask you to remember that God does not create without purpose."

I shivered. "It's still alive . . . isn't it?"

He nodded, biting his full underlip and glancing sadly at the cradle.

"Father"—I hesitated fearfully, trying to summon the courage to continue—"if I don't touch it . . . if I don't feed it . . ."

He shook his head grimly. "The position of our Church is quite clear on such issues, Madeleine. What you are suggesting is murder."

"But surely in this case it would be a kindness."

"It would be a sin," he said severely, "a mortal sin! I urge you to put all thoughts of such wickedness from your mind. It is your duty to succor a human soul. You must nourish and care for this child as you would any other."

I turned my head away on the pillow. I wanted to say that even God could make mistakes, but even in the depths of my despair I could not quite find the courage to voice such blasphemy.

How could this horrible abomination be human? It was as alien to me as a reptile—ugly, repulsive, and unwanted. What right had any priest to insist that it should live? Was this God's mercy . . . God's infinite wisdom?

Tears of exhaustion and outraged misery began to steal down my taut face as I stared at the striped wallpaper before my eyes. For three months I had struggled through an unending maze of tragedy, following the one candle that burned steadily just beyond my reach and beckoned me on—the small, flickering light of hope contained in the promise of new life.

Now that that candle had been extinguished there was only darkness; darkness in the bottomless, smooth-sided abyss of the deepest pit in hell. For the first time in my life I was alone. No one was going to shield me from this burden.

"I think it would be wise if I baptized the child at once," said Father Mansart grimly. "Perhaps you would like to give me a name."

I watched the priest move slowly around the room, a tall shadow in his black habit, collecting my porcelain washbasin and blessing the water within. I had meant to call a son Charles, after my dead husband, but that was impossible now, the very idea quite obscene.

A name . . . I must decide upon a name!

A sense of unreality had descended upon me once more, a numb, unthinking stupor that seemed to paralyze my brain. I could think of nothing and at last, in despair, I told the priest to name the child after himself. He looked at me for a long moment, but he made no comment, no protest, as he reached down into the cradle.

"I baptize thee Erik," he said slowly, "in the name of the Father and of the Son and of the Holy Spirit."

Then he leaned forward and placed the muffled bundle in my arms with a determination I dared not fight.

"This is your son," he said simply. "Learn to love him as God does."

Collecting his lantern and his cloak, he turned to leave me and presently I heard the old stairs creaking beneath his heavy tread, the front door closing behind him.

I was alone with the monster that Charles and I had created out of love.

Never in my life had I experienced such fear, such utter misery, as I did in that first moment when I held my son in my arms. I realized that this creature—*this thing!*—was totally dependent on me. If I left it to starve or freeze to death it was my soul that would burn for all eternity. I was a practicing Catholic and I believed only too seriously in the existence of hell's flames.

Fearfully, with a trembling hand, I parted the shawl that covered the child's face. I had seen deformities before—who has not?—but nothing like this. The entire skull was exposed beneath a thin, transparent membrane grotesquely riddled with little blue pulsing veins. Sunken, mismatched eyes and grossly malformed lips, a horrible gaping hole where the nose should have been.

My body, like some imperfectly working potter's wheel, had thrown out this pitiable creature. He looked like something that had been dead a long time. All I wanted to do was bury him and run.

Dimly, through my revulsion and terror, I became aware that he was watching me. The misallied eyes, fixed intently and wonderingly upon mine, were curiously sentient and seemed to study me with pity, almost as though he knew and understood my horror. I had never seen such awareness, such powerful consciousness, in the eyes of any newborn child and I found myself returning his stare, grimly fascinated, like a victim mesmerized by a rattlesnake.

And then he cried!

I have no words to describe the first sound of his voice and the extraordinary response it evoked in me. I had always considered the cry of the newborn to be utterly sexless—piercing, irritating, curiously unattractive. But his voice was a strange music that brought tears rushing to my eyes, softly seducing my body so that my breasts ached with a primitive and overwhelming urge to hold him close. I was powerless to resist his instinctive plea for survival.

But the moment his flesh touched mine and there was silence, the spell was broken; panic and revulsion seized me.

I dashed him from my breast as though he were some disgusting insect sucking my blood; I flung him down, without caring where he fell, and escaped to the farthest corner of the room. And there I cowered like a hunted animal, with my chin pressed tightly against my knees and my arms wrapped around my head.

I wanted to die.

I wanted us both to die.

If he had cried again in that moment I know I would have killed him—first him and then myself.

But he was silent.

Perhaps he was already dead.

Deeper and deeper into the shelter of my own body I huddled, rocking to and fro like some poor, unhinged creature in an asylum, burrowing away from a burden I could not face.

Life had been so beautiful until this last summer; too easy, too full of pleasure. Nothing in its brief, cosseted length had prepared me for the tragedies that had rained relentlessly upon me since my marriage to Charles.

Nothing had prepared me for Erik!

he only child of elderly, doting parents, I had been a little princess, the center of every stage on which I performed. My father was an architect in Rouen, a successful but eminently whimsical man who loved music and was delighted by the aptitude I showed for that art. From an early age I was regularly trotted out in company to display my voice and my moderate skills on the violin and piano; and though Mama sent me to the Ursuline convent in Rouen for the sake of my soul, Papa's sights were set on more worldly ends. Singing lessons were arranged, to the disgust of the nuns, who considered a girl's voice to be a source of vanity and affectation, and every week I escaped to the professor who had been told to prepare me for the stage of the Parisian opera house. My voice was good, but I never discovered whether I had the talent or self-discipline to conquer Paris. When I was seventeen, I accompanied my father to a site meeting with a client in the Rue de Lecat; and it was there that I met Charles and simultaneously abandoned all thought of a glorious career on the stage.

Fifteen years older than myself, Charles was a master mason whose work my father sincerely admired. Papa always said it was a privilege to place plans in the hands of a man who had such a deep, instinctive feel for the artistry of building, a perfectionist who was never satisfied with second best. Between Charles and my father the average client with an eye to economy had a hard time of it. Perhaps it was because they were so totally in accord professionally that it seemed natural for Papa to welcome Charles into the family once I had made my preference clear. Perhaps he remembered himself as the struggling young architect, with no commissions, who had been obliged to fight Mama's family all those years ago. Perhaps he was simply determined —as he had been throughout my cosseted existence—that nothing should mar the happiness of his only child. If he was disappointed at my decision to throw away a promising future as a prima donna, he said nothing.

As for Mama—she was English, with all the characteristics that that word implies. I think she would rather have seen me respectably —if rather ingloriously—married, than on any Parisian stage.

Charles and I went to London for the honeymoon, at Papa's expense, armed with a list of architectural sites that "must be seen." We didn't see much. It was November, the most dismal of all English months, and for most of our three-week stay the city was shrouded in a thick yellow fog. It was a good excuse to stay inside, exploring the wonders of God's architecture, in our neat, discreet hotel bedroom in Kensington.

On the last day of our visit the sun streamed mercilessly through a chink in the heavy curtains and lured us guiltily from the sheets. We couldn't go home without seeing Hampton Court—Papa would never forgive us!

It was early evening when the landau deposited us outside the hotel steps. While Charles struggled with the unfamiliar coinage and an unhelpful cabdriver, I went into the foyer to collect our key.

"A letter for you, madam," said the bellboy, and I took the envelope absently, tucking it into my muff as I turned to watch Charles enter the foyer.

I still caught my breath at the sight of him, just as I had that first day in Rouen; he was so tall and so unashamedly good looking. And when he saw the key in my hand, his smile mirrored my thought.

We ran up the wide, richly carpeted staircase, laughing and bumping heedlessly into two elderly ladies who were descending with all due English dignity.

"French!" I heard one of them say disdainfully. "What else can you expect?"

Charles and I only laughed even louder. Charles said we should pity the English really. They were all as stiff and cold as Gothic gargoyles —none of them knew what love meant.

Two hours later, as I lay in Charles's arms like a contented, lazy cat, I suddenly remembered the letter in my muff. . . .

It was only after our hasty return to France that I came to realize I had conceived my first child in the same week that both my parents died of cholera.

There was no general epidemic.

An old acquaintance of my father's, visiting from Paris, was taken ill in the course of a convivial evening at my parents' house. Papa would not hear of a friend returning home to be nursed by servants; and that natural, generous hospitality of his killed the entire household.

I could not settle in Rouen after the tragedy. The city had become for me a vast architectural museum, a mausoleum dedicated to my spoiled and happy childhood. The baroque chapel of the old Jesuit college, the Place St. Vivien, the elegant Rue St. Patrice with its splendid seventeenth- and eighteenth-century houses hidden behind heavy portes cochères . . . No, I could not continue to live in a city where every street corner and every fine old building evoked a memory that gave me pain.

It was a month before Charles would permit me to enter my father's house for fear of contagion. We were by then quite certain that I was pregnant and Charles was fiercely and absurdly protective, determined that nothing should place his precious wife and child at risk. He was behaving as though I were the first woman in the world to have a child and his overanxious caution made me curious, slightly amused, and just a little afraid that if it was a girl I should be jealous.

"You shouldn't be so anxious, Charles. Women have children all the time."

"I just want you to take care," he said solemnly. "I don't want anything to go wrong."

I put a hand on his sleeve, oddly disturbed by his intensity. My father's death had evidently affected him far more deeply than I had thought and I was ashamed that, in the selfishness of my own distress, I had failed to realize how he, too, was mourning the loss of a good friend.

"This baby is very important to you, isn't it?" I said slowly. "Anyone would think you were afraid we won't have any more."

He laughed and drew me into the shelter of his arm.

"Of course we'll have more. But there's something very special about the firstborn, don't you feel that, Madeleine? Creating for the first time in your own image. It makes me feel like God."

"Oh, you!" I said affectionately. "You are an artist! Papa always said you should have been a sculptor as well as a master mason."

"I thought of it," he admitted, "quite seriously, in fact, as a boy."

"What stopped you?" I demanded curiously.

"The idea of dying in poverty." He grinned. "Now, be a good girl and come to bed. It's late and my son must have his rest."

While Charles slept I lay awake, seeing the picture that he had painted for me of this very special child. I imagined the sign of the cross made with holy water on the smooth, rounded forehead of a flawless baby . . . the first fashioning of our great love. Charles had promised me perfection and I believed in his vision without question; I had no doubts, none of the normal anxieties that beset an expectant mother. Within the magic circle of our love our happiness seemed safe and assured, protected by foundations that could never be shaken by misfortune.

Everything came to me, of course . . . the lovely old seventeenth-century house in the Rue St. Patrice and the income from my father's many sensible investments.

"You're a woman of independent means," Charles told me pensively, and I sensed his vague unease. He didn't want anyone saying he had only married me for my money. For the first time I became aware of the inner conflicts any man faces when he marries above his station and I began to be increasingly convinced that we should leave Rouen and start afresh elsewhere.

I went through Papa's house, systematically itemizing those sentimental relics of my childhood with which I knew I could not bear to part—Mama's jewelry, Papa's architectural library and files, the small violin on which I had screeched my first ungodly notes. And all the time stilted letters of condolence continued to arrive, expressing regret and respect in the appropriate proportions. Then one morning I opened a letter from Marie. . . .

Marie Perrault, companion of my tedious captivity in the convent, had been my bridal attendant—possibly the plainest bridesmaid that ever was. Even Mama had raised an eyebrow at my choice. I suppose Marie had always been an unlikely friend for me. Even in the convent I had had my following, my own particular set who hung upon my every word and copied my hairstyle and the subtle little touches I added to my dresses. And certainly in looks Marie had nothing to recommend her. She was excessively plain, whey faced and pinched beneath a shock of unfashionable carrot-colored hair, and she had about her that air of timidity which automatically attracts every bully in the vicinity. She must have been about ten when I first took her under the mantle of my protection. The rest of my friends found her boring, and had I given the signal, they would gladly have made her life a misery with the age-old ritual of schoolyard torment. But I did not give it. I allowed Marie to trot after me, like some faithful spaniel, and told the others that I found her useful—which was true enough and yet not the whole truth. I was the prettiest girl in the convent and the most influential by far; my word was law. And Marie remained my friend long after the rest had drifted away to homes scattered throughout Normandy, and ceased to write.

The letter I opened now was entirely Marie—full of clumsy gaffes and muddled sentiments that were written straight from the heart, but probably better left unsaid. She begged us to come and stay with her family in St.-Martin-de-Boscherville, and as I pushed the letter across the table to Charles, I heard him groan. I gave him a look and he subsided into silence. We went down to Boscherville at the end of the week.

Charles survived two days of overpowering Perrault hospitality before deciding that a contract required his urgent presence in Rouen. And the same afternoon that he left, Marie and I discovered that the isolated, stone-walled house on the edge of the village was for sale.

Covered with ivy, sprawling, inconvenient to run, its gardens and orchard entirely neglected by a previous elderly occupant . . . I fell in love with it on the spot.

"It's too far from Rouen," said Charles in horror when he returned.

"It's beautiful," I murmured.

"It needs a lot of work."

"I don't care. Oh, Charles, I want that house so much! It's so—so *romantic!*"

He sighed and I noticed the sun picking out the silver threads that were just beginning to sprinkle his jet-black hair.

"Oh, well," he said, with his familiar air of resigned indulgence, "if it's romantic, then I suppose we shall simply have to take it."

And so we came to the sleepy village of Boscherville.

By May the old house had been completely redecorated and furnished in the latest Parisian style.

It was a perfect little palace, awaiting the arrival of my perfect little prince.

The third of May 1831 is a day I will never forget.

It was hot, unseasonably hot for early May, and I lay on the sofa like a beached whale, fanning myself and demanding drinks of lemonade from the housemaid.

I was tired and peevish. My two-year-old spaniel, Sasha, bounded tiresomely around the drawing room, dropping her ball repeatedly at the side of my couch and wagging her tail hopefully.

"It's too hot to go out in the garden," I grumbled. "You'll just have to wait until Marie comes. Oh, Sasha, do go away! Simonette! *Simonette!*"

Simonette appeared in the doorway, adjusting her apron hastily.

"Yes, madame?"

"Take this silly dog outside and don't let her in again until Mademoiselle Perrault comes to take her for a walk."

"Yes, madame."

In the romping chase that ensued, my new table lamp was knocked to the floor, smashing the white glass shade and spilling colza oil on the carpet. My shriek of fury drove both dog and maid from the room. I was on my hands and knees mopping clumsily and ineffectually at the mess when Marie arrived.

"It's ruined!" I sobbed angrily. "My lovely new carpet, it's spoiled!"

"No, it's not," said Marie, in her maddeningly reasonable fashion. "It's only one patch, really. If we put this rug over it, no one will ever know it's there."

"I don't want a rug there!" I said childishly. "It throws the entire room out of balance. I shall have to have a new carpet."

She sat back on her heels in her plain muslin gown and regarded me thoughtfully.

"That's not necessary, you know, Madeleine. If I were you I'd leave it as it is. No one wants to live in a house that's perfect all their lives, least of all a small child."

I glared at her. I was about to tell her that *my* child would never dream of romping around my lovely house, spilling things on my best carpet, when the baby kicked beneath my heart with such violence that I gave a gasp of shock.

"Nobody asked for your opinion, you little beast!" I muttered, half angry, half amused by this startling reminder of his unseen presence.

But Marie did not smile, as I had expected her to. Instead she turned away and looked intensely uncomfortable.

"I don't think you should say a thing like that, Madeleine. Mama says it's terribly unlucky to speak against the unborn."

"Oh, don't be such a goose!" I scoffed. "It can't hear me."

"No," she said uneasily, "but God can."

I laughed at her, all my good humor suddenly restored by her superstitious absurdity.

"God has better things to do than eavesdrop on the faithful," I asserted confidently. "Think of all the really wicked people in the world, all the murderers and the harlots and the heathens. . . ."

The conversation drifted to other matters and by the time Marie left I had quite forgotten my anger. Charles wouldn't mind if I had a new carpet. "Whatever you want, darling," he would say if I asked, "whatever makes you happy." And, gross and uncomfortable as I was, I could probably contrive to struggle into Rouen once more before the birth.

It was growing cooler now, a fresh wind blowing through the open casements. Sasha was permitted back into the room and, worn out with her walk, fell asleep on what was left of my lap. I watched her head vibrating steadily to the rhythm of the baby's vigorous kicks. . . . He was restless tonight, I reflected indulgently. We always spoke of the coming baby as he. Charles had suspended my wedding ring over my abdomen on a piece of cotton thread and insisted I was carrying a boy. I knew how much he wanted a son; a son to follow him as a master craftsman. . . .

Through the half-open door I listened drowsily to the sounds of Simonette preparing supper. I knew that Charles would be late home. He had accepted a lucrative contract for a huge mansion on the outskirts of Rouen and his men were taking advantage of the light evenings. I did not expect him home before dusk.

The hall bracket clock was just striking six, the sun still streaming through the windows and making a lattice-work pattern on the carpet I intended to change, when they carried him home on a makeshift stretcher. . . .

There had been an accident on the building site—a piece of falling masonry. They assured me that it was no one's fault, that no one was to blame, as though they expected that to be some sort of comfort.

The doctor came and, shortly after, the priest.

Suddenly my house was full of people murmuring platitudes about the child, the child I would have to comfort me in my untimely bereavement.

On the evening of the day we buried Charles I lay alone in our bed —our magnificent new bed that had been a wedding gift from my parents—and felt the new life throbbing beneath the swollen drum of my stomach.

I remember that I prayed for a son, a son to remind me of Charles. Well, now I had one. . . .

*   *   *

Hours had passed since his birth; gradually I became aware of a new day dawning outside the uncovered window.

And with the light I heard again the first plaintive notes of that siren cry which wrapped itself around my brain like a lover's caress. I pressed my hands against my ears, but I could not shut it out; and I knew that even if I ran to the farthest corner of the world I could not escape from him. That sound would still be there in my head, driving me mad with grief.

With weary resignation I went back to the bed and covered the hideous little face with a handkerchief. When I could no longer see him, I found I could control my revulsion sufficiently to handle him.

Dragging myself downstairs, I found a little milk in the kitchen and warmed it.

Later, while he slept in a room full of summer sunlight, I sat in a chair feverishly fashioning the first garment he ever wore.

A mask. . . .

Looking back, I don't know how I would have managed without Marie and Father Mansart, for I quickly learned what a slender and ethereal thing popularity is.

My status in the village evaporated overnight. No one came near my house—it was as though they had painted a red cross on my door, as they used to do in the old days to warn passersby that those within were contaminated with the plague. Even in this bright new century, where science makes new leaps with every year that passes, superstitious fears still rule most small rural communities like Boscherville. Hearsay tales are inclined to grow out of all proportion, but in this case imagination and malice would have been hard put to embroider the lurid truth. When I finally ventured out into the village, I found myself shunned like a leper. People walked the other way when they saw me approaching, and when I had passed by, I would be deeply aware of the nudging and cruel gossip that was taking place in my wake. Father Mansart warned me not to take the child out in public; and though he did not say so, I knew it was because he feared for our safety.

Marie came most days, in spite of the displeasure of her parents and the censure of the village. She overcame her own horror and timidity for my sake and taught me the true meaning of friendship; I was now entirely dependent upon her for companionship and comfort.

The expensive cradle lay forlornly in the attic bedroom, whence I had quickly banished it; and for most of the time it was mercifully silent. He never cried unless he was hungry and that, thank God, wasn't very often. It was as though some deep-rooted sense of self-preservation prevented him from seeking any other form of comfort.

I suppose my distaste at handling him must have communicated itself to him from his earliest days, and indeed, he gave me so little trouble in those first months that I was able to shut him out of my mind for hours at a time. I never went near him unless I was forced to; I never smiled at him or played with him; I assumed he would be an idiot.

It was Marie who hung a string of little bells across the cradle, out of pity; and one morning she drew me upstairs, against my will, and made me stand outside the open door.

"Listen!" she said.

I heard the familiar, random tinkling of the bells, the lonely sound of a solitary, neglected baby amusing itself, which I had heard so many times before and from which I now turned in guilty haste.

"I'm baking," I complained uneasily. "The cake will burn."

"Let it!" she said rather shortly. "I want you to hear something . . . listen!"

Surprised by her tone, I did as she asked, and as I listened, I became aware that the bells were not being struck at random, but deliberately, in a repetitive pattern which formed a short phrase.

It had to be a coincidence, a freak chance, but even as I told myself this, the phrase shifted, altered, and settled itself into a new pattern which was repeated, without variation, several times.

"This is no ordinary child," said Marie quietly. "How much longer do you think you can continue to shut him away up here, trying to pretend he doesn't exist?"

I turned and fled downstairs, slamming the kitchen door shut on the sound of the bells which had seemed to follow me.

I had not allowed myself to think beyond the possibility of caring for some mindless animal. My child was a hideous monster and somehow the thought that he might be exceptional in any other way only filled me with terror. If Marie was right, I knew my predicament was going to grow worse.

It was not going to be possible to ignore the mind that was developing rapidly behind the little white kid mask.

One evening, roughly six months after his birth, there was a terrible storm. The wind rattled the glass in the casements and howled down the chimney, making the fire flicker and smoke. Rain pelted madly on the roof, thunder rolled directly overhead, and each flash of lightning lit the entire room for a split second.

I hated to be alone in a storm. I looked for Sasha, who was also terrified of thunder and should, by rights, have been cowering under my skirts by now, but she was not there. The door into the hall was ajar and I assumed she had gone upstairs to hide under the bed.

Suddenly I heard a great crash from the attic bedroom, the sound of something heavy falling to the floor, and I ran up the staircase in alarm.

From the doorway of Erik's room I could see the empty cradle lying on its side . . . and in the center of the room, some distance away, the big spaniel apparently worrying a small, white bundle.

"Stop it, Sasha!" I screamed. "Leave it alone! Sasha! *Sasha!*"

To my astonished relief the dog trotted obediently to my side and sat down, waving her plumed tail back and forth across the bare floorboards.

I hardly dared to look at the little bundle. If she had taken him for a rat I could hardly blame her. . . .

As I steeled myself to go and pick him up I realized, with a shock, that there was no need.

He was coming to me!

I began to back away instinctively onto the landing, but I was unable to take my eyes off the painful, stubborn, shuffling movement with which he was dragging himself across the room. And then, with equal horror, I realized that he was not making for me, but for the dog.

Sasha was watching him warily, her head on one side, her ears pricked with curiosity. When he laid hold of one paw with his sticklike fingers, she growled deep in her throat, but she did not bare her teeth.

I found that I was rooted to the spot, unable to make a move to prevent this from happening. I watched, with frozen fascination, as he pulled himself up into a sitting position, using the animal's fur for leverage, and then stretched out one hand to grope uncertainly toward her face.

"Sasha!" he said, very slowly and distinctly. "Sasha!"

I took hold of the bannister for support; I had to be dreaming this!

"Sasha! Sasha! Sasha!" he repeated steadily. The dog pushed her nose down into the little masked face and I heard the dull thud of his head striking the bare floor when he overbalanced. I cried out sharply, but I was still unable to move.

I watched the dog paw him gently.

And then, for the first time, I heard him laugh.

Three months later he was walking and mimicking my words like a wretched mynah bird.

It was impossible to ignore his presence now—his voice and his interfering hands seemed to be everywhere, and the only respite I knew was in those few hours when he climbed into Sasha's basket and slept curled up beside her. He called me Mama (God knows why, I certainly didn't teach him to!), but I am very much afraid that in those early days he believed the dog was his mother. She seemed to have taken a liking to him, treating him with the sort of rough affection she might have shown a large puppy. Marie told me I should not allow it; she said it wasn't right, that I was raising him to think he was an animal.

"It keeps him quiet for a few hours," I retorted wearily. "If you think you can do any better, you can take him home to your mother!"

That was the end of that conversation!

*   *   *

I tried very hard to be reconciled to the situation, for though I could not express any physical affection, I was determined to have the satisfaction of educating him.

His abnormally accelerated development showed no sign of slowing down. By the age of four he was reading the Bible with beautiful clarity and mastering exercises on the violin and piano that I had not attempted before my eighth year. He climbed like a monkey and there was nothing I could place beyond the reach of his determined hands. He repeatedly dismantled my clocks and threw the most appalling tantrums at his inability to put them back together. He could not bear to be defeated by inanimate objects.

Soon I began to be a little frightened of his awesome progress. I had been uncommonly well educated for a girl—Papa himself had taught me sufficient geometry to comprehend the science on which all architecture is based. But I was beginning to see that Erik would soon be quite beyond me. Figures fascinated him, and from the basic principles I taught him he fashioned calculations that I could not follow, however patiently he explained them to me. He had discovered my father's architectural library and spent many hours poring over the sketches of Laugier and the Abbé Cordemoy, Blondel and Durand. And he drew endlessly, obsessively, on any surface that was available. If I did not keep him continually supplied with paper, I would find his designs on the flyleaf of my father's books, on the reverse side of his plans—even on the wallpaper up the side of the stairs.

When a pair of needlework scissors disappeared from my workbasket I thought nothing of it, until I found an intricate castle lovingly engraved into the polished mahogany surface of my dining-room table. Those scissors did an incredible amount of tasteful wreckage, and though I turned the house upside down and beat him mercilessly in my fury, I was never able to discover where he hid them.

But there were mysterious and inexplicable voids. He seemed incapable of distinguishing right from wrong, and though he could draw like a seasoned artist, he could not—or would not!—write. If I put a pen into his hand and told him to copy out a Hail Mary he became instantly clumsy, as dull and stupid over the simple task as the most backward of children. I could not beat him into submission, though I am ashamed to admit that I often attempted to do so. He had a will of iron, which I could not bend, and a spectacular temper which frequently reduced me to violence. Exhaustion, and fear of doing him a serious injury, made me reserve calligraphy as a penance from which he might be released for good behavior.

But music was the keystone of his extraordinary genius. Music welled up from some bottomless pool within him and flowed like a ceaseless fountain through his fingertips, making an instrument of virtually every object that fell into his inventive hands. He could not sit at the table without unconsciously beating time with his heels against the back of his chair or tapping out a rhythm on his plate with a knife. A slap would check him momentarily, but within a minute his eyes would glaze over as he slipped back into his secret inner world of sound. In the early days, when I sang the old operatic arias to pass the hours of solitude, he would leave whatever he was doing and come to sit by the piano in wondering silence. Shortly before he was five I allowed him to take over the accompaniment for me, and if I failed to master a difficult tonality he would stop playing, point out the offending note, and sing it perfectly pitched with the intimidating, dizzying purity of his faultless top register.

Already he was beginning to make Mozart look like a dull plodder by comparison. But all the time that he sat composing haunting refrains, or playing the piano with a dexterity far beyond his years, I knew that his incredibly fertile mind was plotting fresh, awesome mischief beyond my imagination.

"Where are you going, Mama?"

I paused in the act of fastening my cloak and turned to find him standing in the doorway.

"You know perfectly well where I go every Sunday, Erik. I'm going to Mass with Mademoiselle Perrault and you must stay here until I come back."

He twined his fingers around the handle of the door.

"Why must I always stay here?" he demanded suddenly. "Why can't I come with you and hear the organ and the choir?"

"Because you can't!" I said sharply. I was beginning to wish Father Mansart had never told Erik about the organ and the choir—I had had no peace since his visit last week. "You must stay here in the house where you will be safe." I added.

"Safe from what?" he challenged unexpectedly.

"Safe from—from . . . oh, stop all these silly questions, do you hear? Just do as you're told and stay here. I won't be that long."

I swept out, pushing him before me with one gloved hand and locking the door of my bedroom, as I always did whenever I left him alone. It was the only room in the house that contained a mirror and he was forbidden to go in there; but I did not trust his obedience to last once I was out of his sight. He was insatiably curious.

He followed me down the staircase and sat forlornly on the bottom step, watching me through the mask.

"What is it like in the village?" he asked wistfully. "Is the church very beautiful?"

"No," I lied hastily. "It's very ordinary, quite ugly in fact. It wouldn't interest you at all. And the village is full of people who would be unkind and frighten you."

"May I come with you if I promise not to be frightened?"

"*No!*"

I turned my back on him, to cover my alarm. That threat had never failed to silence him before. I was concerned to find that his obsessive love of music was now strong enough to overcome a fear I had steadily fostered since he was old enough to talk. My instinct was to protect him from a world which would inevitably seek to do him harm. Even Marie and Father Mansart agreed that I must keep him away from people, and total isolation seemed to be the only answer to my dilemma.

I knew that ignorance and superstition would destroy him. Careful as I had been not to parade his presence, my windows were still smashed at regular intervals and more than one ugly, abusive letter had been pushed through my door, advising me to leave Boscherville and take "the monster" with me. It took enormous courage for me to face the grim, unwelcoming silence of the congregation every Sunday, to sit in the rear pew with Marie and hold my head high, pretending not to notice the primitive hostility all around me. Nobody wanted me here, but my presence was a mark of my defiance, a symbol of my refusal to be driven from my home and hounded from one village to the next.

It was also my one escape from a house I thought of increasingly as a prison. My house—that quaint and pretty house of which I had been so proud—was now no more to me than a dungeon in the Bastille. Returning from Mass, the first sight of its ivy clad walls was enough to make my heart sink; but the thought of the child behind its carefully locked doors, waiting patiently and trustingly for my return, always forced my lagging footsteps down the garden path. Lately, as I approached, I had been aware of the white mask pressed against the window of the attic bedroom and I sensed his growing anxiety that one day I would walk out of the house and never come back.

"Don't sit on the stairs!" I said harshly. "Go and study your text for the day and then copy it out."

"I don't want to."

"I am not interested in what you want to do!" I replied coldly. "I expect to find it finished by the time I return."

He was silent as I reached for my purse; then suddenly he announced with decision:

"I'm not going to study my text. I'm going to make it disappear so that you can't find it . . . like the scissors. I can make anything disappear if I want to, Mama . . . even a house!"

He jumped off the stair and ran past me into the drawing room, as though he expected to be hit; and when he had gone, I leaned against the wall, trembling with apprehension. I tried to tell myself that this was just a silly, childish threat, devoid of any meaning other than vain protest. But I could not stop shaking and I found myself unable to step out through the door. I was afraid to go now, afraid to leave him to his strange, unchildish devices. I dared not think by what terrible means he might contrive to make the house disappear!

When I had regained my composure, I took off the cloak and walked into the drawing room. I found him sitting on the rug before the fire with Sasha, staring fixedly at the flickering flames in the hearth.

"I've decided not to go to Mass today," I told him unsteadily.

He turned to look at me and clapped his hands in unveiled satisfaction.

"I knew you would," he said. And laughed.

I had been his jailer; now he was mine. I felt as though I had been sealed up in a tomb to serve the corpse of a child-pharaoh in its afterlife, and I fiercely resented the captivity which he had forced upon me. Love, hatred, pity, and fear circled around me like carrion crows, spinning me wildly from one peak of emotion to another, until I hardly knew myself anymore when I looked into the solitary mirror that adorned my bedroom. I was thin and haggard, with a strange wild-eyed look, and though the contours of my beauty remained, I looked ten, fifteen years older than my twenty-three summers. It was as though all the harshness and cruelty which I was driven to show him etched itself, line by line, upon my face, a grim testimony to the endless circle of violence which characterized our life together.

It was during that year that he began to explore the mysterious power of his voice. Sometimes, almost without my noticing, he would begin to sing softly, and the hypnotic sweetness would lure me from my tasks and draw me toward him, as though by an unseen chain. It was a game he played, and I came to fear it more than any other manifestation of his curious genius. I put away the operatic scores which we had studied together and refused to teach him anymore, for I had begun to be afraid of the manner in which his voice was manipulating me. It seemed evil somehow, almost . . . incestuous.

Father Mansart now came regularly to celebrate Mass in my drawing room and spare me the ordeal of appearing every Sunday in church. And that first time he heard the child sing, I saw his eyes fill with tears.

"If it were not blasphemy to think such a thing," he muttered slowly, "I would have said I had heard the voice of God here in this very room."

In the tense, resonating silence that descended, I felt my own heartbeat thundering in my throat. I saw the eyes behind the mask meet mine and their glance was triumphant, somehow masterful. He had heard, and worse, he had understood. I dared not think what he might begin to fashion from that knowledge.

I shivered as Father Mansart beckoned him forward and told him solemnly that he possessed a rare and wonderful gift. I wanted to scream, but I was silent. I knew the damage was already done.

They walked together to the piano, the priest's hand resting on the child's bony shoulder.

"I should like to hear you sing the Kyrie, Erik. You know the text, I believe."

"Yes, Father."

How meek he sounded, how innocent and vulnerable he looked, standing beside the heavily built priest. For a moment I doubted my own senses; I wondered if I was feeding on brain-sick fancies brewed by this penal solitude.

Why had I come to fear the extraordinary bell-like purity of his childish treble?

"Kyrie eleison . . . Christe eleison."

Lord have mercy upon us . . . Christ have mercy upon us.

Three times he sang the invocations to heaven, and with each phrase my will receded before a wave of aching longing that made me long to reach out and touch. Whatever spiritual ecstasy Father Mansart derived from those throbbing notes, my response was utterly and unequivocally physical.

The words were for God; but the voice, the exquisite, irresistible voice, was for me and it pulled like a magnet somewhere deep and unseen inside my body.

Before the next phrase took breath, I had slammed the lid down on the piano with a violence that narrowly missed trapping the priest's fingers. The sudden appalled silence was broken only by my hysterical sobbing. Father Mansart looked at me in amazement, but in Erik's eyes I saw fear and great misery.

"You are overwrought," said the priest briskly, as he pressed me into a chair. "It is understandable. Great beauty is often perceived by human senses as pain."

I shuddered. "He is not to sing again, Father. . . . I will not permit it."

"My dear child, I can't think that you mean that. Forbidding expression to such a gift would be positively unkind."

I sat upright in the chair, staring beyond the priest to the child who now wept silently beside the piano.

"His voice is a sin," I said grimly. "A mortal sin. No woman who hears it will ever die in a state of grace."

As Father Mansart recoiled from me in horror, one hand strayed instinctively toward his crucifix, while the other gestured abruptly for Erik to leave the room. When we were alone, he looked down on me with an odd mixture of pity and distaste.

"I think you have been too much alone with your burdens," he said quietly.

I bit my lip and looked away from him.

"You think I'm mad."

"By no means," he replied hurriedly, "but certainly it would seem that your judgment has been affected by the strain of your solitude. Whatever you believe you hear is only the voice of your own confusion. You must try to remember that he is just a young child."

I got up and went to the bureau which stood in the corner of the room. A shower of papers tumbled out when I opened the glass door, and from the pile at my feet I snatched up a handful of musical scores and architectural sketches and pushed them into the priest's hand.

"Is this the work of a child?" I demanded coldly.

He took the papers to the light and examined them carefully.

"I would not have believed it possible for a child of his age to copy with such astonishing precision," he said after a moment.

"They're not copies," I said slowly. "They're originals."

He turned to protest, but was silenced by my expression. Placing the papers on the table, he sat down in a chair and stared at me in awe as I stood clasping my hands around my arms and shivering.

"It frightens me," I whispered. "Too much, too soon . . . it isn't natural. I can't believe such gifts are heaven sent."

The priest shook his head gravely.

"Doubt is the devil's instrument, Madeleine. You must close your mind to it and pray for the strength to guide the child's soul to God."

As he leaned forward to take my hand I realized that he was trembling.

"I have been remiss in my calling," he said feverishly. "I will come as often as my duties permit to instruct him in the doctrine of our Church. The boy must be taught very quickly to accept the will of God without question. It is extremely important that genius of this stature is never permitted to stray from the teachings of our Lord."

I said nothing. The priest's intense uneasiness was merely a grim echo of my own growing certainty that the forces of evil were steadily closing in around my unhappy child.

I felt desperately in need of the guidance of the Church, but the inner light of conviction was no longer there. The harder I prayed, the less hope I had of being heard. My crucifix was merely a cunningly carved piece of wood, my rosary just a meaningless string of beads. My faith had weakened to the point where I allowed myself to be seduced by a sung Mass rendered shamelessly and sensually beautiful. I had sunk to a wickedness that I dared not even confess.

"Tell me what to do," I said in despair. "Show me how to keep him from evil."

The fire fell into ashes, and as we talked long into the night the priest warned me very seriously against any attempt to muzzle Erik's unique talents.

"A volcano must have its natural outlet," he said mysteriously, "it must not be driven in upon itself. If you feel that you can no longer train his voice, then you must permit me to do so. Let me teach him as though he were any other chorister in my choir. I will steep him in the music of God and the ways of the Lord, and in time heaven will grant you only pleasure from his voice."

I stared at the sad, gray remnants of the dead fire.

How could I tell him it was the pleasure that I feared?

He was five when we had our confrontation over the mask. Until that terrible summer evening he wore it with unquestioning obedience, removing it only to sleep and never setting foot beyond the confines of the attic bedroom without it. So fiercely unbending was my regime that he would no more have considered appearing without it than he would have considered appearing naked—at least that is what I thought until that night.

It was the evening of his fifth birthday and I was expecting Marie for supper. I hadn't invited her. With her stubborn grain of well-meaning she had issued an ultimatum, insisting that I celebrate an event which until now I had contrived to ignore.

"You can't continue to let the occasion pass unmarked," she told me with a curious finality that brooked no opposition. "I shall bring him a present and we shall all take supper together in a civilized manner."

I spent the day in the kitchen, with the door closed, contriving to keep myself busy so that I need not be reminded of the reason for this grim farce. I might have been preparing to feed the entire village. Batches of cakes and tarts issued in an insane procession from my oven, but still I went on mixing and stirring in the still, stifling heat, like a woman possessed. And all the time I worked I was aware of the piano playing softly in the drawing room. He did not come pestering, like a normal child, begging to lick the spoon or steal a cake with the healthy impatience of his age. His complete indifference to food was merely another source of conflict between us.

At length, when I went in and told him to go upstairs and put on his best clothes, he turned on the piano stool to look at me with surprise.

"It isn't Sunday . . . is Father Mansart coming to say Mass again?"

"No," I replied, wiping my hands on my apron, and not looking at him directly. "It's your birthday."

He stared at me blankly and I felt a perfectly unreasonable irritation rising inside at the shameful necessity of explaining this basic phenomenon.

"The anniversary of your birth," I said shortly. "You were born five years ago today and the event should be celebrated."

"Like a requiem?"

For a second I wondered if he was mocking me, but the eyes fixed on mine were entirely innocent and puzzled.

"Not exactly," I said with difficulty.

"Then there won't be a Dies Irae?" I heard the sudden disappointment in his voice. "Or an Agnus Dei?"

"No . . . but there will be a special supper."

I saw his interest shrivel and his glance wander back to the score on which he had been working.

"And a present," I found myself adding suddenly. "Mademoiselle Perrault is bringing you a present, Erik. I expect you to remember your manners and thank her nicely."

He turned to look at me curiously and for a horrible moment I thought I was going to be obliged to explain that too. But he said no more, only continued to gaze at me thoughtfully.

"Go upstairs and get changed while I set the table," I told him hastily.

As I pulled a tablecloth from the drawer, I was aware that he had made no effort to move.

"Mama."

"What is it now?" I demanded irritably.

"Will you give me a present too?"

I put the napkins out on the table with a trembling hand.

"Of course," I replied mechanically. "Is there something particular that you want?"

He came to stand beside me and something about his taut silence made me suddenly very uneasy. I sensed that he was afraid of my refusal, so no doubt whatever it was he wanted was going to be highly expensive.

"May I have anything I want?" he asked uncertainly.

"Within reason."

"May I have two of them?"

"Why should you need two?" I inquired warily.

"So that I can save one for when the other is used up."

I began to relax. This didn't sound very alarming . . . nothing more extravagant than a ream of good quality paper, by the sound of it. Or perhaps a box of sweets. . . .

"What is it you want?" I demanded with sudden confidence.

Silence.

I watched him playing with the napkins.

"Erik, I've had quite enough of this silly game now. If you don't tell me what you want straightaway, you will have nothing at all."

He jumped at the sharpness of my tone and began to twist a napkin between his thin fingers.

"I want—I want two . . ." He stopped and put his hands on the table, as though to steady himself.

"For God's sake!" I snapped. "Two what?"

He looked up at me.

"Kisses," he whispered tremulously. "One now and one to save."

I stared at him in horror and without any warning burst into uncontrollable tears and sank down at the table.

"You must not ask that." I sobbed. "You must never, never ask that again . . . do you understand me, Erik . . . never!"

He shrank from my noisy grief in horror and backed away to the door.

"Why are you crying?" he stammered.

I made a mighty effort to control myself.

"I'm not . . . crying." I gasped.

"Yes, you are!" he shouted in a voice that was suddenly ugly with rage. "You're crying and you won't give me my birthday present. You made me ask—you *made* me ask—and then you said no. Well, I don't want a birthday. . . . I don't like birthdays. . . . I hate them!"

The door slammed behind him and a moment later I heard the echoing bang from upstairs.

I sat where he had left me, staring at the napkin he had thrown on the floor.

When at last I stood up wearily, it was to see Marie walking purposefully up the garden path, with a parcel under her arm.

As we sat down together at the table I was dreadfully aware of the empty place setting.

"Where is he?" asked Marie, broaching the subject that had been between us since her arrival.

"In his room," I said grimly. "He won't come out. . . . I've called him several times, but you know what he's like. There is nothing to be done with him when he flies into one of his tantrums."

Marie looked at the parcel she had placed on the chiffonier.

"Does he know it's his birthday?"

"Of course he knows!" I said angrily.

Lifting the lid off the tureen, I began to ladle soup a little wildly into her bowl, trying desperately to recapture the determined, busy mania which kept my terrible thoughts at bay. As long as my hands were moving, my mind remained blissfully numb and I could avoid facing my own wicked inadequacy as a mother. A mother who could not bring herself to kiss her only child; not even on his birthday; not even when he begged. The tragic dignity of his request had unnerved me so much that my hands were still shaking. I spilled soup on the cream lace of the tablecloth and mopped at it with a muttered curse.

The door behind me opened and I stood rigid, watching Marie's face turn white and her hand fly instinctively to her mouth. The horror in her eyes lasted for only a split second before she regained her composure sufficiently to force her slack lips into a strained smile.

"Good evening, Erik, dear . . . how nice you look in that new suit. Come and sit beside me and have your supper. Then afterward we shall open your present."

When I turned and saw him standing there in the open doorway, without the mask, my heart seemed to stop dead in my breast. He had done this for spite; he had done this to punish and humiliate me. . . .

"How dare you!" I spat. "How dare you do this, you wicked child!"

"Madeleine . . ." Marie half rose in her chair, one hand out-stretched to me in a nervous gesture of appeal. "It really doesn't mat-ter—"

"Be silent!" I snapped. "I will deal with this without your interfer-ence. Erik! Go back to your room and put on the mask. If you ever do this again I shall whip you for it."

He shivered and the grotesquely malformed lips puckered, as though he was about to cry, but still he stood there stubbornly, both hands clenched into fists of defiance.

"I don't like the mask," he muttered. "It's hot and it hurts me. It makes sore places."

I could see those places now. Beneath the hollow sockets of his eyes the livid flesh, thin as parchment, had been rubbed raw by the con-stant pressure of a mask which was evidently too tight. Because I did not look at him more closely than I had to, I had failed to notice how much he had grown.

"Go to your room," I repeated unsteadily. "I shall make a new mask after supper, and you will not come down without it again. Do you hear me, Erik? Never!"

"Why?" he demanded sullenly. "Why must I always wear the mask? No one else has to."

A red mist of rage swam before my eyes, an explosion of fury that blew the last shreds of my self-control to pieces. I flew at him and began to shake him so savagely that I heard his teeth rattle.

"Madeleine!" sobbed Marie helplessly. "Madeleine, for pity's sake—"

"He wants to know why!" I screamed at her. "Then he shall know . . . by God, he shall know!"

I dug my nails into the thin material of his shirt and dragged him from the room, up the stairs, before the only mirror in the house.

"Look at yourself!" I spat. "Look at yourself in the mirror and see why you must wear a mask. *Look!*"

He stared at the glass with such dumb, disbelieving horror that all the fury shriveled and died within me. And then, before I could stop him, he screamed and flung himself at the mirror, pummeling the glass with his clenched fists in a mad frenzy of terror.

The glass shattered. Shards flew in all directions, embedding themselves in his wrists and fingers, so that suddenly he was bleeding from dozens of lacerations. But still he went on screaming and pounding the fractured mirror with bloody hands; and when I tried to restrain him he bit me—he bit me like a wild animal that was out of its mind with fear.

A hand fell on my arm. Marie's voice, oddly cold and determined, told me to go downstairs and find bandages. When I returned, she had coaxed him from the debris of smashed glass and was picking the slivers from his fingers with a pair of tweezers. I could not watch. . . .

I waited for her in the drawing room, but she did not come back down again. I assumed she had put him to bed and was sitting with him; I did not dare to go upstairs and see. Worming my way into the farthest corner of the sofa, I spent the rest of the night stitching steadily at a new mask and staring into the empty hearth.

Shortly before dawn, when he woke screaming from the first of what proved to be a long succession of nightmares, she came into the room with a candle in her hand, looking gray and drained . . . and angry.

"He's asking for you," she said grimly. "God knows why, but it's you he wants. Go upstairs and comfort him."

She stood in front of me like an avenging angel and I shrank from her strangely uncompromising figure.

"I can't," I whispered. "I can't go to him."

Without warning she suddenly leaned forward and dealt me a resounding slap across the cheek.

"Get up!" she stormed. "Get up, you spoiled, sniveling brat! All your life you've been spoiled . . . by your parents, by Charles, by me . . . everyone pandering to Madeleine, dear, pretty Madeleine. Well, it's not enough simply to be pretty, do you hear me, Madeleine? It doesn't excuse you from human obligations. It doesn't permit you to poison a child's mind and cripple his soul. You should hang for what you have done to him since he was born . . . you should burn!"

She struck me again and then turned away, sobbing hopelessly and sinking into the chair beside the hearth. And shocked as I was, I found myself remembering the day I had found her in the dormitory at the convent, standing on the bed to avoid the huge spider that sat peaceably in her path to the door.

"Get rid of it, but don't hurt it," she had begged me with white-faced intensity. "It can't help being ugly."

I had dropped a book on the spider, in my brisk, heartless manner, and squashed it nicely. She had refused to speak to me for days after. . . .

I could not get that picture out of my head, as I dragged myself up the staircase, with one hand against my burning cheek. I could not forget that mangled spider. . . .

The floorboards creaked beneath my feet and I heard renewed terror in Erik's cry.

"Mama? Mama?"

"Hush," I murmured. "It's me, Erik. . . . Hush, now."

I heard him sigh with relief as I walked into the room. One small bandaged hand groped briefly in my direction, then subsided wearily back on the coverlet.

"I don't feel well," he complained fretfully.

"I know." I sat stiffly on the edge of my bed, thinking how small he looked in its great expanse, how small and how helpless. "I'm sorry. Go back to sleep now and you'll feel better in the morning."

He clutched at the coverlet in alarm.

"I don't want to go to sleep," he panted. "If I go to sleep it will come back . . . the face! The face will come back!"

I closed my eyes and swallowed hard over the lump which seemed to be blocking my air passage.

"Erik," I said helplessly, "you must try to forget about the face now."

"I can't forget it," he whispered. "It was there in the mirror and it frightened me. Did you see it, Mama, did you see it too?"

"Erik, the face will never hurt you."

"I don't want it to come back!" He sobbed wildly. "I want you to make it go away forever!"

I took a deep breath and looked down on the little corpse face against the pillow. The deep-socketed eyes were staring desperately into mine, seeking the reassurance that I alone could give. And I knew then that, in spite of his rapidly burgeoning genius, he was still too young to bear the reality of this burden.

"The mask will make the face go away," I said, as gently as I could. "As long as you wear it, you will never see the face anymore."

"Is the mask magic?" he demanded with sudden, passionate interest.

"Yes." I bowed my head, so that our eyes no longer met. "I made it magic to keep you safe. The mask is your friend, Erik. As long as you wear it, no mirror can ever show you the face again."

He was silent then, and when I showed him the new mask he accepted it without question and put it on hastily with his clumsy, bandaged fingers. But when I stood up to go, he reacted with panic and clutched at my gown.

"Don't go! Don't leave me here in the dark."

"You are not in the dark," I said patiently. "Look, I have left the candle."

But I knew, as I looked at him, that it would have made no difference if I had left him fifty candles. The darkness he feared was in his own mind and there was no light in the universe powerful enough to take that darkness from him.

With a sigh of resignation I sat back on the bed and began to sing softly; and before I had finished the first verse, he was asleep.

The bandages on his hands and wrists showed white and eerie in the candlelight, as I eased my skirts from his grasp.

I knew that Marie was right.

Physically and mentally, I had scarred him for life.

I became altogether reliant on Father Mansart for the sensible management of Erik's soul and intellect. When he suggested sending examples of the child's designs to the School of Fine Arts in Paris, I made no murmur of protest. I knew that he had an old acquaintance there, a friend who had once shared his education at the Lycée Henri-Quatre and now lectured on architecture. If Professor Guizot could be persuaded to take an interest in my son, I was ready to accept whatever advice or assistance he might be prepared to give me. Erik was already showing signs of boredom, and when he was bored he was unbearably badly behaved and inclined to dangerous mischief. He could not be sent to school and I had little chance of engaging a tutor suitable to his extraordinary needs; Professor Guizot seemed to be my only hope of preserving sanity, and I awaited his visit with a growing degree of desperation.

He did not hurry down to Boscherville and when he finally arrived, I sensed he was extremely skeptical. Like Father Mansart, he was in late middle age, portly and a little pompous in bearing. In spite of his studied courtesy it was quite obvious that he considered he had been dragged from Paris on a wild-goose chase. I believe it was only out of a sense of obligation to an old school friend that he had come at all, and he appeared determined to look upon the occasion as a little holiday. He seemed more interested in discussing the possibility of duck shooting in the neighboring village of Duclair and it was with a feeling of increasing despair that I finally suggested, rather pointedly, that he might like to talk to Erik.

"Ah, yes," he observed with a sudden, quite unmistakable coolness entering his voice, "the child prodigy. By all means show him in, madame. I'm sure I shall not need to detain him overlong."

He measured me with a look of unveiled suspicion and I felt myself flushing hotly beneath his glance. When Erik came into the room, I saw the professor's guarded surprise at the sight of the mask, but he made no comment. He shook hands with the boy and waited patiently for him to climb onto a chair at the dining-room table, before placing a sheet of paper in front of him and asking him to name what he saw.

"It's an arch," said Erik politely, "a basket arch."

"That is correct." I heard mild astonishment in the professor's voice. "Perhaps you would like to show me the keystone."

Erik pointed.

"The abutment and the impost?"

Erik pointed again and I saw the professor frown.

"Center, span, haunch, and crown," he barked in quick succession. "Voussoirs . . . extrados."

Erik's finger moved unerringly across the sheet and I heard him give a faint sigh of boredom at this dull and apparently pointless exercise.

The professor took out a handkerchief and passed it across his mottled forehead; he suddenly looked uncomfortably warm.

"What is the springing line?" he demanded with abrupt aggression.

"The level at which an arch springs from its supports," Erik replied calmly.

The professor sat down unexpectedly and stared at the child.

"Draw me ten different types of arches and name them," he ordered.

Erik glanced across at me impatiently. I knew he was insulted by the simplicity of the task, but when I glared at him he picked up his lead and began to draw with swift obedience.

I withdrew from the room at that point and left them together. Three hours later, when the professor joined me in the drawing room, he was in his shirtsleeves. He look disheveled and exhausted, not at all the worldly, rather supercilious gentleman who had entered my house with such aplomb shortly after noon.

"Madame," he said solemnly, "I must thank you for permitting me the most remarkable experience of my entire academic career."

I had the grace to remain silent, for I sensed he had something difficult to say and that he was not a man to whom gracious apology came easily.

"I have to confess that I came here today fully expecting to expose a rather clever hoax," he admitted uncomfortably. "When I received those designs in Paris my first thought was that my old friend had become the victim of a confidence trick. I'm afraid I suspected you, madame, of taking advantage of a kindly and overcredulous nature for your own spurious purposes."

I stared at him without comment and he spread his thick hands in a gesture of defeated wonder.

"What can I say to you, madame? You must already be well aware that your son's advancement is little short of preternatural."

I clasped my hands together in relief.

"Then you admit his genius?"

He shook his head slowly. "Genius is a human attribute. What I have seen today cannot be defined by any word that is known to me.

His aptitude is quite beyond belief. Madame, I should find it extraordinarily difficult to resist shaping such boundless talent."

I closed my eyes briefly, feeling as though a great weight had been taken from my shoulders. The professor fell silent for a moment, fingering the jacket that lay over one arm, and suddenly all my uneasiness returned.

"I understand from Father Mansart's letter that there is a serious physical deformity that precludes his attendance at any of our usual seats of educational excellence."

"That is correct," I said faintly, aware that my heart had begun to sink.

"Forgive me, madame . . . but would it be improper to inquire . . . ?

"The mask." I bit my lip. "You wish to know the reason for the mask."

"I must admit to finding it somewhat eccentric, even disturbing. In this age of enlightenment one hardly expects to find a child imprisoned in such a fashion. Surely no accident of birth, however severe, can warrant so primitive a measure."

My head jerked up at the ignorant criticism.

"You wish to see?" I demanded coldly. "You are prepared to show no disgust—no fear that would distress him?"

He smiled faintly. "I think you will find that I am a man of the world," he asserted with contemptuous confidence.

"And you will not allow what you see to interfere with your previous judgment."

Now he was quite plainly insulted.

"Madame, we are not living in the sixteenth century! This is an age of empirical and rational judgment."

"So you think," I said.

With a shrug I went to the door, called Erik into the room, and removed the mask.

I have to admit that Professor Guizot was as good as his word. He lost his high, port-wine coloring as the blood fled from his pendulous cheeks, leaving them gray and flaccid; but not by a flicker of his eye or a twitch of his white lips did he betray what he must have felt when he looked at the child's dead face.

When we were alone once more, I indicated the chair by the fire.

"You may sit, if you wish, monsieur."

"Thank you." He sank down by the hearth, arranging his jacket across his knees with a furtive gesture of shaken nerves. "I wonder if I might trouble you for a glass of water?" he said huskily.

I brought him brandy instead and he accepted it without question, gulping at the rich brown liquid with relief before setting it down on the little circular table beside him with a trembling hand.

"I think you will allow the necessity of a mask," I said.

"Yes," he replied, in a tone of deep feeling, "I very much fear that I do."

"And?" I prompted inexorably.

He glanced at the empty brandy glass with regret, but I did not offer him any more; a terrible fear and anger was starting to build inside me.

"I had intended, if you were agreeable, to take the boy into my own household, where I might instruct him at my leisure and make arrangements for him to take his baccalaureate. But now I see such an arrangement would not be possible. My wife, you understand, is of a nervous disposition, and we have inquisitive neighbors. . . . No, I fear it is quite unthinkable. I have my position in society to consider."

I clenched my fists. "You will not teach him."

"Madame . . ." he protested helplessly.

"I knew! I knew you would refuse once you had seen!"

"Madame, I beseech you to be reasonable. This child—"

"Is a monstrous freak!"

"I did not say that," he retorted with dignity, "and I must beseech you not to put words into my mouth. I have every intention of teaching him, I assure you, but it could not be done in Paris where I am so much in the public eye."

"How, then?" I whispered.

He got up from his chair and laid one hand on my arm in a fatherly fashion.

"I do not consider he will require the constant supervision demanded by most students. It will be a question of providing guidelines and stimulation. This case is a challenge, madame, a test of my professional ingenuity. You may rest assured that I shall establish a means of study entirely appropriate to the rather singular circumstances in which we find ourselves."

I felt tears of gratitude welling up into my eyes and turned away hastily before they could fall.

"You are very kind," I murmured.

"My dear lady," he sighed, "I am not kind . . . I am fascinated."

It was as well that I had been left in comfortable circumstances at Charles's death, for otherwise the cost of Erik's unique education would have pauperized us. I was obliged to lease my father's house in Rouen in order to provide him with the tools of his study, but I did not begrudge him the only happiness I was capable of giving. Father Mansart lined every room in the house with bookshelves and month after month the obscure and weighty tomes—some of them rare editions—continued to arrive from Paris, accompanied by instructions and lecture notes from the professor. He came himself, at regular intervals, to spend the entire day closeted with his eager pupil.

"One day," he told me, with barely concealed excitement, "this boy will astonish the world."

When he spoke of the Grand Prix de Rome and of his determination that Erik should be the youngest ever entered for that coveted prize, I made no comment. Nor did I correct the child when he spoke of the five years he expected to spend studying architecture at the Villa Medici, as a pensionnaire of the French Academy. Neither I nor the professor was prepared to admit to ourselves that castles in the air were the only things Erik would ever be given the opportunity to build. Like two ostriches we buried our heads in the sand and refused to look on the ugliness of reality.

I dared not think of the life which lay ahead of Erik beyond the protection of my door, in a world whose sole purpose would be to mock his grotesque appearance. I dared not begin to anticipate the future.

But I could not deny him his dreams.

Even then I was aware that dreams were all he could ever have.

A few months after he had begun to study architecture with Professor Guizot, Erik asked me for a mirror.

I was taken so completely by surprise that I did not know what to say to him. My first instinct was to refuse, but since my instincts where he was concerned were usually wrong, I decided to yield to his bizarre request. Fetching a small hand mirror from the drawer in my room where I was careful to keep it hidden, I gave it to him with uneasy reluctance. He never spoke about "the face," but since I was still regularly awakened by a single scream of terror from his room, I assumed the memory still troubled him.

He took the mirror from me with exaggerated care, as though it were a poisonous snake that might bite, and turned it hastily facedown upon the table. He was panting a little, as though he had been running hard, and I sensed such fear in him that I was sorely tempted to snatch the mirror away. But I resisted the urge and waited.

"If I took off the back," he began hesitantly, "Would I still be able to see . . . *things?*"

"No," I said steadily, "the reverse surface of a mirror reflects no image. You will see nothing at all."

His sigh of relief was painfully and unmistakably audible.

"It has a safe side, then," he muttered to himself. "That's good." He glanced up at me uncertainly. "May I look inside, Mama?"

"If you wish."

I watched him remove the backing from the mirror with dexterous fingers and prize up a loose corner of the tin foil.

"It's only glass underneath!" he cried, in astonishment. "It's only glass and a piece of tin! How could the face get inside?"

I felt cold with misery as he looked up at me. All that brilliance, all that learning, and still the simple truth of this eluded him.

"The face was not inside, Erik, it was outside. A mirror merely reflects an image of any object that is placed in front of it."

"Then how are the images changed into monsters?" he demanded seriously. "Is it magic? Will you show me how it works?"

I felt sobs massing in my throat, and as I took up the mirror and looked into it, I was aware of him straining to see over my shoulder.

"Oh! It's not working!" he exclaimed with disgusted disappointment. "There's nothing there, it must be broken."

I altered the angle of the mirror so that my image swam abruptly into his view and he gave a cry of delight.

"Look!" he shouted in great excitement. "There's two of you! The magic has changed."

"Erik . . . there is no magic. Whenever anyone looks into a mirror they see a reflection of themselves . . . nothing else but themselves. A mirror has no power to show a monster unless that monster stands before it."

"But I saw one!" he insisted angrily. "I *saw* one!"

I laid the mirror face downward on the table in front of him.

"Yes," I said gently, "I know what you saw."

I left him alone then and went into the adjoining room to wait for the first scream of understanding; but it did not come. When I looked in, I saw that he was playing with the mirror, holding it carefully at an angle which did not show him his face. Presently I heard him go upstairs and when I went to retrieve the mirror from the table, I found it gone.

He came down to supper, seeming perfectly calm, and asked if he might have the mirror to keep. Surprised and relieved, I agreed to his request without question, hoping that the trauma of acceptance was now behind us.

But next day, I found the mirror broken into half a dozen pieces, each one laid carefully facedown on the chest of drawers in his room. When I asked indignantly why he had done this, he explained patiently that it made better magic that way. And he proceeded to prop the pieces of glass above a drawing at angles which produced a strange, distorted maze of reflections.

"You see, Mama, you were wrong about mirrors," he said triumphantly. "You can make all sorts of magic with them. I wonder what they would show if I bent them? Do you think they would go soft enough to bend if I put them in the fire?"

"I've no idea!" I said with horror. "And don't you even think of trying such a silly trick! All you will succeed in doing is burning yourself. Erik . . . Erik, are you listening to me?"

"Yes, Mama," he said innocently. But he did not look at me as he said it, and I was immediately suspicious of such easy acquiescence. He did not normally give in so easily.

I would have taken the pieces of glass away from him on the spot, but I hesitated to provoke one of his terrible rages, which would only end in a savage beating. Perhaps I should be glad that he had overcome his irrational terror of such a simple everyday object. And if he burned himself . . . well, he would not do it again.

I decided to leave well enough alone.

"Madeleine."

Marie came into the kitchen, and as she closed the door behind her with a furtive gesture, I became aware that her earnest face was creased with anxiety.

"I think you should know," she continued uneasily, "that Erik has asked me to buy him some glass and tin . . . and a glass cutter. He gave me this and begged me not to tell you."

She held out her palm to display a hundred francs and I frowned.

"So that's where the money went . . . I had my suspicions. What did you say to him?"

She sighed. "Well, of course I knew the money couldn't possibly be his. I told him it was wrong to steal . . . and—and he just looked at me as though he didn't understand a word I was saying."

I nodded grimly. "He understands only what he wishes to understand. All he cares for at the moment is satisfying this morbid obsession with illusion and magic. And he knows how much it angers me— I told him last week he could not have that glass."

"What on earth does he want it for?"

"He wants to make mirrors—can you believe it? Magic mirrors that will show him only what he wants to see. For hundreds of years the Venetians kept the secret of their craft from the rest of the world and now this child—this *crazy* child—thinks he can start making mirrors in an attic bedroom. Thank God I never told him about the mercury or he would have demanded that, too, I suppose! What in God's name makes him behave like this?"

Marie laid the money on the table and looked at me thoughtfully.

"I think you must let him have this glass which is so very important to him," she said after a moment.

"Oh, really!" I retorted coldly. "Perhaps you think he should have the mercury, too, so that he can poison us all when the fancy takes him."

She shrugged uneasily. "Madeleine, if you don't give that glass to him he will simply find a way of taking it for himself. Do you want him to start breaking your windows?"

I stared at her in horror. "You think he is capable of such wickedness?"

She shook her head slowly.

"I don't think he would consider it wickedness, Madeleine—simply the next logical step toward his objective."

"The end justifies the means . . ." I said softly, looking inward. "That is the teaching of the devil."

She was silent, looking at the floor, and I knew that in her heart she was forced to agree.

At the end of the week, when I presented him with the glass and tin foil, I had to turn away from his cry of delight. He disappeared to his room for the rest of the day and that evening I found him rigid with fury at his failure.

"There must be a better way," he muttered, "I shall ask Professor Guizot when he comes tomorrow."

"Mirrors?" echoed the professor vaguely as Erik pounced on him at the front door next day. "Well, of course, we've always used tin and mercury for the backing up till now."

"Mercury!" I saw Erik stiffen with annoyance. "I didn't know about the mercury!"

"It hardly signifies," continued the professor jovially. "No one will be using that laborious old method much longer. I believe a new process called silvering has recently been discovered in Germany."

"Germany," Erik repeated solemnly. "How far away is that . . . ?"

The dining-room door closed behind them and I heard no more.

From that point I made it my business to keep Erik supplied with any material he asked for, no matter how bizarre the request might seem. Glass, metal, nuts and bolts and springs . . . they were toys that I no longer denied him, for the simple reason that I dared not.

I was beginning to understand the danger of attempting to block the natural outlet of an active volcano.

I was also beginning to understand Father Mansart's urgent concern for Erik's soul.

E ver since he was old enough to walk, I had taken the precaution of locking Erik in his room at night, partly for his protection, but chiefly for my own peace of mind. He was eight when I made the unwelcome discovery that barred windows and a locked door were no longer sufficient to contain his captive imagination.

Father Mansart came to me one morning in considerable anxiety, telling me that there was great unrest in the village and that I must take more care to keep Erik inside at night.

"I don't understand you." I frowned. "You know quite well that he is never permitted to go beyond the garden."

The priest shook his head. "Madeleine, he has been seen by more than one person in the church grounds. And last night several witnesses insist they heard the organ playing at midnight."

"But that's not possible, Father," I protested. "I myself locked him in his room at eight o'clock."

"Did you leave the key in the door?"

"Yes. But that is exactly where I found it this morning. Even if he had contrived to push the key from the lock and slide it underneath the door, he could hardly have locked himself in there again once more."

"I fear that with Erik all things are possible," said the priest gravely. "I think I had better talk to him."

To my intense dismay Erik made no attempt to deny his escape; he admitted it quite freely and only bowed his head when Father Mansart rebuked him for the sin of deceit.

"I wasn't doing any harm," he protested, looking at me anxiously, as though he expected me to beat him in front of the priest.

"Then what exactly were you doing?" I shouted.

"There are foxes in the forest," he said quietly. "I like to watch their cubs playing in the moonlight. Last spring they—"

He stopped, aghast at my expression. I could not believe that he had been roaming as far as the Forêt de Roumare for a year or more without my knowledge. I saw very clearly then what had happened, how his gradually mounting confidence had persuaded him to venture deeper and deeper into the village, where the beautiful Romanesque church pulled like a lodestar.

"How do you get out of your room?" I demanded.

"Oh, that's easy," he admitted. "I just unscrew the bars on the window and jump into the tree outside."

I closed my eyes in horror. His room was at least twenty feet above the ground and the tree he referred to was far enough away from the window to make that jump positively suicidal to anything but a cat. I didn't bother to ask how he managed to get back in . . . no doubt it was by a method equally lunatic.

"You stupid boy! You could have been killed!"

He looked at the floor. "Everything is so beautiful at night and no one sees me," he murmured.

"Well, last night you were not only seen, you were heard!" I snapped. "By now the entire village must know you were playing the organ in the church."

"Oh!" he said miserably. "I thought if anyone heard they would think it was a ghost."

"Erik," said Father Mansart, intervening hastily as he saw me clench my fists, "what you have been doing is very foolish and puts both you and your mother at risk. It must not occur again. If you continue to alarm the village in this fashion there may be unpleasant . . . reprisals."

Erik made an instinctive movement toward me and then froze.

"You understand what I mean by reprisals, don't you, my child?"

"Yes," Erik whispered with horror. "But why—why would they hurt me? I haven't done any harm. Why do they all hate me?"

The priest spread his hands uncomfortably.

"Men hate the things they fear . . . and they fear those things which they do not understand."

Erik touched the mask hesitantly. "My face"—he faltered—"they hate me because of my face?"

Father Mansart took his arm. "Come, child, let us pray. We shall ask God to grant you patience and understanding—"

"No!" Erik pulled away from his grasp abruptly. "I'm not going to pray anymore! Why should I? God doesn't listen to me."

"Erik!" I gasped. "You will apologize to Father Mansart immediately and beg God's forgiveness for such terrible blasphemy."

He was stubbornly silent.

"Go to your room," I said icily. "I will deal with your disobedience later."

There was an appalled silence when he had left us. I sank into the hearthside chair and stared at the priest.

"What can we do?" I breathed.

"He must not be allowed to leave the house again," said Father Mansart, after a moment. "I will return later to board up his window and place bolts on his door."

"Board up his window. . . ." I echoed wretchedly. "Must I now shut him up in a room without natural light?"

"I fear there is no other way to protect him," the priest said sadly.

That night there was a great disturbance outside in the road, a crowd of village boys throwing stones and shouting obscene abuse. I was so furious that in spite of the priest's warnings, I threw open my bedroom window and challenged them.

"Go away!" I screamed. "Go away and leave me and my son in peace!"

"Bring out the monster!" they chanted rudely, in response. "Bring out the monster and let us see him, lady."

A clod of filth struck me on the cheek. I heard the sound of a downstairs window smashing and held my breath with terror as someone began kicking the front door.

"Be off with you!" stormed Father Mansart's voice from a little distance down the road. "You young devils! I promise you this night will earn you penances enough to keep you on your knees for a month! Yes . . . I know your names . . . every one of you! Be off, I say!"

The voices grew fainter and less belligerent as their owners skulked away into the falling dusk.

Running down the narrow staircase, I wrenched open the front door and buried my face against the priest's habit.

"Oh, Father! I thought they were going to break into the house and take him!"

"I don't think they would dare to go that far, my dear, but certainly I couldn't answer for what they would do if they caught him wandering alone. Is he safe upstairs?"

I nodded.

"Good. I shall remove the glass from his window and fit a bolt at the top and bottom of his door. I think that will contain him . . . indeed, it may well be that after tonight he will be too frightened to try to escape again."

"What is to become of him?" I whispered in despair. "What in God's name will become of him?"

"It is not for us to foresee the future," replied the priest evasively. "I will go to him now, if I may. I rather think I shall find him ready to pray once more by now."

I tried to smile, faintly. "You have forgiven him his blasphemy, then?"

He made a philosophical gesture.

"If that is all that heaven is ever required to forgive in him we shall be fortunate indeed," he said.

And taking the candle from my nerveless hand, he lit his way to the top of the silent house without another word.

*   *   *

On Sunday I walked down into the village with Marie, to shame the parents of our tormentors. It was some years now since I had worshiped in the magnificent abbey of St.-Georges-de-Boscherville. Content to hear Mass like an invalid in the privacy of my own home, I had allowed myself increasingly to assume the habits of a recluse. And I began to see that there was perhaps some justification for the general belief that a madwoman and a monster inhabited the secluded house on the outskirts of the village. I must not continue to hide away like a mole in its burrow; I must show that I was prepared to fight for our right to be left in peace.

Throughout the service I was aware of heads turning furtively in my direction. A muted whispering permeated the sermon, and even the priest's steely gaze was not sufficient to quell it. My resolve trembled and I had a horrible urge to run out of the old church, but still I sat there stiffly, with my gloved hands folded over my prayer book, willing the service to come to an end.

"Ite missa est . . ." said Father Mansart at merciful length; and as the congregation shuffled to its feet I avoided the communal gaze by staring fixedly at the cherubs which decorated the transept.

Following Marie into the nave, I dropped my prayer book in my agitation, and the reverberating thud echoed unnaturally loud up into the vaulted roof. My glance went automatically to the gallery, and in the suffused light from the clerestory window I saw the figure of a young man looking down on me thoughtfully.

He made a formal little bow when he realized that I had seen him, and the unfamiliar courtesy of his gesture covered me with confusion. I had forgotten how to respond to such gestures in my years of solitude, forgotten how to play the simpering, empty-minded coquette. I felt extremely uncomfortable, and yet it was very hard to break that first revealing moment of eye contact.

"Who is that man?" I asked Marie, as we walked out into the fierce sunlight which was bathing the village green.

She smiled. "That is the new doctor, M. Barye."

"How long has he been in Boscherville?"

"About two months. But they say he will not stay. I believe he has very few patients because everyone still prefers to call in Doctor Gautier."

"How stupid!" I said, rather more sharply than I had meant to. "Doctor Gautier was in his dotage ten years ago—the man must be eighty at least."

Marie shrugged. "Well, you know what the village is. Mama says she would never dream of being examined by such a young man and she most certainly would not permit him to attend me."

"What does your mama suggest the young man do in the meantime? Is he to starve in the gutter until his beard turns gray?"

"Hush!" said Marie urgently. "He's coming out, he'll hear you."

Against all the instincts of good breeding I turned to look and found the young man's eyes once more fixed upon mine. Again he made that elegant little bow and bade us a good morning before going on his way with obvious reluctance.

Marie took my arm and with one accord we began to hurry down the road, away from his retreating figure. Suddenly, inexplicably, I found myself giggling, like the silly, frivolous creature I had once been; suddenly I was back in the convent, halfheartedly denying my interest in a handsome singing master.

"But of course I don't care for him, not a bit, not a bit. . . ."

Seventeen once more, a pert little butterfly testing her wings after the restrictive, chrysalis years of a strict Catholic upbringing. Seventeen and ready to devour life in one eager greedy swallow. . . .

The dusty, sunbaked road outside my house swam abruptly back into my vision and the sun winked on the new pane of glass that Erik had fitted into the dining room window. Eight years old and already he was as swift and efficient on simple tasks as the best workman in the village.

Why did I have the guilty feeling that I was about to commit the ultimate betrayal of his trust?

*E*tienne!

Étienne Barye! How quickly it happened! How quickly he changed from the urbane young doctor who greeted me with such studied civility every Sunday after Mass; how quickly he became the brightest star in my dark and empty sky.

Within a few short weeks it seemed to me that I thought of nothing but him and that time was measured by the deadly length of hours which separated our secret assignations. For eight years I had lived like a nun; perhaps it was inevitable that I should fall in love with the first handsome man to look on me once more with desire.

He knew my history, of course. There were only too many eager to relate the grisly details in the hope of sparing a good-looking young man the curse of my kiss. Stubbornly he ignored the warnings of doom and continued to present himself each Sunday at the end of my pew. I would place my hand upon his sleeve and sweep down the nave, displaying haughty indifference and defiance to those who watched with disapproval.

He was younger than I, with firm, well-sculptured features and eyes that were inclined to stare with scorn at people he despised. And he despised most of Boscherville, dismissing its inhabitants as provincial and bigoted. The few patients he had managed to acquire were soon irritated by his arrogant and rather abrasive manner and his association with me ensured that he added no more to his practice. I myself quickly learned to defer to his opinions, finding our time together too precious to be wasted in argument. I lived in constant fear that he would abandon what he referred to as "this tedious little backwater" and return to do research in Paris. His restless intelligence and intolerant impatience were far better suited to the laboratory than the drawing room of a querulous patient. It was only a question of time before he came to accept that himself.

He was insatiably curious about Erik, asking me deep and probing questions and often making notes of my replies. His interest, he assured me, was purely scientific; he wished to build up a case study. Repeatedly he asked to see the child, but that, for many reasons, I would not permit. At the back of my mind an uneasy feeling was growing that he would not hesitate to pin Erik to a dissecting table in order to satisfy his curiosity.

"Madeleine," he chided gently, as I increasingly shied away from his persistent inquiries, "you must not be so suspicious of the scientific mind. I thought you trusted me."

I looked away. I was growing to love the man, but I did not trust the scientist; I feared the lust for knowledge that lurked like a ravening wolf in his cool blue eyes.

Rising from his sofa, I walked away to the window, staring out at the village green and the old church which towered to the sky just beyond.

"You ask too many questions," I murmured.

"Of course!" He tossed the notebook aside and came to stand beside me, throwing off the impersonal, clinical manner like a soiled apron. "Insatiable curiosity is not a very attractive quality I'm afraid. Forgive me, Madeleine."

His hand was insistent on my arm, but I did not turn to look at him.

"Sometimes I think all you want from me is answers." I sighed.

He turned me slowly around until I faced him.

"Not all," he said.

And kissed me.

"Who is that man?" Erik demanded abruptly.

He was waiting for me in the hall as I let myself into the house, and there was a hard accusing look in his eyes as he stared at me.

"Who is that man?" he repeated stonily, when I failed to answer. "Why does he walk with you alone?"

It was almost four months since I first met Étienne, but I had been very careful that Erik should not see us together. Obviously tonight I had not been careful enough.

"If I choose to walk with a man it is no concern of yours!" I retorted angrily.

Hanging up my cloak, I made to walk past him, but he blocked my path to the drawing room and suddenly I knew a moment of intense fear. He stood as high as my shoulder now and was deceptively strong in spite of his skeletal frame.

"Who is he, Mother?"

It was the first time he had ever used that word to address me, and the contempt in his voice was quite terrifying.

"His name is Étienne," I found myself saying breathlessly. "Étienne Barye . . . he is a doctor. Now, let me pass, Erik. I will not be questioned in this tiresome and impertinent manner. I . . . ."

My voice wavered to a halt as he continued to stare at me coldly.

"He is a friend," I stammered. "You must understand, Erik, that I have a perfect right to have friends like anyone else in the village."

He made a movement toward me and instinctively I took a defensive step back.

"I do not wish this friendship to continue," he told me inexorably.

The eyes behind the mask were like gimlets; I had never seen him look at me like this before. I retreated down the hall until I felt my back against the front door, but still he advanced toward me with curious, unchildlike menace. I struck out at him, in sudden fear, but after that first hesitant blow, rage overwhelmed my apprehension at his unspoken threat.

"You!" I screamed. "You do not wish? How dare you speak to me like this! You ruined my life the day you were born—ruined it . . . *ruined* it! I hate you, I hate the very sight and sound of you . . . your devil's face and your angel's voice! There are plenty of angels in hell, did you know that? I wish to God you were there with them, where you belong. I wish you were dead, do you hear me? I wish you were dead!"

He seemed to shrink, almost to shrivel, in front of my eyes. Whatever he might have been a few seconds before, he was only a child now, recoiling in disbelief from a punishment beyond his worst imagination. It was as though all the ugly emotion that had been festering between us since his birth had erupted into a single, massive boil and finally burst, drowning us both in its poison. And I knew, as I looked at his crushed misery, that he would carry those words with him to his grave. Nothing I could say or do would ever wash their corrosive stain from his mind.

As I hovered beside him, unable to express my grief and remorse, he suddenly took his hands away from the mask and stared at me with a wretchedness that was utterly beyond tears.

"I hate you too," he said with slow, pained surprise, as though it was something that had only now been revealed to him. "I hate you too."

And turning away from me, he groped his way slowly up the stairs like a blind child.

Erik did not speak of "the man" again. From that time he displayed complete indifference to my increasing absences, not even bothering to look up when I returned to the house. He wrapped around himself a cloak of impenetrable silence and spent most of his time working alone in his room, with only Sasha for company.

The dog was growing old and obese, entering that period of rapid decline which besets so many canines around their tenth year. Erik carried her patiently up and down the steep stairs that were now beyond her, bathed her rheumy eyes, and sometimes sat for an hour at a time feeding her by hand. But I was not convinced he understood that the inevitable moment of parting might be close at hand. And since it was not a thing I could comfortably discuss with him, I asked Father Mansart to raise the subject instead.

Their quiet voices were only just audible to me in the next room, where I sat sewing. Yes, said Erik calmly, he knew that Sasha was old and would not live forever, might not perhaps live beyond the next year or so. But he understood that God would take her to live in heaven and they would not be separated forever.

I felt, rather than heard, the priest's quick intake of breath, the breath he had taken to correct his pupil's childish but unacceptable error in doctrine. He asked Erik to understand that, though God had compassion for all his creatures, it was to man alone that He had granted an afterlife. Animals, said Father Mansart solemnly, have no souls. . . .

There was a heartbeat of silence and then, without warning, a scream of indescribable grief and rage, which seemed to rip my head apart. I rushed into the drawing room in time to see Erik seize the clock from the mantelpiece and smash it in the hearth. And then, to my absolute horror, he picked up the coal tongs and lashed out at the priest, shrieking terrible obscenities, words I did not even think he knew. When I tried to get between them, the tongs caught me with full force on my shoulder, slicing clean through the velvet into the flesh.

The priest dragged me back, out of the range of the wildly flailing weapon which was hacking indiscriminately at everything in its path.

"My God!" I breathed. "He will wreck the entire room! Let me stop him—"

Father Mansart's answer was to pull me through the door, shutting it hastily behind him. A savage barrage of blows struck the panels in our wake and the door began to splinter. But as I caught at the handle, the priest snatched my hand away.

"You must not approach him . . . he does not know you."

I stared at him in disbelief. The sounds of frenzied destruction continued in the room beyond and the priest's face was deathly pale, his lips set in a gray line of pain and grief.

"I have failed," he muttered wearily. "I have failed him and I have failed God."

"I don't understand you," I gasped. "Are you telling me he is mad?"

The priest shook his head grimly. "This is not madness, child—this is possession! If you go to him now I think he will kill you. We must wait until whatever demon now has him in its grip grows tired of its sport and departs."

I looked at the blood soaking steadily into my sleeve. "Will—will it happen again?" I stammered uncertainly.

The priest sighed. "Once a suitable host presents itself to the forces of darkness . . ." he spread his hands in a helpless gesture, before continuing.

"Tomorrow I will perform a ceremony of exorcism," he said unhappily.

Exorcism. . . .

Blackness closed in around me and Father Mansart caught me as I swayed.

"Exorcism!" said Étienne, in disgust. "That priest is a stupid meddler who properly belongs in the Middle Ages. This is not a case for the Church, but for a medical institution."

"An asylum," I muttered. "You mean an asylum for the insane!"

Étienne sighed. "I wish you would not resort to such emotive terms. The child appears to suffer from a degree of mental disturbance, which under the circumstances is really no more than what I would expect to find. There are few things more hazardous to the equilibrium of the human mind than the freakish genius you have described to me." He placed one hand upon my arm before adding quietly, "My darling, you really must begin to give serious thought to the question of an institution."

"But . . . they are terrible places, are they not? One hears such dreadful tales of cruelty."

"By no means," replied Étienne calmly. "Some are better than others, I won't deny that, but I happen to know of an excellent place where he could be kept out of harm's way. He could have his books and his music . . . he'd be quite happy . . . or at least as happy as he's ever likely to be on this earth."

Étienne leaned back on the riverbank and watched the Seine flow past through half-closed eyes. He had a brisk, uncompromising manner of dealing with emotion, a manner that negated both passion and sentiment. His boundless optimism was capable of cloaking the most unpleasant proposals in a respectable, acceptable garb. A quick decision, a signature upon the committal papers, and all my problems would be over. He made it sound so easy and so right.

Leaning over, he pressed me back against the tussocky grass, and I was glad to surrender to his insistent lips. It meant that I did not have to think, to argue with myself. For a few blissful moments there was only physical delight and spiritual release and I pulled him closer, fearing the moment when he would draw away.

Ten years ago, I do not believe that I would have loved him, for ten years ago I could not have borne to be told what to think and what to do in such a cavalier fashion. Now there was nothing I wanted so much as to be safely locked in his arms and sheltered from the ugliness of reality. We were lovers in all but the fullest sense, for he was too logical, too rational, too sensible, to take the risk of ruining me. He craved a respectable existence, in keeping with the dignity of his profession, and I knew that these hole-in-the-corner assignations were likely to pale in time. Not unreasonably, he wanted some promise of a future.

But what future could there be when I dared not even invite him for dinner for fear of provoking Erik's violent rage?

I knew this state of affairs could not continue indefinitely; and already there was a soft-footed intruder, whispering with insidious determination at the back of my mind, telling me now what I think I had known from that very first moment in the nave of the church.

This man would marry you, if you were free.

If I were free of my misbegotten child.

If I put him in an institution for the violently insane. . . .

I was very quiet as we walked back along the riverbank, and long before we came in sight of the village I suggested it would be wiser for me to continue alone.

"People are beginning to talk. In your position you cannot afford a scandal."

He put one arm around my shoulders and tilted my face up to his.

"Madeleine," he said gently, "there doesn't have to be a scandal . . . you know that, don't you? All I am asking is that you let me examine the boy and give you my professional judgment on his mental state."

But I knew that that judgment had already been made, and desperate as I was, I was not yet ready to play Judas.

"You will think about what I have said?" he insisted.

"Yes," I said dully, "I will think about it."

But I knew that I would not.

tienne was right about the exorcism; it was a thing I should never have permitted. If Erik was not possessed before the ceremony took place, he most certainly behaved as though he was once it was over.

His respectful attachment to the priest was gone for good. He refused to continue the vocal training that had given them both such delight; but, worse than that, he refused to hear Mass or to have a crucifix in his bedroom. I did not dare to insist, for he had begun to behave so strangely that I found myself growing truly afraid of him. Curious things began to happen in the house when he was near. Articles disappeared, almost before my very eyes, only to return again once I had ceased to search for them. I knew he was responsible, but when I challenged him, he only shrugged and laughed and told me that we must have a ghost.

Then one day, when a cup had leapt from its saucer and smashed itself in the grate, I discovered a finely pared length of thread attached to the broken handle, and I turned on him in fury.

"You did that, didn't you! You made it happen!"

"No!" He backed away from me in sudden fear. "How could I have done that? I wasn't even near it! It was the ghost!"

"There is no ghost!" I shouted. "There is no ghost—only you, with your infernal threads of silk! Look at it! You haven't been so clever this time, have you? This is one trick I can see straight through."

He was silent, glaring at the gossamer thread as though his own incompetence angered him. I could almost hear his furious determination that next time there would be nothing to betray his hand.

"There will not be a next time," I said calmly, and saw his head jerk up in alarm that I should have read his thoughts with such ease. "This wickedness is to cease right away, do you hear me?"

"It isn't me," he repeated with childish stubbornness. "It's the ghost. The ghost that Father Mansart tried to send away."

I shook him wildly by the shoulders, until the mask dislodged itself and fell to the floor between us.

"Stop this madness!" I shrieked. "Stop it at once! If you don't I shall do what Doctor Barye advises and send you away to a terrible place for mad people. *Yes!* That frightens you, doesn't it? Well, I'm glad! I'm glad it frightens you, because perhaps it will make you stop this insane behavior. I promise you, Erik, if I send you away to an asylum you will never come back—never! They will tie your hands behind your back and shut you away in a dark place until you die and you will never, never see me again! Now, will you stop? *Will you?*"

I let go of him abruptly and stood back, panting for breath, while he knelt on the carpet at my feet and replaced the mask hastily, with shaking hands. I could feel his terror, it was like a physical force, but for once I felt no guilt or remorse at my harshness. The two of us were approaching a dangerous precipice and I knew that if I did not take control of him now, we would both finish in an asylum.

"What would you do," he whispered softly, not looking at me, "if I were no longer here?"

"I would marry Doctor Barye," I said, goaded to the lie by sheer desperation. "He has already asked me and you are all that prevents the marriage taking place. So, you see—you had better take care and do as I say. Now, look at me! Look at me and promise there will be no more of these—these happenings."

He continued to kneel on the floor, winding the thread of silk tightly around one skeletal finger until the white tip turned blue where he had cut off the circulation of blood.

"Erik!"

Quick as a grasshopper he leapt out of reach of my hand and ran to the door, where he paused to look back at me defiantly.

"There is a ghost," he told me steadily. "There is a ghost here, Mother. And it's going to stay with you forever and ever!"

I stood looking after him, one hand against my throat and the other outstretched to him in a hopeless gesture of supplication.

I suddenly felt very cold.

That night I heard the voice for the first time. A voice that was familiar and yet strangely altered, singing so low and soft that at first I was barely aware of its sweet hypnotic tone.

The voice was close beside me, so close that it seemed if I stretched out a hand I should surely touch it. But as I stood up curiously and moved toward it, the voice retreated before me.

I stopped and stared at Erik, who was grooming Sasha on the mat before the fire. He seemed absorbed in the task and quite unaware of my agitation.

The voice was curiously muted, a distant eerie breath which seemed to beckon me out of the room and up the staircase. I followed with helpless fascination, and as I entered my bedroom, the wordless melody seemed to gather strength and center itself upon the statue of a shepherd boy which stood on my marble-topped chest of drawers.

I drew closer and now it was unmistakably clear to me that the statue itself was responsible for the humming. I gazed at it in amazement and as I did so, I became aware that I was no longer alone in the room. Erik was suddenly beside me, watching me watch the statue. He had removed the mask and his lips were set in a grim line of silence.

And then I knew.

I drew back my hand very slowly and deliberately, letting him see my intent; but he did not even blink and the soft, seductive humming never faltered.

When I struck him across the mouth, it seemed to me that it was the statue that cried out in pain.

I understood now how he had employed those long dismal hours of solitude; I recognized the new achievement that he had added to his curious misarray of talents. I remembered the present which Marie had brought him on his fifth birthday; a present which had remained unopened and which I had later locked away in my bureau as totally unsuitable.

An antique copy of *Le Ventriloque ou L'Engastrimythe*.

"I thought it would interest him," she had explained, when I took her to task for her stupidity. "I only wanted to amuse him. But if you think it best that he should not have it, then of course you must keep it from him."

I should have known that nothing could be kept from Erik once his curiosity was aroused. How could I have been stupid enough to think that he would not remember the only birthday present he ever received, or that a simple lock would be sufficient to keep him out of my bureaus? The book was never missing whenever I had cause to open the cabinet, but of course he was too clever and secretive to have made a mistake as elementary as that. If he wished to keep something to himself there was no one more adroit at covering his own tracks than this curious child, part cat, part fox . . . part nightingale.

The shepherd boy continued to sing to me, and though I understood the secret of this illusion, I found myself compelled to listen to its haunting beauty. At first I listened against my will, swearing each time that I would destroy the wretched figure as soon as it was silent. On several occasions I lifted my hand to dash it to the floor, but each time I was restrained by some unseen force which seemed to emanate from deep inside my own body.

And then, little by little, I began to abandon my senses to its growing power; I became unable to distinguish between illusion and reality. The voice not only sang now, it talked, and I soon found myself acceding to its numerous little requests. I humored it when it told me it was cold by the window, and moved it to the table beside my bed; and when it sulked like a child and told me it would not sing unless I kissed it, I bent obediently and laid my lips against its cool, lifeless cheek.

There was indeed a ghost now, but its spirit was beyond the power of exorcism and I embraced its presence with wondering delight. Slowly I was crossing the enticing bridge that had opened up before me, following a magic rainbow which beckoned me ever farther into a dangerous and unknown land. . . .

How much of it was a dream, the product of long-repressed emotions, and how much was due to Erik, I cannot say. I was drowning willingly in the quicksand of this growing fantasy, and it seemed to me that physically we drew even farther apart during this time, meeting only in the strange spiritual oasis of sound.

I scarcely saw him, but when I did he was very restrained and civil, almost quaintly adult in his manner toward me. And as he grew older and more fiercely independent before my very eyes, it seemed to me that the voice of the figure in my room grew correspondingly younger, more petulant and demanding, with every day that passed. Increasingly it seemed to punish me, first with stubborn silence and then with tears. And soon my head rang day and night with the persistent, heartrending cry of an inconsolable baby.

I could not eat or sleep. Night after night I walked my room in despair, cradling the statue against my breast, until at last it lay beside me in my bed, silenced only by the touch of my hand. I spiraled farther and farther down into this dark dream, until the dominance of this cold porcelain tyrant began to touch every aspect of my life.

I no longer went to Mass and refused to see Father Mansart when he came to the house. And when Étienne remarked upon my pallor and my distracted air, we quarreled violently.

"What is the matter with you, Madeleine?" he demanded uncertainly. "You're like a hunted fox, staring over your shoulder all the time. What is it you are listening for?"

"Nothing!" I said sharply. "I'm not listening for anything."

But even as I lay in his arms, in a house on the far side of the village, the sound of crying still filled my ears and made me too restless and agitated to respond to his caress.

At length, rebuffed and disturbed by my strange coldness, he sat up and looked at me with irritation.

"If you do not wish to be touched, I would prefer you to tell me and have done with it. There really seems no purpose in prolonging an exercise in mutual frustration."

I got up like a sleepwalker and went to the door. Étienne ran after me, and as I looked at him I could see anger and concern warring on his face.

"Tell me what is wrong," he demanded.

I shook my head. "I have to go," I said bleakly. "I should not be here. I've left him crying."

Étienne frowned slightly. "Erik?"

I turned to him impatiently. Why on earth should he think I was talking about Erik when it was the baby who cried? I had opened my mouth to tell him this, when I suddenly remembered the dreadful word *asylum* and Étienne's brisk, uncompromising sense of logic.

If I told him, he would think I was mad.

"I don't understand," he persisted, reaching out for me.

I avoided his grasp with an urgency that was suddenly very close to fear. All I wanted now was to get out of this house as quickly as possible.

"Madeleine!" He cornered me by the door and his grip on my wrist seemed like a jailer's. I began to struggle wildly.

"Let me go!" I shouted. "I will not be treated like a specimen for observation at the School of Medicine!"

He let go of me in astonishment and I wrenched open the door.

"For pity's sake, Madeleine, let us discuss this calmly."

"I don't want to discuss anything. I don't want to see you again, Étienne . . . ever!"

I saw the pain and bewilderment on his face. For once he had no words ready, no nice, neat, empirical solutions to offer. Science and logic alike failed him in the face of my devastating unreason.

"I can't believe you mean that," he said with disbelief. "What has happened, Madeleine . . . what has happened to make you turn from me like this?"

"Nothing has happened," I told him distantly. "I must go."

"You can't go—not like this. *Madeleine!*"

He caught my hand once more, but I only stared at him unseeingly as the sound of crying swelled in an unbearable crescendo inside my head. I might have been looking at a total stranger. His words were empty mouthings that had lost their power to move me and at last I saw his arm drop helplessly back to his side.

He made no further attempt to stop me leaving, and as I left his house I was aware that he would be too proud to seek me out against my spoken wish. A few months ago the prospect of his indifference would have broken my heart; now I welcomed it with curious relief.

One by one I was closing the windows that looked out on the world beyond my prison, retreating behind the strange barricade that Erik was patiently erecting around me.

The day that I walked away from Étienne was the day that I finally turned my back on reality and locked the door.

A curious contentment descended upon me when I finally abandoned myself to the dream and ceased to function with any pretense of sanity; when I accepted that heaven had looked with pity on my plight at last and sent me the perfect, beautiful baby that Charles had promised; when I accepted that I had two sons.

One was a monster, a genius of inhuman and terrifying dimensions; but the other was as enchantingly normal as I could ever have wished and his welfare was my consuming obsession. I could not bear to be parted from him.

Strangely, Erik showed no jealousy of this new interloper. At my request he carried the old cradle down from the attic bedroom, without a murmur, and watched me caress the carved wood when he had set it beside my bed.

"You're happy now," he said quietly. "You don't want to marry Doctor Barye now that you have the baby. . . . You'll have to stay and look after it, won't you?"

I nodded dreamily as I bent over the cradle and began to arrange the lace coverlet. After a moment I remembered to thank him for being so helpful.

"If I'm helpful you won't send me away, will you?" he persisted. "You'll let me stay here with you both."

"Yes," I said vaguely, "I expect so. . . ."

He gave a little sigh, I could not tell whether of relief or satisfaction. I think he lingered awhile, watching me. I was not aware of the moment when he slipped silently from the room.

*   *   *

When Marie got out of her chair and stared at me, her face was as white as the collar of her gown. I could not think why she should look at me like that. I had merely asked if she would like to look at the baby.

She did not reply, she simply went on staring at me and I wondered, with surprise, if she could possibly be jealous. I watched her grope her way across the room to the piano where Erik sat watching us.

"Your mother is very sick," I heard her tell him in a low, strained voice. "I am going to ask Doctor Barye to come and see her at once."

"You must not do that," he said steadily. "Mother doesn't like Doctor Barye, she doesn't want him here in this house. If you bring him here, I will not let him in."

"Erik . . ." she protested helplessly, "you must try to understand that—"

"I think you should go now, mademoiselle."

His voice cut across her wavering tone with devastating authority and I saw her stare at him for a moment with a disbelief that bordered on fear. Then abruptly she rushed back to me and began to shake my arm.

"Madeleine . . . listen to me. I'm going to fetch your cloak and take you down into the village at once. I'm going—"

Her voice broke on a gasp of terror as Erik's long fingers closed around her wrist.

"I think you should go now," he repeated ominously. "I want you to go."

She pulled away from his grasp and steadied herself against the mantelpiece; I saw with vague curiosity that she had begun to cry.

"I must tell Doctor Barye," she muttered feverishly to herself. "I must tell him what terrible things are happening under this roof."

"She doesn't want him here." I watched her back away as Erik began to walk steadily toward her. "And she doesn't want you, either . . . interfering . . . asking questions . . . you tire her."

Marie stopped crying and looked at me, as though she could not believe that I made no move to correct his astonishing impudence. When Erik brought her cloak and handed it to her, she took it from him without another word and followed him from the room like a sleepwalker.

"You must not concern yourself," I heard him say calmly as he opened the front door for her. "My mother is quite well, but she does not want visitors anymore. Good day, mademoiselle. Thank you for calling."

If she made a reply, I did not hear it. I listened instead, with calm indifference, to the sound of the key turning in the lock and the bolts sliding into place.

At length he came back into the room and stood beside my chair, looking down on me solicitously.

"Shall I play for you?" he asked.

"Yes," I said dreamily. "Mozart . . . the Piano Concerto in C major."

He sat down at the piano and began the cadenza, playing from memory with his familiar effortless brilliance, and wrapping me in a warm cocoon of languorous sound that floated me ever farther from reality. I had no thought, no desire, now but to be left alone in a world entirely fashioned and furnished by his imagination.

The day drifted, as all my days were beginning to drift, in a calm, unquestioning haze of dependence. All decisions and conscious thought had been taken from me; I was merely a contented spectator, able to observe with strange detachment.

All day he sat and worked on a series of designs for a building unlike anything I had ever seen before—a building so extraordinary and bizarre that it was only the elevations—front, rear, and side—which made it recognizable to me as a structure at all. I waited patiently for him to finish and begin to play for me again, but he was transported by a fierce, elemental frenzy of creativity which I dared not disturb. Repeatedly he screwed up sheets of paper and flung them into the fire with angry frustration. And when Sasha whined for attention and pawed at his hand, he picked her up impatiently and shut her outside in the dark garden.

That last action was so utterly out of character that it penetrated the stupor of lethargy which gripped me. In that moment I suddenly saw him as the grown man he would become—totally consumed by his obsessive quest for perfection, formidable and frightening in his ruthless drive to create. He would be nine this summer, and already he was touched with the awesome, unpredictable majesty of the ancient Greek gods. A time would come, as Father Mansart had foreseen, when he no longer acknowledged the barriers that confine and unite the human race. He would be a law unto himself, untroubled by tiresome mortal questions of right and wrong.

A soul entirely lost to God.

It was dark when he finally laid his lead down with a sigh of exhausted satisfaction. I saw him glance automatically over to the hearth and check in surprise.

"Where's Sasha?" he demanded with concern.

"In the garden." I frowned. "Don't you remember, Erik? She was annoying you and—"

"You shouldn't put her out into the garden at night, Mother. It's too cold for her now that she's old."

I sat in my chair, tried and condemned by his unwavering certainty, and dimly troubled by this curious lapse of memory.

Would he always forget these deeds which he did not wish to remember?

Before I could collect myself sufficiently to reply to his accusation, the dull whining outside the front door changed to a frenzy of barking as Sasha deserted her patient vigil on the doorstep and rushed to the gate.

"Look!" shouted a voice in the road. "There's the monster's dog!"

Through the window I caught the glare of lanterns and a moment later a barrage of stones began to rain in the direction of the gate. When Sasha gave a yelp of pain, Erik leapt to his feet and rushed to the door; but I reached it first.

"No!" I screamed. "Don't you see they're trying to lure you out there? They'll kill you if you go out to them. . . . Erik!"

The eyes behind the mask were an insane yellow gleam of rage. When he threw me aside, with a violence that knocked all the breath from my body, I struck my head on the newel post at the foot of the stairs. For a few moments I was too dazed to do anything except cower on the floor, listening with disbelieving horror to the ugly voices of the mob and Erik's awesome rage.

Laughter and shouting . . . a man's high-pitched scream of pain
. . . Sasha's frenzied barking rising to a crescendo and ending in one
long, piteous howl.

And then Erik's shriek of demented anguish.

"I'll kill you! I'll kill *all* of you!"

Swaying dizzily to my feet, I staggered to the open doorway, but the
lanterns were already swaying and bobbing away down the road,
driven off by the demonic fury of an outraged child. When Erik struggled back down the paved path with Sasha in his arms, I could see at
once from the unnatural angle of her head that her neck had been
broken by some savage blow.

I stretched out my hand to him, but he pushed past me as though I
didn't exist. Stunned with shock, I followed him into the kitchen,
where I found him kneeling beside the bloody bundle of fur, his thin
shoulders shaking with the harsh violence of his sobbing.

In the light from the oil lamp I was able to see that his mask had
been torn off in the struggle and his yellow flesh slashed in several
places. Blood was trickling into his eyes, and as he lifted a hand to
wipe it away, I suddenly caught my breath. The blood on his shirt was
not Sasha's, as I had first thought. The stain was growing, welling
outward, fed by some unseen knife-wound within.

An icy coldness gripped me as I laid a trembling hand on his sleeve.

"Come away now," I whispered. "There's nothing more you can do
for Sasha."

"I must bury her," he said with dull despair. "I must bury her and
sing her requiem."

"You can't!" I breathed in horror.

"She *will* have a requiem!" He sobbed. "A requiem to take her soul
to God!"

"Yes," I said hastily, praying silently that I would be forgiven for
condoning this blasphemy. "But not tonight. You've been stabbed,
Erik, don't you realize that? You must come and rest while I attend to
the wound."

"I must bury her," he repeated, as though he had not heard a word
I had spoken. He swayed to his feet, and though the red stain on his
shirt spread alarmingly, I knew that I could not prevent him.
Wounded and broken with grief, he was still stronger than I, still

capable of throwing me across the room if I resisted his wild determination.

Lifting down a lantern, I lit his way into the orchard at the back of the house without another word.

I wept as I watched him struggling to dig a grave in the iron-hard soil. He would not permit me to help and I crouched on the grass beside Sasha's slowly stiffening body, stroking the matted fur and wincing at the labored sound of his every breath. Listening to the trembling notes of the Dies Irae, I closed my eyes and clung to the crucifix around my neck.

"Forgive him, Father . . . forgive him! He is only an angry child. He does not understand how he sins. . . ."

When it was done, Erik stumbled back to the house and collapsed on the sofa in the drawing room. I ripped open the sodden shirt, but there was so much blood that I could not immediately locate the site of the wound and I felt panic closing in around me.

"Madeleine!"

I turned with relief to find Étienne standing in the open doorway, his hat in one hand and his bag in the other. In a single stride he seemed to be beside me, bending over the sofa in alarm.

"Who did this?" he demanded with cold fury.

"I don't know. There was a crowd . . . men, boys. . . . They killed the dog. He struggled with them and then. . . Oh, God, Étienne, is it serious?"

He frowned as he probed the wound with expert fingers.

"It's missed the lung, he's been very lucky. Heat some water, would you, and bring some salt."

I did as I was told and returned to watch anxiously as Étienne worked on my son with deft efficiency. He was very calm and there was no indication in his manner that this patient differed in any respect from his others.

Erik lay very still, watching him with guarded hostility.

"Are you Doctor Barye?" he demanded warily.

Étienne smiled briefly in acknowledgment.

"Why are you helping me?"

"I am a doctor," said Étienne, with a gentle patience that quite took me by surprise. "It is my duty to help those who require my skills.

You have been a very brave boy, Erik. I am going to give you something that will make you sleep now."

To my surprised relief Erik accepted the draught without a murmur
of protest, and within a few minutes his breathing had become even
and his eyes closed wearily.

Étienne closed up his bag and stared at the face on the cushion.
Now that he was no longer hiding behind the barriers of his professional dignity, I could see the shocked pity and disbelief that had crept
into his eyes. He reached out and took my hand absently.

"I have never seen anything like this before," he said slowly. "This
is not a simple case of disfigurement . . . it's almost as though . . ."
He fell silent, groping for words and ideas that were just beyond the
reach of his sharp mind, and I sensed the deep frustration of a man
whose moment of inner vision confronts the insurmountable boundaries of existing language and knowledge.

"Lamarck defined two laws governing the ascent of life to higher
stages," I heard him mutter to himself. "Is it possible that there could
be another determining factor—a spontaneous alteration of a life-
form?"

His musings were beyond my comprehension, and after a moment
he abandoned the vain struggle for expression and came to put his
arms around me.

"I can't condone the behavior of the village, but at least I can
understand it now. Madeleine, you can't possibly continue to keep
him hidden away in this house; they'll never leave you in peace after
this. For his own sake you must permit me to put him in a place of
safety."

"An institution . . . an asylum for the insane?"

I covered my face with my hands, but Étienne pulled them gently
away and forced me to look at him.

"You must face the truth, my darling. You can't contain him any
longer within these four walls. I have heard enough to know that he is
already quite beyond your control. Rightly or wrongly the village fears
him, and wherever you try to take him it will be the same—hatred,
persecution . . . violence. This time it was the dog, next time it
could be you. You have to think about your own safety . . . your own
sanity."

"Sanity?" I whispered uneasily.

He shook his head gravely. "Marie Perrault came to me this evening. She was very worried about you, Madeleine, she begged me to come and see you. Why else do you think I would have come here without invitation?"

I tried to turn away from him, but he caught my arm.

"I won't stand by and see you driven out of your mind for the sake of a freak accident of nature. I'm very sorry for the child, but there's nothing I can do for him except put him beyond the reach of the ignorant."

"Étienne—"

"No . . . listen to me, just listen! Let me make the arrangements and when it's done we'll go away from here, far away where no one knows you, to a place where you can begin to forget. I love you, Madeleine, and I know that you love me. There's no reason in the world why we should not make our life together once you are free of this monstrous burden."

Erik stirred on the sofa with a drowsy moan.

"Can he hear us?" I demanded anxiously.

"I'd be most astonished if he could. I gave him enough laudanum to make him sleep the clock around."

Even so I was uneasy. Picking up his bag and hat, I drew him out into the hall and closed the door; and once we were there, I handed him his belongings and asked him to go.

"Madeleine"—he sighed—"you haven't listened to a word I've said."

"Oh, yes, I've listened," I said sadly. "I've listened and I've understood . . . and I've made up my mind. If I did as you suggest I know that I should only come to hate myself—and in time I should begin to hate you. Go away from Boscherville, Étienne . . . go right away and forget you ever saw me. That's all you can do now, because I won't abandon my child. Not even for you."

He looked at me with despair.

"The midwife had no right to let him live," he said darkly. "If I had attended his birth he would never have drawn a single breath."

I smiled faintly and touched his hand.

"You would not have done that, Étienne. You would have saved him then, just as you have saved him now. You are a good Catholic."

"But I'm a bad doctor!" he said grimly. "A bad doctor, and a very great fool."

I said nothing. He put on his hat with dignity and opened the front door.

"I'm going back to Paris at the end of the month," he told me steadily. "If you change your mind in the meantime you know where to find me."

"I won't change my mind."

He reached out and touched my cheek gently.

"No," he said sadly, "I know that you won't."

A moment more he looked at me with regret, and then he was gone, striding away down the path between the swaying beech trees, without a backward glance.

There were tears in my eyes as I locked the door, but my movements had a new purpose and steadiness; I was no longer operating like a sleepwalker in a trance. The dream was gone, I was awake now.

Returning to the drawing room I covered Erik with a blanket; he did not move and I judged him to be deeply asleep. A strange calm came over me as I looked down on him, a curious sense of resignation. For the first time since his birth I felt at peace with myself.

I lifted the figure of the shepherd boy from the chair where I had dropped it in the panic of the moment and placed it, without emotion, upon the mantelpiece, where it belonged. It had no power to move me now, I was no longer its mindless slave.

I had only one child. One child, whose mind I had warped and twisted, whose affection I had spurned, and whose heart I had repeatedly broken. But I did not want him dead and I did not want him shut away.

I did not want these things because I loved him.

More than Étienne; and now at, at last, more than myself.

When I looked in the mirror in my room, I no longer saw a spoiled, inadequate child, brooding bitterly on the cruelty of her fate. For the first time I saw a grown woman in her place.

It could not be too late to repair the harm that I had done. I would not let it be too late. Tomorrow, while he watched, I would gather all the masks together and throw them on the fire.

The sun woke me, stealing over my face like a warm caress.

Sitting up with a start, I glanced at the clock and saw with concern that it was already late morning. I had tumbled into bed the night before, like a spent swimmer who has struggled to a far-off shore, and slept like the dead for almost twelve hours. Flinging a wrapper around my shoulders, I hurried downstairs to the drawing room, where the heavy curtains were still closed.

Even in the dim gloom I saw at once that the room was empty.

"Erik?"

My voice echoed eerily in the gloomy silence and my slippered footsteps seemed unnaturally loud as I ran back up the stairs.

"Erik, where are you?"

When I threw open the door of his room, shafts of harsh, brilliant light struck me full in the face and forced me to shield my dazzled eyes with a gasp. It was a few moments before I was able to focus on the source of these cruel rays, and then I saw that his odd collection of mirrors had been set out at angles around the broken remains of the shepherd boy, to reflect a maze of macabre images that took my breath away with shock.

I knelt in the sunlight beside the high altar of a child's imagination and stared dumbly at a message so plain, so unequivocal, that it might have been written across the glass in blood. I could see now that the figure had not been smashed in anger, but carefully severed by a glass cutter with a ritual precision that left the head and limbs recognizably intact. I was looking at the remains of an execution, staring down upon a dismembered body that asked nothing more of me in this world except burial.

I continued to kneel on the floor, surrounded by his few treasures . . . my father's architectural library, a cupboard full of musical scores, a chest stuffed with a weird collection of magical devices. The violin that I had given him when he was three lay abandoned and forgotten at the foot of his bed. I could see that he had taken nothing with him in his headlong flight from the house; and I knew, without looking, that my purse remained untouched on the chest of drawers in my room.

This grim gesture of childish sacrifice showed me every painful thought which had led him to this final act of despair.

I had given him life, but now he chose to take no more from me. And in the tomb-like silence of this sunlit room, his last, unspoken words rang in my ears like the tolling of a passing bell.

Forget me. . . .

Erik
1840-1843

I remember it was pitch black the night I ran away from my home in Boscherville. There was no moon and as I pushed through the dense undergrowth in the birch and pine forest of Roumare, clumps of nettles stung my hands. I wasn't usually so clumsy, but tonight my head was clouded with a haze of laudanum and I stumbled and fell several times. The wound beneath my rib cage had begun to bleed again with the exertion and I was aware of a warm stickiness seeping once more beneath my shirt; but I did not stop. I only pushed on and on—as though my life depended on this headlong, desperate flight—without knowing how or whither I fled.

I was not afraid of the dark anymore; I had long since learned to love the kindly veil that shielded me from hating eyes. I had become a creature of the night, passing unseen through the darker shadows of the woods, absorbing the wonderful mysteries of nature, while those who loved harsh daylight slept easy and ignorant in their beds. I was as nocturnal as a badger; and like a badger, I knew my only enemy was man.

There was no plan, no coherent thought, in my head, just a deep instinctive need to get away, far, far away, from my mother's house. Sasha's death had shown me that my mother would never be safe while I continued to lie beneath her roof. As I lay half drugged on the sofa, I realized that there were only two alternatives open to me: I could let them shut me away in that terrible place for mad people or I could run away. I chose to run.

When the dawn came I found a stream where I could drink, and built myself a shelter of branches and frosted leaves. It was no palatial edifice, hardly the work of a great architect, but it shut out the knifing winds of that freezing Norman spring. When it was finished, I crept inside and lay there through several risings and settings of the sun. I was exhausted enough to have slept through the pain of my body; it was the pain in my mind that kept me awake, the pain of words which cut deeper than any metal blade.

Freak of nature.

Monstrous burden.

A place where you can forget.

I thought of my mother. A dreadful clarity of vision showed me her relief at finding me gone, and I pictured Doctor Barye consoling her in his eminently sensible and practical fashion, while privately congratulating himself on this astonishing piece of good fortune. She was free now. They would go away together to a place where no one knew her, where she could forget me and be happy.

I wanted her to be happy. She was so beautiful when she smiled at the statue of the shepherd boy. That was why I made it sing for her—so that she would be happy and smile and not want to send me away to the asylum. I never meant to make her mad. When she first began to rock the empty cradle in the attic bedroom, I was afraid that she, too, might be sent to that terrible place of which she had told me. So I made everyone else go away instead. Father Mansart, Doctor Barye, Mademoiselle Perrault . . . I made them all disappear, one by one. I can make anything disappear, if I really want to. Anything except my face.

Even in my earliest memories my mother was always cold and remote, like a beautiful distant star, always beyond my reach. I think I was born knowing that I must not touch her, but it was a long time before I understood the reason for her revulsion and hatred. Even when she dragged me in front of that mirror and showed me my face, I did not at first understand. I thought the horrendous thing in the glass was some nightmare creature sent to punish me for my disobedience, and for a long time I was afraid to remove the mask in case it came back to haunt me.

The truth came to me slowly, and with the dawn of realization I developed an irrational fascination for mirrors. As I began to play with the cruel, unfeeling pieces of glass, I learned that they could be warped and manipulated, made to show to others an illusion of the sort of nightmare they showed to me. My preoccupation with illusion made my mother angry. She said it was a sick fancy and that if I did not conquer it and turn my thoughts to God, I would most certainly end as a madman.

I was always being told to turn my thoughts to God, as though I were some especially wicked creature with more than one mortal's fair share of original sin. In point of fact I was a perfectly devoted and dutiful little Catholic—until the day I learned that animals have no souls.

I have no memory of what took place once that dreadful revelation had been made to me. I do not know what I did to make Father Mansart decide I must be exorcised—it must have been something bad! I only know that after the grim ceremony took place, I discovered that I hated the priest, and I hated God too—God, who denied an afterlife to my only friend. Why should hateful men have souls when my precious Sasha was condemned to be eaten by worms, returned to the clay as though she had never existed? I could not bear to be told that when we parted it would be forever.

Sasha! As far back as I remembered she had always been there, a warm, comfortable, welcoming presence who never turned from me. She looked upon my face without its mask and licked my bare cheek with her rough pink tongue. She let me kiss her smooth, soft head and sometimes, when I was working, she would push her nose into my hand and demand to be caressed.

When I looked at her lying at my feet, with her beautiful golden fur all matted with dirt, I swore to be revenged upon the whole human race for this crime that my faith considered unworthy of the confessional. I learned how to hate the night that Sasha died. It was the first time I felt that mindless lust for blood, the uncontrollable, insatiable urge to kill . . . and kill . . . and kill!

The first time—but not the last.

It was bitterly cold beneath the bed of leaves, and my trembling breath left little clouds in the damp air. In the stiff, whitened grass beside my head, I noticed a spider weaving its purposeful way. Mademoiselle Perrault was afraid of spiders. I had put one on her shawl once, a particularly large and ugly specimen, not unlike the one I saw now, and her scream of fright had been awesome to hear. My mother was not afraid of spiders but she hated them all the same—she hated all ugly, unlovely creatures. Whenever I saw a spider in the house I would rescue it before she got the chance to squash it with her broom. Sometimes I used to dream I was a spider, scuttling in a terrified search for some safe dark hole where no hating human could find me. I used to dream of spinning a great sticky web that would swallow all the people who threw stones through our windows and shouted ugly things. In the dark I would slip out along a thread of silk and gloat over their helplessness, before paralyzing them with one single bite.

I have often thought that I would have been quite happy as a spider.

Even a spider has the right to a mate.

Hunger drove me at length from my shelter, forcing me to push on through the densely wooded area, walking by night and sleeping by day. An ironic quirk of fate had blessed me with astonishing powers of recovery, and the knife wound was now healing to a crusted brown weal which encouraged me to discard Doctor Barye's bandages. His prompt treatment had prevented infection. He had probably saved my life, but I did not see this as a thing I should be grateful for; indeed there were times when I came to hate him more for that single act of pity than for anything else.

I was vaguely aware that the forest would bring me out on the road to Canteleu. My instinct was to hide from people, but challenged by my growing need for food, that instinct was beginning to grow weaker every day. My clothes were torn and filthy, clinging to me like damp rags after so many nights spent sleeping on the ground, but that discomfort was lost beside my ravening hunger.

I was not accustomed to hunger. In her half-crazed insistence that I should eat and not remind her of a starving skeleton, my mother had constantly set before me an obscene procession of dishes. Food was forced upon me like a punishment; it was as though she had sought to atone for some past neglect in this respect that filled her with perpetual guilt. I had developed sleight of hand at a very early age, simply as

a means of conveying this unwanted food to Sasha, beneath our table
—and I often thought of heaven as a place where no one would need
to eat again. But that was before I truly understood what it meant to
starve. I had had nothing but water for nearly a week and I was light-
headed with a desperation that was driving me steadily back into the
inhabited world.

When darkness fell once more I left the shelter of the forest and
ventured out onto the open road, where a blaze of winking lights
beckoned welcomingly. Lights meant people, and where there were
people there was also food that might be stolen. I stumbled on until I
reached an encampment of tents and caravans, pitched on a broad
patch of common land and backed by the deeper mass of the forest.

Gypsies!

I knew very little about these mysterious people and what little I
knew was mostly bad, gleaned from snippets of conversation between
my mother and Mademoiselle Perrault. They were heathen masses
(according to my mother that was the worst crime imaginable); they
stole children (particularly children who did not eat their supper—this
last with a hard look at me); they were vagabonds, unwashed and
unprincipled ruffians who should never be permitted to settle near
decent folk.

Gypsies were like spiders then. My mother did not like them and I,
in consequence, felt a sneaking comradeship with such social outcasts.

Even so I was wary and fearful of discovery as I crept into the camp.
A group of horses had been tethered to a post on the inner ring of the
settlement and their warmth and beauty momentarily swayed my purpose. I reached up instinctively to caress one smooth, velvety nose and
that was my undoing, for the horse whickered nervously at my unfamiliar touch and at once a restlessness passed through the peaceful
tethered animals. Instantly a dog began to bark and a man's voice
cried out an angry warning that someone was meddling with the
horses.

Suddenly lanterns came at me from all sides. Instinctively I dropped
to the ground and hid my face with my arms, bracing myself against
anticipated blows. I was grabbed by the shoulders and dragged along
the frosted, leaf-mold floor to the enormous campfire which flickered
and flared against the clear spring night. And there I was flung at the

feet of a small man with a jet-black moustache and a single gold ring dangling from one ear, who prodded me ungently with his foot.

"Get up!" he commanded coolly.

I scrambled to my feet and looked around frantically for some avenue of escape, but I quickly saw that I was surrounded.

"Do you know what we do with thieves?" the man demanded. "Little thieves who won't show their thieving faces? We roast 'em, like hedgehogs . . . and then"—he leaned forward and pulled me close to his swarthy-skinned face—"and then we *eat* 'em!"

I saw no reason to disbelieve this threat, and my gasp of horror was greeted with loud bellows of delighted laughter.

"Better show your face then, hadn't you?" continued the man calmly. "If you don't want to finish on the campfire."

I clutched hold of the mask in defiant terror, aware of the curious anticipation on every face that was rosy-hued by the firelight.

"Oh, let him go," said a woman in gaudy-colored skirts. "Poor little devil looks as though he's starving. Look at his arms, they're like sticks. Give him some food and let him go, he's not done any harm after all."

"How do you know he's done no harm?" I heard a man shout behind me. "We don't trust gorgios, do we? Sneaking gorgios? What was he doing hanging around the horses? I say turn out his pockets and see what he's stolen first."

"And take off the mask!"

"Yes . . . take off the mask!"

The cry was taken up like a chant, and I was passed around the fire from one set of hands to another, struggling all the time to hold on to the mask.

"Take off the mask, dearie, and let's have a look at you."

Fingers were fumbling at my temples and I began to scream and kick out wildly.

"No—*no!* Please don't . . . *please!*"

"Listen to that—a gentleman's manners, if you don't mind!"

"Is he a Bourbon prince who missed the tumbril?"

The laughter was growing louder and wilder all around me.

"Got blue blood, have you, dearie—shall we open a vein and find out?"

My arms were pinned behind me and I strained violently to free myself. A strong hand came down beneath my chin and tore the mask away; and suddenly there was a deathly hush broken only by a single Romany oath.

In the terrible silence I saw them all staring at me, on their faces a mixture of expressions ranging through utter disbelief to fear.

"Let me go," I whispered faintly. "If you let me go I promise I won't come back."

They were closing in around me, like wolves in a pack. I saw the flash of a knife in the firelight and I screamed, for I suddenly knew that it was all to be endured again—the mindless violence of an angry, unreasoning mob.

Then everything went black and I knew no more of what they did to me that night.

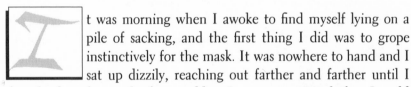t was morning when I awoke to find myself lying on a pile of sacking, and the first thing I did was to grope instinctively for the mask. It was nowhere to hand and I sat up dizzily, reaching out farther and farther until I drew back at the touch of a metal bar. It was some time before I could focus clearly, and then I saw that there were bars all around me.

I was in a cage!

Trembling with fear and bewilderment I lay back on the rags and shut my eyes tightly. I was so completely disoriented that it was easy to persuade myself that what I had seen was just the product of a fevered dream. I would wake up soon and find myself back in the attic bedroom, with Sasha lying at my feet. I waited to wake up, and while I waited I touched my swollen lips with the tip of my dry tongue and tried to call out.

"Sasha . . ."

"Quick!" said a voice beside me. "Run and fetch Javert—he told us to fetch him as soon as it was awake."

"Aw, what's the hurry? Let's have some fun with it first. Here, get hold of this stick—go on, get hold of it! What are you scared of? It can't get out."

It!

I lay very still, willing this nightmare away. It was only a dream, only a bad dream that would end. . . .

When the sharp piece of wood splintered against my forehead, sending a shower of pricking specks into my eyes, I tried to crawl out of their reach, but they simply pursued me to the other side of the cage. I could see now that there were three of them, two thin olive-skinned Gypsy boys with black hair and dirty faces and a little girl in a torn dress, who hung back and began to cry.

"Don't, Miya . . . don't hurt it like that!"

"Oh, shut up, Orka, or I'll put you in the cage with it. Come on, Vaya, let's find some stones."

A huge shadow fell across the floor of the small cage and I heard the crack of a whip. Without waiting to be told, the children fled across the camp, possessed by one shared, instinctive fear; and as the door of my cage was unlocked, I turned to look up at my new master.

My first impression was one of size—immense size. He seemed to fill the entire cage, an enormous man with a great paunch of a belly which hung grotesquely over his tight belt. He bore no resemblance to any of the small, slender, rather graceful men I had seen around the campfire the night before; he did not look like a Gypsy—but he looked every inch a rogue. His eyes, sunk in a fat face which glistened with sweat even on this cold spring morning, were narrow and infinitely cruel as they rolled over me in a critical fashion.

"Remarkable," he mused to himself. "I've waited all my life to find something like this—something truly unique. They'll come from miles around to see a living corpse. Yes, that's it, that's what I'll call you—the Living Corpse."

I backed away from him against the bars of my cage and slumped down in a crumpled heap against the cold metal rods.

"I have to go home now," I said stupidly. "My mother will be looking for me."

"The devil she will!" He sniggered. "Have your little coffin all made up for you, will she?"

"Coffin?" I stared at him without comprehension.

"That's where corpses sleep, isn't it?" he replied obligingly. "Now, there's an idea! I'll have a coffin made for the cage. No harm in heightening the effect with a prop or two."

And with that he locked the cage once more and left me staring after him with dull stupefaction. My mind was quite blank, as empty as a worm's, a numb, frozen mass that flatly refused to perform the simplest feat of reasoning. I could not understand any of those few words that had been spoken to me in my native French—he might as well have spoken Russian. I did not understand why I was in a cage or what was going to happen to me, but I had sensed sufficient threat from the man's manner to be thrown into a mindless panic.

I began to claw frantically at the lock.

In other circumstances, with a calm, rational brain and a single hairpin, I could have freed myself in minutes, but there was nothing in the cage to have served my purpose, even if I'd had the presence of mind to look. That single clumsy lock had the power to reduce me to total impotence. I hit and bit at it like a wild animal, and not once in all the time that followed did I ever return to attack it with the full force of my intellect and my extraordinary manual dexterity. Even after all these years I am still unable to explain that strange mental paralysis, except to acknowledge that the mind is capable of erecting barriers far stronger than any physical fence. Such is the key to all illusion, and God knows it was a key I learned to turn often enough on others. For me, at that moment, the illusion of captivity was so complete that even had he left the door unbarred I sometimes wonder whether I should not still have sat there, staring through the bars, like a hopeless chained animal who knows no better than to wait patiently and endure.

I lay back on the pile of sacking and watched the pale sun sink into a dull glow behind the forest. The children came back with their sticks, but I fear they found me poor sport, for this time I made no attempt to escape from their tormenting. I let them draw blood with indifference, almost without feeling, and receiving no response, they soon grew bored and drifted away to more lively entertainments.

At dusk the man called Javert returned and pushed a tin platter of disgusting stew and a patched blanket through the bars of the cage.

I sat up hopefully.

"Please, sir, may I go home now?" I whispered.

I was like a very small child, repeating the only phrase in its repertory; and when I continued to repeat it day and night, he grew angry and struck me.

"Can't you say anything else, you stupid creature? I'm fairly sick of your whining bleat. Now, get this into your addled brain—if you have a brain at all, which I'm seriously beginning to doubt—you're *my* discovery, *my* creation, and *my* fortune! They tell me you won't eat— well, I've trained too many animals to fall for that old trick. You'll eat of your own accord, or I'll force every mouthful down your ugly little throat by hand. You're not going home—and you're not going to die on me, either, have you got that, you witless little monster? You'll do as you're told or you'll suffer for it, understand me? Now, pick up that bread and eat it—*eat*, God damn you!"

He caught hold of my head and began to force the rough, grainy bread into my mouth until I gagged and retched; but strangely, instead of angering him further, that merely served to make him very calm and coldly determined.

"Very clever," he said quietly, "but if you think that's going to stop me, you're very much mistaken. I'm a very patient man, though you might not think it. I can sit here all day and if need be all night, so it's up to you, little corpse, it's entirely up to you how long you want to go on being stubborn."

I do not know how long this torture lasted; it seemed like hours. The stars were winking in the sky and he was as soiled and stinking as the floor of my cage, before I reached the limit of my endurance and capitulated to his physical strength and his unwavering determination. When I finally took the piece of bread from his hand and began to nibble it wearily, he stood up and wiped his hands on my sacking bed.

"I like an animal that knows its master," he said with satisfaction. "There's never been one yet that defeated old Javert."

When he came to me next day I did not make the mistake of refusing to eat or asking to go home, but asked instead what he intended to do with me.

He seemed surprised by my question.

"I'm going to exhibit you, of course, what else would I do with you!

People pay well to see freaks, don't you know that . . . don't you know *anything* about the world?"

I stared at him in horrified disbelief.

"They will pay," I stammered, "pay to *look* at me?"

"Of course—and pay handsomely too. In a few weeks' time, when word gets around about my new attraction, they'll be queuing all around this cage as far back as you can see."

A flood of revulsion swept over me and I started to shiver and vomit uncontrollably.

"Damn it!" he said irritably. "The greatest find in the world and what does it turn out to be? A puking brat! Just my luck!"

Storming out of the cage, he hailed a passing child, who immediately began to cower with fear.

"You—fetch me some milk and look sharp about it. Move!" He turned to glower through the bars at me. "And you'd better keep that down, you little skeleton, or I'll beat you senseless!"

I did not answer.

I knelt on the floor and began to pray silently that God would let me die before this terrible new shame was forced upon me.

I began my life as a freak exhibit with my hands and feet bound to the bars of the cage, so that I could not hide my face from the prying multitude. My first appearance had been a disaster that produced something dangerously close to a riot when the angry crowd demanded their money back; they could see nothing because I cowered in a corner with my arms wrapped around my head. They insisted they had been cheated and Javert—fearful of impending violence—promptly sent two men into the cage to bind me.

I screamed and kicked and bit like a wild animal, but I was no match for the strength of two full-grown men, and within a few moments I was secured with my arms at full stretch, like Christ on the cross, so that it was impossible for me to turn my face from view. Javert entered the cage and tied a rope around my neck so that I was forced to lift my head from my chest. As my skull jerked back against the iron bar, I opened my eyes involuntarily and saw people stepping back in delighted horror.

"Mother of God!" exclaimed a woman, pulling a screaming child into the shelter of her skirts. "Let us pass . . . for pity's sake let us through!"

The crowd parted a little to allow her to drag the hysterical infant away, but other children had also begun to scream and I could not take my eyes from their open, shrieking mouths. It was as though I saw myself once more in that mirror and shared with them all over again the horror of that first sight . . . but no horror could compare with the burning degradation, the unspeakable humiliation, of this obscene exposure. Panic numbed all other senses and I began to twist and pull like a frantic unbroken horse until the rope cut into my throat.

"Look!" someone shouted. "It's going to strangle itself!"

"How disgusting! Such things should not be shown in public. . . ."

A new ugliness was rapidly infecting the crowd. They had paid good coin to be titillated and entertained, not disturbed and discomfited. My raw anguish was offensive to some, and once more Javert was faced with angry demands to return the viewing fees.

My cage was hastily withdrawn from view. I do not know how much money I cost him on that occasion, but it was sufficient to bring him to me a little later in a towering rage. He whipped me savagely for ruining his exhibition, but at the very moment when blessed unconsciousness promised to embrace me, he cut me down from the bars and stood over me with his arms aggressively folded.

"Well?" he demanded coldly. "Have you learned how to be silent now . . . or do you need a further course of instruction?"

I lay at his feet, staring in disbelief at the huge weals that were rising on my bare arms; my head spun and there was blood in my mouth from where I had bitten my tongue. But there was only one thought in my head, only one desire. . . .

"Give me back the mask," I whispered.

"What?" He stared at me curiously.

"The mask. . . ." I repeated dizzily. "Give me back the mask . . . please!"

Suddenly, without warning, Javert began to laugh, slapping his whip against his gross thigh and then leaning forward to poke me with the crop.

"Now, you listen to me, little corpse, and listen good. No one's going to pay to see a bloody mask, but half the women in France will swoon at the sight of your face. Don Juan himself could not have drawn more skirts in one afternoon. But I won't have any more of that cursed screaming, so be warned. You drive away any more customers as you did today, and it'll be a bad lookout for you. I'll flay every scrap of skin off your miserable body if you ever behave like that again in public."

I clenched my fists and stared up at him in crazy defiance.

"I won't be seen. . . . I won't be stared at. . . . I won't. . . . *I won't!*"

Surely he would kill me now. He would bring down his great fist and smash my suicidal impudence to pulp. I waited desperately for the end that would release me, but he did not strike me again. Instead he regarded me thoughtfully, as though he measured every lesion on my body and weighed it against the time when I could be exhibited once more.

"I suppose I could always gag you," he mused slowly to himself. "It's the screaming that does the harm . . . makes the women jumpy and spooks the crowd. Yes . . . I think I'll gag you next time. A beating's soon forgotten, but a gag—a gag will put an end to your defiance once and for all."

Next day we moved on. I did not know where we were going, nor did I care; time and place had ceased to have any meaning for me. But he kept his promise. The next time I was exhibited I was gagged and bound in an upright coffin, in a position where it was physically impossible for me to do myself harm. I was silent now, and this time no one complained or wanted their money back.

I was an enormous success, Javert told me with satisfaction, when he came that night to feed me like a trained dog. When I had learned to be sensible, he would remove the gag and permit me to earn my keep with a little more comfort. I watched him put the key to the lock in his pocket and walk away whistling cheerfully and I thought how much I hated him, how I wished that he were dead.

The wind whistled around the bars of my cage that night as I lay listening to the camp dogs barking intermittently and hating . . . *hating!*

But hating could not keep me warm.

Long before the campfires burned out I laid the coffin flat on the floor, crept back inside its narrowness for shelter, and fell asleep.

The gag defeated me, as Javert had known it must. His violence and cruelty concealed an innate shrewdness, a crude, instinctive sort of wisdom that showed him new and more subtle ways to conquer rebellion. It wasn't long before I came to accept that I was only adding to my suffering by my own stubbornness; and, though my flesh still crawled with revulsion when the crowds pressed around my cage, I learned to display the silent indifference of a dumb animal. That was what they wanted, what they came to see—an animal, an oddity . . . a *thing!*

Increasingly I ceased to feel that I belonged to what is loosely termed the human race. It was as though I had tumbled onto some alien planet where I found myself unable to take revenge upon my tormentors except in the dark prison of my mind. There, in that uniquely private domain, where I was free of chains, I conjured a thousand horrible deaths for those who came to prod and stare. I learned to live almost entirely in my mind, creating a landscape of my own and peopling it with the devices of my captive imagination. My world was strange and beautiful, an entirely new dimension where music and magic held sway. It was a second Eden, where I alone was God, and at times I retreated so far into it that I became indeed a living corpse, comatose and trancelike, scarcely breathing.

And yet, however far I retreated, there was always a part of me that remained bitterly aware of reality. My mobile prison jolted me across the length and breadth of France, from one fair to another, and I was kept in conditions of animal squalor until I feigned sufficient obedience and resignation to suggest that my spirit was entirely broken. Humility was the price of those moments of privacy which basic human dignity demands. My mother had taught me to conduct myself like a gentleman, to be fastidious in my person and courteous in my demeanor. I could not bear to live like an animal.

I begged to be allowed out of the cage, to attend to matters that demanded privacy, and this request so amused Javert—that mannerless pig!—that he came to release me in person and stand guard over my ablutions with his pistol. I knew that if I made any attempt to escape he would shoot—not to kill (I was too valuable an exhibit for that) but to maim sufficiently to ensure I should not get far before he caught me.

When I demanded clean clothes he laughed out loud and told me he had never known a corpse so particular about its shroud.

"You'll be wanting a dress suit next," he sneered. "Quit your bleating, you draw good enough crowds as you are."

I turned very slowly to look at him.

"I could draw more," I said, driven by desperation to sudden boldness. "I could draw twice as many people—if you made it worth my while."

He lowered his pistol and beckoned me nearer; his instinct was to mock, but his own inherent greed made him curious.

"What blather is this?" he demanded cautiously. "You're the most ugly creature that ever walked God's earth—that's your livelihood and my good fortune. Why else would anyone want to pay to see you?"

"If you place lilies in the coffin with me . . ." I said slowly, "I could make them sing."

He pushed the pistol into his belt and rocked to and fro on his heels, bellowing with laughter.

"God help me, brat, you're a raving lunatic. You'll be the death of me, I swear it. Going to make lilies sing, are you? And just how are you going to do that, I'd like to know?"

At this time—before I turned my attention to my own setting—I still considered Bach's Mass in B minor to be the worthiest interpretation of the Latin text. It was from that composition, so beloved of Father Mansart, that I now chose the Agnus Dei which apparently issued from the petals of a wild daffodil beside Javert's boot.

"Agnus Dei . . . misere nobis . . ."

Without emotion I watched Javert's fat face sag in disbelief as he bent and plucked the flower at his feet. He held it to his ear and I heard his sharp gasp of astonishment when I let my voice ring sweetly in his head. He changed ears and abruptly my voice changed direction; he threw the withered bloom to the floor and walked away from it and I tapered the sound accordingly so that it seemed to him my voice had grown distant.

Then he came and stared at me intently, placing a thick, dirty finger on my throat and starting violently when he felt the faint vibration of my vocal cords.

"How is it possible?" he muttered, more to himself than to me. "I've seen enough ventriloquists in my time—but I've never heard anyone produce a voice like that." He caught me roughly by the shoulder and gave me an angry shake. "I should beat you for keeping this secret from me, you little devil! When I think of the money I could have made already . . ." He released me abruptly and stood back. "Still, no matter, you'll sing tonight. I'll get hold of those lilies if I have to raid a churchyard grave—"

Suddenly he became aware of my pointed silence.

"Well?" he demanded uneasily. "Why that mum, codfish look? Cat got your tongue, has it?"

I stared at him in defiant silence and he immediately began to bluster like a bully who senses the first scent of defeat.

"All right, what's going on in that twisted little head of yours? Out with it!"

I shrugged my shoulders and turned away.

"If I agreed to sing," I told him calmly, "there would be conditions."

"*Conditions!*" He caught me by the neck and pressed his huge thumbs against my windpipe in a strangling grip. "Conditions, is it? I could slit your throat for you here and now."

Very slowly I began to smile; and I suppose the utter absurdity of his empty threat must have been instantly apparent to him, for even as he spoke he let me go and I became aware that he was breathing noisily through his nose in a futile attempt to govern his fury.

"Conditions," he repeated, enunciating the word with some difficulty through clenched teeth. "Well, what are these damned conditions? Name them, you insolent little bag of bones, and have done with it!"

I sat on the grass, staring away across the straggling camp with complete indifference to his growing agitation. I let him wait . . . and sweat.

"I won't sing without the mask and I won't sing in a cage," I said steadily. "If you want to make a bargain with me, you can begin by giving me my own tent."

"If I want . . ." he began incredulously. Then suddenly he seemed to recover from his stupefaction and became coldly practical. "Impossible," he continued—but without rage, I noted. "How could I trust you to stay?"

I stared at the floor to hide the tears which were suddenly stinging my eyes as I gazed squarely into the bleak future.

"I have nowhere to go." There was an edge of weariness and resignation in my voice. "Give me privacy and a little comfort and I will stay and make your fortune in return."

He stared at me suspiciously.

"So you say. Just supposing I chose to trust you, there's still the crowd to consider. They'll want to see your face. What's the point of the coffin and the lilies if they don't see your face?"

I considered this resentfully, for I knew he had made a valid point.

"Very well," I conceded at last. "I agree to remove the mask at the end of the performance. But only for a few minutes, just long enough to shock. My face remains covered until that moment and the rest of the time is my own, to do with as I please."

"You don't want much, do you?" There was a sneer in his voice, but something moved behind his hard eyes, a look that was almost a grudging sort of respect.

"I could beat you to a pulp, but I couldn't make you sing—that's it, you little rogue, isn't it, that's what you're telling me?"

"No," I told him grimly, "you couldn't make me sing." We stared at each other like wary enemies, and after a moment he made an abrupt gesture for me to accompany him to his tent, striding off across the field and resisting the temptation to look back to check that I was following.

For the moment I was the victor.

Strange as it may seem, once I had gained that small measure of freedom, I no longer occupied myself with thoughts of escape. All my life I had been sheltered from the outside world, and I was as yet too ignorant of its ways to survive alone. I wished to eat at reasonable intervals and have a roof of sorts over my head; Javert provided the basic necessities of life and I chose to remain obediently at his side for much the same reasons that tie a stray dog to a cruel master. His authority was the boundary of my world at a time when I was still child enough to need such boundaries and the sense of order and place they bestowed. I belonged to him; perhaps for no better reason than that I simply needed to belong.

Moving became an integral part of my life, and I quickly learned to embrace the instinctive restlessness of the Gypsies and absorb their mystical ways. I soon recognized the signs that other Romany travelers had left in their wake, signs that pass unnoticed to the eyes of the uninitiated. A birch twig denoted danger ahead, white feathers the presence of chickens in the area; branches of fir announced a wedding. Silent and observant, I soon became as steeped in Romany customs and skills as any Gypsy born on the open road.

Once it was discovered that my eyes were adapted to the dark better than any cat's, I was immediately singled out for the ancient practice of *chiving drav*. In the tent of a gap-toothed old woman, famed for her herbal knowledge, I was taught how to prepare a poison capable of killing a pig without contaminating its blood. And then, at

dead of night, I would be sent creeping into a nearby farm to adminis-
ter this poison to some unfortunate beast. Most Gypsies will not
thieve at night for fear of encountering the spirits of the dead, but, as
Javert pointed out with drunken wit, the dead were hardly likely to
object to my presence. Next morning, when the farmer was puzzling
over the mysterious demise of his pig, one of the tribe would appear at
his door, begging for food. Almost invariably they would be presented
with the carcass, the farmer being anxious to get it off his hands,
fearful lest the death heralded some deadly outbreak of disease.

I hated this practice and never ate meat procured in this manner. It
became known as one of my eccentric ways, that I would go hungry
rather than share in such a meal; and eventually, as the performances
in my tent grew steadily more professional and lucrative, I refused to
undertake this distasteful task anymore. The night that I threw the
vial of *drao* on the campfire and told the tribe to procure their own
miserable carrion in future was a strange turning point. No one moved
to punish me, no one struck me to the ground for my disobedience;
and it was then that I suddenly came to realize I was not without
power.

Power!

The concept began to appeal increasingly as I perfected my ventriloquist's skills and sat long into the night devising increasingly complex
magical tricks to enchant the crowds. By the time I had passed two
summers with the Gypsies my fame was already beginning to run
before me, and the camp was growing unusually prosperous as a result.
I was the main attraction at every fair; people came for miles to see me
perform. And though I still hated the moment of unmasking, there
was a certain satisfaction in the breathless hush which greeted my
singing and my displays of legerdemain.

Power!

Once I had begun to seek it actively, power came to me in many
curious and unexpected ways. My period of instruction in the wisewoman's tent had sparked an acute interest in the herbal properties
she sold at all the summer fairs. She had remedies for every conceivable human disorder; and since anything that caused the human race
to suffer was inevitably of consuming fascination to me, I began to
study her skills with stealthy industry. She was ugly enough herself to

be largely untroubled by my presence, and I think she was flattered by my questions. But when I began to experiment with tried and trusted remedies, she was furious and threatened to put a curse upon me. I think that would have been an end of my tuition, but that same night she was stricken with a fever that yielded to none of her proven recipes. The rumor went around the camp that she was dying of a deadly contagion and with cold and pitiless logic the tribe repitched their tents at a safer distance.

"Surely someone will go to her," I protested uneasily.

Javert looked up in mild surprise from the stick he was patiently whittling

"There's nothing to be done for a mortal fever," he told me placidly. "It's only common sense to keep away."

A strange fury gripped me, a fury that owed virtually nothing to pity, but a great deal to mortal impotence and complacency. There was no better way to raise a demon in my brain than to tell me a thing could not be done.

Impossibility was not a concept I acknowledged.

I got up quietly, without breathing a word of my intention, and crossed the void to the old woman's tent.

I could see as I looked at her that she was in a very bad way and I felt the same frustration I had once experienced when I dismantled my mother's clocks—unbelievable irritation in the face of my own inadequacy and limited competence.

Well . . . I had learned very early to master the mechanism of a clock. And I would not be defeated this time either—not by some miserable pestilence invisible to the naked eye!

I was not moved by any feeling of common humanity or affection. This was simply a challenge I could not resist.

While the old woman lay moaning on her pallet, completely insensible of my presence, I pulled out the ancient copper pans and began to heat an infusion of my own. . . .

She lived.

The infection spread all over the camp, afflicting almost half of the sturdy Gypsy children, who had seldom known a day's illness in their lives. Those who were treated with the traditional infusions died; the three who were treated with mine lived.

Beginner's luck, perhaps, but of such strange and timely coincidences legends are born. After that incident the tribe began to treat me with increasingly wary respect. The entire encampment, riddled with superstition, took to explaining my rapidly expanding skills as a natural talent for dealing with unseen forces. A story went around the campfire that I was the scholar of ancient Gypsy legend, the tenth graduate of the College of Sorcery, who had been detained in payment to serve as the devil's apprentice. It was said that I knew all the secrets of nature and magic and that I rode a dragon which dwelt high in the mountains of Hermanstadt and slept in the caldron where thunder was brewed.

The change in my status was remarkable. Small children no longer threw stones and chanted names when I appeared. If I passed by their tents in the daytime, they would run away from me, as though I were the devil in person, shrieking for the mothers, who now used my name as the ultimate threat to enforce obedience.

"Hush! Or Erik will come and take you to his tent and you will never be seen again."

Boys of my own age, who had made my life a misery during my early months with the tribe, now left me alone, fearing a terrible retribution if they angered me. And since it was comfortable to be free of their torment, I did everything in my power to foster the growth of my grim reputation.

Power!

I was beginning to acquire quite a taste for it, to see it as a very satisfactory substitute for happiness . . . for love.

By the time I had spent three summers with the Gypsies, I was pleasantly aware that everyone in the camp regarded me with some degree of unfounded terror.

Yes . . . everyone was afraid of me by then; everyone except Javert. Legend though I might be, I was still his creature.

And he never let me forget it for a moment.

avert was not a true-born Romany, not even a *poshratt,* or a half-breed. He was a *chorody,* a wanderer tolerated purely for his skills as a showman, and I soon began to understand that, though he traveled with the Gypsies, he was no more a part of their tightly knit community than I was.

At some point in his past he had had a nodding acquaintance with an education. Unlike the rest of the community he could read, and from time to time odd remnants of culture would surface inexplicably through the layers of his inherent vulgarity. It was Javert who told me the legend of Don Juan and added the great lover's name to the odd collection of nicknames with which he delighted to address me. At first it was just another insult, no more hurtful than anything else; but as I grew older, and more aware of the meaning behind his mockery, I began to hate that name of Don Juan more than any other.

Javert was forever prating of lovers, and yet no woman ever came to his tent. Since he was no man's blood brother, there was no father in the camp who would have accepted a bride price from him, and in my innocent ignorance I simply assumed that this was the reason that he had no wife.

He strode into my tent one evening without warning, as was his wont, and leaned over me, breathing vile spirit fumes into my face. I could see at once that he was drunk—and when he was drunk, he was dangerous; I knew I would have to take care.

"Working . . . always working," he remarked unpleasantly, pushing a fat finger into the mechanism of a new device which lay on the table before me. "What an industrious little corpse you are!"

When an unseen spring snapped shut on his finger, I received a blow to the head which tumbled me to the floor.

"Damn you!" he snapped. "You made that happen!"

"I did not!" I flared with indignation, since for once I was telling the truth. "It was an accident."

"Yes, I daresay," he sneered. "You're very good at arranging accidents, aren't you? I've noticed how many little misfortunes befall me when you are around."

I was silent, wondering with alarm whether he could really have guessed just how much mischief I was responsible for. That fall from his horse, for instance . . . the inexplicable collapse of his tent. Silly, irritating, commonplace misfortunes that I had thought him incapable of connecting with me.

I looked up into his face, saw with terror that he knew everything, and waited for the punishment to fall.

I didn't have to wait long.

Abruptly he snatched the mask from my face, slashed it to pieces with his ugly knife, and flung the pieces at me. Then he stared at me.

"No tears?" he frowned. "You disappoint me, little corpse. And surely you know better by now than to disappoint old Javert."

He reached out and struck me repeatedly across the face with the back of his huge hand, but I remained silent, staring at him with dry-eyed loathing. And at length, remembering that I was to perform that night, he abandoned his attempt to make me cry.

"A man at last," he said begrudgingly, "no longer a sniveling brat. You'll be wanting a wage next, I suppose."

I judged it safer to remain silent as he loomed over me. I had learned to distrust these moments of apparent generosity—they were usually the prelude to fresh violence or humiliation.

"How old are you?" he demanded unexpectedly.

"I don't know." I kept my eyes on the floor.

"You don't know?" He sniggered suddenly. "Surely you have a date of birth, like anyone else! Or perhaps you weren't born at all. Maybe you just hatched out of an egg like a lizard."

A looking glass shattered in my memory and I shivered.

"I don't know," I repeated shakily. "My . . . she . . . it was never spoken of."

He passed the sleeve of his shirt across his nose and grinned, show-ing a row of yellow, gapped teeth.

"Well . . . I daresay there was nothing much to celebrate. It's a miracle no one dropped you on the fire before you drew a breath. But I'd say you must be eleven or twelve by now—that seem about right to you?"

I nodded warily, wondering where this strange line of questioning could be leading.

"Well, then," he continued affably, "another year or so, if you keep drawing these crowds, I might see my way clear to paying you a wage. Of course, it would depend on whether you continued to give satisfac-tion—on stage and off, if you take my meaning. I like boys who know how to show their gratitude . . . in a manner of speaking."

I stared at him blankly. "I don't understand," I whispered.

"Don't worry, you will!" He laughed and cuffed me playfully around the ear. "Yes, you'll understand, all in good time. You're very clever, I grant you that—a sight too clever for your own good at times—but you don't know everything. There's a thing or two that I can teach you when I've a mind to do it. And if you're willing to learn, if you're willing to *please* . . . well, you might find me very generous."

I had no idea what he was talking about, but his tone and soft, almost feline manner made me cold with apprehension. This curious amiability cloaked an unknown threat as yet beyond my comprehen-sion, and I was afraid to ask any more questions. I had the feeling that for once I did not want to know the answers.

He sucked his bleeding finger, spat upon the earthen floor, and sauntered to the flap of the tent. In the doorway he turned to look back at me and there was a curious expression on his face.

"I never had a corpse before," he mused.

And then he was gone, leaving me alone with my ignorance and my fear.

I waited nervously during the following months for this nameless disas-ter to overtake me, but my life continued as before and nothing worse befell me than the beatings with which I was already familiar. I had learned to accept physical pain with a show of indifference. If my performance was not perfect, if I crossed my master with a casual, unconsidered word, I knew exactly what to expect. But my split skin and bruises healed quickly and I was careful never to make a mistake more than once. I had learned how to survive.

At some point during the following year we crossed the boundary into Spain, traveling steadily in the direction of Catalonia. The annual fair at Verdu had been a traditional meeting place for Gypsies since the fourteenth century, and an atmosphere of suppressed excitement permeated the camp at the prospect of emotional reunions with blood brothers. At night the tents and wagons disgorged their occupants around the campfire, the fiddlers struck up a merry refrain, and the Gypsy girls danced for their menfolk, weaving in and out of the flickering light, trailing long scarves over bare, suntanned arms . . . graceful . . . *sensual.* . . .

This was the time I had learned to love above all else, when the magic of the Gypsies unfolded before my eyes as I lay a little distance away, watching, listening, absorbing, yet silent and unseen, like a snake in the dry grass. Their culture was a universe removed from the respectable middle-class existence I had known before, a life steeped in the love of music and governed by an instinctive, abiding respect for the forces of magic and mystery. To a Gypsy every stream, forest, and hedgerow is peopled by invisible sprites and demons that must be constantly appeased by incantations and charms. The occult holds a powerful grip and fortune is determined by the turn of a tarot card. I was fascinated by the secrets of divination and enthralled by their music, which opened up new vistas to my formally trained ear. It was music that acknowledged no artificial boundaries. Dispensing with chords, transition, and intermediate modulation, its freedom was utterly intoxicating.

I listened and I learned and all that I absorbed found expression in the secret world within my tent, in music or illusion. No part of me was untouched by their inspiration, but I did not acquire those heightened concepts of beauty and mystery without pain.

I had been a solitary child, content with my own company, neither knowing nor desiring companions; but now I looked out upon a very different world, a world of gregarious, tightly woven people, who were not forbidden by unspoken taboos to touch each other or be public in that touching. Every evening that I watched them together, fighting, laughing, loving, made the awareness of my own difference increasingly sharp and hurtful, threw a cold new light on my inner misery.

Perhaps, if I had not tumbled among Gypsies, I should not have been made aware of the female form at such an early age; perhaps I should have enjoyed a few more years of sexless, boyish innocence. Gypsy women are not light and lascivious in their ways—virgins are highly valued and only to be bought for an accepted bride price. But love, once sanctified by marriage, was not a private thing and couples embraced freely around the campfire, displaying their pleasure in one another's bodies without shame. That spring in Verdu it seemed to me that the whole world was pairing off together, sharing a universal secret that would always be closed to me. And suddenly it was not enough to be the devil's apprentice, the star turn of an increasingly famous traveling show.

All I wanted was to be like everyone else.

While the wedding celebrations were at their height, the fiddles throbbing with that extraordinary love of life which is so peculiar to Gypsies throughout the world, I slipped away into black, shapeless night and stole what I needed from the wisewoman's tent.

I could live with cruelty and hatred; it was the happiness of others that I could no longer endure, the sudden realization that none of my talents was ever going to win me acceptance as a human being. My tent might be comfortable now, I might be free to come and go as I pleased, but in all essentials I still lived in a cage, surrounded by invisible bars. The world wanted nothing from me except the gratification of the sensory organs of sight and sound.

I was alone and nothing was ever going to change that.

Perhaps it was time to leave this world behind.

he night was dry and still, silent except for the far-off throb of fiddles and the gentle whirr of crickets in the tall grass. Enormous moths hurled themselves at my lantern and bounced off my mask as I fled away from the settlement, where the Gypsies danced with growing wildness as liquor began to flow more freely and the flames of the campfire leapt up against the black Spanish sky.

When I was certain no one could see me, I tore off the mask and threw it at the crescent moon which gleamed pale and uncaring upon my frenzy of grief. Then I sat upon the dusty road and examined the little bottle I had stolen from the wisewoman's tent. It contained sufficient poison to kill the whole camp. I did not intend that there should be any mistake over the dosage.

Unscrewing the little glass stopper and checking at the bitter aroma which emerged, I hesitated. The magic talisman of death was in my hand—my skeleton's hand—and all that prevented me from using it to escape from this nadir of despair was the sudden nagging relic of a memory I had thought long discarded.

Father Mansart's homily on the deadly sins of murder and suicide had been impressed on me at an age when most children are struggling to master the Credo. Murder and suicide, he had told me grimly, were equal crimes in the eyes of the Lord and brought an undiscriminating damnation upon the perpetrator. The suicide lies in an unhallowed grave and the gates of heaven remain closed to him forever.

"Life is never ours to take, Erik. If you remember nothing else of what I have taught you, remember that."

They were virtually his last words to me after the exorcism and I had stared through him, as though he did not exist, pretending I could not hear a word he said.

But now I remembered and I gazed at the poison in my hand with horror. Suppose it was true that by this act I closed the door on one suffering merely to open another leading to one infinitely worse . . . and this time without natural end?

Appalled by the possibility, I flung the little bottle to the ground and watched the dry earth swallow up the liquid that trickled out. A sense of hopelessness washed over me as I bent mechanically to retrieve the mask, but before I could replace it I was startled by a cry in the darkness behind me.

I stopped and listened intently and once more the voice wavered out in the darkness, this time on a low moan of pain. Moving instinctively in the direction of the sound, I climbed a rocky outcrop, unfaltering and fearless with my cat's eyes and the peculiar agility which had once caused my mother to liken me to a monkey.

On the other side of the rocks the lantern showed me a crumpled heap of brightly colored skirts and a pretty face that was familiar to me from the campfire.

"Dunicha?" I whispered.

She looked up at me and screamed with an ugly, piercing intensity that took me by shocked surprise; I had forgotten for the moment that I was no longer wearing the mask.

Her screams jangled every nerve in my body and I was suddenly overcome with blind fury.

"Stop it!" I snapped, shaking her wildly by her thin shoulders. "Stop that screaming or I shall do you all the harm you fear and more!"

That silenced her. She swallowed her screams with a sort of gulping sob and cowered back in my grasp, like a terrified rabbit in the jaws of a wild dog.

I let go of her contemptuously.

"Where are you hurt?" I demanded with cold indifference.

She was shaking violently and her teeth were chattering with fright, but she managed to indicate her left foot, which I saw was twisted at an unnatural angle.

"Will you let me look?" I said.

She was too frightened to refuse. Over my Gypsy garb I still wore the long magician's cloak that I affected for performances. Removing it, I tore a strip from the bottom and then wrapped the rest of the robe around her shoulders, for it was bitterly cold beneath the clear mid-April sky and her skin was chill and moist with shock. I felt the broken bone in her ankle at the first probe of my fingers and immobilized the joint as best I could. She fainted when I touched her, though whether from pain or sheer terror it was impossible to tell. I wasn't unduly concerned or surprised, and at any rate it made my task that much easier.

When I had finished, I sat down on a nearby rock and waited for her to come to her senses. The light of my lantern traced the curve of her breast and a thought came to me that I hastily pushed away in disgust. I did not touch her; and after a while the urgent desire to do so ebbed away, leaving me calm and cold once more, entirely in control of my body. That first adolescent stirring of desire was fierce but transient, and I felt curiously triumphant at having mastered it. I was suddenly quite warmly disposed to this girl who had made me feel that I need never fear the ravages of love. Lust was nothing special after all, simply a rush of blood, an animal instinct that I could contain and control, just as successfully as I controlled my voice. This girl was pretty but I did not love her, so perhaps God had been merciful after all and not made me as other boys; perhaps I would never love anyone. Elation and relief surged through me at the thought and I wished she would wake up so that I could begin to thank her for this wonderful sense of release. Lust was nothing, and I did not love her. I did not love her and I no longer felt the need to die of crushing misery. Everything was going to be all right after all.

She opened her eyes upon my face and looked hastily away with a shudder.

"I have never seen you before, without the mask," she whispered.

"Really!" A little of my warm gratitude shriveled, and with it all desire to thank her. "You must be the only person in the camp who has not, then. Perhaps I should charge you for the privilege of a private viewing."

Fear returned to her eyes. I sighed and picked up the mask, which lay beside me on the ground, replacing it with a gesture that had become second nature to me.

"You have nothing to fear," I said quietly. "I'm not going to hurt you. I never hurt anyone."

"But, you said . . . before . . . you said—"

"Oh, that!" I gave a little shrug of indifference. "That was only because you made me angry. I hate it when people scream at me. All those stupid women screaming and fainting around my cage—you can't imagine how much I hate it!"

She sat up a little, her eyes still wary upon me, but her breath coming with greater ease as the mindlessness of her terror abated.

"Everyone says that you are evil, that you work for the devil as an apprentice and—"

"And ride a dragon!" I finished for her derisively. "Do you honestly think I would stay with Javert if I had a dragon to ride?"

She smiled faintly. "I suppose not. How strange it is to talk to you just as if—as if you were like everyone else."

A sick cold wave passed over me and I suddenly had the horrible feeling I was going to cry . . . just when I had thought I was done with crying forever! That quiet, unthinking little comment completely shattered my composure and my newfound resignation.

"I *am* like everyone else!" I burst out angrily. "Inside, I am just like everyone else! Why should that seem so strange?"

She was silent, staring at me curiously, and I found I could no longer meet her gaze. She did not understand what I was telling her; but at least she was no longer afraid of me. I supposed that was something.

"What were you doing out here alone?" I asked after a moment. "Why are you not at the wedding feast?"

Something passed across her face, a fleeting look of guilty defiance.

"That's none of your business!" she said rather sharply.

I stared at her in honest disbelief, for I suddenly saw there could be only one explanation for her absence.

"You have been meeting a lover?" I breathed in awe. "A *gorgio* lover?"

She glared at me. "And what if I have?"

"Your father will beat you and drive you from the camp if he finds out," I said uneasily. I knew there was no worse crime a Gypsy daughter could commit than to betray her proud race with a gorgio. Mixed blood was deeply frowned upon.

When her angry bravado abruptly disappeared and she burst into noisy tears, I did not know what to do.

"Where is your lover?" I demanded uncomfortably. "Why has he left you here alone? Is he coming back for you?"

Her face contorted with rage and she beat her clenched fist on the hard ground.

"He promised to marry me, the Spanish pig . . . he promised! Oh, they are right about gorgios, filthy, lying gorgios! May the devil rot him! I hope his manhood shrivels and drops off on his wedding night!"

I was glad that I was wearing the mask, for I knew I had turned furiously red with embarrassment. Three years among the Gypsies had not hardened me to their healthy, unashamed vulgarity.

"What are you staring at me like that for?" she demanded with hostility.

"I wasn't staring."

I was hastily apologetic. Not only was she no longer afraid of me, she now seemed to remember that she possessed at least five years seniority. A cold aloofness had crept into her voice and I felt myself growing younger and more stupid by the minute beneath her contemptuous glance.

"They will come looking for you soon," I told her. "They must not find you here."

I leaned forward to give her my hand, but she recoiled in disgust.

"Don't touch me!" she spat unexpectedly. "If you touch me I shall scream until the whole camp hears and comes to find us!"

I was stunned. We had conversed like human beings; now suddenly I was an animal again. Then, as I looked at her face in the light of the lantern, as I saw the sly, secret smile of satisfaction cross her lips, I suddenly understood her purpose.

"No one will believe you!" I gasped. "No one will believe it was I who lured you to this place."

"Oh, you didn't lure me," she said simply. "I was taken by force."

"In silence?" I inquired with trembling sarcasm. "Without a single cry of protest?"

"I fainted—from terror." She was staring fixedly into the distance, as though she were watching a play being acted out in front of her. "Who would doubt the truth of that?"

No one, I admitted to myself with cold horror. No one would doubt her. I had cultivated a reputation for evil out of all proportion to my years. No one now was going to waste any time wondering whether I was too young to rape a pretty girl.

I backed away from her, shaking my head in slow disbelief. Then panic overwhelmed me and I fled back the way I had come.

I was sobbing with rage when I reached my tent. Grabbing the few belongings I had accumulated over the years, I rolled them into a sack, with a feverish desperation that seemed curiously at odds with my earlier mood of suicidal despair. Once she told her tale, I knew that I would wear the dead man's shirt. Forgetting their individual fears, the entire camp would rise up against me to take revenge for such a violation. I was not afraid of death anymore, but I was still sufficiently a child to fear the protracted torture that must precede it. They would do terrible things to me . . . indescribable things. . . .

I was so wrapped up in my own terror that I did not hear the footstep behind me until it was too late.

A hand fell heavily on my shoulder.

"Well, now," said a familiar voice in my ear. "What's all this haste? Leaving, are we . . . leaving dear old Javert without so much as a by-your-leave?"

He twisted me around to face him, digging his fingers into a point on my neck which caused me paralyzing pain. The soft menace of his voice and the narrow intensity of his gaze held me breathless with fear.

"Leaving without a word of gratitude after all I've done for you," he continued thoughtfully. "Looked after you like my own flesh and blood and now you think you'll up and off. Oh, no, my dear . . . I don't think so. You don't escape from old Javert as easily as that."

As his free hand ripped the buttons from my shirt I gave a gasp of shock. The shameful, nameless horror that had been hovering above me like a breath of foul air had now descended so unexpectedly that I was powerless to struggle against his strength. As I watched him take off his belt I knew instinctively that this was to be no simple beating—this was a terror as yet beyond my imagination.

His hand slid caressingly down my body beneath the open shirt and I shivered.

"How cold you are," he complained. "As cold as the dead, ice water running in your veins. But no matter, I shall soon warm you."

"Please—" I jerked away from his hand and he laughed as he forced me to the floor.

I began to fight in earnest then, with a savage desperation I should not have employed simply for my life.

"That's better," he said with strange satisfaction, "that's much better. You're surprisingly strong, aren't you? I see I could not have delayed this last little lesson much longer. No one else will ever want you as I do—certainly no woman! Do you know that? Do you realize the great honor I'm about to do you? No . . . of course you don't. Proper little innocent you are, for all the tales they tell about you around the campfire. Pure as driven snow in spite of all your clever tricks. Well, not for much longer. This, my dear, is the end of your innocence."

He put one hot hand between my legs and then I understood; I did not know how it would be possible, but deep inside I understood what was going to happen to me.

Rape!

Why had I thought that was a fate reserved exclusively for women?

I stopped fighting and lay perfectly still, watching him discard his dirty clothes on the floor beside me.

"I see you've decided to be sensible," he remarked. "That's good, that's how I like it. A healthy struggle to whet the appetite—and then, a little accommodation."

"What must I do?" I whispered hollowly.

"Take off your clothes and the mask and then . . . I'll show you."

I sat up warily, controlling my senseless panic. No sudden movement, nothing to cause him alarm. I saw him relax visibly at this evidence of my weary resignation. When he turned away carelessly to kick off his boots, my hand closed on the hilt of the knife that was protruding from beneath his discarded belt.

I waited just long enough for him to turn back to me, then I plunged the knife up into the obscene, wobbling mass of flesh which concealed his gut. I was shocked and thrilled by the extraordinary intensity of my pleasure as I felt the knife slide effortlessly between the layers of skin and buy itself up to the hilt; shocked that I should register that extraordinary sensation precisely where his indecent hand had touched me.

I watched Javert's eyes bulge in incredulous disbelief, his mouth sag and quiver on a soundless gasp, his hands clutch helplessly at the fountain of blood which spurted from him when I calmly removed the knife. I gazed at the crimson torrent with dispassionate, almost academic surprise; it was as though I had burst a skin of wine. There was time to wonder at this curious phenomenon . . . there seemed to be all the time in the world.

He was on his feet, lurching desperately toward the flap of the tent, when I sank the knife into his ribs, this time striking jarringly against bone. His hands closed over mine as I jerked the blade free, but his strength was draining rapidly away and he could not hold me. I swung my arms free in an arc and brought the knife down for the final time, implanting it squarely in the sweating hollow of his throat.

He fell like a stone at my feet. I stared down at his mutilated body with panting ecstasy and watched his jerking death throes without a flicker of remorse or revulsion. It had been so easy and so incredibly satisfying that I could hardly believe my good fortune. Five minutes ago I had been an innocent, terrified child; now I was a man, with a remarkably efficient murder to my credit.

I felt intoxicated with power as I wiped the knife clean on Javert's shirt and tucked it into the sack which still lay on my pallet. Quietly, unhurriedly, I gathered up the sack and made my way to his tent, where I quickly located the leather bag in which he kept the profits from my performances. There was nothing furtive or frightened about the manner in which I crossed the camp and calmly took my favorite horse from the tethered group. I no longer feared discovery; no man would lay a hand on me again and live to boast of it. I was leaving now because I chose to leave; and I left not in fear for my own safety, but in contempt for my past weakness, my childish terrors, and my spine-less despair.

The end of innocence. . . .

I had outgrown the limitations of this petty little tribe of wanderers; I no longer needed the dubious protection of a perverted villain. My childhood was at an end and the world beckoned to my unique talents. I had only just begun to explore the vast empire of my mind, and now its frontiers stretched ahead of me like a far horizon. I wanted to consume every note of music ever written, to absorb all the world's knowledge, and master arts as yet unconceived by humanity. I no longer needed boundaries . . . wherever I found them in the future I would tear them down, forging in my wake new wonders to astonish poor credulous mankind. Creation—and destruction—were the only lusts I would acknowledge henceforth. I would be like God, an abso-lute force; beyond question . . . beyond restraint.

The end of innocence. . . .

Like Adam I had eaten of the tree of knowledge and been con-demned, in consequence, to wander the face of the earth. But my Eden was full of cruel nettles and vicious thorns. . . . I could not look back on its loss with any regret. The chains of conscience with which a parish priest had sought to shackle me were broken now beyond repair. Losing the fear of death, I had lost all respect for the lives of others. Tonight I had been made to see that life was cheap and easily spent, a poor cowering creature of the daytime that could be snuffed out as easily as a candle's light.

Death was the ultimate power and I his eager, willing apprentice.

Murder was only another art for me to master!

Giovanni
1844-1846

I often come to sit alone in the rooftop garden now.

When the warmth of the Roman sun at noon begins to draw the stench of the city's squalor, I like to nod drowsily upon the travertine bench, breathing the heady scent of Luciana's potted plants. Sometimes, bending to take a cutting with fingers that are twisted and deformed almost beyond recognition by arthritis, I remember the loving care Erik lavished upon these flowers; I remember how tenderly he nursed them through the ravages of Luciana's feckless neglect, and the way he would sometimes pause to caress a smooth, green leaf, as though he was silently willing it to grow. Over the succeeding years they have flourished into magnificent blooms, just as he once flourished beneath my guiding hand. These flowers, this white stone bench, and the mysterious models lining the walls of my cellar are all I have left to remind me of those two years that altered the landscape of my world forever.

Memories! Memories are like fireflies darting across the surface of my mind, showing me here and there images so sharp and vivid that I catch my breath in wonder before the vignette disappears, sinking like a pebble into the quicksand of regret and recrimination. Perhaps they are right, those who say behind my back—as I know they do!—that I had begun to lose my faculties long before the tragedy. But I hope they are wrong. I would like to think that I was as sane as anyone else that day when I first saw Erik; I would like my story to stand as the last will and testament of a man sound in mind.

I remember quite clearly the dark stillness of the empty streets as I walked down to the site; I remember the aching heaviness in my heart as I brooded on the letter which had drawn me from my bed, restless and disturbed, before dawn was in the sky.

It was an unremarkable morning, a day that promised to be like any other; and in the gray light, rain had awakened the pungency of excavated earth, bringing the familiar scent of wet sand and cement to my nostrils. Some master masons hate a site at sunrise, when first light cruelly underlines the limits of their daily achievement. So little accomplished yesterday, so much to be done today! But for me dawn was a time of inspiration. I could not remember a period in my life when an unfinished building had not been my reason for waking, eating . . . breathing. It was only when a contract was completed that I felt dissatisfaction creeping upon me, a sense of loss that was almost bereavement. Erik understood that. Erik understood things that most boys never even glimpse; but right from the beginning the depth of his passion to create made me fear for him. In my mind there was always the uneasy knowledge that one day there would inevitably be the great commission, the glorious challenge to which he would give every ounce of his being and from which he could not bear to part; the beautiful, full-term child of his imagination that he would kill to possess.

I came to know him as a gentle, sensitive genius, but I never deceived myself upon that one point. The boy had killed long before he ever came to me, that much was quite obvious at our first meeting.

I remember that before we had exchanged a single word, his knife was already drawn upon me. . . .

He was trespassing.

As soon as I stepped onto the site I became aware of a thin, boyish figure gliding like a ghost over the gray ramparts of the scaffolding, a strangely eerie sight in the light of the rising sun. I did not cry out in angry indignation, but stood for a moment watching the boy draw his fingers caressingly across the wet masonry. After a moment he stood back, lifting his arms to the walls like a Druid priest communicating with some heathen god, and his hands began to move with a rhythmic series of swoops, as though he were molding the very air around him. It was one of the strangest and most beautiful sights I had ever seen.

There was something intensely mystical in this curious communion that made me want to go on watching him with breathless fascination; but my foot touched the edge of a poorly balanced mason's point and sent it crashing to the ground. The boy leapt down from the scaffold with the ease of a young panther and in a second he was upon me with his knife drawn.

I was startled by the sight of the white mask. The eyes behind it were as tense and wary as any wild animal's as he gestured for me to back against the stonework and clear his path into the street. With hindsight I know that I should have listened to his instinctive wisdom and let him go. But I was never a coward and my curiosity had been intensely aroused. With his knife gleaming barely a half inch from my throat, I merely raised my hands ironically and demanded to know if he usually dealt old men such scant civility.

I didn't seriously expect an answer and I was unprepared for the sudden lowering of the knife and the look of uncertainty which replaced the feral aggression in his eyes.

"*Monsieur?*"

The instant he spoke I was aware that, in spite of his outlandish Gypsy attire, this was no young backstreet cutthroat, intent on murdering me for the sake of my purse. The single word was so beautifully pitched and modulated that I found I had no desire in my head other than to hear him speak again.

"Do you speak Italian?" I demanded curiously.

"Yes, sir." He seemed astonished to find himself being questioned with common civility.

"You are trespassing on private property . . . do you understand I could have you arrested for that?"

The knife was instantly raised again, but with a weary halfheartedness that suddenly gave me the courage to push his hand away.

"Put that damned thing down, for heaven's sake boy, you make me quite nervous. There—that's better. Now . . . tell me what you were doing here."

"I wasn't stealing!" he said quickly, looking down at the knife rather helplessly, as though suddenly uncertain what he ought to do with it now. "I wasn't doing any damage—"

"I can see that," I said with dry irony. "Nobody ever did any damage to stone simply by stroking it."

"*Oh!*" One hand went to the mask in a gesture of agonized embarrassment. "How long have you been watching me?"

"Long enough to know I wasn't watching a thief at work," I said. "Interested in stonework, are you . . . care to see the plans, perhaps?"

He looked at me warily, as though trying to decide whether he was being mocked, but I saw him abandon his natural suspicion when I reached inside my coat for the papers.

"Thank you," he said automatically, taking the sheets from me and spreading them out upon a dry patch of ground beneath the scaffold. He reminded me of a little boy who has had good manners drummed into him by a long and painful process, and I was taken aback when he suddenly gave a cry of rage that was almost a sob.

"No, it's wrong!" he said furiously. "It's *quite* wrong, not a bit like I —oh, how can you bear to build anything so vulgar?"

I gave a slight sigh, unnerved to remember that my first response to those plans had been oddly similar.

"The building is being erected to suit the specifications of a very rich and vulgar client," I explained patiently. "An architect must eat, you know, and so must a master mason. If we built only to satisfy our own inner vanity we would very soon starve."

I watched him stare darkly at the design.

"I would rather starve!" he said with extraordinary passion. "I would rather starve than build ugly houses!"

I believed him. The tone of his voice affected me with deep unease —it was as though *ugly* was the worst expletive in his dictionary.

"Are you apprenticed here in Rome?" I inquired after a decent pause.

"No, sir." Was it my imagination or did he stiffen at the question?

"But you have an interest in architecture, do you not? You love fine buildings?"

"I studied a little once," he admitted cautiously. "A long time ago, when I was a child."

He could not have been much more than thirteen and yet he spoke of childhood as though it were many decades behind him. He puzzled and worried me with his sad, wary dignity and his whiplash reaction to threat. I wanted to know who he was, where he came from, and why he combined the manners of a young gentleman with all the instincts of an experienced street killer.

Strangely the mask remained the least of my curiosity. . . .

"I have other works in progress," I told him quietly, "and I think you will find that not all my clients are without taste. If the company of an old and opinionated man is not uncongenial to you . . ."

I spread my hand to indicate the street beyond, and after one last moment of hesitation, born of God knows what terrible experience, he stood up and followed me.

A strange elation surged through my thin veins as I began to walk away, not looking behind, trusting that he would not stab me in the back or simply flee at the first opportunity. My inner depression had evaporated like the morning mist, leaving behind an odd, pulsing happiness, an awareness that somehow I had stumbled on something very rare and precious.

For a moment I thought I knew exactly how Christ must have felt when he called John.

It was hard, not looking behind me. He made no more noise in walking than a cat, and since it was as yet too early to see his shadow on the walls we passed, I had the oddest sensation of being trailed by a ghost.

The contract I wished to show him lay on the south side of the city, outside the ancient Roman walls, and was within a few weeks of completion. I could tell by the quick intake of his breath that the sight pleased him; I was rather pleased with the result myself. For the last fifteen years or so I had dealt mainly in contracting, but I had never released control of the high-precision work. The fine carving in relief on the capitals and cornices, the cutting of tracery and archmolds, I still considered my exclusive province, despite the slow creep of arthritis, and here I could show him the good taste of pure, clean lines and understatement, a skill that merely released the natural beauty of stone.

He was impressed. He didn't say anything, but his silent approval washed over me like a warm tide and made me feel as though I had just submitted my master's piece to the ancient Masonic lodge. An odd feeling that, in a man who had spent forty-five years at his craft!

I permitted him to prowl all over the empty, echoing building, touching, asking questions, occasionally volunteering a criticism that struck me dumb by its pertinence and vision, its uncanny mirroring of my own instincts.

And then, as we were disturbed by the arrival of the master carpenter and his apprentice in the courtyard below, the boy at once shrank out of sight against a bedroom wall.

"I must go," he said uneasily, the eyes behind the mask already seeking the shortest path to flight.

I laid a hand on his thin arm to detain him.

"Where do you live?" I demanded suddenly.

"I don't live anywhere." He was staring at my hand where it rested on his arm, making no effort to shrug free of my grasp, merely staring as though he could not quite believe I had touched him without intending to inflict pain. "Sometimes I travel with the fairs for a while. I heard there was one in the Trastevere, so I left my horses outside the city walls and came to look while the streets were quiet. . . ."

As he spoke absently, he put one finger on the back of my hand, gently tracing the knotted veins that ran through my dry and wrinkled skin, so roughened and whitened after years of contact with stone dust.

"I must go," he repeated sadly.

"But you'll come back," I insisted, wondering a little at my inexplicable reluctance to see him disappear for good into the labyrinthine streets of Rome. "You will come back, won't you. . . . I still have so much to show you."

More men were arriving now in the courtyard beneath us, hailing each other and cursing the heat which was already beginning to hang oppressive in the airless sky and wring a heat haze from the damp ground. The boy looked down through the unglazed window, and every line of his painfully thin body mirrored the anguish of despairing conflict. I knew then—as perhaps I had known from the first moment I saw him—that he was deep in trouble, dragging behind him the chains of some unspeakable crimes. The darkness in his soul cast a shadow that seemed to embrace my own, and as I looked at him I had the strong feeling that I was watching him drown before my very eyes in the black waters of his own past. I suddenly felt a deep urge to throw the rope that would pull him from that poisoned lake; for, whatever he might have done—and there was unquestionably *something!*—I could not believe he was evil, not when he had touched my hand with all the silent wonder of an innocent child.

"Come back!" I repeated steadily. "Tomorrow at dawn I will meet you here."

He turned and looked at me searchingly, as though he wished to read on my sagging face the quiet sincerity that he heard in my voice.

"Tomorrow at dawn," he echoed softly.

There was a sound of heavy footsteps crossing the floorboards of the landing outside the room and instantly, without a word of warning, the boy slid through the empty window casing to drop almost soundlessly into the courtyard below.

When I went to look out the window, I saw that he was already gone.

I was a practical man and, had anyone asked me, before that strange and disastrous interlude, I should have said a most unlikely candidate for spiritual revelations. At fifty-eight I was old in a craft that traditionally claimed life early. Constant dust and fine chippings clog a stonemason's lungs over the years, while the sheer grinding hard labor of the job wrecks the muscles of the fittest. Few of us reach the age of forty without the racking cough that heralds the grave, but I had been more fortunate than most; it was only in the past year or so that my lungs had begun to show the familiar ominous signs of decay.

There had been some distinguished moments to my career. My work with Giuseppe Valadier on the Piazza del Popolo had established my reputation as one of the foremost master masons in Rome. My private tenders received such favorable viewings that I turned inevitably to contracting and became a man of substance as well as a master craftsman; in consequence it was more than ten years since I had taken an apprentice.

My last boy had been a serious disappointment to me. Six months of slovenly work and a single piece of impertinence were sufficient to convince me that the lad was quite unworthy of the knowledge I had to impart. I canceled his indentures without compunction and declined to accept any further recommendations, telling myself that I was now too old and too set in my ways to struggle with inept hands and suffer the general disruption engineered by a boy around the house. I know that few in the trade now take an apprentice into their home; they are content to let the boys remain under their own roofs, growing soft with the attentions of their mothers. I myself had always favored the old ways, the grand traditions of the Gothic builders. A young mason should model himself upon his master in every way, and how is that possible unless that boy sits at your hearth, eats your salt, breathes your air, your views, your entire being? No . . . the old ways were best for anyone with the patience left to use them, but the contracting system had inevitably brought decay in its wake. Too many boys were now content to pick up a mere smattering of knowledge, preferring to travel the countryside in building gangs rather than apply themselves diligently to the hard discipline of a seven-year apprenticeship. Soon there would be no master craftsmen left, only powerful, soulless contractors who had no interest in whether their buildings would still be standing a thousand years from now.

I was old and my lungs were beginning to heave like the creaking leather in a pair of ancient bellows, but I cannot pretend that was the sole reason for my nebulous discontent, the nagging sense of frustration that somehow robbed me of all pleasure in my success. Even in my prime I had never found an apprentice who wasn't glad to complete his daily quota of work, eager to return to a boy's amusements, fighting and carousing on the streets of an evening or lingering in dark alleyways with a new sweetheart. I used to tell myself that it would be different when I had a son to follow me into the trade, but though I sowed my seed with diligence (and enthusiasm!) I waited in vain for the ultimate reward. Three daughters, plain, dutiful girls who married well and never gave me a moment's trouble; a ten-year dearth, in which I largely abandoned hope and tried to resign myself to my fate.

And then . . . *Luciana!*

My wife wept with chagrin the night that Luciana was born and I myself hung dutifully over the cradle, preparing to hide my bitter disappointment. But the moment I parted the covers to look at her I was lost in wonder at the sight that greeted me. She did not look like the wrinkled prune that I had come to believe typified my newborn children. Even then she was beautiful, and her tiny little hand closing around my finger was only a symbol of the tenacity with which she wound herself around my heart in the following years.

Luciana never got along with her mother, not even as a small child. I was forever coming home to complaints of insufferable behavior and a hot, tragic, tearstained face burrowing into my coat. I never dreamed then that I should one day find myself sending her away from home for the sake of my own sanity. I never dreamed . . .

But I will not think of Luciana! Not now!

I will think instead of the boy; the boy who should have been my son. . . .

"I want to see everything," he said in answer to my question, when we met that following dawn with all the ridiculous stealth of young lovers, *"everything!"*

"That's a tall order," I said with a smile, "but if you really want to see the city in one fell swoop you can't do better than to climb the Janiculum. That hill commands the finest view of Rome. You won't see everything, but you'll see enough."

We were silent as we climbed the steep road that wound its way beneath the pine trees to the crest of the hill, but our silence was companionable and gave me a chance to observe him more closely in the open light. He was leading two of the most beautiful horses I have ever seen, one black and one pure white; both mares, I noticed, each carefully groomed and bearing well-balanced packs, but no saddles or harness.

I asked him how he managed to control the animals without a bit.

"I never use a bit," he said coolly. "It is an unnecessary cruelty. These horses choose to carry me, there is no question of control."

I realized then that he was not leading the creatures; they were simply following him like dogs. When we stopped he made no effort to secure them, merely lifted a hand to caress each one briefly before turning away to look at the view.

"Oh!" he said.

Hardly a word, more a simple sigh of ecstasy, a sound that I sometimes hear still in my restless dreams, the sound of a soul lifting from the clay. As I watched him drift toward the edge like a sleepwalker in a trance, I had the sudden horrified suspicion that he wasn't going to stop, but simply keep on walking right out into the treacherous void beneath.

I ran forward to catch his sleeve and drag him back a step to safety.

"Be careful!" I said urgently. "The ground is unstable here, you must keep away from the edge."

"Keep away from the edge," he echoed dreamily to himself. "Must I always keep away from the edge?"

Something in the odd, otherworldly quality of his voice sent a shiver running through my gut—for I knew he was not talking to me, but to some terrible unseen presence that was suddenly at his side. Something that had claimed him before and now returned briefly, like an absentee landlord checking its rightful property.

I shook his arm violently and he opened his eyes to look at me with blank confusion, as though it was not me he had expected to find beside him. After a moment he seemed to remember where he was and turned once more to look out over Rome, as though nothing untoward had taken place.

"What is that flat façade over to the right?" he demanded, suddenly alert again.

"Santa Maria d'Aracoeli," I said, glancing at him uneasily. "The shallow dome is the Pantheon and just behind it stands the Quirinal Palace. Over to your left"—I swept my hand in the direction I wished him to look—"you can see the drum of Castel Sant'Angelo. That great park in front of you is the Villa Borghese and the two towers on the edge of it—no, you're not looking—just there, do you see?"

"Yes, sir . . . the two towers. To what do they belong?"

"The Villa Medici."

He reacted to those words as though I had struck him, turning away, with clenched fists, as though he could no longer bear to look on the vista which had given him such delight only moments before.

"You have heard of the Villa Medici?" I asked curiously.

"Oh, yes," he said, in a voice which seemed to be plummeting down some bottomless abyss into darkness, "I've heard of it!"

He drew a sharp intake of breath and then continued as though he was repeating text and verse of some lesson learned by heart.

"The villa was built in the sixteenth century for Cardinal Ricci di Montepulciano and passed to the Medici family in 1576. In 1803 it became home to the French Academy after the Palazzo Salviati was sacked and burned during the revolution. The Academy is open exclusively to artists, musicians, and architects. Entry is determined strictly by competition—*the Grand Prix de Rome!*"

Powerless to comprehend the black bitterness suddenly pulsing through him, I could only stare and wonder how a Gypsy boy had come by such knowledge, and why the mention of it should be capable of throwing him into the grip of such violent rage.

He flung away from me abruptly, returning to the horses as though he intended to ride off without another word; but as the white mare gently nuzzled his masked face I saw control return slowly to his tense body. And after a moment he came back to me with hesitancy.

"I'm sorry," he said simply. "I didn't mean to be uncivil. If you can forgive me, sir, I should greatly like to see whatever else you care to show me."

A strange, disturbing boy, and yet the more I saw of him the more strongly drawn I felt toward him, the more convinced of our mutual need of one another.

I accepted his disarming apology without hesitation or comment.

"Come," I said, with a simplicity that matched his own, "let me take you to the Colosseum."

Over the course of the following two weeks we continued to meet at intervals, and those days when I did not see him were filled with a restlessness that I found hard to comprehend. He parted with personal information with the greatest reluctance, as though the smallest confidence might leave some gaping hole in his defenses against the world. Questioning him presented all the ease of prizing open a reluctant oyster shell, and yet I could not rid myself of the certainty that gentle persistence would ultimately show me an extraordinary pearl.

It was almost a week before he told me his name and the occupation he was pursuing at the fair in the Trastevere.

"I do magic," he admitted with a little shrug of self-contempt. "Not very good magic really, not yet—but people are very easily amused."

And showing me his empty palms, he reached up with a graceful, theatrical flourish to pluck a purse out of thin air and drop it carelessly into my hand.

The purse was mine!

"I see you don't starve," I observed dryly, replacing the little leather bag in my pocket. "Why didn't you keep it? That was your intent, wasn't it? And I wouldn't have known."

"It didn't feel right," he sighed.

"You keep others, though."

"Oh, yes," he confessed cheerfully, "all the time."

"You're not ashamed of stealing from people, then?"

"No," he said, "I don't like people"—there was a moment of hesitation before he added in a whisper that was barely audible—"as a rule."

I thought of the Trastevere, one of the least respectable districts in Rome, home to charlatans and rogues of the worst kind; and I thought of his hands, those slim, nimble instruments of mischief that could be so much more nobly employed if only . . . if only . . .

I repressed an impulse to sigh.

"I think you ought to see the Vatican" was all I said.

I made sure we arrived at Saint Peter's when the great basilica was deserted, save for the odd devoted pilgrim; and for two hours or so I watched him explore the extravagant architectural splendors of previous centuries. His wondering delight made me feel young again, as though I were being reborn through his vision, and that day, as I answered his whispered questions, it was as though I, too, were seeing Saint Peter's for the first time. The colors seemed more vivid to me, the sweep of the barrel-vault ceiling more awesome, the perfect harmony of the basilica's proportions more inspiring. I had never felt quite so close to God before, so utterly sure of His benign existence.

The great church echoed with a throbbing silence as we came to stand before the bronze statue of Saint Peter. I paused to make the customary reverence, pressing my forehead briefly to the right foot where the bronze toes had been worn smooth and featureless by the caresses of thousands of pilgrims through the centuries. I looked at the keys of heaven held close against Saint Peter's heart and the upraised right hand which symbolized hope to countless sinners; and I stepped back automatically, expecting Erik to repeat my gesture.

He stared at the statue with academic admiration, but he did not move to touch it, and I was aware of something ominous in this very deliberate omission of respect.

"They say," I prompted uneasily, "that when a sinner kisses Saint Peter's foot he receives the first hope of God's salvation."

Erik turned slowly to look at me.

"There is no God," he said with sad, quiet certainty. "There are beautiful churches, there is beautiful music . . . but there is no God."

I stood and watched him walk away down the silent nave. I had been unable to persuade him to look at the *Pietà*, Michelangelo's celebrated masterpiece which depicts the Virgin holding her dead son. I had wondered at the time at the cold civility with which he declined my suggestion.

Now I was afraid I understood.

When I came out onto the steps he was standing in the center of Saint Peter's Square gazing at the double colonnade surmounted by statues of saints and martyrs. But as I approached, he hastily turned his attention to the huge obelisk in the center of the square, which had been the work of Egyptian heathens in the first century before Christ. The meaning of his gesture was painfully clear to me; he did not want to hear about God. If I questioned that statement in the basilica our curious relationship would be at an end; I would never see him again.

In response to his fierce, silent plea I found myself swallowing the indignant platitudes that were threatening to trip off my tongue.

"When does the fair leave the Trastevere?" I demanded.

"Tomorrow." He did not look at me.

"Tomorrow I have business at the travertine quarries in Tivoli," I said brusquely. "I shall be on the Tiburtina road at dawn. You had better make up your mind in which direction you want to travel."

It was my turn now to walk away in anger.

I felt him watching me unhappily, but I made damned sure I didn't look back.

The next day, when I found him waiting for me on the ancient Roman road and saw that both the mares were with him, I knew a moment of relieved satisfaction.

It was the best part of twenty miles to the foothills of Tivoli, but the horses were fresh and we made good time. The quarry master was an old acquaintance who had good reason to be grateful for the business I had put his way over the years. He made no difficulties when I told him I would like to put a boy at the stone face for an hour or two.

"New apprentice?" he asked, with obvious surprise.

"Possibly," I said guardedly.

"Well, you surprise me, Giovanni. I wouldn't have thought you could be bothered trucking with a boy these days, not when you employ some of the best rough-masons in the city."

I frowned and he threw up his brawny arms in mock defense.

"Mind your own business, Luigi," he said to himself with good-natured humor. "Nobody wants to know what you think, right?"

"We'll need some tools," I reminded him pointedly.

"Be my guest, Giovanni. You've had enough stone out of this quarry in your time, you know you don't need to ask."

The sun was beating down mercilessly, making a white hell of the quarry as it shimmered in a cloud of choking dust motes. I had chosen a quiet area, well away from the main working parties, and Erik stood in his shirtsleeves touching the dirty white stone face with disdainful fingers.

"I didn't think it would be like this," he said, "it's so pockmarked and porous and . . . *crude.*"

"It's not the most beautiful stone in the world," I admitted coolly, "but it was good enough for Caesar and it had better be good enough for you too."

He laughed suddenly, the sound reverberating around the quarry and lightening my heart with its spontaneity and boyish innocence.

"Please show me what to do, sir," he said, with a simple humility that almost made me forgive his atheism.

As I put the age-old tools of a hewer into his hands, I told myself it was not too late to say to him: *"Let there be light."*

It was after midnight when we returned to Rome, but the streets were still full of revelers. Music continued to spill out of the taverns and the cafés, while around the obelisks and fountains in the many piazzas friends lingered to talk of Young Italy with noisy exuberance.

I felt the boy tense at the sight of the crowds, saw his hand slip automatically to the knife in his belt, and I led him hastily down the quieter back streets until we reached my house.

"What place is this?" he demanded cautiously when I indicated he should dismount and follow me into the small courtyard.

"This is where I live," I said.

He took a step back from me.

"Why have you brought me here?" he whispered.

The horror in his voice, the sudden fear flickering into his eyes, told me everything. This boy had suffered abuse from a man in its worst form, and I felt a great anger welling up in me against that unknown tormentor.

"I have brought you here to sleep in safety off the streets," I told him steadily. "There will be no payment asked of you of any kind."

"You would let me sleep here?" he said doubtfully. "You would take beneath your roof a thief and a—"

He stopped abruptly, cutting off the word I dreaded to hear before it could take breath, and we tended to the horses in silence before I went to open the door and beckon his hesitant figure over the threshold.

He came in slowly, with a nervous reluctance that reminded me poignantly of a hungry animal venturing in from the wild against the warning of instinct. As I moved around the big, stone-walled living room, lighting the oil lamps, he stood with his arms clasped tightly against his chest, gazing around with a bewilderment and wary disbelief that tightened my throat. I realized with a touch of despair how daunting was the task that lay ahead of me if I chose to build on the unstable ruins of this devastated soul.

I left him for a moment while I went to the cellar to fetch a jug of wine. When I returned I found him standing in front of the old spinet, running his fingers soundlessly along the dusty keys with a gesture of longing.

"Who plays this?" he asked suddenly.

"No one now," I admitted with a sigh. "It's been in the family for many years, but none of my children were musical. I've been thinking of getting rid of it—it takes up a lot of room and it only gathers dust."

Again he touched the wood with lingering regret.

"How can you think of doing that?" he said unhappily. "It's such a beautiful instrument. . . . I wish—"

"Yes?"

He was silent.

"You know how to play?" I persisted.

He nodded, still staring at the keys.

"It could be moved to the cellar," I said quietly, "if you wish."

He looked up at me in astonishment. "You are saying I may stay here. Why?"

I shrugged my shoulders slightly.

"Perhaps I need an apprentice," I said.

Silence. I watched him turn away, both hands covering the mask for a moment.

"I lied to you when I said I was not apprenticed," he said softly. "I am already sworn to a master."

I did not need to ask who that master was, not when I could already see Death's mark upon him like sheep brand.

I went to the empty hearth and sat down in the fireside chair to fill my pipe calmly.

"You don't think perhaps you're a little young to be so certain of your calling in life?" I said after a moment, not looking at him as I spoke.

Again he did not answer and I put the pipe down on the tiles without lighting it.

"Indentures can be broken at any point during an apprenticeship, Erik, however dark the profession. Even the harshest master cannot hold you to a craft against your choosing. And remember, however long and faithfully you may have served as a bondsman, once those indentures are broken you will never have the right to call yourself a master of that trade."

Still he was silent, staring at the old spinet, and from the taut set of his shoulders I was able to sense the fierce struggle taking place inside him, his real reluctance to abandon the only other master who had ever shown him hope of security and pride. The devil is capable of commanding loyalty and respect from an apprentice; his charisma can be a formidable thing. Perhaps after all I was wasting my breath. . . .

The keys beneath Erik's long fingers began to depress in a series of richly melodic chords which lingered on the air for a moment, with an echoing sweetness, before expiring into the thick silence.

Then at last he turned to look across the room at me.

"I should like to see the cellar, please," he said.

For the first few weeks I confined him to the masons' yard, permitting him to work only in the absence of my other workmen and under my exclusive supervision. He still showed no inclination to remove the mask, and I knew this grim eccentricity would inevitably bring him trouble on a building site. He would not survive long there without some basic knowledge of the craft beneath his belt.

Very soon he was dressing stone as though he had been born with a mason's ax in his hand. Each batch of mortar that he made for me was of an exactly uniform consistency, and I would dearly have liked to know how he managed to do that every time, without fail. One measure of fine-ground Italian pazzolona, two of clear river sand, one of fresh burnt lime—the formula is simple enough, yet most apprentices make an utter botch of their first attempts to make decent mortar. God knows I received enough angry cuffs from my own master in the early days before successfully mastering the process.

Perhaps I should have resented the ease with which he absorbed my skills, but I could only wonder at his startling capacity to learn. He seemed to be at one with the stone, instinctively sensing its strengths and weaknesses, handling it with reverent respect, as though it were a living entity. He refused to wear the mason's gloves that would have protected him from the painful shards and splinters; he always liked to feel the stone beneath his bare hands and often pointed out a fault in the grain that might have escaped many a more experienced eye.

The day came, far sooner than I had hoped, when I knew there was nothing more he could learn in this stone-walled nursery, so I took him down to one of my sites and placed him in the charge of a layer I trusted. There were several young laborers working there, and I noted the nudges and meaningful glances that were exchanged between the lads with great misgiving.

When I returned to the site at noon, the men were resting from the unseasonable heat and I was immediately aware, from the ominously swift manner in which Gillo Calandrino approached me, that there had already been trouble.

"That new boy is a menace!" the man said grimly, as he wiped his dusty hands upon his mason's apron.

I frowned. "You don't find him willing to learn? Attentive . . . respectful?"

The man gave a grunt that might have been a stifled snort of laughter.

"I've no quarrel with his willingness to learn, sir. I've had my brain picked clean by his questions all morning—he's sucked me dry as sponge!"

"Well, then, what is it?" I demanded, with rising irritation.

"Begging your pardon, sir, but I'd say he's not quite right in the head. He damned near killed two of our lads a half hour back. I've had to send Paolo home to get his arm dressed. And it was a nasty knife wound. . . . I doubt if he'll be able to work for the rest of the week."

"I assume the boy was provoked," I said coldly.

"I wouldn't know anything about that, sir," said Calandrino, suddenly evasive and unable to meet my eyes any longer, "but I do know he behaved like a mad savage. When I went to break it up I thought he was going to go for me too—and I don't mind telling you, sir, I thought twice about tackling him with that knife in his hand. He knows how to use it, there's no mistaking that."

"But he didn't harm you."

"Well . . . no," the layer admitted reluctantly. "Seemed to come to his senses after a moment and back off. But you can't blame the lads, sir, it was only a bit of fun. Stands to reason they'd want to get a look under that mask, I mean, any normal boy would."

"I thought you said you didn't know what happened."

The man went very red beneath his suntan and gave a little shrug.

"Boys will be boys, sir, but if you want my opinion that one should be locked up! There's one or two slates loose there, if I'm not very much mistaken!"

"I'm not interested in your opinion!" I said with measured fury. "I look to you to keep better control on a site during my absence. If you can't do that, maybe it's time you found yourself another position. As for the laborers, you'd better tell them I don't employ them to indulge their curiosity on my time. Any more trouble and I'll see them all turned off! Do I make myself plain?"

"Yes, sir." The man looked dumbstruck at my tone.

"Well, what are you waiting for? Get everybody back to work!"

With a resentful glance Calandrino made to turn away.

"Wait," I said abruptly. "Where's the boy now?"

The man jerked his thumb toward the top of the scaffolding where, by shielding my eyes, I could just make out the distant figure hunched perilously against the fierce sun.

"You let an untrained lad climb up there?"

"He didn't stop to ask my permission, sir," said the layer with a cool sarcasm that this time I chose to overlook. "Just shot up like a bat out of hell before any of us could blink. The lads were taking bets that he was going to jump off."

I made a gesture of dismissal and the man strode away, muttering under his breath.

Taking the scaffold in easy stages I climbed to the dizzying height where the boy sat staring straight into the sun. He got to his feet hastily when he heard me coming and stared at me with tense expectation; I knew he was waiting to be dismissed.

"Are you hurt, Erik?"

"No, sir." He sounded astounded that I should have asked.

"Come down, then. I need your help this afternoon."

Without waiting for him to reply I returned to the ground. And for the rest of the day, as he followed my instructions to the letter, I was aware of his eyes constantly coming to rest on me with puzzled gratitude.

A week later I overheard the men talking as they prepared to leave the site at sundown.

"As soon as the master's gone we'll jump him, agreed? Get that mask off and see what's underneath."

"Yes—and give the clever little bugger a few tokens of our appreciation!"

"If any of you have got any sense you'll leave him alone. Don't you realize who he is yet?"

As Calandrino's voice cut in and silenced the rest for a moment, I listened to the taut anticipation that had suddenly settled on the group.

"You saying you know who he is?" That was Paolo, admittedly never overly quick on the uptake.

"Mother of God!" Calandrino paused a moment to hawk and spit. "I should have thought it was obvious to anyone with a half a brain by now. How long is it since the master took an apprentice . . . must be ten years at least!"

"So?"

"So no one else thinks it just a little odd when the old man turns up with a boy in a mask and starts behaving like a hen with one chick?"

"You're not suggesting—"

"Yes I am suggesting! Christ, why not? The master was no more above a bit of skirt in his prime than anyone else, right? And when a man with a clutch of daughters gets himself a son on the wrong side of the blanket it goes against the grain to leave him there. But he's a Freemason, isn't he . . . mighty respectable, past master and all that . . . can't have it all around the lodge that he's no better than the rest of us! So he thinks maybe a mask is going to cover everything, including his past. Well, you've seen them together—think about it! It makes good sense and just goes to prove what I've been saying for the past six months now—the master's been one brick short of a load ever since the old lady died and he had to send the girl away!"

"*Santa Maria!*"

"Exactly! I'm telling you, the whole pack of us could find ourselves turned off if anyone else sets about that lad. I say we're best keeping well out of it. No good ever comes of meddling in a master's affairs . . . and the boy's no trouble if you leave him alone. Does more than his fair share without complaining to the old man that he's been put upon. . . ."

I stood listening with a curious mixture of emotions while my men continued to drag my good name cheerfully through the mire. I wasn't sure how I felt about this. I had half a mind to stride out from behind the wall that was concealing me and turn them all off for their insolent assumptions; but I was not unaware that my silence now could be Erik's shield. Simply by saying nothing and allowing this monstrous slander to put down roots I could protect him from further pain at their hands. I could buy the boy a little more time to find his feet and perhaps lose the instinctive belief that the whole world was his enemy. For some reason he had had the astonishing stroke of luck not to be recognized for his performance at the Trastevere fair. Perhaps, when performing, he had worn some fantastic mask more in keeping with the status of a magician . . . perhaps there were days when he had simply chosen not to appear at all. I didn't know, I couldn't account for it; but I *was* aware that luck didn't come his way very often, and I didn't feel inclined to deprive him of its benefit now. And so I chose to hold my peace.

Even as I came to this decision I saw it was no great sacrifice. Rumor had presented me with a son and I could not quite find it in my heart to complain; I found that I did not begrudge the boy the silent protection of my name.

Once the men had left the site I withdrew from the shadows behind the half-built wall to watch Erik gathering up the tools that had been used that day—all the trowels, squares, plumb rules, and chisels which were my personal property and must be safely locked away in the masons' yard at night.

When he had finished he went over to inspect the work that had been completed, studying the beds as though he wished to commit the exact position of each mortared joint to memory. The light was failing rapidly now—it was the first week of October—and there was a threat of storm in the still air.

"Erik!"

He started so violently at the sound of my voice that I knew he had believed himself to be alone.

"Leave that now, boy, tomorrow is another day."

He stared at me in bewilderment; right to the very end that was a concept he never seemed able to understand.

"Rome wasn't built overnight, you know," I added, beckoning him to my side. "You need patience to master this trade. Come along now, it's time to go home."

I waited for him to pick his way across the site with the sling of tools over his shoulder. He moved like a cat, with a lithe, flowing grace that made him oddly pleasing to watch—in spite of his height he had none of the gawkishness normally associated with his age.

We fell into step together and began to walk through the steadily darkening streets toward the masons' yard. I couldn't see his face, so of course I can't swear to it, but I am sure he smiled at me for the first time that night.

I made no attempt to set boundaries or to limit the nature of the work I permitted him to tackle. Ignoring time-honored traditions and increasingly resentful workmen, I simply permitted him to develop at his own staggering pace. Within six months he could random-chisel, fine-chisel, rub, or work fair exactly to my specifications and I was already allowing him to set square ashlar. He could keep beds and joints full and square for their whole depth and preserve the outer arrises so that the work, when set, was close and solid throughout. And whether he was fixing arch springers or cutting grooves for lead flashings in a stone parapet, it was never necessary to inspect the quality of his finished work. He had only one standard. If he felt he had made a mistake he was never too proud to ask for my correction. But he rarely made mistakes; and those few he did make were never repeated.

The question of indentures never arose between us. I knew by the end of the first month that I could never hope to imprison him with the age-old chains of my craft. So I gave him his freedom and was rewarded in my turn by the single-minded self-discipline of a boy who simply chose to serve me for a time upon his own unspoken terms; who, though he would not be my bondsman, never showed me anything less than absolute respect.

Slowly, over the months, I became aware of that respect changing steadily into guarded affection. As the winter drew on I found a series of minor tasks that would keep him at my side for another hour or so of an evening. I needed a fire built, the figures in the ledger kept up-to-date, estimates drafted; but in time I was able to dispense with these transparent ploys as he found the confidence to linger at my hearth of his own accord.

At the end of February, when the mild weather suddenly turned against us and put a stop to all outside work, I watched him grow restless and wondered uneasily if he intended to leave me. He asked if he might go and draw in Florence for a few weeks and I agreed without a murmur of protest, for I had always known it would not be possible to hold him against his will. As I watched him ride off into the snow I did not expect him to return. He had already told me that it was his intention one day to study the architecture of the whole world, and I felt that Rome must inevitably lead to Naples and Pompeii; Apulia to Bari; Athens to Egypt. That raging appetite for knowledge could not be contained beneath my roof, and I feared the wanderlust that would inexorably pull him ever farther from my restraining hand.

But in the last week of March he was back, pausing in the courtyard to unpack the dozens of sketches he had completed as proof of his industry. As I lay once more, in the early hours of the morning, listening to the distant notes of his violin, I realized how deeply I had missed his elusive presence in the house, the odd, haunting pleasure of his shy companionship.

One day he would leave and not return, I knew that was inevitable. But I found I could not bear to think ahead to a time when he would be gone from my life for good.

The year turned on its unfailing cycle and the approach of summer brought a series of humid, airless days that made me pressingly aware of my years and my failing health. In the first week of June Rome began to swelter with a merciless heat that sapped my strength and sent me staggering out into the courtyard one evening, coughing like a consumptive in a sanatorium, and desperately seeking air.

The lantern suspended from the outer wall showed me the ominous flecks of blood upon my handkerchief, and in the brief pause between the spasms I stared at them with grim resignation. Suddenly, without a sound, Erik was beside me and I saw that he, too, was staring at the bloodied linen with pained understanding.

"You are very ill, sir," he said with quiet concern.

I made a breathless philosophical gesture and stuffed the handkerchief into my pocket, because I saw that the sight of it distressed him.

"All masons come to this fate in time, Erik—there's no cure been found for a lung full of grit and dust. But I reckon I have a good year or two left in me yet—there's no cause to look so alarmed, boy."

He hesitated a moment and then produced a small vial which he had evidently been concealing behind his back.

"If you care to try this," he began diffidently, "I think you will find it gives some ease."

I took the vial from him and unstopped it, releasing a pungent, yet not unpleasing, aroma of herbs.

"Where did you come by this?" I inquired with puzzled interest.

"I made it," he confessed awkwardly. "I was taught by the Gypsies to understand herbal properties."

I took an experimental sip and pulled a face.

"Kill or cure, is it, lad?"

He laughed at that. More and more now he was beginning to accept my gentle teasing, learning to laugh at his own seriousness, even at his occasional mistakes.

"You should try the cure for gout," he volunteered unexpectedly. "That really is cause for complaint. It tastes like a skunk's urine and keeps a man on the privy for a week. It doesn't work either," he added as a wry afterthought.

I finished the potion and returned the empty vial to him with a smile.

"Perhaps you could give me a hand up those stairs now," I said.

"Oh yes." He sounded utterly startled by the suggestion. "Of course. . . ."

He came forward to offer me his arm with a sort of dumbstruck wonder and I put my hand on his shoulder, permitting him to take my full weight on his slim, yet surprisingly strong, frame. When we reached my room he lowered me tenderly onto the bed and then knelt to remove my boots.

"Good night, sir," he said gently. "I hope you can rest now."

I was already pleasantly drowsy. Whatever he had given me was calming the spasm in my chest and acting like a powerful opiate. I saw him glance briefly around the chamber as though to make sure he had not overlooked anything that might appertain to my comfort. He went across to close the wooden shutters at the window, and when he returned to set a glass of water on the table beside the bed, I reached up on impulse to squeeze his cold hand.

"You're a good boy, Erik," I said fondly. "I'd like to think you won't ever let anyone persuade you otherwise."

He held on to my fingers for a moment, enclosing them between his palms, and I became aware that he had started to tremble. My God . . . the boy was crying . . . crying because I had spoken kindly and touched him with affection!

"Erik . . ." I whispered helplessly.

"I'm sorry!" he stammered, dropping my hand and stepping back from the bed hastily. "I'm very sorry! Please forgive me!"

And before I could say a word to stop him he fled from the room.

I lay back on the pillows, staring at the stuccoed ceiling. The turbulence of his fiercely repressed emotion made me wonder yet again how I was going to approach a situation that could not be avoided much longer.

For I had not been entirely honest with him when I led him to believe that I lived alone as a widower, attended only by an old woman who came in to cook and clean and the occasional dutiful visit from matronly daughters living some distance outside Rome. Eleven months had slipped away and still I had not found an appropriate moment to confess to my sin of omission.

It was June already and soon, very soon now, Luciana would be coming home for the summer.

hen Luciana was three years old her mother and I had a row which must surely have been heard by the pope in the Vatican.

It began with Angela—then an ungainly girl of thirteen—running onto the building site with her skirts flapping madly around fat ankles.

"Papa, Papa, come quickly! Mama's locked Luciana in the cellar and she's screaming the house down. She'll choke if she doesn't stop, Papa, but Mama says she won't let her out till suppertime."

I left the site with a face like thunder—all my men staring at me with roughly veiled sympathy. Even at three Luciana was already notorious in her own right.

I could hear the screaming when I was still two streets away, and I felt my temper rising as I stormed into the house.

"Don't you *dare* let her out, Giovanni!" Isabella shrieked as I made for the cellar. "Don't you dare undermine my authority with that wretched child again!"

I swung around at the top of the cellar steps as she caught at my arm.

"How dare you do this!" I shouted. "How dare you make me look a fool in front of my men! Locking a baby down in a dark cellar . . . you must be mad."

"She's not a baby, she's three years old, and if she doesn't learn to do as she's told soon, I promise you she won't live to be four. I've had enough of her tantrums, do you hear me, Giovanni? I have had *enough!* It's all your fault. . . . you've ruined her, ruined her since the day she was born, and now no one can do a thing with her, including you."

I ran down to the cellar, kicked open the door, and picked up the sodden, hysterical bundle which lay in a pool of urine and vomit on the stone-flagged floor.

On the stairs I paused to fix Isabella with a look of contempt that made her shrink against the wall. I was so beside myself with fury that I thought I might actually strike her for the first time in our twenty-five years of marriage.

"It's not her fault that you couldn't give me a boy!" I said with bare control. "If you ever do this again perhaps I'll find someone else who can!"

And so it went on throughout Luciana's turbulent childhood—the rows, the scenes, the interminable conflict between Isabella and myself. Where once we lived in perfect harmony there was now only constant discord, and all of it shamelessly propagated by the exquisitely pretty child whose willful winsomeness was the delight of my late middle age. Surrounded as I was by a colorless crop of females, Luciana seemed like a mischievous ray of sunshine peeping between dignified clouds; I was always powerless to resist the enchanting pout and the overly ready tears.

Ten years on, I was finally obliged to admit that what had been so utterly irresistible at three was not half so beguiling at thirteen. A widower by then, a full decade older and less able to cope with the spectacular manifestations of Luciana's unstable personality, I was beginning to understand that Isabella's fears had not been without ground. The child began to run wild when her mother died. She lived for a brief time with Angela and wreaked such havoc in her sister's household that I was forced to admit the need to send her away to a place where she might learn the harsh lessons of self-restraint.

The convent school I chose was near Milan, far enough from home to discourage any thoughts of running away, yet close enough to the aunt who undertook to take charge of her in the brief Christmas and Easter vacations. Always beguiled by the prospect of novelty, Luciana departed cheerfully enough for Milan; but within a fortnight I had received the first of a series of tragic little letters.

Dearest Papa,

I am so very unhappy here. The nuns are very unkind and none of the girls like me. . . . Please, please change your mind and say I may come home to you at Christmas after all.

That letter kept me awake all night. I got up before there was a glimmer of light in the sky and wandered distractedly down to the nearest site . . . and it was there that I saw Erik that first time and gained the strength to resist the artful pleas of my wicked little daughter.

I determined to keep to my original intention for once. Luciana would not be allowed to come home until summer.

But now summer was upon me and still I had not told him.

Why?

All over Rome the bells were ringing and calling the faithful to early-morning Mass. As I came out into the courtyard, adjusting the set of my hat, I tried to pretend I had not noticed Erik quietly pruning the Chinese wisteria that crept up the trellis work. He never came with me to Mass and I firmly resisted the temptation to ask him to do so. The boy's devotion to me had grown to the point where I strongly suspected he would cut off a finger should I once suggest that I had need of it. If he ever returned to the faith I wished it to be for love of God and not for love of me. . . .

It was Sunday, a good day to make a resolution and stick to it, and I determined that as soon as I returned from Mass I would tell him about Luciana. But just as I was pulling on my gloves there was the sound of carriage wheels in the street outside and I frowned. I wasn't expecting visitors. . . .

She flew into the courtyard to my unready embrace like a little bird let out of its cage, her heavy hair flying out behind her like a cloak of black silk and her piquant face flushed with excitement.

"Papa, Papa, I'm home! I thought I'd never get here, it's been such a horrid journey, so hot and tiresome! Oh, Papa . . . what's the matter, aren't you pleased to see me?"

"Luciana . . ." I held her eager little figure slightly away from me, as one might seek to fend off the attentions of a lovable but overexuberant puppy. "My darling girl, what are you doing here? I didn't expect you for another week!"

"Oh, I know, isn't it wonderful? Sister Agnes and Sister Elizabeth have the fever and we've all been sent home early because of it."

"Surely there should have been some notification, Luciana—a letter at the very least."

She pouted prettily. "Oh, we were all told to write home, and, Papa, I really did mean to do it, but somehow I just never seemed to have a moment. And I knew it wouldn't matter, I knew you'd be here. . . . Oh, Papa, please don't be cross with me, not on my first day home."

I kissed her hot cheek helplessly and turned to look at the tall figure who had silently taken refuge behind the riot of trailing foliage. The moment I had been instinctively avoiding could be avoided no longer.

"Erik," I said quietly, yet with an unmistakable note of command in my voice, "I would like you to come and meet my youngest daughter, Luciana."

For a long moment he did not move and then slowly, reluctantly, he unfurled himself from the shadows to glide across the courtyard beneath the shelter of the cloak in which he had hastily shrouded himself. He glanced at me briefly, with pained surprise, and I had the uncomfortable suspicion that his face might well have turned as white as the mask that hid it.

Luciana was staring at him—but not as I had expected her to stare, with vulgar, tactless curiosity. Her eyes were resting on the mask with a sort of glazed fascination and she seemed to be holding her breath as she held out her hand to him.

Erik bowed gracefully, but his hand stopped just short of her gloved fingers and I noticed that he took great care not to touch her.

"Mademoiselle," he said softly, "I must ask you to pardon my intrusion upon a private moment of reunion. Sir"—he turned to make exactly the same little bow of courtesy to me—"I should be glad if you would excuse me . . . ?"

There was nothing I could do in the face of his icy formality except make the signal of assent that freed him to return to the house without a backward glance at either of us.

When he had gone Luciana clutched my arm with urgent and barely concealed excitement.

"Oh, Papa," she breathed, with that ominously familiar note of subdued hysteria in her voice, "who *is* he?"

The peaceful idyll of pupil and master came to an end with Luciana's return, just as I had secretly feared it must. She appeared in our quiet, ordered firmament like a spectacular shooting star, and in her wake the bond that had been growing steadily between Erik and myself suffered inevitable strain. He no longer came to dine at my table, preferring to eat alone in the cellar. Nor did he come to sit anymore of an evening beside my hearth, and permit me to delve at my leisure into the bottomless wonders of a unique imagination.

His response confirmed the deep-rooted unease which had held me silent all these months. It was inevitable that a boy who so worshiped beauty in every form would be dumbstruck by Luciana's heartrending loveliness, and I was not surprised that his immediate reaction should be to bury himself behind a wall of silence and retreat to the cellar like a wounded animal going to ground. I had expected him to back away in pained horror from a situation that threatened to strip away all his natural defenses.

What I had not anticipated was Luciana's response to his guarded aloofness, the inner misery and outrageous bad behavior that his determined reserve and cold correctness provoked in her. They scarcely met —he made very sure of that—but those occasions when they did were charged with the intolerable tension generated by Luciana's hurt pride. The boy ignored her because he was afraid to betray himself to further pain, but Luciana could not bear his apparent indifference. And she began to demand his attention with rudeness, sarcasm, and ridicule—the very things life had taught him to expect.

For a month I was forced to stand by helplessly, watching my headstrong daughter fall in love not with a living, breathing boy, but with a dream, a fantasy inspired by the primeval mystery of the mask. Once I chose to look with Luciana's eyes, it was very easy to see and understand the primitive allure of that almost regal dignity, the curious, hypnotic quality of that unique voice. Beneath my roof I was sheltering a young prince of darkness. The sensuality of power radiated from his every gesture, but he remained entirely unaware of his extraordinary ability to attract. There were women here in Rome—women all over the world—who would have gladly sunk themselves in his shadow, had he only known it, had he dared to look beyond the cage in which he had determined to imprison himself. But he was blind to the most essential element of his own magnetism. Someone had taught him to expect only rejection and revulsion in this world and now, in the natural shyness of youth, he was merely repeating to himself whatever painful lessons he had been forced to learn by rote in childhood.

Day after day I watched him suffer the cruel agony of first love. He did not speak of his feelings to me—how could he?—but in every swing of his mallet, every thrust of his chisel, I felt his pain, and my helplessness grieved me. I watched him driving his young body to the breaking point on the site in an effort to escape from the intolerable reality of loving a shallow, frivolous child who was entirely unworthy of him. And I could say nothing and do nothing because the bitter truth was that that shallow, unworthy child was my daughter and I loved her dearly in spite of her selfish triviality.

All I could do was pray that the end of summer would release them both from this powder keg of unexploded emotion. When Luciana returned to the convent there would be another year of grace, a whole year for them to grow up and away from feelings that they were both —for vastly differing reasons—emotionally incapable of expressing in an acceptable manner.

During that terrible month of subdued hostility and repressed yearning, it was the one peg upon which I hung all my hope of peace.

I was a fool.

I should have known my daughter well enough by then. . . .

She wasn't pretending when she told me she was too ill to go back to Milan. Luciana never needed to pretend. From earliest infancy she had always possessed the ability to make herself thoroughly ill whenever it suited her purposes, and now the eyes that looked beseechingly into mine were unquestionably fever bright, and her pulse throbbing beneath my fingers like a butterfly's wing.

I went downstairs grimly to dismiss the waiting carriage and ask

Erik to prepare an infusion. I had no confidence in the remedies of apothecaries, but I did have the greatest respect for the boy's herbal knowledge.

"She is ill?" One hand went to his throat in an instinctive gesture that betrayed his anguished alarm.

"It's nothing serious, just a low fever, but she will not be able to travel for a while. I thought perhaps you might know of something—"

"Yes," he said hastily, "there is something . . . she wouldn't take anything bitter, though, would she? Perhaps I can sweeten it with honey."

And he turned away with an air of distraction that only heightened my growing concern.

"I don't want it!" said Luciana mutinously when I presented the potion an hour later. "You know I hate medicines, Papa."

"Very well," I said coolly, "I shall tell Erik that you refused to take it like the baby that you are."

She sat up suddenly, pushing back the heavy hair from her flushed face.

"Erik?" she echoed wonderingly. "*Erik* made this for me?"

Reaching out her hand she took the little wooden goblet from me and swallowed its contents without another murmur of protest.

And that was the moment when I finally acknowledged defeat. I was too old, too sick, and too generally weak minded where she was concerned to make a stand on any issue that Luciana had determined to fight.

She didn't go back to Milan.

The tragedy had already begun.

I never went down to the cellar.

From the very first I had respected the boy's right to privacy, his deep-seated need to have one place that he might call his own. So, although I was annoyed to learn that Luciana had been prowling about there during his absence, I could not resist a small, unworthy flicker of curiosity.

"It's so strange down there, Papa," she said with awe. "The floor is covered with drawings and sheets of music, and all the shelves where Mama used to keep preserves are full of . . . *things.*"

"What sort of things?" I demanded uneasily.

"I don't know, Papa, they're not like anything I've ever seen before. There are lots of coils and wires, and when I touched one it shot sparks."

"You have no business to be interfering with things that do not concern you," I said mechanically. "Keep out of that cellar in future, do you understand me?"

"Yes, Papa." She sighed.

I was alarmed. Concern overcame my dislike of prying, and when I was alone once more I picked up a candle and lit my way down to the cool chamber that ran beneath my house.

I realized as I gazed around in astonishment that I had entered the laboratory of an extraordinary inventor. My knowledge of science was somewhat perfunctory, but I thought I recognized apparatus that appertained to the study of electrical impulses. And there was more, much more that I did not even begin to understand, row upon row of working models—at least I *assumed* they worked—whose very mystery seemed oddly threatening. The boy labored fourteen hours a day on my sites and yet still retained the energy to sit up most of the night tinkering, drawing, composing. I remembered noticing now that even on the sites his interest was turning increasingly to engineering problems, to solutions that lay beyond the compass of a master mason. Once or twice he had made such astonishingly crack-brained suggestions that I had been tempted to laugh out loud at him.

But perhaps after all they were not simply the ludicrous notions of an absurdly fevered imagination. . . .

I went back upstairs, determining that I would say nothing about what I had seen. I trusted his common sense sufficiently to be reasonably certain that he was not about to blow my home off the face of the earth in the course of some crazy experiment.

But I was disturbed by this fresh evidence of his inability to rest with my daughter in the house. I wondered what ran through his tortured mind during those hours of darkness when ordinary mortals lay snoring peacefully in their beds.

And my primitive, wordless unease continued to grow.

At the end of spring Luciana's shamelessly scheming mind prompted her to hit upon a new means of luring Erik from the cellar. She wanted to transform the old rooftop garden into a beautiful arbor, and part of her scheme was a new travertine bench which she required the boy to carve.

"You *can* do that, I suppose?" she inquired with an airy insolence that made me quite ashamed of her. "A bench—it won't be too difficult for you, will it?"

"No, mademoiselle . . . it won't be too difficult." He spoke with guarded courtesy as always, but there was an unmistakable edge to his voice that suggested he was not prepared be pushed very much farther. I determined then that I would be present throughout the course of this enterprise.

Twenty stone urns were delivered from the marketplace, and in due course Erik carried them up to the rooftop garden and filled them with soil.

"I can do the rest," Luciana insisted. "I don't want you interfering with my new plants. Boys know nothing about flowers. You ought to get on with that bench now, I don't want you to take all summer."

He turned away in silence, picked up his tools, and went over to the great slab of travertine that awaited his attention.

For a couple of weeks Luciana tripped enthusiastically around the paved rooftop with a small watering can in her hand; but then, predictably losing interest in maintaining the pretense, she started to sit beside him each evening as he worked, occasionally making scathing comments on his progress.

"You're very slow, aren't you?" she said one night. "I thought you would have finished that bit by now!"

"*Luciana!*" I said sharply, looking up from my Bible to give her an angry warning glance. "Go and look after your flowers."

She got up with an impatient toss of her head and went away to fetch her little brass can.

"What's the matter with these stupid plants?" she said after a moment's disgusted contemplation of the urns. "Why are all the leaves turning yellow and falling off like this?"

I sighed and remained silent, but as I returned to my book, I was surprised to see Erik put down his chisel and go over to touch the withering blooms with angry regret. It was the first time I had ever seen him approach her of his own accord.

"They're dying of neglect," he told her shortly. "Can't you see that?"

"They're *not* neglected!" she flared. "I water them every day. Every day without fail!"

"You haven't watered them for over a week!" he snapped suddenly. "Look at the soil, it's rock hard!"

"Oh, *you!*" Without any warning Luciana threw the little brass can at him. "You think you're so clever, don't you . . . the all-seeing, all-knowing oracle! How dare you tell me I'm too stupid even to grow flowers! How dare you!"

She burst into tears and ran below, and suddenly there was silence in the garden. Erik bent to pick up the can, placing it on the edge of the balustrade when I approached.

"This parapet is crumbling very badly," he said uncomfortably. "The stonework really ought to be renewed, sir."

I agreed with him, permitting him to avoid a subject which he very obviously did not wish to discuss.

"That's a job you can tackle in the autumn when we're slack," I said quietly. "I'll get the stone ordered from the quarry for you in September. Better finish that bench first, though. I can see you're making a good job of it. And don't allow yourself to be rushed, boy. Even the most difficult customers have to learn patience."

"Yes, sir." He looked away, out over the old city where the light of a thousand winking oil lamps was just beginning to show in the gathering dusk.

I left him and went to the edge of the stairs. When I glanced back I could see that he had filled the brass can from the water butt and had already begun to move like a shadow between the urns.

Very late that night, when the sound of the old spinet in the cellar drew me from my room, I found Luciana sitting on the stone staircase with her knees drawn up beneath her chin. She was barefoot and shivering in her night shift, but listening with such fierce intensity that she did not know I was there until I put one hand upon her shoulder and made her start guiltily.

"Hello, Papa," she said in a sad tone. "Have you come to listen too?"

"You shouldn't be sitting here like this in the cold," I told her. "You should be asleep."

"He plays so beautifully." She sighed wistfully. "I've never heard anyone play like that before. Sometimes I sit here for hours just listening to him. Oh, Papa, I wish I'd worked harder at everything. . . .He makes me feel so very small and ignorant."

I was silent, sitting beside her and feeling the cold stone creeping slowly into my old joints.

"Luciana . . ." I said at last, "I'm going to write to the Mother Superior in the morning and tell her you will going back to school in August."

She turned and buried her dark head against my shoulder.

"Please don't send me back there again, Papa. I'm quite old enough now to keep house for you."

"My dear little girl, you've no idea how to keep a house."

"I could learn!" she insisted fervently. "I really will learn, Papa. Please don't send me away again. I'll miss him so much!"

She held me in a suffocating embrace, as though simply by clutching tighter and tighter she believed she would be able to hold on to what she really wanted.

"I'll die if you send me away!" she said passionately. "I'll die!"

Music filtered up from the cellar and swirled around us like a gentle, enveloping shawl.

I felt the pointed bones in her shoulder which showed me where the weight had dropped from her these last few months; and I knew that for once this inveterate little liar was telling me no more than the simple truth.

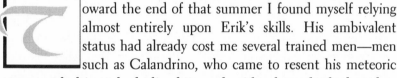oward the end of that summer I found myself relying almost entirely upon Erik's skills. His ambivalent status had already cost me several trained men—men such as Calandrino, who came to resent his meteoric progress and ultimately declined to work with a boy who had made a mockery of the apprentice system within two years.

By this time I was accepting work purely for the sake of Erik's experience. Arthritis was twisting my fingers out of all normal proportions and I was aware that I would soon be unable to hold a chisel; I wanted Erik to take over the business from me.

During that final contract I found it easier to employ itinerant laborers and place all of the laying under the boy's supervision. I had given him responsibility for every aspect of this new job; he had done all the costings, and though I had gone over the estimate with a fiercely critical eye, I had been unable to pinpoint any naive oversight or extravagance. The client accepted the estimate without demur and then conveniently departed to Florence for the summer. Consequently there was no need for him to know that the building of his property had been placed largely in the hands of a fifteen-year-old boy.

The construction proceeded in the orderly manner which characterized all of Erik's work. He had absolute authority in my absence and his formidable, brooding presence upon the site ensured that there was neither conflict nor slacking among the men. He was very tall now, massively boned and muscular, almost inhumanly strong, and staggeringly competent; one glance at the uncompromising eyes behind the mask was sufficient to quell anyone's inclination to argue a point. And yet he was always fair, ready to acknowledge a hard worker or encourage a beginner; he showed all the signs of becoming a good master.

They were up to the first level when one of the men went sick and I was obliged to engage a new laborer temporarily. I thought nothing of it when the fellow told me he had worked his way down through Italy from Milan—it was not unusual for a laborer to travel in search of work.

But there was something alarming about the quick, startled glance that the man gave Erik when they met, something over and above the normal surprise engendered by the prospect of working beside that mask.

By siesta time I had gathered enough from the throbbing whispering running like wildfire all over the site to know that whatever secret Erik had chosen to hide was a secret no longer. This man had seen something—not in the Trastevere perhaps, but elsewhere—in Milan or Florence, wherever there are fairs to be attended.

And now he had told what he knew.

I turned him off at the end of the day, but I knew it was too late to repair the damage he had done. The atmosphere on the site reminded me of the timeless lull before an electrical storm, and I could see from the sudden tension in Erik's eyes that he was fully aware of the change that had come over the men.

It wasn't long before the whispered word *monster* reached my ears and I heard it with terrible sorrow, for it merely confirmed my own inner understanding. I had guessed long ago that the boy hid some very serious deformity behind that mask, something he had never found the courage to reveal to me. In many quiet little ways I had tried to show him that his fears were groundless, but he had never been ready to read those signs; and I had been forced to wait patiently for the day when he finally trusted me enough to show me his face in the privacy of our home. Now, as I began to understand the enormity of the burden he carried with him, I saw that day was never going to dawn. . . .

Danger was pulsing all around him, like molten lava waiting to engulf him in an unguarded moment, and I watched him change in response to this unspoken threat. Suddenly he was a feral animal once again, scenting the imminent reality of attack; a young tiger waiting in grim threatening silence to repel the challenge that never came. His natural authority—and his reputation for a quick and savage knife hand—kept the threat hovering narrowly at bay. But the vigilance required of him was unremitting, and he began to come home from the site at night too tense even to think of eating.

It was the same week that Luciana had taken it upon herself to dismiss my housekeeper and take over the duties herself. . . .

"What's wrong with my cooking?" she demanded in that ominous tone, when Erik had chosen yet again to go straight to the cellar without explanation or apology.

"There's nothing wrong with your cooking," I said, valiantly spearing a stringy forkful of a dish I had yet to identify, "nothing at all."

"He hasn't even bothered to come and see what it is."

"The boy's weary, for God's sake, Luciana! He only wants to rest."

As the delicate, tinkling notes of the old spinet drifted between us, Luciana's fists clenched upon the table.

"He's not too weary to play, though, is he?" she said fiercely. "He won't be too weary to sit up all night drawing and messing around with bits of wire! Only too weary to eat a meal I spent hours making!"

And snatching her own untouched plate off the table she rushed away to slam pots and pans in the kitchen.

When Luciana had gone to bed, I sat for several hours staring into the empty hearth, smoking steadily, and refilling my pipe at intervals, trying to think what to do for the best.

Toward midnight, reaching a sudden decision, I knocked once on the door of the cellar and went down the steep stone steps without waiting for a reply.

Erik had been working on the accounts. The huge ledger stood open on the table behind him, lit by a wilting candle on either side, a spray of ink across the page betraying the startled haste with which he had got to his feet at my unexpected intrusion. I fancied I could almost hear his accelerated heartbeat, and it saddened me to see him returning inexorably to his instinctive, distrustful wariness.

"I've been wanting to have a quiet word with you, Erik."

"Yes, sir. . . . I know." He turned away to close up the heavily ruled ledger. "The accounts are all up to date now, everything's in order. I'll be packed and gone within the hour."

Glancing beyond him, I saw that the old saddlebags were already laid out waiting on his pallet, and I knew then that had I not made the decision to come down here tonight, I would have found the cellar empty in the morning.

"You were going to leave without a word?" I accused him indignantly. "Why?"

He stared at the ledger. "Because . . ." he said with difficulty, "because I didn't want to wait until you asked me to."

I had a sudden great desire to strike him a smart cuff around the ear.

"You foolish boy!" I said testily. "Why in God's name should you think I want you to leave?"

"I'm causing trouble. . . ." He would not look at me. "I ought to go now before it's too late."

"I never heard such absurd drama! You'd better come upstairs at once before I really get very angry with you."

I marched back up the steps and he followed me in uncomfortable, meekly obedient silence, just as though he were an errant son . . . sat hastily where I told him to sit and accepted the wine I gave him without further protest. I was well aware that it was going to be impossible to talk to him, in the manner that I wished to talk to him, while he sat there stone cold sober, wearing his tension and his habitual reserve like an impenetrable suit of armor. So for a while I discussed the business of the day and steadily refilled our large Venetian glasses, obliging him to keep pace with me. It didn't take too many glasses before I saw that his free hand was no longer clenched on his knee, but trailing limp and relaxed over the arm of his chair.

I spoke of many things that night, some that I had meant to, some that I had not. I, too, was feeling the wine by now, and it filled me with a morbid certainty that this opportunity would not come again, that we were all of us caught in a relentless current that might soon become too strong to swim against.

The oil lamps faded and went out, one by one, but I did not trouble to replenish them as I spoke of the grand Masonic ideals, the responsibilities of manhood. I spoke of God, the Grand Sovereign Architect of the Universe, who measures us all by the Square and the Plumb and the Compass; I spoke of goodwill and charity and tolerance.

And at length, choosing my words with as much care as I could muster, I spoke of the extreme vulnerability of young women. . . .

He asked no questions, made no comment, but he did not look away and I knew he was listening, trying hard to accept what must seem so much at odds with the reality of his life. I asked tolerance and forbearance in the face of cruelty and scorn and I knew it was a hard path I showed him, a daunting journey from which it would be all too easy to turn aside. He wasn't ready to accept a crucifix, and yet without some symbol of hope, something to touch, to hold on to, in those dark moments of despair, I feared he might soon be lost to the temptations of angry violence.

In my desk lay the silver compass that Isabella had given me in our happier days, before Luciana was born. It had been in my mind to give it to him many times, but I had never found a moment in which the appropriate words could be spoken.

I gave it to him now, knowing I could not afford to wait any longer, and he accepted it with the confused, tongue-tied embarrassment of a boy entirely unused to receiving gifts. His faltering gratitude hurt me and made me take refuge in a brusqueness I had not intended.

"Well . . . it's no use to me anymore when I can hardly hold a lead straight. Just see you put it in a safe place, that's all, and don't go losing it."

He pocketed the compass with some difficulty on his second attempt, his fingers oddly clumsy and uncoordinated with the wine. By now I could see he was struggling to keep dutifully awake.

"Get yourself off to bed, boy, you're well and truly shipped," I said ruefully.

Watching him get unsteadily to his feet and negotiate his way with slow determination toward the stairs, I called him back. The eyes behind the mask gazed vaguely in my direction and I wondered how many of me he was seeing in that moment.

"Erik . . . I hope you'll never become so good at building walls that you can't see when they need to be pulled down."

He hesitated, staring at me with fuddled uncertainty.

"I'll . . . see to that first thing, sir," he muttered, as though he hoped that was the appropriate reply.

Since there was quite clearly no point in trying to say another rational word to him tonight, I let him go before it became necessary to carry him down those stairs to bed.

I went on drinking for some time after he had left me, feeling that I had made a rather miserable botch of the proceedings. What, after all, had I achieved by getting the boy so blind drunk that he could hardly stand?

In the morning he probably wouldn't remember a thing I'd said to him!

I had little enough cause to feel proud of my wisdom as father or guardian in the months that followed either. Indeed, almost everything that happened seemed to confirm my growing impression that I was simply a foolish, rather incompetent old man who was rapidly losing his grip of things and ought not to presume to give advice to anyone. Much good it was to hold forth on the ancient Masonic values of manhood, when I was quite plainly incapable of controlling my daughter and maintaining order in my own household.

Throughout that summer Luciana was like a blind puppy snapping in angry confusion at a thing she could neither see clearly nor understand. She lacked the language to express her infatuation, and Erik, the ability to believe in its existence; there seemed to be no end to the innumerable ways in which they managed to hurt each other.

In self-defense the boy began to work longer and longer hours at the site, using lanterns to light the scaffolding after dark. Some nights he did not come home at all. The wonderful inventions which lined the walls of his cellar began to gather dust and the old spinet stood silent in its corner. Luciana sulked in his absence and greeted him with wounding sarcasm at his return. My furious rebukes went unheeded. Erik had withdrawn so deeply into himself that it was impossible to approach him on any subject that did not pertain to work. I could not reach either of them; I could not halt the relentless spinning of the whirlpool that was sucking them ever deeper into darkness.

Then one morning I woke to hear their voices echoing up from the cellar; Luciana's petulant, with an angry hint of tears; and Erik's so instinctively defensive that it had affected a chilling indifference bound to infuriate.

"What are all these things, anyway? What do they do?"

"Please leave them alone, mademoiselle."

"I want to know. . . . Explain them to me!"

"You could not possibly understand."

"Oh, really? Am I so very stupid, then?"

"That is not what I said."

"No, but it's what you meant! Or did you perhaps mean something else? Yes, that's it! I know now why you're afraid to show me these things—it's because they don't work, isn't it? *They don't work!*"

"Everything in this cellar works!"

I heard the dangerous note of rage explode in his voice; and I heard Luciana's fury rise to meet it in head-on collision.

"Well, *this* doesn't work!" she cried suddenly, "—not anymore! Or *this!* Or *this!*"

My God, I thought in alarm, *he'll kill her. . . .*

The crash of glass and metal on the stone-walled floor reverberated all around me as I started down into the cellar to intervene; but Erik was already rushing up, taking the steps two at a time. He pushed past me roughly without a word, and such was his violent fury that I did not dare to lay a restraining hand upon his sleeve. It was the first time he had ever treated me with discourtesy, and I was stunned by the uncomfortable suspicion that he had not even recognized me.

I let him flee from an urge to kill that was so real, so very nearly ungovernable, that it still pulsed around me like a lingering scent. Then I looked down at the stupid child who remained in ignorance of the tragedy she had almost provoked.

She was kneeling on the floor now, staring at the remnants of her willful destruction.

"Luciana," I said with cold displeasure, "go to your room at once!"

She did not move to obey me, but reached out instead to touch the broken glass with reverence and remorse.

"How can he love these things, these bits of wire and metal?" she whispered. "How can he love these things and not love me? Am I not pretty enough?" She lifted her tearstained face and looked up at me with anguish. "Oh, Papa . . . *Why* does he hate me so much?"

The senseless futility of everything overwhelmed me and took away my anger, leaving me feeling very old and tired.

"He doesn't hate you, child," I said wearily. "He only hates himself."

She stared at me, and her face creased into a frown of confusion.

"I don't understand," she began doubtfully. "Why should he hate himself?"

I came down into the cellar and sat heavily on the pallet where Erik must occasionally have slept.

"Luciana—the mask. . . ."

I saw her stiffen. "I don't want to hear about the mask," she said stubbornly, putting her hands to her ears with defiant childishness. "I don't want to hear those hateful rumors that the laborers are spreading. They're only jealous of him because he's so quick and clever and everyone knows he could take over from you tomorrow."

"Luciana—"

"I don't believe them!" She got up abruptly and backed away from me toward the stairs. "I *won't* believe them, Papa, I know it's not true!"

"But if it were—"

"*It's not true!*" she screamed with a hysteria that twisted her pretty face into unlovely folds. "He's *not* ugly, he's *not* some kind of monster! I won't let him be ugly, Papa. . . . I won't *let* him be!"

The intense irrationality of her emotion effectively silenced me. I suddenly saw there was nothing more I could say on the subject, and with the deepest misgiving I was forced to let her go.

I did not go down to the site that day, feeling that Erik would prefer to be left alone. Luciana remained in her room; the house was shrouded in silence and the day ticked away steadily, hot and humid with a fetid air drifting in from the Tiber. Suppertime came and went but we did not eat, and occasionally I looked up at the clock on the mantelpiece with a sigh. Nine o'clock, ten o'clock—and still there was no sign of Erik.

At eleven o'clock Luciana came downstairs and demanded that I go and fetch him from the site. I refused. The boy would come home when his temper had cooled and not before; until then I intended to leave him in peace.

She disappeared for a moment and returned with a shawl around her shoulders.

"If you won't fetch him back, then I will," she said tearfully. "I want to tell him that I'm sorry."

I stared in amazement. As far as I was aware, Luciana had never said she was sorry for anything in the entire course of her life.

"Papa," she said tremulously, "Papa . . . I'm going to ask him to take off the mask."

Somewhere deep in my mind an alarm bell began to ring, and I shook my head.

"You're not going anywhere at this time of night," I told her firmly.

"But Papa—"

"For heaven's sake, leave the boy alone!" I shouted suddenly. "He doesn't want you to see him, not you or anyone! You're driving him out of his mind, Luciana. . . . He wanted to kill you this morning, did you know that?"

She gasped, staring at me out of eyes red rimmed in a chalk-white face.

"He wouldn't hurt me—I know he'd never hurt me!"

I turned away impatiently and reached for my pipe.

"You know nothing about him, absolutely nothing! You're provoking him beyond all human endurance."

Her mouth opened and shut wordlessly at the cruelty of my stinging insult; then slowly she subsided to the floor and began to cry.

For an hour I sat in my chair and watched her weep without speaking a single word of comfort. Then I went over and picked her up, carrying her upstairs with her head on my shoulder just as I used to do when she was a small child. It was pitifully easy to do—she could not have weighed much more now than she had done at ten.

When I laid her on the bed she looked at me with abject despair. "I have to see him, Papa," she said quietly. "I have to see him."

I knew she was right; there was now no other way to end this terrible midsummer madness that was threatening to destroy us all.

I sat in my room for a couple of hours staring at the wall and occasionally passing a handkerchief across my forehead. It was almost two in the morning, but the heat was still stifling, and at length, knowing there was no possibility of sleep, I wandered up to the rooftop garden where it was cooler.

For want of anything better to do I began to water the flowers, and thus hidden among the shadows, I escaped Erik's attention when he crossed the roof with a slow, dragging step and flung himself down on the travertine bench. He put one arm along the back of the seat, laying his head against it in an attitude of complete exhaustion; and when he did not move again I began to wonder if he had fallen asleep and it might be safe to steal away unseen.

"Erik!"

Luciana's unexpected whisper startled him like the crack of a pistol; he leapt to his feet and stood rigid, keeping his back to her as she approached.

"I want you to take off the mask," she said simply and without arrogance. "*Please* take off the mask."

"You must excuse me, mademoiselle," he said stonily, keeping his face averted as he swung past her. "I have work to finish."

"I will *not* excuse you!" she cried after him. "You *don't* have any work to finish! I want you to take off the mask, do you hear me, Erik? I want you take it off *right now!*"

I made up my mind quite suddenly and stepped out in front of him as he made for the stairs.

"Sir?" He stopped and glanced behind, like a fox who senses the hunters drawing in. I laid a hand on his sleeve.

"Erik, we've gone beyond the question of choice."

"I'm sorry. . . . I don't quite—"

"I think it would be best if you simply did as my daughter has asked."

He was utterly motionless, staring at me with such pained horror that I was forced to avert my eyes from the crumbling ruins of his trust.

"You are asking me to do this thing?" I heard disbelief trembling in his voice. "You are *ordering* me?"

"If an order is what it takes," I said sadly, "then I am ordering you. God Almighty, boy, you must see this can't go on any longer."

He swayed slightly, putting out a hand to steady himself against the balustrade, and I moved automatically to give him a supporting arm. But before I could touch him he lifted his head and the light of the hanging lanterns showed me in his eyes a naked loathing born of black despair and disillusion.

I realized then the enormity of the crime that I had committed; I realized when I saw that look of hate which seemed to squeeze all the breath out of my lungs. I had been a father to him; I had shown him honesty and hope and led him to believe there might after all be a chance for him to live with pride and dignity among the human race he so distrusted. For love of me he had begun to abandon his deepest instincts and grope tentatively and painfully toward the certainty that I did not care what lay beneath the mask.

Now in a single ill-considered moment, the result of my own exhaustion and despair, I had reached up and pulled that castle of dreams down around him. I had demanded the one thing he had trusted me never to ask of him; and if I had plunged a dagger through his heart I could not have destroyed him more effectively, I could not have given him more intolerable anguish.

As I watched the boy I knew shrivel and die before my very eyes, I saw an awesome stranger take his place, a grim and oddly frightening stranger who no longer waited to hear any further worthless words of mine.

"You want to see?" he said in a toneless voice that seemed to belong to a sepulcher. *"You want to see?* Then look!"

As he spoke he began to move with a dreadful, measured calm toward Luciana, and I felt a paralyzing dread flowing through my veins. They were standing face-to-face when he ripped off the mask and I saw her mouth drop open in a soundless scream, her hands fling upward to fend him off. The defensive gesture seemed to madden him, and he reached out as though he intended to drag her closer to the terrible horror he had revealed.

I cried out in warning but my voice was lost in the primitive, animal panic which sent her running from him, running across the rooftop garden to throw herself against the balustrade which finally blocked her line of escape. Again and again I see it happen . . . the crumbling stonework giving way beneath the weight of her body and tumbling her, in a shower of flaking mortar, into the courtyard that lay two stories beneath.

Silence settled once more over the roof, disturbed only by the last, sickening shift of the stones; and the lantern light showed me the void that now gaped in the balustrade, like a lost tooth in the mouth of some grim nightmare creature.

Without urgency, without hope, I turned numbly and groped my way down into the courtyard where my daughter's broken little body lay surrounded by a shroud of decayed masonry. I had known she must be dead and even had one last flicker of hope remained with me, it would not have survived that first sight of her split skull, the slow grayish ooze upon the flagstones. Time and place had ceased to have meaning and the world seemed very far away from the silent void which closed around me as I carried her into the house and laid her on the creaking leather couch.

I did not hear his step, but I was aware of his presence just behind me, like some great black specter.

I did not turn. I felt that if I looked around I would be turned to stone, calcified by the bitter venom of his rage and grief. I did not fear the horror of his face—I could have looked upon that sight with equanimity at any time. But I feared his eyes now, those bottomless pits of sorrow that would only mirror my pain. I heard his ragged, sobbing curse and I knew I must not look at him. . . . I would go mad if I looked.

Silence stretched between us like a stone wall and became the final separation. The oil lamps, still burning in their brackets, showed me his shadow moving slowly across the wall beyond the couch, a huge and silent shade slipping out into the night beyond my door, where darkness waited to reclaim him like a fond parent.

When he was gone . . . only when he was finally gone . . . was I able to weep.

The shadows are creeping steadily across the rooftop garden now . . . another bleak and meaningless day is ending. I have sat here once again until sunset, brooding, remembering, reproaching myself for the folly which emptied my life, the last mistake which killed my daughter and destroyed a unique boy.

Erik . . . I can say now what I could not say that night when Luciana's hand lay cooling in my grasp and I was struck dumb by outraged grief. You were not to blame for her death. Whatever blame there was I have long since taken upon myself.

You were the child of my imagination, the son that God withheld, and I learned to love you in your slow and painful striving for the light.

Tomorrow these flowers you cared for will lift their faces once more to the sun, stretching up proud and true to acknowledge their creator in all their beauty.

There was so much beauty in your soul, Erik, so much beauty that I fear now, because of one old man's folly, will never see the light of day.

In darkness you came to me.

And in darkness you left. . . .

Nadir
1850-1853

shraf was a magnificent ruin of palaces. There had been, over the centuries, as many as six different royal residences contained within its huge wall of circumvallation, all beautifully laid out in their time with stone terraces, canals, cascades, and lovely *aiwans*. But once the Hall of Forty Columns burned down, little was done to restore the opulent glories of former years, and an air of shabby decay hung over the Bagh-i-Shah and the Garden of the Seraglio. In the enormous grounds orange trees and gigantic cypress ran riot among a jungle of wildflowers and weeds. The court came to the maritime province of Mazanderan for a brief period each winter, to escape the harsh bleakness of Tehran's plummeting temperatures, but only infrequent, fleeting visits were made during spring and summer. So for much of the year the area suffered the neglect peculiar to deserted property, with scorpions and small lizards sunning themselves peacefully on the terraces. I had always thought it a shame; Mazanderan is a place of great natural beauty and deserved better from its imperial masters. It was said that the new shah intended to make changes; and since he appeared to me to be every bit as vain and pleasure loving as his predecessor, I thought it quite likely that he would soon come to require a residence more in keeping with his station than these crumbling relics of the past.

This was the second time in a week that I had received a direct summons to the palace, and once more I went there with a quaking heart, wondering what fresh unpleasant commission was about to be foisted upon me. Even in this tropical backwater we were not immune to the religious uprisings that had been taking place in the capital. The execution of the Bab in July had not put an end to the unrest, merely exacerbated it, with the result that the name of Babi had become a convenient label for any dissident and sufficient excuse for their elimination. Babi activity was reported everywhere, and I, as chief of police, had found my prisons bursting at the seams like everyone else's, until the executions brought their own form of relief. The stinking, decaying bodies had been publicly displayed as a timely warning to those who might still be tempted to voice their heresies. No wonder the flies had been so bad that year, issuing like a plague from the malarial swamps and lagoons along the Caspian shore. . . .

I never asked to be made daroga of Mazanderan, and I am obliged to confess that there were times when I thought I should rest far easier in my bed as a lowly secretary. There were hundreds of us shahzadeh in Persia, all entitled to claim imperial descent from the thin smattering of royal blood that ran in our veins. The shahs had always exercised a peculiarly excessive talent for paternity, and blatant nepotism had run riot for countless years because of it. Until someone died and freed a post more suitable to my regrettably squeamish nature, daroga of Mazanderan I would remain. I had a modest estate, a son, and a respectable position in society to support—I couldn't afford to be overly particular about the nature of my employment in the royal service. The post gave me a good pension and brought me to court sufficiently often to enable me to keep a wary eye on those next in blood who were frantically trying to appropriate it behind my back. Rampant corruption and blatant backstabbing were the inevitable results of our system of government; the Persian court was not a place where a wise man took his eyes off an enemy for a single careless moment.

Passing through the Sublime Porte, which led into the palace complex, I was directed out into the gardens, to the wooden pavilion which had been hastily and halfheartedly erected to replace the Hall of Forty Columns. Already it looked ready to fall down, the product of inferior design, poor materials, and idle workmen. Persia was slowly stagnating after a glorious past; evidence of decadence and decay was everywhere.

I prostrated myself dutifully on the highly patterned carpet at the foot of a Turkish divan and gave the prescribed greeting to the king of kings.

"May I be your sacrifice, Asylum of the Universe."

Unmoved by the essential absurdity of my address, the shah looked up from the cat which was arching beneath his caressing hand, and made the brief gesture which raised me to my feet.

"Daroga! You're late."

"A thousand apologies, Imperial Majesty."

I bowed my head in assumed humility and he was satisfied. I wasn't late and we both knew it, but he was young, barely two years on the throne, and still felt the need to establish his querulous authority. Now that I had become the humble penitent, we could come to business.

"Have you interrogated the Samarkand fur trader, as I instructed?"

"Yes, Imperial Majesty." I got all the good jobs—the ones that no one else at court would touch. It had taken me two months to track down that wretched fur trader and extract his garbled, incredible tale.

"And what is your opinion of the man's honesty?"

"He was a simple man, Your Majesty, a very simple man. I would say he lacked the imagination to embroider such a story."

The shah sat upright on the divan and the Siamese cat—his special favorite, a gift from the royal court of Siam—sprang down on the carpet, tossing her fantastically jeweled collar and eyeing me with a look of pure malevolence. It was a serious thing at this court to make a feline enemy, but no matter how I tried, I never had the knack with cats.

"So it is true, then," mused the shah thoughtfully. "He does indeed exist, this miraculous magician who sings like a god and performs wonders beyond all imagination. The khanum will be delighted. She has already said that such a phenomenon would be wasted in Nijni-Novgorod. He must be brought here at once, the khanum desires it."

I remained respectfully silent, not daring to voice my thoughts. Like the rest of the court I was heartily weary of satisfying the whims of the shah's mother. Beautiful, heartless, and politically shrewd, she had been the power behind the throne for the last two years and would continue to rule our lives with her caprices until her son broke loose from her maternal dominance. There was, regrettably, no sign of this happening. The shah had three principal wives and innumerable concubines, but no woman in the harem had yet shown herself capable of emerging from the khanum's shadow sufficiently to challenge her insidious influence. We all went in fear of "the Lady."

"I intend to entrust this little matter to your worthy care, Daroga," the shah continued, watching the cat circle me with an ominous swish of her tail. "You will prepare to leave for Russia at once."

I opened my mouth to protest and shut it hurriedly as the shah's expression hardened into displeasure.

"As you wish, O Shadow of God."

As I bowed myself out backward, my foot trod on something long and sinewy. There was a spitting screech of rage, and an unsheathed claw lashed at the bare skin above my ankle. Another infernal cat! Praise Allah, not the shah's favorite this time, but one sufficiently esteemed to win me a frown from the imperial brow and a rebuke that brought sweat glistening on my upper lip.

"You are clumsy today, Daroga."

I mumbled profuse apologies like an idiot, but my efforts at conciliation only won me another vicious scratch from the indignant animal. Allah, how I hated cats! The miserable creatures were all over the palace, filling the rooms with the stench of their urine. It was considered a particular privilege to be sprayed by one of the royal cats—one was not expected to exclaim in disgust and rush off to change into clean attire. Indeed I have known a courtier to cut the coattails from his jacket rather than disturb the Glory of the Empire while she slept. The animals had their own servants and rode in velvet padded cages whenever the court moved. Some of the especially favored even had pensions! Men have been thrown into prison for far less heinous crimes than treading on the tail of a royal cat; I knew I was fortunate to escape so lightly.

I left the palace in an angry daze. It was never safe to leave court for an indefinite period, but my resentment had deeper roots than that, deeper and infinitely more painful. This mission threatened more than the security of my post. . . .

I had been aware, for a year or more, that all was not well with my son's health. He suffered a strange disturbance of vision and there was a weakness of the muscles in his arms and legs that was growing imperceptibly more pronounced with the passage of time. In spite of the reassurance of several doctors, I remained uneasy. We Persians were not noted for our skill in medicine—even the shah himself had dispensed with our native physic in favor of the services of a French physician. I did not wish to leave my home at this time and yet I knew I had no choice. To refuse an imperial commission was to court the shah's displeasure, and I knew of no quicker road to ruin and death.

That night, as I patiently explained to Reza why I must leave him in the care of servants during the period of my absence, I suddenly realized what a great disservice I had done him by failing to provide him with another mother. I had had my share of concubines, but since Rookheeya's death I had never been remotely tempted to avail myself of the four wives to which my religion entitled me. It had seemed disloyal somehow. Whenever the itch of manhood was upon me, I simply availed myself of the services of a woman in my household and continued to push all thought of marriage into the background. But now, staring at Rookheeya's pale and delicate child, I wondered if I had not betrayed them both with the selfishness of my grief.

There were tears, as I had known there must be. I had encouraged the boy to be overly dependent upon my affection, and now I could not even tell him when I would be back. So to buy myself smiles instead of tears, I told him that I was being sent to find the greatest magician who ever lived. And I promised him that, once my mission was accomplished, I would bring this eighth wonder of the world here to our home before I took him to the shah. How easy it is to distract a child with promises! If only guilt could be so easily appeased!

Watching Reza limp clumsily out of my apartments, I heartily cursed the khanum, whose accursed whim was forcing these bleak months of separation upon us. As for the mysterious genius I was now condemned to pursue, I wished he had never drawn breath to sing and enchant that garrulous fur trader from Samarkand. Better that he had drowned in the Volga rather than perform those astonishing tricks which had caused his fame to be carried from the wastelands of Russia by the trading caravans.

A thousand curses on you, Erik, I reflected bitterly, how I wish that you had never been born!

In order to arrive at Nijni-Novgorod before the end of the Great Yarmark, as its famous summer fair was known, I was obliged to cross the Caspian with precious little delay. Rumor travels at a leisurely pace on the back of a camel, and the tale that had excited the khanum's bored imagination had been the best part of twelve months in reaching us. I had no time to assemble the elaborate entourage so beloved of the traveling Persian. I took with me a mere handful of servants—among them my trusted Darius—and we traveled as lightly as possible in the interests of speed.

I prefer to forget as much as I can about the sea crossing, which was surely as disagreeable as any crossing could have been. The summer storms were unimaginably bad, and our small vessel was tossed about like a piece of driftwood. I was in a vile humor by the time we reached Astrakhan, and the first thing I noticed about this famous Russian town was not the towering minarets of its dozen mosques, or the graceful cupolas of its innumerable churches, but the disgusting smell of decaying fish, which seemed to pervade the whole city.

I retired at once to a mean-looking, insubstantial wooden lodging house, leaving Darius to arrange our passage up the Volga by steamer. The landlady served a meal which seemed to consist chiefly of cabbage soup, cucumber, and watermelon, and I was gazing at this noxious fare, trying to decide whether I dared to send a mouthful down to my outraged stomach, when Darius returned, looking anxious. The Great Yarmark at Nijni had only a few more days to run and the steamer on which he had accordingly booked our passage was due to leave at noon.

Abandoning the watermelon in disgust, I watched our baggage bump unceremoniously down the rickety staircase. The indignation of the landlady was extremely vocal. When Darius joined me at the waterfront I noticed there were streaks of cabbage soup on his robe. If I hadn't been so furious, I might have been amused.

I suppose a leisurely trip up the Volga is a pleasant thing to those who are not burdened by severely limited time and a nerve-racking sense of urgency. Certainly my fellow Moslem travelers appeared to be enjoying themselves. Five times a day I joined them on the paddle box of the steamer to turn my face to Mecca and prostrate myself in prayer, but I am ashamed to admit that my mind often wandered from the ritual invocations. There was no thought in my head except the success of this mission, for only success would buy me a swift passage home to my son. We had arrived far later than I had first calculated, and I knew that time was against me now. Cursing the stately pace of the steamer, I paid a visit to the engine room to inquire whether our speed could not be increased. All I received for my pains was a lecture on the mechanics of steamer navigation and a tart re-minder that things had been far worse in the days of the old *mas-chinas*, which had only recently receded from the waterways. Didn't I realize that it used to take as many weeks to complete this journey as it now took days?

"Admire the scenery and be patient," advised the old captain.

I wasn't interested in the scenery. The wooded hills of the Jigoulee, the idyllic coves and bays, were quite lost on me as I stared unseeingly into the distance, willing the boat to make greater speed. Sixteen hundred miles stretched endlessly before me as the days slipped away like sand in an hourglass. Saratov; Samara; Kazan. . . .

And then at last the square whitewashed monastery of St. Macarius loomed up on the right bank and I realized, with intense excitement, that I was finally within five hours of my goal.

Heavily laden barges were moving up and down the congested river on either side of us, often passing so close that it was a miracle we avoided a collision. The country on the right bank had assumed a new aspect—a high, mountainous range now rising abruptly from the plain below. We turned sharply to avoid a sandbank and at that point I was afforded my first glimpse of Nijni's imposing setting. I saw the gilded cupola of the cathedral and the white crenellated wall of the ancient kremlin. The old town was reposing serenely under the shadow of its fortress, as though mildly surprised by the frenzy of activity that was taking place on the river below it. Later I was to think how much Nijni-Novgorod resembled the man that I had come to find—aloof, formidable, full of astonishing contradictions.

When we disembarked on the quayside, I sent my servants to acquire lodgings in the *haute ville*. I waited only long enough to ascertain an address, before hiring a droshky boy to drive me through the town to the western quarter, of which I had been told. Darius came with me, insisting that the fair was full of thieves and rogues and that it was not safe for a gentleman to venture into the throng alone.

Throngs there certainly were. The little Tartar horse could barely make headway against the tide of traffic that was sweeping out of the fair. No Persian bazaar could compare with this chaos. Crowds on foot, in carriages, and on horseback, droves of cattle, carts laden with jars and casks and boxes of every description, all served to hamper our progress, and I was amazed to see such activity so late in the day. Rain teemed down steadily, and the horse was up to its fetlocks in a quagmire of mud that suggested such torrential downpours were a depressingly regular occurrence. But neither the rain nor the mud discouraged the remarkable number of dévots. On virtually every street corner that we passed there was a sacred shrine or image, surrounded by hysterical men and women, all flinging themselves down in the mud before the lighted candles and crossing themselves with feverish urgency, as though their lives depended on the gestures.

"Christians!" said Darius beneath his breath, and in his voice I heard all the ancient contempt of Islam for the unbeliever. I shared his beliefs, but not his contempt. I knew there was no God but Allah; I accepted that no infidel would ever be admitted to paradise—and yet I had made many friends in the Catholic missions in Persia, men whose moral integrity I respected even as I pitied their religious misguidance. They had no hope of heaven, but here, on this earth, I saw no reason to deny them civility or friendship. I could not hate with the indiscriminating simplicity of my servant.

So I made no response and we rode on in silence—though perhaps *rode* is hardly the right word to describe our progress. We lurched from side to side, we were constantly jostled, almost overturned, in the melee, and stinking mud was thrown up in our faces from all directions. At length I was forced to admit the need to abandon the road until the crowds lessened. The little droshky boy—a grimy-faced urchin—seemed delighted to relinquish the struggle and gladly directed us to an eating house, where we were served a passable dish of chicken and rice and unending pots of lemon tea.

Returning to the streets an hour or so later, I was dismayed to find that, though the livestock and carts had disappeared, the numbers on foot had increased tenfold. It seemed to me that half the world was bent on entering the western faubourg tonight in search of food and entertainment. There was plainly no point in attempting to navigate our way through this press of bodies by horse and cart. I paid off the droshky boy and we continued on our way by foot.

In no time at all we were lost. My Russian was not all that it could have been, and my attempts to gain direction sent us on a long series of false trails. Most of the bearded merchants and grave-faced Orientals appeared to be as bewildered and confused as I was myself. It was some time before we managed to reach the famous Kunavin suburb.

This area was situated at the farthest western extremity of the fair and was given over entirely to the pursuit of dubious pleasures. As darkness closed in, groups of drunken, riotous revelers lurched out of the eating houses and began to pick fights with each other on their way to the gambling dens and the whorehouses. Darius took out his knife and urged me to seek shelter, but I shrugged off his anxious restraining hand. I could not sleep tonight without discovering whether my prey had already flown. Fairs were scattered throughout the length and breadth of Russia, and I felt cold with panic at the prospect of failure at Nijni. I was condemned by the imperial edict to wander the entire face of this huge, bleak country until I found that damnable magician. I would walk these streets all night if necessary before I abandoned hope of an early success.

An hour later I turned a corner and came face-to-face with the very sight I was looking for—the Kirghiz tent that had been described to me in such painstaking detail by the Samarkand fur trader. Oval shaped, like an enormous beehive, the huge black shadow seemed stark and rather sinister amid its gaudy and disreputable surroundings. I was surprised and unnerved to find that, having struggled so far to come upon this moment, my first impulse should be to turn and run. As I stood in that half-lit street I was overwhelmed by a powerful presentiment of ill omen and tragedy, unlike anything I had ever experienced before. All my instincts warned me against stepping into that domed tent which suddenly seemed so strangely and irresistibly threatening. My legs were like lead as I bade Darius remain where he was and hesitantly lifted the rush matting that served as a door.

It was like stepping into a mysterious womb. Everything before my eyes was red, the walls, the rich Persian carpet on the floor, the pennants suspended from the concave roof. Soft, subdued candlelight and a heady aroma of fragrant oils and incense made the atmosphere weigh down upon me like an enchanting cloud. A strange, heavy lethargy began to creep over me, and I had to blink to clear my head before I could focus on the man who reclined upon the floor cushions.

In stark contrast to the warm opulence of his surroundings, he was dressed from head to foot in black, and his face was entirely concealed behind a white mask. The effect suggested power, a cold and thrilling majesty; it was as though I had stumbled upon one of the ancient gods of mythology. He did not look up when I entered, and for a long time he continued to tinker with an intricate trick casket, while I hovered by the doorway, troubled by a growing sense of invisibility.

He ignored me so completely that I began to be persuaded that he was quite unaware of my presence, and consequently I allowed myself to stare at him with vulgar curiosity. I could not help noticing his fingers, which were extraordinarily thin, scarcely more than bones. They were of positively inhuman length and they moved with a graceful skill and dexterity that was oddly fascinating. Mesmerized, I stood and stared; and then suddenly I became aware that he was watching me stare. The scrutiny of those unblinking eyes behind the mask made me very nervous. There was something sinister, almost reptilian, in the stillness of that black-clad figure, something that reminded me uncomfortably of a cobra poised to strike.

"The performance is over for tonight," he said in faultless Russian. "If you wish to see my skills you must come back tomorrow."

My mouth dropped open in astonishment, for nothing in his grim and austere appearance had prepared me for his voice. Even in that cold, clipped comment its astonishing beauty was quite unmistakable. Only those who heard him speak and sing will ever know just what a voice could be, for it was necessary to *hear* the extraordinary resonance and depth of timbre to truly understand the magnitude of his power. I never expected to hear such a voice outside paradise. To encounter it here, in this drafty, ill-lit tent, held its own kind of terror, for who was he—*what* was he?—to be possessed of such divinity of sound? That first moment when I heard him speak I wondered whether I beheld an angel or a devil; and even now, after all these years, it is a question I still ask myself. For each time I thought I finally knew the answer, he would only confound me once again.

But that was in the future. Now there was only the present and the need to gather my wandering wits in the face of his brisk dismissal.

"I beg your pardon for this intrusion," I said hastily, lapsing into Persian in my confusion. "Please understand that I do not come here simply as another credulous spectator, impertinent enough to expect a private performance."

"You are certainly impertinent," he retorted coldly, in my native tongue. "State your business with me and be brief."

He spoke to me with the arrogance of a king, and involuntarily I found myself slipping into the automatic deference that I normally reserved for the shah.

"Sir, your fame has carried many miles, even farther than you may have imagined. I have come from Persia to extend to you the personal invitation of the *shah-in-shah.*"

Even as I spoke, I knew I was grossly exceeding my commission. I had been told to fetch this man, in much the same way as I might have been required to obtain a performing monkey. But suddenly I was deeply aware that it was not going to be so easy.

He laughed softly, a sound which made all the hairs on the back of my hand stand on end.

"So you think I come and go on the whim of kings, like other men?" he challenged.

No," I said quietly, "I can see already that you are not like other men."

He leaned back on the cushions, studying me with some curious emotion that I could not fathom.

"You speak more truly than you know, Persian. You may do better to remain silent!"

He rose and I felt cold with apprehension as he took a step toward me; I knew that I had angered him, but I did not know how or why.

"Suppose I do not choose to accompany you to Persia? What will become of you . . . *King's Messenger?*"

The menace in his voice had become indescribable, and his physical nearness was a thing of terror. I was suddenly aware that nothing could save me now from his unspoken threat except scrupulous and painful honesty.

"If I fail in my mission I shall lose my position at court, my livelihood, and quite possibly my life," I told him simply.

He was silent for a moment, regarding me thoughtfully, and I sensed that he had begun to smile behind the mask.

"What is your position?" he demanded unexpectedly.

I made him an ironic little bow of courtesy. "I am the daroga of Mazanderan."

"I see." He folded his arms beneath the enveloping black cloak. "Then I may take it that the chief of police has come with armed men?"

"No, sir, I come alone, save for a servant who waits outside." Allah! Why was I telling him this?

He laughed again, but this time there was no heart-stopping menace in the sound.

"That, if you will forgive me for saying so, is remarkably careless of you. I trust you conduct your business with greater efficiency at home!"

His mood had changed abruptly with my ignoble confession. He was still playing with me, as a cat plays with a mouse, but gently now, with sheathed claws. Refusing to rise to his bait, I maintained a dignified silence, and after a moment he shrugged and went to a corner of the tent where water was bubbling steadily inside the brass urn of a samovar. Removing the little china teapot from the top of the charcoal, he poured a single cup, added a slice of lemon, and offered it to me. I accepted this sacred gesture of Russian hospitality with great relief. In this country tea was a natural preliminary to business—indeed a natural preliminary to all civilized negotiation; more agreements were struck in the teahouses than anywhere else. So at least it seemed I was not to be thrown out of his tent without a full hearing.

"What does the shah offer in return for my services?" he inquired abruptly.

I took a gulp of the scalding tea for courage.

"Wealth . . . honor . . ." He made a gesture of impatience, as though these things were of no interest to him, and I took a deep breath as I baited my final hook. *"Power."*

He placed the teapot back on the charcoal and swung around to look at me.

"Power?" The resonance of his single word quivered in the air between us, and I knew that at last I had struck the right chord.

"If you please the shah and the khanum, your word would be law."

"For a time."

"For a time," I agreed, knowing it was useless to lie, "but . . . during that time . . ." I spread my hands in an expressive gesture that was not wasted on him.

"Yes," he said slowly, "I understand your meaning."

"Then—you will come with me? If you agree we could leave tomorrow."

He snapped his fingers irritably.

"Your persistence begins to annoy me, and you will find I don't care to be annoyed—not even by the daroga of Mazanderan. Go now. You will have your answer when I am ready to give it and not before."

I knew that if I said another word I should lose all the ground I had made; so, infuriated though I was by his arrogant autocracy, I merely bowed and left him. My fate hung entirely on his whim, but I suddenly wished that I had come too late after all, that I had been unable to find him.

I did not know what dreadful chain of events I had set in motion that night, but a deep uneasiness came upon me as I contemplated his presence in Persia.

The sense of menace and ill omen was still with me long after I had left his tent. It was dawn before I was able to sleep that night, and when I did I heard his voice echoing through my restless dreams like a curious echo of doom.

eturning the following evening in good time to witness the performance, I was truly staggered by the sights which met my eyes. Such ingenuity and baffling sleight of hand as virtually defied belief! I was dizzied by the assault on my visual senses, and my brain reeled as all my concepts of gravity and time were turned upside down and inside out in merciless succession. All the laws which govern the universe were challenged within that tent. Some of the illusions were positively supernatural, and long before the show was at an end, I was quietly convinced that I stood in the presence of a genie, created from fire more than two thousand years before Adam. I noted uneasily that he was left handed. Every Moslem knows that the devil is left handed—it is for this reason that we always take care to spit to the left. My fingers felt instinctively for the amulets that hung at my neck, an outstretched hand made in silver and the dried eye of a sheep, killed at Mecca on the great day of sacrifice. Both were powerful protective agencies, and I had never felt more in need of their protection. I took care not to meet his gaze directly, for I already feared his evil eye.

The crowd in the tent became hysterical when the performance ended, surging forward, showering the floor with coins and clamoring for more marvels like greedy, wide-eyed children. But he turned away, telling them, with a note of weariness in his voice, that they had seen all he was prepared to show today.

They refused to go. Closing in around him like a pack of hungry animals, they began to demand, with mounting frenzy, that he should take off his mask and sing for them.

"Show us your face!" they shouted. "Show us your face, Erik, and let us hear the devil sing!"

His thin hands clenched convulsively into fists of rage and I felt a moment of stark fear that he would refuse; for if he did, I expected to be trampled in the ugly mob violence that would surely follow.

Then, without warning, his hands sprang open and stripped the mask away.

The silence that descended was awesome; it was as though everyone in the tent had ceased to breathe. I was standing very close to him, close enough to feel myself sway a little with shock when that horrific skull was revealed before my bulging eyes. The fur trader from Samarkand had never spoken of this; perhaps he had been afraid that it would discredit a tale already larger than life, for certainly no one who had not seen would ever have believed in such living horror. I could not take my eyes from him. I stood and stared like a mannerless peasant, aghast by an unparalleled, inhuman ugliness that was made somehow all the more terrible by the hatred that looked out of his sunken eyes and the pain that twisted his grotesquely deformed lips. In that tense moment before he began to sing, I sensed his deep and overwhelming loathing of the crowd.

And then I forgot everything as the real magic was revealed to me for the first time.

Nothing I had seen till now could compare with the wonderful alchemy that turned sound into liquid gold within my ears and washed me out of that dimly lit tent on a swift moving tide of ecstasy. For he sang of love, and with every nuance of his voice I saw Rookheeya reaching out to me across the endless void which separated us. Every word and every note brought us closer, so close that I found myself holding out my arms to her embrace.

Then silence fell once more and the vision was gone.

My throat closed and I wept, as so many were weeping all around me.

When the song ended the crowd drifted from his tent in soundless wonder. There could not have been a single person present who was not severely shaken and deep in private thought. He had conjured every remembered sadness from our racial memories and distilled it to a peak of unbearable beauty. No human mind could have tolerated more pain that evening; he had been revenged upon us all.

When the tent was empty, I watched him replace the mask mechanically with hands that trembled with emotion, and I wondered what terrible anguish of the past enabled him to express such an exquisite refinement of grief.

A remarkable physical change came over him as soon as his hideous face was out of sight. His shoulders straightened and his entire frame once more exuded the mysterious strength and power that I had sensed last night. A moment before he had seemed like an old man; now he might have shed thirty years in as many seconds, and I was once more aware that he was in the prime of manhood, probably a few years younger than myself.

"You have come for your answer, I suppose," he said grimly, when I continued to linger pointedly by the velvet-covered table.

"You will be greatly honored in Persia," I reminded him. "Anything you desire will be yours."

"No one in this world can give me what I desire," he said shortly, "not even the shah of Persia."

"But . . . you will come with me?"

He raised his shoulders in an elegant, scornful shrug.

"Apparently," he said, and turned away to relight the charcoal in the samovar.

The following day coincided with the end of the great fair, and the mass exodus from Nijni-Novgorod began in earnest. There were no immediate passages to be had on the paddle steamers, which were now full of rich merchants heading for home, and the best I could arrange was a place for our party aboard a barge grossly overcrowded with people, chests of tea, and bales of cotton.

We traveled as far as Kazan by river and there, very early in the morning, I chanced upon him unloading his horses with an air of quiet determination.

"What are you doing?" I demanded in alarm. "This is no time to go ashore."

"I intend to travel no farther like a crate of tea," he told me calmly. "You, of course, may do exactly as you please."

"You can't seriously mean to travel to the shore of the Caspian by land!" I gasped.

He glanced at me carelessly across the horse's mane.

"Perhaps I do not choose to continue at all. I don't care to be confined in such disagreeable proximity to the human race."

Sensing defeat, I did my best to be conciliatory.

"I admit the journey has not been comfortable—"

"Comfort has nothing to do with it," he muttered.

"I have every hope of transferring to a steamer at Samara, in which case we shall reach the Caspian in a matter of days."

"I am not interested in speed," he retorted sharply. "Only in privacy. If I am to continue this journey at all, it will be by land."

I lost my temper. "That's ridiculous!" I flared. "Such a journey would take us weeks—*weeks!* How am I to explain this unpardonable delay to the shah?"

He spread his hands in an arrogant gesture of indifference.

"Perhaps you would prefer to explain your failure instead. Good-bye, Daroga . . . enjoy the remainder of your voyage aboard this floating packing case!"

As he turned and began to lead his horses ashore, I grabbed at his sleeve.

"Wait!" I knew that if I permitted him to disappear into Kazan now I should never succeed in tracking him down a second time. "Give me time to arrange the unloading of my own belongings and we shall proceed as you wish . . . exactly as you wish. But I warn you now that the imperial displeasure is not a thing to be lightly risked. The king of kings does not like to be kept waiting."

"The king of kings must learn patience," said Erik coldly, "like everyone else."

That was the first occasion that I bowed to his capricious whims—the first of many, had I but known it.

Before we left Kazan, he insisted on visiting the mausoleum which stood roughly a mile outside the town. Since I had now abandoned all hope of a swift return to Persia—and because I did not trust him out of my sight for two minutes!—I was forced to accompany him through the dank, ill-smelling catacombs to admire the bones of those who had died three centuries ago at the siege of Kazan.

Human remains made me nervous and I was horrified when he began to assemble the relics of an entire skeleton, placing it patiently, bone by bone, into a bag.

"What do you want with that?" I demanded uneasily. "You're surely not going to take it away with you."

"But of course," he replied calmly. "I have rarely seen such a perfectly preserved specimen. Look . . . it is possible to see where the knife chipped the rib bone on penetration."

"How can you tell it was a knife?"

"I have dissected sufficient corpses who died of knife wounds to know that the signs are unmistakable."

"Dissected!" I stared at him aghast. "You have performed *dissections?*"

"From time to time. It is the only way to reach any true understanding of the human body. I have an academic interest in the physiology of *Homo sapiens* . . . a certain *curiosity,* you understand."

The way he spoke of the human race was oddly unsettling. It was as though he did not include himself within the species at all. A shiver passed through my body, and I was deeply relieved when we were out in the sunlight again. I asked him no more questions. I did not want to know what kind of a man collected skeletons from tombs and dissected dead bodies to satisfy an "academic interest."

Several times before we left Kazan he devastated me with fresh evidence of utter amorality. Walking with him through the streets of this "Little Moscow" one night, I was horrified to observe that, each time we passed a wealthy Tartar merchant, a leather purse would appear briefly in Erik's hand on its way to some hidden repository in his cloak. It seemed to me that these purses were leaping into his fingers by magic alone, for though I watched him closely, I was never able to register the moment when his hand dipped effortlessly into a capacious pocket. Later I began to understand that the only reason I had seen anything at all was because he wished me to see. He appeared to enjoy shocking me, and I am forced to admit that though his company was certainly highly disconcerting, it was never for one single moment dull! I was like a well-behaved child playing truant from school in the company of a perfect rogue. When he offered to teach me the trick, I actually hesitated for a moment, weighing the consequences of being caught, before refusing with a show of righteous indignation.

But reality descended upon me abruptly once we left behind the Tartar splendor of Kazan. During our interminable trek through the primeval forests that lined the banks of the Volga, I suffered many uneasy moments. We were a small party, completely vulnerable to the bands of robbers who roamed the waterways in search of foolhardy and unwary travelers. Darius slept with a loaded pistol beside his pallet and persuaded me to do the same. But Erik seemed utterly indifferent to the danger, often disappearing by himself into the thick of the forest without warning or explanation and remaining absent from the camp for several nights.

On closer acquaintance I found him moody and changeable; it was never possible to predict his humor or anticipate the moment when good temper would abruptly give way to bad. He was subject to fits of black melancholy, and when such a mood came upon him he would withdraw into his tent and refuse to move any farther, neither eating nor speaking for days at a time. Anyone who disturbed him at such a moment did so with considerable risk to life and limb, for as we quickly learned, he had a violent and ungovernable temper. And then again, just as unpredictably, he would become amusing and sociable once more, showing off his astonishing skills as magician, musician, and ventriloquist, stunning us all with each fresh evidence of his inexhaustible ingenuity. In such a mood he was occasionally prepared to linger by the campfire and humor my curiosity with tales of exotic travel. He seemed to have lived for a time in most of the countries that cover Europe and Asia, and in India he had spent a brief sojourn among the mystics in the tented empire of Karak Khitan that lies south of the western Himalayas.

He was a born storyteller. Extraordinary legends fell from his lips with a rhythmic and compelling intensity that held the listener spellbound. I learned more of the secrets of the world during those weeks of travel than I could ever have done in a whole lifetime of study; but of his personal history I gained very little insight. He never spoke of the life that must once have been his in the days before he began to roam the earth, driven by an insatiable lust for knowledge. He hid his past, just as he hid his face, and even the most innocuous attempt to pry was greeted with hostility.

We had traveled in this manner for several weeks when the weather abruptly turned against us. For days in succession heavy clouds rolled in over the Volga and rain sluiced down from the iron-gray sky in a relentless sheet that turned the ground beneath our horses' hooves into an impassable quagmire. We were soaked to the skin as we rode, and it was impossible to dry our clothes at night around the inade-quate braziers in our tents. The steamy tropical heat of Mazanderan seemed very far away, and in this unseasonably cold and cursedly wet spell I took a cold that left me coughing like an old man. By the time we reached Kamichin, where the storms closed in and made further travel out of the question, I was burning up with fever.

Darius covered me with the driest blankets he could find and I spent a wretched night listening to the rain drumming incessantly on the stretched hide of the tent. By morning pain was knifing through my chest with every breath I took.

I was still struggling to draw air into my lungs when Erik strode unexpectedly into my tent and bent over my pallet.

"Your servant told me you were ill." His eyes examined me with shrewd concern. "How long have you had pain on breathing?"

"A few hours," I said sullenly. "This filthy climate and your stub-bornness are entirely to blame for it."

He put a cold hand on my forehead and I gasped at his chilling touch. It was not a natural coldness, such as I could safely have attrib-uted to the weather, but rather the stone-cold, bloodless chill we asso-ciated with death, a coldness that would remain unchanged even in the fierce heat of Mazanderan. I twisted my head away from a touch that reminded me so uncomfortably of mortality.

"Inflammation of the lungs," I heard him mutter. "I shall prepare an infusion that will help."

"So you're a doctor, too, are you?" I said rudely. "Is there no end to your accomplishments?"

He rose and looked down on me with extraordinary calm.

"I have certain skills that you may have cause to be glad of. But, of

course, if you would prefer to rely on the remedies of your idiot servant, that is certainly your privilege."

He walked out of my tent without a backward glance and I lay
glaring at the leather walls with feverish irritation. Why should I trust
him? He was as likely to poison me as anything else, particularly after
the manner in which I had insulted him. I did not feel inclined to
submit to dubious Gypsy cures. Inflammation of the lungs! What
could he know of it?

I remember very little of the following days. I plunged into a realm
of fevered nightmares, through which I was only dimly aware of Darius tending me and a strange, dark, faceless shape that occasionally
bent over my pallet to utter some scathing challenge.

"*Try*, damn you! I can do nothing for you if you're just going to give
up!"

Each time I heard that voice I had a vague impulse to struggle up
and hit its owner, and for a little time the darkness would recede from
me. But I was growing very weary and all I really wanted to do was to
slide effortlessly down into the welcoming oblivion, down, down, down
into the peace where Rookheeya waited patiently for me.

And then there was the music.

Music soft and soothing as a waterfall . . . music that coaxed my
unwilling soul back up into the light with its sweet, unspoken promise.

Trust me, follow me, let me show you the way to her side.

I believed in the music. . . . I followed it without question.

And when I woke in the grayness of my tent with only Darius
beside me, I wept at the cruelty of its fiendish deception.

"He said you would wake weeping, if you woke at all, master," said
Darius quietly. "He said I was to take no notice and give you this."

Darius lifted me from the pallet and trickled a little foul-tasting
syrup down my throat.

When he laid me down again I saw the Koran lying beside my head.

And then I knew just how close to paradise I had been.

If my extremity of illness had aroused Erik's concern, certainly my
convalescence appeared to bore him utterly, for he did not come near
me again until I was back on my feet. And when I made some tentative reference to gratitude he only laughed rather scornfully and told

me that my death would have proved most inconvenient to him at this point in the proceedings.

He stayed with me on that occasion until quite late in the evening, taking advantage of my weakened state to win a hefty sum of money from me in successive games of chess. But at length, when he grew bored with my uninspired play, he got up, put the chessboard away, and tossed his winnings down on my pillow.

"What is this?" I demanded in surprise.

He shrugged. "You're tired, it wasn't a fair contest. But beware—tomorrow we shall treble the stakes and believe me, I shall show you no quarter."

He turned and strode out of the tent without another word, and in his wake the wind blew the flaps apart. As I struggled over to tie them shut I glanced out and saw it happen.

A man in Kalmuck dress came at him from the undergrowth with a knife, but before I could utter a word of warning, Erik had rounded like a wildcat on his assailant.

A thin lasso whipped through the air, neatly garroting the intruder with one swift, savage jerk, and the man fell dead in the churning mud almost before I had time to blink. I was dumbstruck by that lightning reflex, an automatic, merciless response which betrayed all the instincts of a jungle predator to whom killing is as natural and commonplace as breathing. He had killed before, many times; of that simple fact there could be no question of doubt.

As I stood at the mouth of my tent gaping in open-mouthed horror, Erik bent down to release the lasso with a careless flick of his fingers and replace it in some unseen repository in his cloak. He was utterly composed and detached; had he wrung a chicken's neck instead he could hardly have displayed less emotion, and this deadly calm unnerved me as much as the ruthless, unthinking speed with which he had killed.

Pushing the body aside with his foot, he glanced up and saw me standing there, staring at him like some witless idiot.

"Go back inside your tent, Daroga," I heard the frown in his voice. "I should find it enormously tedious to have to save your life a second time."

And with that he turned on his heel and disappeared into the enveloping darkness.

I returned to my bed deeply shaken and tried to reconcile myself to this new and most unwelcome knowledge.

He was not merely the greatest magician, the most remarkable ventriloquist, and the most accomplished musician I had ever seen. He was also the most coldly efficient murderer.

Only the most suicidal fool would fail to treat him with wary respect.

The small ship that waited for us in Astrakhan harbor was still flying the imperial flag, and Erik's vanity was sufficiently mollified by the sight of it for him to board the vessel without protest. I promised him privacy during the voyage. . . . I would have promised him the moon and the stars to get him safely out on the Caspian Sea, where I could be reasonably certain that he could not contrive to vanish on me again.

The final stage of our journey was mercifully uneventful, and at length we sighted the great chain of sandhills that ran along the edge of the Mazanderan seacoast. Behind them lay the *murdabas*, or dead waters, an endless succession of stagnant lagoons surrounded by dense jungle, swamps, and quicksand. Every manner of reptile wallowed in those stinking morasses, and clouds of mosquitoes hummed incessantly in the pestilential air. The maritime provinces were a death sentence to unacclimatized Europeans, and once we had landed I made haste to the gentle air of Ashraf, where the sweet, familiar scent of cypress trees waited to embrace us.

The little houses with their sloping roofs, wide verandas, and stained-glass windows had never looked more beautiful, and though I knew we should press on inexorably to Tehran, where the court was in residence, Allah himself could not have commanded me to go a step farther without a sight of my child.

If I had hoped to impress Erik with the grandeur of my estate and my royal descent, I was quickly disappointed.

"I understand that princes outnumber the camels and fleas in Persia," he remarked with gravity.

I felt myself flush. Allah, he had barely set foot in the country! How had he managed to unearth that most wretched of proverbs so soon?

He studied my discomfort for a moment with quiet amusement.

"Never mind, Daroga," he said softly. "If I am ever seized by the need to shed royal blood, at least I now know where to find it."

I sensed the smile behind the mask, and in spite of my annoyance I could not help laughing with him.

"You will have to learn to muzzle your tongue at court," I warned him seriously. "Merciless wit is a very dangerous possession."

"I shall try to remember that . . . and in the meantime, all mockery aside, I am truly honored to sleep beneath your royal roof tonight."

I was moved by his genuine courtesy, astonished to see him shed his cold, abrasive manner and assume instead the demeanor of a perfect houseguest, charmingly civil and appreciative. This invitation to my home seemed to mean something deeply significant to him, and if it were not for the mask I could almost have believed I was entertaining a young gentleman from the British mission.

We sat together on the veranda in quiet civility, while my curious servants plied us with caleans, coffee, and ices; and it was there that my son stumbled upon us, while his attendant hovered apologetically at a distance, expecting rebuke.

"Father! You've been away for so long! I thought you were never, ever going to come back!"

I untwined myself from the urgent grasp that I had missed so much and set the boy back on his feet, steadying him when he seemed to lose his balance.

"Reza," I reproved gently, "this is no way to conduct yourself in front of guests."

Erik stood in silence as the child turned his vague, wandering glance toward him.

"May your heart never grow narrow, sir," came respectfully enough;

and then, with a sudden burst of excitement that would no longer be contained within the prescribed limitations of decorum: "Oh, sir . . . are you *really* the greatest magician in the whole world?"

"Some have called me that."

Erik's voice was oddly gentle. He took the child's outstretched hand and turned it over in his grasp so that it seemed for a moment as though he studied the palm.

"Oh, please say you will show me some magic before you leave!"

Erik glanced briefly, questioningly, toward me and I gave him a sad, helpless shrug.

"I would be delighted to," he said kindly, "and for you, Reza, there shall be something very special . . . something no human ear has heard before or shall hear again . . . no, not even the shah himself."

I saw the spellbound look on my son's face as he raised his hands instinctively toward the source of that extraordinary voice.

"Will you show me now, sir?"

"Tomorrow," Erik demurred. "I'm afraid it will have to be tomorrow. Can you be very patient and wait till then?"

"Reza, you are forgetting your manners!" Discomfited by the strange communion that I sensed between them, I spoke more sharply than I had intended. "Return to your quarters now and I will come to you later."

"Yes, Father." I heard the hurt surprise in my child's voice as he permitted his attendant to lead him away.

A tense silence descended on the veranda in his absence. Erik returned to the white wicker chair and examined the dregs of his coffee cup with odd intensity.

"How long has the boy's sight been failing?" he demanded abruptly.

"Perhaps eighteen months."

"And the weakness of the muscles came later?"

"Yes." I swallowed my own coffee with difficulty. "I am told it is a childish malady which he will grow out of in time."

Erik sighed as he set the cup down on the table.

"This is a progressive and degenerative sickness, Daroga."

I stared at him. "Then . . . you do not think he will regain his sight after all?"

"I do not think it is a thing you should hope for," he said evasively. "And now I have work to attend to. . . . Perhaps you would be good enough to excuse me from supper tonight."

I inclined my head and was left alone to brood upon his words.

My servants told me that lights burned in his room all night and that when he eventually emerged from the apartment next day he was carrying a curious doll-like figure.

Sometime later I saw the figure for myself in Reza's quarters. It was not a doll, but an automaton, dressed in the robes of a Russian peasant, bearing a fiddle in one hand and a bow in the other. As I watched it bend stiffly from the waist and place the fiddle beneath its chin, I smiled involuntarily and waited for the simple gesture to be repeated. I had not seen such fluid refinement in a clockwork mechanism before.

"That's very clever—" I started to say, but Reza clutched at my arm urgently.

"Wait, Father, it's not finished yet . . . listen!"

When the figure began to play, swaying gently to the rhythm of its own melody, I was intrigued, but not yet dumbfounded. I told myself that I was listening to an intricate musical box—an ingenious, but scarcely world-shattering, invention.

When the tune ended Reza told me to applaud.

"It won't play again until we do," he insisted gravely.

I hid a smile. *Erik,* I thought with quiet amusement, *what an incorrigible showman you are!* And I clapped politely to humor the child.

When the figure did not move, I assumed its clockwork mechanism had run down.

"You must clap with enthusiasm to satisfy an artist's insatiable vanity," said Reza severely. "That is what Erik told me."

Puzzled, I put my hands together with greater vigor.

"Louder!" said Reza with a touch of imperiousness in his voice that I had never heard before. "Louder, Father!"

The palms of my hands began to sting, but just as I was thinking I had had enough of this childish nonsense, the Gypsy figure bowed with condescension, replaced the fiddle beneath its chin, and began to play a different tune.

Three times I repeated the prescribed procedure and each time the music was different. I thought I recognized the same melody, but the sequencing altered subtly on each occasion so that it was virtually impossible to determine which was the original phrase and which the cunning variation. The more I struggled to pin the illusion down, the more confused and frustrated I became at my inability to govern my scattering senses.

But at least there was one simple hoax I would expose. Erik had evidently built some kind of delay into the mechanism. All I had to do was wait, without applauding, and the cunning little device would betray itself by playing again. I was so determined to place the invention within the realm of my comprehension that I gave no thought to the needless disappointment I might cause my son in revealing the secret of this trick.

"Don't clap," I ordered suddenly. "Let us see what happens."

We stood and waited in the resounding silence. Without applause the curious little automaton remained mutely aloof, and I fancied it was staring at me with some of its maker's contempt.

"I told you it wouldn't work!" said Reza sullenly. "I told you what Erik said."

"I don't want to hear what Erik said!" I shouted, suddenly furious at the boy's slavish parroting of that name. "Give me the key and I will wind it up again."

"There is no key."

"Don't be absurd, child, of course there must be a key!"

I snatched up the figure and began to examine it angrily, but it was just as he said. I could find no way of controlling this automaton, and I was suddenly overwhelmed by a fierce, mindless urge to smash it against the wall in fury.

"Stop shaking it," sobbed Reza. "You'll break it. . . . Please, Father! Please give it back to me!"

Slowly I came to my senses and relinquished my maniacal grip upon the figure. Allah! What had come over me to make me act like a demented, petulant child?

"Reza . . ." I hurried across the room to the floor cushions where the boy had crawled to take refuge with his precious toy. "Reza . . ."

He turned his face away from me into the satin pillows and shrugged off my hand.

I was stunned by the unexpected rejection and appalled to realize how thoroughly I had deserved it.

I crept from the room in shame and leaned against the door, trying to regain my composure. After a moment I heard the child clapping frantically.

And then those slow, strangely maddening notes began to play all over again. . . .

Late that evening I found Erik sitting on the edge of the fountain in the courtyard garden, lazily trailing his long fingers in the spray. I wanted to ask him how the automaton worked, but the memory of my intensely irrational behavior that afternoon held me silent.

Mosquitoes buzzed irritatingly around us as he accepted the bowl of sherbet that I offered.

"Your wife has been dead for some time," he said unexpectedly. "Since it is not customary for those of your faith to confine themselves in a monogamous manner, I must assume that you loved her very much."

I looked up, outraged by the impertinence of this remark, and was silenced by the extraordinary compassion in the eyes behind the mask. His pitying glance took my breath as effectively as a blow to the spleen and filled me once more with that terrible sense of ill omen. I became aware that I had started to tremble.

"Does the child resemble her?" he persisted with sadness.

"Yes." My voice was a thin, reedy whisper; suddenly all I wanted to do was run from this.

"I am very sorry," he said.

And replacing the untouched sherbet on the wicker table, he disappeared through the full-length windows on the garden wall of the house.

I sat very still, staring at the smooth olive-skinned hands which lay limply on my lap. If the shah's personal physician had told me my son was dying, I would have refused to believe him; I would have gone on clinging stubbornly to the last straws of hope like a drowning man.

But I could not close my mind to the meaning of Erik's carefully veiled insinuation; I could not deny his mystical inner knowledge of things beyond my simple understanding.

My son was dying. And this strange masked man—who killed without a qualm of conscience and seemed untroubled by morality of any kind—was moved to generous pity for my plight.

He was still ruthless, dangerous, and shockingly amoral.

But I found that I no longer thought of him as a cold and heartless monster.

We lingered at Ashraf many days longer than had been my original intent, for I was sunk in a despair that no longer admitted to the urgency of the shah's displeasure. What did it matter now whether I kept my post, my favor, my petty position in society; what did anything matter anymore? Soon I would have lost everything that made life dear to me.

My resentful bitterness resolving itself at length into fierce need of a woman, I sent for a girl who had served me well in the past and lost myself eagerly in the soft welcoming curves of her body. It meant nothing, but it brought physical relief; a few moments of delirious pleasure and blessed forgetfulness that permitted me to function as the man Allah had created. I pitied any man who was denied the slaking of such simple healthy need in the form of a wife, a concubine, even a prostitute. But when I thought of such a man, my mind instinctively shied away, unwilling to contemplate vicarious pain on behalf of another. I did not wish to think of what that face must inevitably have denied to Erik—for now, I had quite enough pain of my own.

Reza spent those few days almost entirely in the company of a magician whose voice and astonishing skills held him utterly mesmerized. For hours at a time he would sit at Erik's feet, like a young addict in an opium den, begging shamelessly for another story, another song, and I marveled at the tireless good humor of a man scarcely notable for equanimity and patience. Sometimes he would teach the boy a few simple tricks, guiding the child's hands with all the unseen skill of a clever puppeteer.

"That's good . . . that's very much better, Reza. . . . You may show your father now. . . ."

Their voices drifted past me, echoing through the distant chambers of my wretchedness, until at last I roused myself sufficiently from this stupor of inactivity to announce our departure.

I was unprepared for the violence of Reza's reaction.

"Why must he go so soon? Why can't he stay a little longer?"

"Reza, the shah has commanded his presence at court. You know that."

"But you don't have to go *now*, not straightaway. . . ."

"The shah—"

"I hate the shah!" shouted Reza passionately. "I hate him!"

I had never seen my son behave like this before, and I was alarmed by his outburst. Erik stood staring out the window, with both arms crossed beneath his cloak, and I sensed that for once he was truly discomfited by what he had precipitated.

I signaled to a hovering servant and told him to take the child to his apartments at once, but as soon as the man laid hold of his shoulder Reza flung himself down on the floor and began to pummel the blue tiles in a frenzy of rage. My son, that quiet, well-behaved child, had without any warning become a savage, mindless little beast; and I was bitterly aware that I was going to be powerless to control him without resorting to undignified physical force.

"Reza!"

The voice from the window was immeasurably soft, hardly more than a whispered breath; yet it made itself heard above the ugly noise of the child's hysteria, and immediately there was silence in the sunny, white-walled chamber.

"Come to me."

Into the gentle, mellifluous tone there had crept an irresistible note of command. As I watched, Erik stretched out one hand and seemed to draw the child across the room to his side with a single gesture that pulsed with terrifying force.

I became aware that I was holding my breath with a sort of dull horror. The same voice which was manipulating my child's mind was holding me in a frozen impotence that utterly denied all power of intervention; I felt as though I had been drugged by a massive dose of poppy syrup.

Reza was perfectly calm now, though the tears still stood gleaming on his flushed cheeks.

"Will you come back?" he whispered tremulously.

Erik placed one skeletal finger beneath the boy's chin and tilted his face upward into the light.

"I will return as soon as my court duties permit. But if you cry when I leave, your father will forbid me to come here. You have behaved very badly in his presence. . . . Go to him now and ask for his forgiveness."

The child came to me like an automaton, with all the humility and deference that his master had commanded, and I forgave him graciously, in a mindless response to that superior unspoken will.

I *felt* the precise moment that Erik chose to release us from his hold; it was like the cutting off of some unseen electrical current.

Even had I not already known him for a ruthless murderer, I should still have acknowledged him that day as the most dangerous man in the world.

We left for Tehran the following morning, taking the old caravan road from the Caspian through the entrancing glens and ravines of the Elburz Mountains. Huge vines had woven themselves like tapestry threads through the tangle of tree stems that clustered together in this thickly forested area. We made camp on a floor carpeted with wild strawberry plants, and at night, as we listened to the distant roar of a tiger, we saw the eyes of a leopard winking just beyond the firelight.

There was snow on the top of the Demavend volcano, which is the highest peak in Persia, and though the mountain pass was not yet prey to the blizzards and treacherous avalanches that would be commonplace in winter, a cruel wind knifed through our warmest garments and made us bow our heads against the storm. My servants did their best under difficult circumstances and we dined nightly on mutton ragout, kabobs, and pilaf; but by now I was heartily weary of the road.

When we finally approached Tehran, the sight of the city's ugly mud
wall, circular towers, and forty-foot moat was one which gladdened my
heart. If I had ended a pilgrimage to Mecca, I could have not felt
more relief. My task was almost completed, and soon I would be free
of my strange, disquieting companion.

As we passed beneath a gate adorned with glazed tiles and were
admitted to the city's interior, I heard Erik exclaim in disgust at the
sight of the narrow, filthy streets and the uncovered drains.

"What squalor!" he muttered darkly. "What shameful poverty!"

I felt inclined to agree with him, but I had no desire to appear
critical of the shah's personal extravagance and greed.

"Certainly," I admitted warily, "the condition of the people is to be
regretted."

"The condition of the people is not at issue," he said coolly. "It is
the city itself that appalls me. Have you no architects in Persia?"

"There are worse places in the world," I muttered.

"Not many, Daroga, not many. This is the most disgraceful example of a capital city that I have ever seen. The whole area is a stinking
midden bereft of a single building worthy of my attention. And that is
exactly what I shall tell the shah when I see him."

"Allah!" I breathed with feeling. "You'll be executed before dawn!"

"Yes . . . I daresay," he agreed.

I looked at him with despair.

"If you really intend to tell him that, you had better learn to moderate your language." Reaching inside my coat I brought out a folded
sheet of paper and handed it to him. "These are some of the prescribed forms of address. I advise you to commit them to memory
before your audience."

He studied the paper for a moment and then burst out laughing.

" 'Salutations, O Glory of the World!' " he said in a wickedly mincing tone. " 'Let me be your sacrifice, O Shadow of God!' Do you
honestly expect me to mouth this nauseating garbage?"

"I know it may sound a little absurd to European ears—"

"It's worse than absurd, Daroga—it's an insult to human intelligence!"

"It's merely a court formality." I sighed. "It doesn't mean anything."

"Then if it doesn't mean anything, it won't matter if I don't say it," he retorted with infuriating logic. "I have no intention whatsoever of groveling like some ridiculous worm simply to satisfy the colossal vanity of your king. I will speak to him with common civility and nothing more."

"Oh, very well," I said irritably. "Insist on this mad infringement of etiquette if you must. But at least be sure you always call him sir."

The laughter died out of his eyes without warning and the look that replaced it turned me cold with fear.

"There is no man on this earth to whom I would ever accord that respect again!" he snapped.

I did not dare to question that abrupt statement, and we continued our journey toward the Ark on the northern side of the town in grim silence.

As soon as we entered the palace complex I lost him. One moment he was at my side as we walked through the maze of connecting rooms, and the next he was gone; it was as though he had simply vanished into the walls.

This trick was not unfamiliar to me by now. Several times during our tedious trek through Russia he had performed this singular feat, abandoning me without warning or compunction the moment his attention was caught by some unusual feature on the landscape. I had once lost him for more than a week on the Aktuba branch of the Volga, where much of the sixty-five-mile area is covered with ancient ruins. But I could not believe that he would dare to disappear now, a bare half hour before his appointed audience with the shah!

In mounting panic and fury I trailed all over the sprawling building, muttering obscenities I seldom felt obliged to use, and calling upon ever more colorful parts of God's anatomy for aid. I questioned every guard and servant that I passed, but no one, it seemed, had seen a man in a mask; if they had done so they would most certainly have remembered.

Removing my *kolah* I wiped sweat from my brow with the back of my hand.

Damn you, Erik! Damn you! When I get my hands on you I'll wring your infernal neck for this. . . .

My frantic wanderings brought me eventually to the door of the Council Chamber. No, I thought, surely not . . . he wouldn't dare. . . .

Pushing open the heavy door I checked in aghast disbelief.

Erik was sitting on the Peacock Throne, patiently prizing a diamond from the mass of gems which decorated the chair's lofty backrest. I stood and watched with horrified fascination as he reached into his pocket, withdrew a handful of cut glass, and selected a piece to replace the jewel he had just removed.

"Allah have mercy!" I gasped.

He turned to look at me without alarm or surprise.

"Oh, there you are," he remarked calmly, as though he had been expecting me. "Would you care for a diamond . . . a little keepsake to remind you of our happy journey together?"

I put out a hand to steady myself against the wall.

"Come down from there," I said weakly. "If you are discovered it will be the end for both of us!"

In answer he touched the mechanism at the rear of the throne and set the circular star of diamonds spinning wildly in a kaleidoscope of scintillating rays that blinded me for a second.

"There are rubies and emeralds, of course, if you prefer," he continued imperturbably, "but they would be harder to replace. It would be very much more convenient to me if you simply settled for a diamond."

"Are you out of your mind?" I almost screamed. "For pity's sake come down and let us leave this room before it is too late."

"Oh, Daroga"—he sighed—"what a truly boring little fart you are at times!"

He came slowly down the two steps, which were decorated with salamanders, and paused to examine one of the seven jeweled legs which supported the platform.

"This is a very great work of art," he remarked conversationally. "I shall have to come back later and have a better look at it."

I was outraged by his brazen impudence.

"If you ever come back here again, I shall have you *arrested!*" I snapped.

He came to stand beside me thoughtfully.

"I don't think that would be very wise, my friend. You really might find one or two things rather difficult to explain."

As he spoke I became aware of something hard and cold nestling in my ear, and from that orifice I duly removed the diamond I had seen in his hand only moments earlier. The meaning was very clear. If I dared to speak of what I knew outside this room, he would simply plant that diamond upon my person again without a single scruple and name me as his accomplice.

When he saw that I was speechless with fury, he went to the door and glanced out into the deserted corridor beyond.

"What remarkably lax security," he said pleasantly. "I find Persian complacency quite beyond belief."

"Does that justify theft?" I demanded.

"Stealing from a thief is no theft," he replied mildly.

From his sleeve I saw him draw *my* watch upon its familiar pocket chain and glance at it briefly.

"We're late!" he said severely, for all the world as though it were my fault. And tossing the watch at me with a careless gesture, he walked out of the room.

I followed him with the uneasy demeanor of a faint-hearted criminal, not daring to contemplate how many more diamonds might be missing from that throne.

If I had been a Catholic, I suppose I would have crossed myself. . . .

The shah had agreed to receive us in the Gulistan, that vast garden court which Europeans called the Rose Garden. Its winding paved avenues were lined with pines, cypress, and poplar trees to create shade from the merciless sun, and all the flower beds, tanks, and lakes were separated from each other by neat gravel paths. Water ran perpetually down the innumerable little iron bridges lined with blue tiles, and Erik seemed as delighted as a child by the sight of the teeming fish, the elegant swans, and the noisy waterfowl.

"Swans are ugly when they hatch," he said enviously, "and yet they grow to be the most beautiful and majestic of birds. That is one of life's pretty little miracles, is it not? Like the snake, which sheds its skin, and the caterpillar, which turns into a butterfly. *Metamorpho-*

sis. . . ." His voice grew soft and distant as he continued, "Yes . . . that is the true magic in this world . . . but it's a secret that has never been revealed—not even to the tenth graduate of the College of Sorcery. Would you like to be turned into a swan, Daroga?"

I must have looked vaguely alarmed at the prospect, for he suddenly laughed.

"Don't worry," he said rather sadly. "If such physical alchemy really lay within my power, I certainly wouldn't waste it on you."

"Come," I said, plucking at his sleeve and glancing over my shoulder uncomfortably. "You must not keep the shah waiting any longer."

Ahead of us a beautiful kiosk could just be seen nestling among the trees and it was here that we found the Glory of the World, surrounded by a collection of his feline favorites.

Toward me the pampered creatures displayed their customary response to intruders, a spectrum of behavior ranging from supreme indifference to overt hostility. But slowly, one by one, they left their embroidered cushions to rub their heads against Erik's legs. They behaved like dogs greeting the return of a beloved master, fawning upon him and competing with each other jealously for his caress. I was astonished by this unprecedented display, and so, I could see, was the shah. Without waiting for the correct obeisances to be made, the young man got up from his chair and came forward with undisguised curiosity.

"Remarkable," he muttered to himself. "I have never before observed such a phenomenon . . . never. Daroga!" A quick jerk of his wrist indicated my dismissal. "You may leave us. Come, my friend," he continued, turning to address Erik pleasantly, "walk with me in the gardens and let me hear of these extraordinary gifts for which it seems you may be quite justly famous. . . ."

I lingered in the gardens for a couple of hours, and at length I saw Erik returning alone down the wide path which led to the lake. Once more he paused to admire the swans. As I drew near, he began to scatter little cakes of *gaz* on the water, and the birds dipped their long necks greedily to devour the mixture of manna, honey, and pistachios. The *gaz* was succeeded by *arjil*, then fondants and Turkish delight, and I was interested by the implication of this sideplay. If the shah had honored him with sweetmeats at their first audience, then his favor was most certainly assured. . . .

"Who on earth is that funereal creature in the mask?" demanded a hearty voice in my ear.

Turning hastily I found the grand vazir standing beside me and just beyond him his little party of sycophants, the usual obsequious toadies who always manage to attach themselves to a prominent man. Mirza Taqui Khan was married to the shah's sister and in consequence demanded automatic deference from anyone at court who was not already his sworn enemy. He was one of the most noble and incorruptible men in Persia, too innately honest and opinionated, I often thought, to last for long in a court where groveling servility, subterfuge, and blatant bribery were the prerequisites for survival. He was loud in his condemnation of the age-old traditions of corruption, and his fierce determination to drag Persia into the modern world had already caused him to tread on many toes. Petty princelings such as myself had found our pensions reduced in accordance with the grand vazir's sweeping economies. He was in the course of founding a college where the best of European scientific knowledge might be put to good military use, and he did not seem to mind whom he offended in his ceaseless quest for the funding of this precious brainchild. Remaining in cheerful ignorance of an increasing number of ill-wishers, he continued to speak his mind, in season and out, confident that royal status would always be his protection. I was not surprised that he had taken no trouble to lower his voice now as he looked with contempt at Erik.

"That is the new magician, Excellency," I said quietly, hoping he would take a hint from the softness of my voice. I knew that Erik possessed the ears as well as the eyes of a cat and was apt to hear what was inaudible to the average human.

"Magician?" frowned the prime minister. "Ah, yes. I seem to remember some moonshine a while back about a miracle worker. Sent off to find him, were you not, Nadir?—another absurd extravagance for the treasury to foot, I suppose! Never tell me he was worth the cost of that ridiculous journey!"

"He has some remarkable powers, Excellency," I said warily.

"Indeed? Well, I'm perfectly delighted to hear it. It's time the khanum had a new toy to keep her occupied and take her mind away from the young fellow's affairs. No good ever comes of permitting a woman to interfere in politics, you know. I trust that odd bag of bones will be capable of amusing her long enough for me to get on with the serious business of the realm. I'm sure he's an utter charlatan like all the rest, but for now he might have his uses. Extraordinary hands he has—they quite give me gooseflesh! One rather hopes he knows how to keep them to himself. We really have quite enough pederasts at court, do we not, my friends?"

Laughter came on cue from his attendants, and as the brightly colored party moved off again across the gardens, in pursuit of the shah, Erik came to join me in an ominous silence that dispelled any last lingering hope I might have entertained of his ignorance. I knew as soon as I looked at him that he had heard every word.

"Perhaps you would care to see the aviary," I said uncomfortably.

"I have heard sufficient squawking peacocks for one afternoon," he muttered. "Who was that?"

"The grand vazir," I admitted unhappily, "Mirza Taqui Khan."

"Thank you. That is a name I shall take great pleasure in remembering. I assume he has influence?"

"He is the shah's brother by marriage, and his voice is respected by many."

"But not by the khanum," Erik suggested shrewdly, "or—dare one say it—*the young fellow?*"

"There have been on occasion certain differences of opinion."

"How interesting! It may amuse me to follow this family friction more closely—from the Council Chamber, perhaps."

"Erik—"

"It would be pleasant to bathe and change one's funereal garments," he interrupted coldly. "Perhaps you would be good enough to conduct me to my apartment now."

I glanced at him uneasily as we made our way back to the palace; I suspected he would prove a hard and pitiless enemy and I could not commend the grand vazir's wisdom in winning him as such so early in the game.

Erik's apartment was located among some of the finest at court, and I could see that he was mollified by the opulence that met his eye.

He examined the white marble bathroom with satisfaction and returned to arrange himself with languid grace across the Turkish divan.
Painfully thin and angular though he was, he seemed incapable of any
hurried or inelegant movement, and sometimes it was virtually impossible to chart his soundless progress around a room. Like a cat he could
be there one moment and gone the next, without exciting attention. I
found it a disturbing quality.

"These apartments are normally reserved for an officer of state," I
warned him. "You must expect to make enemies."

"I never expect to make anything else," he said.

"What did you discuss with the shah?" I demanded curiously.

"Among other things the appalling architectural poverty of this
city."

My mouth dropped open. "He wasn't angry?"

"No, he was rather interested. He has asked me to design and build
a new palace outside Ashraf. If the result pleases him I shall be permitted to rebuild Tehran."

"Allah!" I breathed softly. "Can you do that?"

"There is nothing I cannot do, if I choose."

"But, Erik, you can't conjure up an entire palace. That requires
professional training—experience of building."

"I have had all the experience I require," he said shortly.

"Are you sure?"

He leapt off the couch, in the grip of some fierce and ugly emotion
that I found impossible to comprehend.

"I learned my skills from a very great master mason!" he spat unexpectedly. "Do you dare to doubt that?"

"No." I backed away from him hastily, aware of cold sweat suddenly
trickling down my temples. "I don't doubt that you can do anything
you say."

Still he advanced upon me and I continued to retreat. I had never
known such primitive, gut-sliding fear, and my terror was touched
with bewildered panic, for I could not think why my words should
have made him so uncontrollably angry.

"Erik"—I gasped—"for pity's sake, I believe you . . . I believe
you. . . . Can't you hear me?"

He stopped abruptly; the hands that had been reaching out for my throat fell limply at his sides and he looked at them with dull bewilderment. I suddenly had the oddest feeling that he was very close to tears.

"I'm sorry," he said wearily, turning away from me. "My temper is truly inexcusable at times. . . . I look for insults even when none are meant. It gets harder and harder to be rational, to pretend that I don't hear what they say. . . . That ignorant fool in the garden! . . . It's him I want to kill, not you—not you. You have shown me nothing but civility. . . ."

He made a gesture of frustration toward the mask and subsided into brooding silence. After a while he drifted to the window and looked out with an absence that made me wonder if he realized I was still there. In his hand he was suddenly holding what looked to me to be a silver compass, turning it around and around with restless fingers.

"He taught me everything," I heard him murmur distantly, "everything! I can't go on wasting all that he gave me. I want to build something *beautiful*—something he would have been proud of. There has to be a purpose in being in this world. There has to be some purpose in living. . . ."

I waited patiently, expecting to hear more, but he did not speak again. His hand was empty now, the compass gone as suddenly and mysteriously as it had appeared. He seemed sunk in a very deep reverie as he stared down into the Gulistan below, and at last, believing it would be both insensitive and discourteous to linger, I slipped quietly from the room and left him alone.

 had hoped that the safe completion of my mission would leave me free to return to Mazanderan to resume my regular and less onerous duties; but later that day I was summoned to the shah's presence and required to stay at court.

"I have a little further task for you, Daroga," said my young master, and my heart sank, for I had a sudden unpleasant premonition of what this task was going to entail.

"I am honored by the opportunity to be of further service, Imperial Majesty," I parroted dutifully; but inside my head a little voice had begun to scream: *Damn, damn,* damn!

"I intend to make you entirely responsible for the safekeeping of my masked friend," continued the shah, twisting his thin wisps of moustache to exaggerate their curl. "You will answer for any harm that befalls him during such time as he continues to please me. It is not, you understand, a task that I can entrust to a simple bodyguard. The commission he is to undertake in Mazanderan is a state secret. I require a man of proven skills and loyalty to keep him under surveillance."

I repressed a shiver. I wanted to say I would have considerably more success following a moonbeam than trying to keep track of Erik's dubious activities; but the shah's steely glance told me exactly what my fate would be if I dared to demur.

"You are the obvious choice for this assignment, Daroga. Already you know him better than anyone else. It would suit my purposes if you persuaded him to trust you. Befriend him . . . win his confidence . . . and keep me informed of any interesting developments. The man intrigues and fascinates me, but I am well aware that he will bear very careful watching."

I bowed my head wretchedly.

"It will be as you command, O Shadow of God," I murmured.

"I have no need of a bodyguard!" said Erik ominously. "I am perfectly able to take care of myself. . . . And as for you, your presence is far more urgently required elsewhere. No one in common charity could possibly expect you to remain here indefinitely. I shall speak to the shah and have you removed from this farcical position at once!"

I begged him urgently to do no such thing.

"You have no understanding yet of how easy it is to fall from favor in this country, Erik. If you refuse to accept my services it will be seen as a failure on my part and I shall be punished accordingly, perhaps by many months in prison."

"Why do you tolerate such gross injustices?" he demanded quietly.

"Why do you not simply ride back to your son and tell the shah to hang himself?"

"All that I possess depends upon the shah's continued favor. My pension and my estate could be stripped from me tomorrow; my son thrown out to die in poverty upon the streets. I beg you to reconsider your request and permit me to serve you in this capacity."

"Have you been commissioned to spy on me?" He sighed.

I made a reluctant gesture of assent and let my eyes drop to the floor.

"Well, that's honest, at least," he acknowledged philosophically. "I shall have to make sure your reports are suitably interesting, shan't I? I don't want the shah getting bored and replacing you with someone more *efficient.*"

I glanced up at him and once again, in spite of myself, I began to laugh.

He was a murderer, a thief, and an unbeliever; but against my better judgment I was beginning to find him curiously likable. . . .

Next day I accompanied him to the boundary which separated the harem from the rest of the palace.

"This is as far as I am permitted to go," I said.

I indicated the two eunuchs who waited to conduct him to the inner sanctum of the khanum and reminded him that their Turkish yataghans would be trained upon him for the duration of his presence in the shadowed world. I did not think it necessary to say more. His entry to this exclusive domain was in the nature of a special dispensation, such as might occasionally be granted to a doctor; it was a privilege he would abuse on pain of the most terrible death.

No one with any pretensions to success at court can afford to overlook the significance of harem intrigue, and I had long ago taken the precaution of opening a private channel of communication within these hallowed walls. It was easy enough to do. Eunuchs are notoriously fond of money and the things it can buy. The physical effects of castration require them to abstain from alcohol, but they love opium, good perfumes, and rich confectionery, and for the right price they are willing to talk to anyone who will pay for their information.

The seraglio was the khanum's domain, an exclusive, evocative world whose insidious influence spread out through the court like a sweet cloud of poisonous perfume. By tradition it was a place of bitter rivalries, cunning conspiracies, and sudden, violent death. To be the mother of the reigning shah was to reach the very pinnacle of power, and the present khanum was a force to be reckoned with, a handsome, vigorous, clever woman who knew how to manipulate her son to the utmost advantage. She ran the harem with a ruthless efficiency, reducing the shah's three principal wives to timid subservience and ruling the concubines with a rod of iron. She spent her days eating sugarplums and occasionally smoking a pipe, and out of her frustrated boredom there had hatched some formidable tragedies. I do not think there was a man at court who did not fear her more than he feared the shah himself. I was willing to pay handsomely for news of Erik's reception in this veiled world of labyrinthine corridors, marbled baths, and hushed whispers. The world of Kismet, where he had yet to find his appointed fate. . . .

He was taken to a small courtyard, and there, surrounded by half a dozen eunuchs, he waited for the khanum to appear on the balcony above with her ladies.

I was told that she kept him waiting there for over an hour and that the eunuchs were growing deeply uneasy as he began to pace up and down like a caged tiger, displaying the angry impatience that was already so familiar to me. They were obliged at last to draw their yataghans upon him, to confine him to the appointed area; but as they closed in upon him, they were suddenly driven back by a shower of multicolored sparks which issued from his fingertips and ignited a perfect circle of flames around him.

When the flames died away, there was slow, mocking applause from the balcony above, and Erik was left staring up at the veiled and majestic woman who had appeared in the gallery.

"I trust," said the khanum softly, "that you have not come all the way from Russia simply to show me fireworks."

"By no means, madame," Erik replied smoothly. "That indeed was a mere trifle, designed to amuse tiresome children."

He indicated the eunuchs with a contemptuous gesture and the khanum laughed outright.

"If that is a mere trifle, then I am eager to see your true skills. And also to see you, my friend. The mask is likewise a device to frighten infants. Remove it!"

He stood very still, his hands clenched by his side, every muscle in his body tensed.

"Madame, I crave your indulgence in this. . . . I would rather not."

"Indeed!" The khanum glanced briefly behind her to silence her whispering women with a single venomous look. "Then perhaps I should remind you that only ladies hide their faces in this country. Remove the mask, or the *children* will be instructed to perform that service for you—and also to take the precaution of removing your head with it!"

Still he made no move to obey her, and the khanum stirred restlessly, made uneasy by such unprecedented defiance.

"If you have no great attachment to your head," she continued slowly, "perhaps you would prefer to share the fate of a Chinese eunuch and carry your genitalia around with you in a small jar of brine."

He made a graceful shrug of mocking indifference.

"Are you so sure a *small* jar would contain me, madame?"

The khanum laughed delightedly.

"I am sure of nothing where you are concerned, my friend, but I warn you now, in deadly earnest, that this is the last time I shall choose to overlook your disobedience on the matter. Take off the mask!"

When the mask landed abruptly at her feet, panic broke out behind her as the younger women hid their faces in their veils and collided in their terrified urge to distance themselves from the dreadful sight that had been revealed.

"Be silent!" snapped the khanum viciously. "The next woman who screams will be beaten to death for her stupidity, I swear it! Now leave me—go, all of you!"

She clapped her hands imperiously and the women dispersed in a flurry of voluminous pearl-trimmed trousers and thin crêpe chemisettes, their many bracelets and necklaces clacking wildly together in their hasty departure.

The khanum placed her elegant hennaed hands on the white latticed stonework of the balustrade and smiled down at Erik with immense satisfaction. She drew a huge diamond ring from her finger and when she tossed it to him, he caught it deftly, almost without appearing to move.

"If your imagination matches your face," she said quietly, "it will make you the most powerful man in Persia."

As he placed the diamond upon his little finger, the eunuchs say that he seemed to smile for a moment.

"Is that a prophecy, or a promise?" he inquired.

Again the khanum laughed.

"That, my friend," she said silkily, "is entirely for you to decide."

It did not take him long to reach that decision. By the time the court left to winter in Mazanderan, he was being called upon to give his opinion at council meetings and remaining present during the grand vazir's private audiences with the shah.

It was impossible to determine the shah's true motives, but he seemed to take a certain delight in baiting his brother-in-law in this fashion.

"Erik has certain interesting proposals to make concerning the Dar al Funun, my brother," he said one day, leaning back on his divan to observe the effect of his words. "I think you should take the trouble to consult him."

The grand vazir stiffened angrily.

"With the greatest respect, Imperial Majesty, I should prefer to rely upon the opinions of qualified men of science in all matters that appertain to the college. I must, with deepest humility, suggest that this is not an appropriate field for the talents of a court magician."

"If I say he is to be consulted," said the shah with deceptive mildness, "then you will consult him. I can assure you that you will find few qualified men of science who can even begin to rival his knowledge—in any field."

The slave who was serving sherbet was forced to withdraw at that point and was therefore unable to give me the grand vazir's reply; but he told me that he saw Mirza Taqui Khan cast a look of pure venom in Erik's direction before the great double doors closed the scene from his view.

I was uneasy and I hoped that the building of the new palace in

Mazanderan would distract Erik's attention from the very dangerous power game that he seemed determined to play.

On our return to the northern provinces I accompanied him to the chosen site—a lovely wooded eminence, half a mile outside Ashraf—and there watched him sketch until darkness fell.

"Are you ready to go yet, Erik?" I sighed at length, as hunger began to gnaw at me inexorably. "We've been here more than eight hours, you know."

"Have we?" he said vaguely. "I suppose you want to eat again. It really isn't necessary to eat more than once a day, you know. Perhaps when you get back to Ashraf you would have some lanterns sent out here to me. . . ."

I honestly believe that from that point, utterly absorbed as he was by this project, he would have gladly forsaken court politics entirely; but he had set a ball rolling down a long slope and it had begun to gather momentum without his aid. Once the preliminary designs for the palace were completed, he began to suffer the irritations that inevitably result when a man makes himself indispensable on too many fronts. Neither the shah nor the khanum was prepared to remit their constant demands for amusement and advice. He had implied omnipotence, and consequently they did not expect him to be subject to the limitations of time and energy which confine ordinary mortals. He was a great magician, and surely a great magician ought to be capable of being in several places at the same time! He was seldom spared attendance at court for more than a day or two, and each time he was parted from the stone and mortar of this slowly rising edifice by a fresh peremptory summons, I was afraid his simmering temper would finally betray him.

The khanum was the worst perpetrator of his irritable frustration.

"I am bored," she complained, stretching languorously on the satin cushions in her private chamber, where, I am told, she had taken to receiving him separated only by a thin gauze curtain. "I am bored, bored, *bored!* What name do you give to this tedious emotion in your country, Erik?"

"L'ennui, madame."

"L'ennui," echoed the khanum softly. "What a charmingly seduc-

tive turn of phrase you Frenchmen have. Do you ever feel . . . *l'en-nui* . . . Erik?"

"Hardly, madame. Time and idleness are both necessary prerequisites to boredom, and God knows I have little enough of either commodity these days."

"Don't scowl at me like that, you wretch!" said the khanum peevishly. "You are sufficiently ugly already without twisting your horrible face in that fashion! In fact you are so incredibly and unbelievably repulsive that it's almost . . . *attractive* . . . in a strange way."

He was silent. I am told she often tormented him in this fashion, seeking to exact some unknown response, but he only stared back at her with stony-eyed contempt.

"So . . . you do not feel boredom, then. What, I wonder, are you capable of feeling . . . *Erik?*"

"Anger," he said softly, "murderous anger. You will find me more than capable of that, *madame!*"

"I think I should like to see you angry," mused the khanum thoughtfully. "Yes . . . I think perhaps it would be very . . . interesting. Anger, too, can be strangely attractive, you know . . . in the right person." The khanum sat up against her cushions suddenly, watching him through the thin gauze curtain with interest. "Tell me, Erik, have you ever had a woman?"

There was a tense, throbbing silence between them.

"Come, I demand to be answered," she prompted abruptly. "Are you a virgin?"

"Madame"—he sighed—"I am very busy."

"Too busy for a woman? No true man is that, my friend. Would you like a woman, Erik? I could arrange it, you know, I could arrange it very easily. And is not that what you surely desire above all things?"

Those who were watching say that his hands closed convulsively on the folds of his cloak and began to twist with a slow savage rhythm.

"What I desire above all things," he said coldly, "is to be left in peace to complete my commission without disturbance."

The khanum frowned behind the open-worked aperture of her veil.

"You think of nothing else these days but that palace. I am jealous of your ridiculous devotion to a pile of stone and mortar. My son demands altogether too much of your time, and I intend to tell him so. You were brought to Persia for my amusement—mine! And you *will* amuse me, Erik . . . one way . . . or another. I forbid you to return to the site until you have devised some new form of entertainment . . . an amusing death, perhaps. Go now and think upon it."

I met him as he left the harem and I could see as soon as I looked at him that he was in an evil temper.

"She wants amusing deaths!" he shouted. "By God, she shall have them!"

He worked like a madman over the following weeks, and within a month it was finished—a strange, hexagonal-sided chamber, entirely lined with thick mirrors, which puzzled me intensely when I was invited to view it.

"What is it?" I demanded curiously as I stared at my own image reflected an infinite number of times.

"It's a torture chamber," he told me shortly.

"A mirrored room?"

"Mirrors can kill, Daroga . . . you may safely take my word for that."

His voice raised gooseflesh on my arms and made me suddenly very relieved to leave the chamber. I did not go back again to look at the *tortures*, but I know of many who subsequently did . . . people who spoke graphically of horrific illusions taking place within a room heated to the temperature of a furnace; illusions so real they reduced the victims to suicide within a few hours.

The khanum was delighted by the ingenuity of her new toy and three black eunuchs were duly required to present themselves in Erik's apartment, bearing variously a great purse laden with gold, a silver-plated hookah, and a plentiful supply of hashish.

He tossed the purse carelessly onto an ivory inlaid table, without even bothering to glance at the contents, but I saw him examine the hookah with interest and soon he was reclining on his floor cushions, with the hookah smoking efficiently between his lips.

Presently he tore off the mask and flung it across the room, laughing uncontrollably at nothing in particular, and I recognized in this irrational behavior the first signs of the drug's intoxicating influence. I had never tried hashish, but I knew of its terrible effects. Soon all his senses would be distorted beyond recognition. Time would telescope inward upon him and the faintest sound would be heard as a deafening roar; ecstatic euphoria would be succeeded by intense physical desire and a savage need for violence.

Some of the worst crimes imaginable have been committed here in Persia under the influence of this particular drug, and I fully understood why the khanum had chosen to reward Erik with hashish rather than opium. She was impatient to explore the darker regions of his incomparable imagination.

Who knew how many more *amusing deaths* still waited to be conjured from the dungeon of his tortured mind?

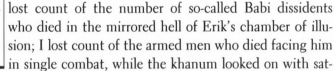 lost count of the number of so-called Babi dissidents who died in the mirrored hell of Erik's chamber of illusion; I lost count of the armed men who died facing him in single combat, while the khanum looked on with satisfaction—each one a victim of the same cunning piece of catgut which I had first seen wielded with such devastating efficiency that night in Russia. The Punjab lasso was a weapon guaranteed to strike fear into the heart of the toughest warrior, a thin, merciless serpent that came to life only in the hands of its master. It amused the khanum to boast that there was no man alive capable of surviving a contest in the arena with her self-appointed Angel of Doom.

Before he came to Persia and fell under her malevolent influence, I do not believe that Erik had ever killed purely for pleasure. But with her drugs and her insatiable demand for novelty she awakened his sleeping hatred of men, releasing a demon of savage ingenuity which he could no longer control.

Increasingly, during this period, he began to escape to my estate, fleeing from the horrors of his own imagination to take refuge in the innocent laughter of a child.

"It's so peaceful here," he told me once, in a rare moment of confidence. "It's the only place in Persia where I don't dream that I am drowning in a sea of blood."

That night I introduced him to an opium pipe, in the hope that its calming somnolence would persuade him to abandon the khanum's hashish. And the following morning, still wrapped in the drug's hazy cocoon of well-being, he said he would like to visit the local bazaar. He was perfectly lucid, but the pupils of his eyes had contracted to telltale pinpoints and I knew that he would never have suggested venturing into a crowded place in daylight if he were in full possession of his faculties.

"Are you looking for something in particular?" I demanded uncertainty, as we entered the noisy lanes with their low-vaulted roofs.

"Birthday presents," he said absently, "lots and lots of beautiful birthday presents. . . . Who are those poor twisted wretches with sticks?"

"Beggars seeking alms," I said with a sigh of resignation. "Let me deal with this, please."

I turned aside to do my religious duty, dropping a single coin of small denomination into each begging bowl as expected and receiving the customary blessings in return. When I glanced around I saw that Erik was emptying gold coins into the bowls behind my back.

"What are you doing?" I demanded with alarm.

"Giving alms," he said, mildly surprised by my annoyance. "What's wrong with that?"

"You idiot!" I snapped, as I saw the word being hastily passed through the crowd. "Surely you know better than to give such reckless sums to beggars at bazaars. You will bring every wretch in the vicinity around our heels, we won't be able to move through the streets in a minute. Come on!"

Catching hold of his cloak I hurried him through the crowds until we were safely lost in the press of camels and donkeys that constituted a caravan passing through from the coast.

The bazaar was typical of any that are to be found in Persia. Most of the shoppers were men, but the vendors were chiefly women swathed in black *chadars*, who sat beside their wares, almost under the feet of the carriages, and ignored the constant rude and colorful injunctions to get out of the way of the passing traffic.

Erik paused by a stall of brightly painted toys and selected a number of purchases which left me in no doubt of the intended recipient of his birthday presents. Numbed on a sweet cloud of opium, he was shopping with needless extravagance purely to please a blind child. And when the woman at his feet named a truly outrageous price I was amazed to see him reach into his purse without demur.

"It is customary to barter before purchasing in a bazaar," I reminded him sternly. "This wretch is asking at least four times what she seriously hopes to receive."

He glanced at the infant on the woman's lap and then at the small, pinched face peering out from behind her shoulder.

"She is poor and has children to feed. I am able to pay the price she asks without hardship. Why should I stand here and haggle with her like a miser?"

"She expects it, Erik. I tell you, it is the custom."

"*Fuck* your customs!" he said succinctly.

I watched dumbfounded as he dropped double the asking price into the woman's trembling hand and waved my servant forward to collect his purchases.

"Now," he said, turning to me cheerfully, "tell me where I can buy an opium pipe and at least a crate of that heavenly poppy cake one burns inside it."

Reza was waiting for us when we returned, in the wheeled chair to which he had become confined during the course of that winter. He was almost entirely blind now, but there was nothing wrong with his hearing, and I saw his face light up at the first sound of his idol's voice.

"Did you get me a surprise?" he demanded eagerly.

"Yes . . . lots of surprises," said Erik softly, wheeling the chair out onto the sunny veranda beyond the garden window. "Come with me and see."

Come with me and see.

No one else said that to Reza now.

Only Erik.

And somehow on his lips those words never sounded sad or absurd.

I had determined to be reconciled to their odd friendship, for whenever I saw them together the sheer magnitude of their respective tragedies made me turn my back on my own jealous uneasiness. I tried to forget that my son had chosen to worship a murderer of questionable sanity.

But one day I received a fright that made me face reality at last. . . .

I walked out into the garden unexpectedly to find my son stroking a handsome Siamese cat, collared with huge diamonds. There was no doubt over the identity of the animal. It was unquestionably the Glory of the Empire who sat there with a king's ransom around her slender neck—the Glory of the Empire, the shah's most favored and treasured possession.

"Are you quite mad!" I said furiously to Erik. "Are you determined to have us all killed for this crazy theft?"

"Stop shouting, you're frightening the child. I shall return the animal before she is missed . . . and who shall say then how she came to lose her pretty collar?"

I sat down on the edge of the fountain, because my legs would no longer support me.

"I don't know how you spirited her away from her guards," I said faintly, "but I do know that if that collar goes missing you will surely be the first to be suspected. How dare you come here and involve my son in this insane crime?"

I saw Reza tense and shrink closer to Erik's darkly cloaked figure.

"Father," he whispered tremulously, "please don't be angry. . . . I asked him to bring the cat. It was only a joke."

"You foolish child!" I snapped. "This is a joke that could cost us all our heads."

Reza's eyes filled with tears, and without warning he flung his arms around the masked man, who had bent over him in concern.

"I don't want to stay here anymore," he sobbed into the muffling folds of the cloak. "I want to go with you. I want to go with you now."

Erik withdrew hastily from the child's clutching embrace, and as he turned away, with the cat in his arms, I signed for a servant to remove the wheeled chair from our presence.

"Well?" I demanded shakily when we were alone once more. "Was that not exactly what you wanted to hear?"

He did not answer. He passed one hand briefly over the cat's neck and in a moment the jeweled collar was gone.

I went up to him, keeping a hard grip upon my turbulent emotions, and obliged him to meet my eye.

"Take what you like," I said quietly. "Pillage the whole world if you must to satisfy your professional vanity. But don't take my child's heart from me just because you can. Don't shut me in that torture chamber, Erik."

He turned to look back regretfully at the house, as though silently taking leave of something very dear to him.

"All sensible men learn to close their doors against thieves," he said sadly.

And tucking the cat securely beneath his cloak he walked away.

The matter of the cat's missing collar was never resolved. The shah raged and had several of the guards thrown into prison for negligence, but if he suspected Erik, as he must surely have done, he kept his own counsel. It did not yet suit him to part with a man who performed so many unique and irreplaceable services. For now he was prepared to overlook the loss.

And yet there were subtle nuances that indicated his growing resentment of a servant who had made himself indispensable. Perhaps it had been amusing, even refreshing, at first, to deal with a man who never used a courtesy title, who spoke to him as an equal and never stooped to fawning flattery. But all novelty pales in time, and the shah was notoriously fickle in his choice of favorites.

Sooner or later, I knew, there would be a terrible price to pay; I only hoped that I would not be present when that day of reckoning finally dawned.

hen the court returned to Tehran, Erik asked that he might be permitted to remain in Mazanderan to oversee the entire course of building. But since the khanum would not countenance his indefinite absence, permission was refused and consequently he was obliged to travel constantly back and forth across the Elburz Mountains all through the spring and summer of 1851.

Watching him grow progressively more tired and short tempered with each succeeding month, I sensed that the continued slights of the grand vazir were beginning to rankle ever more deeply in his mind. The enmity between the two men became increasingly open as Erik began to use his influence with the khanum to overset several of the prime minister's cherished proposals. And when I saw Mirza Taqui Khan storm out of the Council Chamber one sultry, airless afternoon in late summer, I guessed that there had been yet another heated exchange of views between them.

"It is insupportable," said the grand vazir loudly, "truly insupportable, when the opinions of a demented magician are permitted to carry weight in this fashion. How can Persia take her place in the civilized world if her affairs continue to be misdirected by the twisted fancies of this insane monster?"

A terrible hush fell over the prime minister's friends as first one and then another turned to glance in quiet horror at the door of the Council Chamber, where the *insane monster* now stood listening. The grand vazir followed their gaze and then, with an expression of cold contempt, continued to address his audience as if he were unaware of Erik's presence.

"Gentlemen, it is time for us all to consider how much longer the shah will be content to be served by a creature who properly belongs in a cage."

I saw Erik stiffen.

"A cage?" he repeated softly.

The prime minister wheeled around upon him angrily.

"A cage, sir, is where you belong and where I would most gladly see you confined, like the hideous beast that you are. Your pretended claim to humanity is an affront to every honest man at court!"

"Are there any honest men at court?"

Erik's voice was lightly sarcastic and raised a little nervous laughter even among Khan's supporters, but I was not deceived by his apparent calm. I could see from the faint tremor of his hands that he was ready to kill.

"God knows there are fewer since you came!" snapped the grand vazir furiously. "The depravity of your activities stains us all. You are neither an artist nor a scientist—you are a deranged fiend who should have been locked away from the world at birth! Your mind is as distorted as your face. I truly shudder to think what horrendous tales are being carried from court to the European missions!"

Turning abruptly on his heel, the grand vazir walked away, with the members of his entourage hurrying behind him. Erik stared after him, and as I came near I was able to feel the anger that throbbed inside him, like a tense swollen boil.

"A cage!" he muttered darkly, "a cage!"

"Erik," I said desperately, "I beseech you to forget this."

He gave a short, bitter laugh.

"How lightly you speak of forgetting," he muttered, "you who have never known the filth and degradation of a *cage!*"

I was stunned by the pulsing venom in his voice.

"They were only words," I protested, "hasty, ill-considered words spoken in the heat of the moment—"

"By a man with many enemies!" he said softly, still staring down the corridor. He was grimly calm of a sudden, no longer breathing in harsh gasps with one hand clutching fiercely at his chest. And this deadly, stone-cold serenity was somehow infinitely more frightening than his blazing anger.

"If you are his friend," Erik continued with the same unnerving dispassion, "you had better tell that man to guard his back. The planetary alignments in his birth sign are most unfavorable. His stars are against him."

He drew a tarot card out of the air with a flourish and dropped it on the floor at my feet. The card fell facedown, and as I bent to turn it over I found myself looking at a skeleton bearing a scythe.

Death. . . .

When I looked up to protest, the corridor was completely empty; there was no sign of Erik anywhere.

Slowly I tucked the card into my coat and turned away with a heavy heart. . . .

There was no more open show of hostility between the two men, but I did not make the mistake of confusing Erik's restraint with resignation. Like a prowling cat in the shadows he was secretly and silently stalking a reckless prey. He had the ear of the khanum, whose dislike of her son-in-law was well documented, and I suspected that whatever disaster Erik had in mind for the prime minister would be directed through the insidious influence of the harem.

The coup fell in November when, without warning, the shah suddenly summoned four hundred of his personal guard to the palace late at night and had the grand vazir placed under arrest. No accusations were made, no explanations given. The man simply fell from favor with all the abruptness that was commonplace in Persia, plummeting to the ground like a tangled kite and dragging his supporters with him in his wake.

Erik was standing at a window, looking down into the palace courtyard, when the grand vazir, his wife, and two infant children were placed in a *takheterewan.* The curtained litter was surrounded by an armed guard and the dismal torchlit procession proceeded to the main gate and was soon swallowed up in the blackness of the autumn night.

"Where are they taking him?" I demanded.

"To the palace of Fin in Kashan," he replied quietly.

"Indefinite exile?"

"It is enough." Erik made a brief gesture of resignation. "I had forgotten there were children."

I nodded and would have turned away both relieved and satisfied, but still he lingered at the window.

"She chose to go with him," he said after a moment, "his wife, the little princess. She defied the wishes of her mother and her brother and insisted on sharing her husband's fate. I think she would willingly have shared even a cage to be near him."

I raised my shoulders in a hesitant shrug.

"Their affection is well known. Did you expect her to desert him?"

"I have taken from him nothing of value," he said broodingly. "Even in his ruin their love defeats me. I have failed."

"Yes," I agreed with sad, unthinking absence, "there is nothing you can do to destroy the love of others."

There was a moment of silence and then, without warning, Erik suddenly struck both his fists against the window with a violence that shattered the glass.

"I have never accepted defeat!" he shouted. "Never! And I don't intend to begin now! I will find a better way to be revenged!"

As I stared at the blazing eyes behind the mask, I was suddenly afraid that I had quite unwittingly set my own seal upon the grand vazir's death warrant.

Two months passed peacefully enough, without incident, and I began to hope that Erik's vindictive anger had cooled.

The grand vazir remained in captivity, with his wife tasting all his food in order to shield him from the poison that had ended the lives of so many fallen favorites in the past. It was said that his fear of treachery was so great that he never left his wife's apartments for a moment, even to bathe.

I thought often of the beautiful palace of Fin, with its graceful cypress avenues, and its marble canals full of swift flowing water. I thought of a great and noble man reduced by his own folly to a state of cringing terror and I reflected that even if Erik showed forbearance now, there were still many others who would lose no time in seeking the grand vazir's death. A fallen favorite was rarely permitted to live for long.

In January Erik left court unexpectedly. None of his servants could tell me where he had gone or when he would be back, and I was deeply uneasy. I knew he would not have returned to Mazanderan without me . . . so where else could he have gone?

Several nights later, when the whole palace was buzzing with rumors of the grand vazir's murder, I went to Erik's apartments, sick at heart, and determined to wait for his return.

His rooms were filled with an odd assortment of creatures, most of them injured and in various stages of recovery. A lizard limped around a small tank with a tiny splint on its rear leg; a bat with a torn wing hung upside down and eyed me hopefully, as though it expected to be fed; a cat with a bandage swathed over one eye tried to climb onto my lap and made my flesh cringe so badly that I was forced to shut it in the marbled bathroom.

I sat there grimly in this menagerie of hospitalized animals and waited to ask the question that was burning into me like an acid.

Did you kill him, Erik? Did you?

The story was imprinted on my brain by now. I had it by heart, every last treacherous detail, except the one I had to know. . . .

A lady of the harem had been sent to Kashan, bearing news of honorable retirement in Kerbela. Told that the Coat of Honor was even now upon its way to him, the grand vazir had been persuaded to leave his wife's apartments for the first time since his captivity began, to purify himself in the bathing chambers. There he had met with the shah's assassins and, being offered a choice of death, his veins were duly opened with ritual ceremony, in accordance with his last request. The assassins had not yet been named and I was stricken with a terrible feeling of foreboding and despair.

Erik walked into the room shortly after midnight, and if he was surprised to find me waiting there, he gave no sign as he tossed his hat and cloak into the arms of a hovering servant and waved the man away.

"Where have you been?" I demanded curtly.

"Nowhere that is any concern of yours," he retorted with infuriating calm.

"It is my business to know exactly where you are at all times. You know that I am answerable to the shah for your activities."

"Don't exceed your commission!" he snapped suddenly. "I am not a prisoner in one of your petty Mazanderan jails."

I watched him ladle sherbet into a glass with a fine wooden pear-spoon.

"Erik," I said hopelessly, "you must know what I suspect."

"How the devil should I know what you suspect?" he demanded. "I'm not a mind reader!"

"Mirza Taqui Khan . . ." I began hesitantly, "—what do you know of this tragedy?"

"I know that he is dead. I would hardly have called it a tragedy."

"No?" I countered bitterly. "And what of his wife, what of his young children . . . *yes!* . . . you turn away at that, don't you? Did you go to Kashan, Erik?"

He stared at me in silence with eyes that seemed strangely sad.

"Answer me!" I cried, suddenly beside myself with an emotion I could barely control. "Did you go to Kashan with his assassins? Did you?"

Reaching inside his capacious magician's sleeve, Erik withdrew a small enameled casket and handed it to me.

"There is your answer," he muttered grimly. "Take great care how you open it."

I took the casket to an oil lamp and lifted the lid warily. Inside, on the red velvet lining, lurked an angry black Kashan scorpion with its tail curled ready to strike. Disturbed by the sudden light the creature darted toward the raised lid and in my alarm I lost my grip upon the little box and dropped it.

I felt the sting just below my ankle and gave a gasp of shock at the searing pain.

Erik moved like the god of lightning and a second later the scorpion was skewered to the floor with the point of his knife—the same knife, I presumed, that had rendered the last service to the grand vazir.

"You damned fool!" he said in concerned alarm. "I told you to be careful."

Pushing me into a chair he pulled the slipper from my foot, which was already beginning to swell like an angry red balloon. I saw him hold the tip of his knife in a candle flame before he made the incision in my flesh, and then, as the notorious venom coursed through my veins, I felt myself falling.

When I came to myself I was lying on his divan. My foot was throbbing like the devil beneath a layer of linen bandaging, and the room was filled with an unpleasant burning odor. Turning my head with difficulty, I saw Erik pouring a noxious, oily substance into a vial.

He came over to the divan when he saw me move, handed me a goblet, and placed the vial on the table beside me.

"Drink that," he said curtly.

I tasted copper, honey, and vinegar—the prescribed antidote—and my glance wandered to the vial.

"What is that?" I asked uneasily.

"The oil of the scorpion. It will relieve the pain and reduce the swelling."

He sat down beside me on a cane chair and laid two bony fingers on my pulse.

"You'll live!" he said with grim satisfaction. "Next time I warn you to take care, perhaps you will listen to me. How do you feel?"

"Cold and sickened," I said grimly.

He nodded as though I had merely confirmed his expectation.

"That is a natural reaction to a scorpion bite."

"And to murder," I said.

Erik sighed. "You know that there is only one way with enemies in Persia. You've cut down a few yourself in your time as chief of police, haven't you?"

"Criminals perhaps . . . enemies of the state . . . but all by due process of the law."

He shrugged. "Death is death however it comes, legal or otherwise. Why do you plague me with these pointless questions? There were many cutthroats involved in the opening of his veins."

"I'm not concerned with paid assassins—mindless, soulless animals who excel at nothing else. But you, Erik—you love all the beauty in this world. . . .You are a genius in so many different fields. Why do you set yourself beyond the pale of humanity by such a despicable crime?"

He took off the mask and turned slowly to let me see.

"This face, which has denied me all human rights, also frees me of all obligation to the human race," he said quietly. "My mother hated me, my village drove me from my home, I was exhibited like an animal in a cage until a knife showed me the only way to be free. The pleasures of love will always be forbidden to me . . . but I am young, Nadir, I have all the desires of any normal man."

I watched him replace the mask wearily.

"I did not kill the grand vazir," he continued unexpectedly. "Oh, for God's sake, spare me that pitiful look of relief! I can assure you that I fully intended to take part. I went to Kashan for the express purpose of taking his life. The *meerghazab*s had orders not to touch his throat—the coup de grace was to have been mine."

"What happened?" I demanded.

Erik made a gesture of impatience.

"I saw the scorpion and wasted a few precious minutes on its capture. In my absence the fools misjudged his strength and opened too many veins. When I arrived the bath was full of blood and he was already dead. I was so *angry*— you cannot begin to imagine my fury and frustration. I hated him! I hated him for being wise and respected . . . and loved. I hated him for making me look in the mirror of his eyes to see the loathsome thing I have become. . . ."

Erik sank back on the chair beside me and stared at the floor.

"Go on," I prompted grimly, "you had better tell me everything."

"I would have killed them all for their disobedience," he continued dully, "but they were too many in number and already half crazed with bloodlust. I left the bath in haste before my rage betrayed me, and as I walked back through the gardens to my horse, the princess ran from the palace with her hair streaming in the wind. It was dark. She didn't see me until we collided, but as soon as she recognized me she understood that he was dead. She backed away against the palace wall and started to scream. . . . My God, I'll never forget those screams . . . such terrible, demented grief! It made me remember . . . so many things I thought I had forgotten." Suddenly he buried

his masked face in his hands. "She went on screaming"—he sobbed—
"on and on and on. I cannot shut the sound from my head."

I let him weep, relieved beyond measure by this astonishing show of
emotion, the first evidence of a remorse and regret which might yet
save him.

"There is nothing I can do," he said in despair. "I can't turn back
the clock and see this terrible thing undone. It's too late . . . too
late."

"Too late for the princess, perhaps, but not for you." I suggested
with sudden hope, "Erik . . . have you no religion to turn to?"

"I was raised a Catholic," he said slowly, "but I have not heard
Mass since I was a child."

"There are missions here in Persia," I pointed out gravely, "priests
who would hear your confession and grant you absolution."

He lifted his head and looked at me curiously.

"You have no belief in the doctrines of the Catholic church."

"No," I agreed, "but I have a great respect for its morals. And I
would sooner see you an infidel than an atheist and murderer."

He got up and went to open a window.

"A sung Mass is very beautiful," he said wistfully. "I think tonight
perhaps I could begin to compose my own setting of the requiem. I
have neglected my music for too long . . . far too long."

I said no more.

A short time later, when I was able to hobble to my own apartment,
leaning on the arm of a servant, Erik was already too absorbed in the
score to take note of my departure.

*U*nseemly celebrations attended the demise of Mirza Taqui Khan, and those who had suffered inconvenience and straitened circumstances as a result of his sweeping reforms were the first to raise a glass to absent friends. I suppose I should have been among them, but the general hilarity of the court was distasteful to me, and I felt Persia to be a poorer place for the loss of an inherently noble man.

When the princess was brought back to court, prostrate with grief, to be given in marriage to the son of the new grand vazir, Erik came to me in a terrible rage.

"Is this another of your quaint and delightful customs?" he demanded furiously. "Has no one in this godforsaken court heard of a decent period of mourning?"

I raised my shoulders helplessly.

"The shah's sister is his personal property, to be disposed of as he sees fit."

Erik looked at me incredulously.

"Are you telling me the girl is *transferable*, like the grand vazir's signet ring—that whoever takes one must take the other?"

I sighed. "It is often the custom in such matters."

"Oh, I see," he said contemptuously. "Legalized rape is the done thing here, is it? Any man may force himself upon a woman and say it is the custom? My God, what a country!"

And he turned away with such fierce disgust that I felt faintly ashamed of my own race.

I was fully aware that he was by no means indifferent to the opposite sex, indeed quite the contrary. A powerful sexuality informed his
every gesture. Curbed and leashed, expressed in the enormous sensuality of his hands, this sexuality gripped every audience and made him a
uniquely compelling performer. I believe it was this very quality that
had fascinated the khanum, a woman of intense and urgent passions.
If the eunuchs were to be believed, the fancy she entertained for his
presence went far beyond her interest in his magical skills. They say
that each time she watched him kill, the intensity of her pleasure
bordered on sexual gratification, and I had heard a whisper that she
would have invited him to her bed, had she only dared to take the risks
involved. Oddly enough, I would have said that Erik and the shah
himself were the only people in the palace who remained unaware of
that whisper. No one would dare to carry such a tale to the king of
kings, who believed, like all good Moslems, that heaven lay beneath
his mother's feet. But Erik . . . Allah! Had he no eyes to see what
the woman really wanted from him? To be so corrupted with vice and
yet maintain a child's essential innocence! Strange, but whenever I
looked at him I found myself remembering that Lucifer himself had
been an angel before he fell. . . .

I felt cold at the thought of what tragedies might ensue if Erik
should ever open his eyes and fall in love. Surely God, who had punished him so cruelly in his birth, would spare him the cruel travesty of
such sight. . . .

No, I did not seriously believe he was falling in love with the princess. What he felt for her now was only the same angry pity he
experienced for anything vulnerable and damaged. She was merely a
helpless creature who aroused his deep, and astonishingly contradictory, instinct to heal and protect; had she been a bird he would have
mended her broken wing, set her free, and safely forgotten her.

The door of the torture chamber had not closed on him yet and I
could find it in my heart to hope that it never would.

"Are you to perform at the wedding celebrations?" I inquired at
length, seeking to divert his dark thoughts.

He laughed shortly.

"Yes . . . I am to be the skeleton at their little feast. The shah has
already asked me to prepare a spectacular show. I think some trick

with a coffin might be rather appropriate, don't you? I shall have to think about it."

And he turned back to the window already deep in thought.

If I live to be a hundred I know I shall never see a sight more extraordinary than that astonishing trick Erik performed with the coffin.

There was no stage, no visible place to conceal whatever mechanics govern the secret of levitation, and when the sarcophagus began to open a tense, expectant silence descended upon the watching court.

Erik was dressed like a god and wore a mask that had been specially fashioned for the occasion out of beaten gold. He snapped his fingers once and the stone lid of the coffin fell to the floor of its own accord with a deafening thud that made everyone jump. When silence descended once more, he held out one hand and beckoned toward the sarcophagus with a gesture of awesome authority that left everyone holding his breath. I had enough French now to translate the words that he began to weave into soft, enticing song.

Come forth from your dark sleep.
Come to the angel of doom,
And show the living the fate which awaits. . . .

As the last note died, there was an answering shriek from the coffin, a horrible, heart-stopping wail that chilled us all to the bone. And then, with a faint, eerie rattle, I saw the Kazan skeleton rise slowly into the air and come to rest, erect and unsupported, beside its master.

My gasp was lost among the communal intake of breath as Erik took the skeleton by the hand and led it toward the place where the new prime minister stood. I saw the man tremble visibly as the terrible apparition approached, and the shah himself leaned forward in his chair, his face a little paler than normal as he watched intently.

The bony visitor from the tomb raised an accusing finger at the grand vazir; there was a tense heartbeat of silence and then, as Erik clapped his hands abruptly, the skeleton collapsed to the floor in a mass of inanimate jumbled bones.

Swooping forward, like some golden bird of prey, Erik retrieved the skull and from its jaw withdrew the prime minister's signet ring, tossing it at the feet of the stupefied man with a gesture of contempt.

"I trust Your Excellency's son will prove less careless with his secondhand possessions," he said pointedly.

There was a moment of stunned silence, all the court staring at the young shah to see whether they dared to show approval at an astonishing trick so blatantly colored with dangerous political overtones. The moment could not have lasted for more than a second or two, but it seemed like all eternity before the shah leaned forward to toss a large drawstring purse to Erik.

Immediately the court burst into thunderous applause.

Erik bowed and walked away, taking the skull with him, but leaving the rest of the skeleton lying where all might examine it with greedy curiosity. He had no further use for this particular device now, and so arrogantly confident was he of his own unique expertise that he had no qualms in exposing the apparatus of this illusion to the curious gaze of the ignorant. He had made his point and he was satisfied; nothing could have better expressed his contempt for mankind than the utter carelessness with which he abandoned the instrument of this remarkable deception once it had served its purpose.

I saw the shah looking at him as he walked away, and there was a certain coldness in his eyes as they rested on this uniquely favored servant. The political gesture had been aimed at the grand vazir, but neither the shah nor the khanum could escape from the associated ridicule that would always attach to the remarriage of the princess now. I could not help feeling it was remarkably foolhardy of Erik to risk offending his mighty patron in such a dangerously public manner.

As for the new grand vazir, once having recovered from the unnerving experience, his humiliation and resentment were very plainly etched upon his face. When I saw him deep in conversation with his son and their supporters, I felt increasingly uneasy.

Wine is forbidden to followers of the Prophet, but, regrettably, at court, this injunction was very commonly ignored. A slave brought a tray containing goblets and a flagon of arrack to the whispering group and a few minutes later I saw this same man serve Erik on bended knee. For some time Erik lingered, speaking to no one, as was his wont, and viewing the remainder of the evening's entertainment with an aloof and scornful eye. I was drawn into a lengthy, tedious conversation with the undersecretary and a clerk of the foreign office and when I chanced to look around later I saw that Erik had disappeared. Not in itself an unusual event, but this time, for some unknown reason, his sudden absence disturbed me; and excusing myself hastily from the conversation, I hurried through the palace to his apartment.

The rooms were deserted, no servant in sight.

I found Erik alone in the beautiful bathing chamber, vomiting blood with a terrible, choking violence. He looked around briefly and swore when he saw I was there.

"The wine," I said dully, staring at the blood streaking the sides of the great white marble bath. "How many times have I warned you to employ a taster? Where are your servants?"

"I sent them away," he gasped. "And now if you don't mind . . . I should prefer to conduct my final performance without an audience. . . . Ask nicely and I'm sure they'll give you your money back at the door!"

He turned his face away from me and was convulsed once more by the agonized retching that seemed as though it would tear him apart. A little blood splashed up on my hand as I reached out helplessly to hold him steady.

"Go away!" he panted. "I don't want you here. . . . I don't want anyone. . . ."

"Stop wasting your strength," I ordered. "Do you have any idea what you may have taken?"

"No," he muttered. "I've made no study . . . of your crude Persian toxins. . . . I don't make a habit . . . of poisoning people as a rule. It's not a form of death I find . . . *esthetically* pleasing."

"Ground glass would account for the internal bleeding," I said grimly. "There are various substances with which it could have been combined. Most of them produce a protracted and agonizing death."

"How long?" he inquired shortly.

"Those who are lucky die within forty-eight hours, but I have known a strong man to linger up to ten days."

"Ten days," he echoed. "Then . . . I could get to Ashraf?"

I looked down at him in amazement.

"You could never endure that journey in this condition."

"I must," he said. "There are . . . instructions . . . I have yet to give . . . And I must see . . . with my own eyes . . . one last time."

I shook my head. "You'll die on the road long before we reach the palace. Why give yourself so much more unnecessary pain?"

"The pain is nothing . . . compared to the regret . . . the *frustration!* Nadir"—his voice dropped to an exhausted whisper and his hands clenched taut with agony on the rim of the marble bath— "please . . . order a *takheterewan* . . . secretly . . . and take me back to Mazanderan tonight. . . ."

I could not deny such a desperate plea for help.

Against my better judgment I did exactly as he asked.

The outer shell of the Mazanderan palace was nearing completion, sufficient of the building now standing—erected by the hands of more than a hundred laborers—to create a glorious illusion of the past.

The columnar structure, with its double porticoes on three sides, and its soaring, elegantly fluted shafts, echoed back to the glories of the Persian Empire under Darius and Xerxes. But the outer façade was a cunning illusion designed to deceive the mental defenses of an unwary courtier. Within, using the versatility of our high-quality baked bricks and with his own unique technical ingenuity, I knew that Erik intended to create an interior belonging entirely to the future. He had guarded his secrets jealously until now, revealing to the laborers only as much as they needed to know at each stage of construction. But rather than take those secrets to his grave, he entrusted me, at the outset of our mission, with documents that would ensure the structure's completion in the event of his death. I did not dare to look at them, and as I watched his protracted suffering on that never-ending journey, I fully expected to be required to hand them on to the master mason in charge.

When we reached the palace, Erik was carried into the echoing edifice on a litter and there, pulling himself up on one elbow, he looked around incredulously.

"Give me those papers!" he said in a voice that was suddenly thunderous with rage. "And fetch the master mason here to me now!"

He was on his feet when the trembling man came to kneel before him.

"You have not followed my instructions. Why?"

"Forgive me, master," the man stammered. "I did my best . . . but the specifications were so—so complex . . . I did not understand them."

Erik snatched the riding whip from my hand and brought it down across the man's shoulder with a violence that made the fellow stumble backward.

"Next time you don't understand something," he said awfully, "ask, damn you! *Ask!*"

"You weren't here, master," sobbed the man in terror, "you weren't here to ask. It has been more than three weeks since you came to us."

Erik let the whip fall to the ground.

"Yes," he said faintly, "you are right. . . . This is a damnable way to build. Get up now . . . are you hurt?"

"No, master," said the mason, wonderingly.

"You are very fortunate," said Erik with a sigh, "that I lacked the strength to break your neck. Come to my tent now and I will go through the plans with you . . . give you my last instructions. You will listen very carefully—and you will not be afraid to tell me if you do not understand. I swear to you now that as long as you show me honesty I will show you no more anger."

I was present throughout that interview, but the technicalities of pivots and trapdoors and echo acoustics were well beyond me. For three hours Erik leaned on the little makeshift table, explaining and reexplaining with extraordinary patience, occasionally sketching an extra diagram to illustrate a particular point more clearly.

The hands of my watch stood at midnight before the master mason said that he understood everything.

"Are you sure," Erik persisted, "absolutely sure this time?"

"Yes, master."

Erik sighed.

I turned from the flap of the tent in time to see him fall.

By dawn he was delirious, wandering in dark nightmares of the past.

"It was an accident," he whispered, "it was an accident. . . . I didn't mean to make her fall. . . . I didn't want you to see. . . . Oh, Father . . . why did you make me do it . . . *why?*"

As I bent over to place a water bottle to his lips, he clutched at my arm in terrible panic.

"Give me back the mask!" he sobbed. "Give me back the mask and let me go home. . . . I hate it here. . . . I hate this cage . . . this filthy cage!"

He fought with me like a madman for several minutes, and when he fell back on the pallet exhausted I was able to see tears glistening on the mask.

"Where's Sasha?" he suddenly demanded with quiet fear. "*Where is she?*"

"She's here," I said with hesitation. "She's here, Erik, she's—she's quite safe."

He closed his eyes.

"Don't let her out tonight," he begged, twisting his fingers in my sleeve. "Promise me you won't let her out . . . promise me!"

I promised; it seemed to calm him.

When he slipped from delirium into a coma, I had him carried the half mile to my house at Ashraf.

There was nothing more I could do for him now except permit him to die in some semblance of comfort, in a place where he had once shared a child's laughter.

My orders were strict on our arrival: Reza was not to be told of Erik's presence.

But before the end of the day someone had betrayed me and I found I had no option but to wheel the child into that deathly silent room.

"Why did they poison him?" Reza's speech was slurred now and increasingly difficult to follow. I bent down and placed one hand on the child's emaciated shoulder.

"You must understand that he has many enemies, Reza. He has become too powerful. There are many people who hate him and wish for his death."

"If I speak to him, will he hear me?"

"I don't think so, Reza. . . . I don't think he can hear anything now."

"But he might," persisted the child, "he might. Father, may I stay here with you for a while?"

I had no heart to refuse. I wheeled the chair beside the bed, and when the child's fingers groped blindly across the coverlet I leaned over and guided his hand to Erik's thin wrist.

"I want you to wake up, Erik," said Reza simply. "My music man is broken and no one else knows how to mend it."

There was no response from the skeletal figure in the bed.

Over and over Reza repeated his request, with ever shriller intensity, until I knew I could not permit this terrible travesty to continue any longer. Then, as I moved toward the chair with quiet determination, I saw Erik's fingers stir briefly on the coverlet. The child saw nothing, of course, and I wheeled him from the room without speaking of it, not wishing to raise false hope.

And indeed it was not until the following night that Erik opened his eyes and looked up at me with quiet lucidity.

"You should have told me it was broken," he said.

 month later, as we sat together on the veranda taking thick, sweet coffee with crushed cardamoms, a messenger from the khanum arrived bearing a letter which commanded Erik's immediate return to Tehran.

As I watched, Erik got up, brought his hands together briefly, almost in an attitude of prayer, and then opened them to reveal a heavy purse nestling on one palm.

"I never received this message," he said.

"Master?" The man took the purse from him and stared at it with obvious bewilderment.

"You did not survive your dangerous journey through the Elburz

. . . a landslide . . . a tiger . . . a Turkoman—there are half a dozen deaths a solitary messenger could have met. Choose whichever pleases you and disappear. There is sufficient in that purse to ensure you never need to carry messages again. Go now and be sure you do not speak of this to anyone. If you betray me, I promise that I will take the greatest pleasure in personally arranging your extinction!"

When the man had gone I looked up with a sigh.

"She will send again, Erik. This can't buy you more than a few weeks' grace."

"Two months are all that I shall need."

"To finish the palace?" I said in astonishment. "Surely that is impossible."

He looked down on me with great pity.

"I am not speaking of the palace," he said gently.

I felt suddenly cold, as though all the blood had ceased to run in my veins.

"Two months," I echoed. "Erik, surely you are mistaken, he must have longer than that—he must!"

He sat down beside me and leaned forward in his chair, forcing me to look at him.

"Nadir . . . the child does not deserve to suffer all that will very soon lie ahead of him."

"What are you telling me?" I said numbly.

"I am telling you nothing—merely asking you to remember that death can come in many shades. Some are harsh and infinitely painful to look upon; others can be as peaceful and beautiful as the setting sun. I am an artist, and many colors lie upon my palette. Let me paint him a rainbow, and give you the means to decide where it ends."

I let him paint that rainbow.

For two months the kaleidoscope whirled, making beautiful, many-hued pictures that still glow in my memory like fresh oils. The sorcery of an incomparable genius focused like the sun's rays on the tinder-dry imagination of a child. My house was filled with magic and mystery as Erik seemed to cause the very earth itself to yield long-kept secrets. Windows opened into a world of fantasy, and bridges of music spanned deep chasms into a strange and secret realm. It was a timeless

period of wonder, bounded only by the rapid creep of a cruel reality
that no magic could keep at bay.

Two months indeed were all I needed to see the terrible signposts at
which Erik had darkly hinted. The evening that Reza began to choke
unexpectedly on the drink I was holding to his lips, I suddenly understood what horrors lay ahead.

A dull heaviness closed in around me as I sent a servant to fetch
Erik from the palace site.

He came at once; and as he stood before me in his white mask and
his black cloak, he looked every inch the khanum's Angel of Doom.

Taking a vial from his sleeve, he placed a little colorless liquid in a
small glass of sherbet and handed it to me.

"It will be quick," he said quietly, "and he will feel nothing."

I stared at the finality of that glass with horror.

"No," I said with sudden panic, "I can't do this. I will let nature
take her course after all."

He looked at me steadily.

"Nature is a cruel and unfeeling goddess. Will you abandon your
child into her merciless hands?"

Covering my face I turned away from his relentless gaze.

"I am his father . . . how can you know, how can you understand,
what it means to take life from your own child?"

He was silent for a moment; then I felt him lay his fingers briefly on
my arm.

"This is no longer your burden," he said softly. *"Wait for me here."*

Once again experiencing that curious paralysis of will, I watched
him take up the Koran and pass into the adjoining room.

Time slid through my limp grasp and there was a sluggish throbbing
in my head that seemed to extend to all my muscles. His voice was like
a dead weight in my mind, dragging me down and numbing all inclination to resist.

The moment of choice had been taken from me and now the last
sound my son would hear was the voice of an infidel . . . an unbeliever. . . .

Swirling, drowning in that bottomless lake, I grasped the knife of
my faith and freed myself from the strangling weeds that were settling

around me like a shroud. I broke loose from the spell that bound me and rushed into the silent chamber beyond.

Save for the muted glow of a candle in the prayer niche, the room was in darkness now. All the windows along the garden side of the wall had been pushed wide open to admit the wind that was blowing in from the Caspian Sea.

Erik turned as I entered the room. For a moment the wind took his cloak, making it swirl out around him as he came toward me with all the slow majesty of a winged angel returning to earth.

"There is no God but Allah and Muhammad is his Prophet," I whispered hoarsely.

There was a faint answering sigh in response, the barest flutter of breath from Reza's slack white lips.

The boy was already dead when Erik laid him in my arms.

e do not bury our dead in coffins.

Washed and shrouded, Reza's small body was committed directly to the earth, in accordance to the customs of my faith. I dutifully opened my doors to those who came to pay their condolences; I saw that the coffee and tea and traditional halvah were served, and on the fortieth day the women of my household covered their heads while verses from the Koran were intoned solemnly and prayers said to send the spirit of the departed to paradise.

When all was done that needed to be done, I went back to court. Erik was already there. The morning after Reza's death an armed guard had arrived with orders to escort him to Tehran, and I believe he was relieved to go with them. I was unable to express my confused and contradictory emotions. I let him ride away without speaking the word which might have lifted that leaden shroud of grief and guilt from his shoulders. This time he did not look back at the house and I knew he would never set foot on my estate from choice again.

I had barely arrived at the Ark when I received orders to wait upon the shah, and I went to his chambers with careless indifference, prepared to accept whatever punishment was doubtless to be visited upon me for aiding and abetting Erik's lengthy period of absence. I half hoped for imprisonment, since that at least would spare me the daily ordeal of attending my child's unhappy murderer.

I found the shah sitting at a marble-topped table, poring over the plans of the new palace with odd intensity. The sun streaming in from the window reflected on the diamond clasp which held an egret feather in place upon his *kolah*. When he glanced up and made a quick gesture for me to rise from my obeisance, the feather danced like a coy woman in the faint breeze that blew in from the open casement.

"Have you seen these plans, Daroga?" he demanded abruptly.

I hastened to assure him that I had not. Knowledge is a very dangerous thing in Persia, and sick at heart though I was, I was not yet ready to contemplate execution with any equanimity. Erik's interior designs for the Garden of Echoes had always been a closely guarded secret. What tales had been carried from Mazanderan to arouse the shah's suspicions now? Did he know of the documents Erik had entrusted to my care? Did he know of my presence during that desperate consultation with the master mason?

The shah drew heavily on a calean and regarded me steadily with eyes that always reminded me of a hawk's.

"Tell me, Daroga," he began conversationally, blowing a stream of smoke in my direction, "does my masked friend consider himself adequately rewarded for his services . . . extraordinary as we grant them to be?"

"Your generosity has always been without question, O Shadow of God," I said warily.

"You have not answered my question!" snapped the shah with unexpected irritation. "The sultan . . . the emir . . . they, too, would be generous to a man of such singular talents."

I was silent, aware that the ground beneath my feet had become dangerously unstable.

The shah set his water pipe aside in order to lock the plans safely into the drawer in his desk.

"I have it in mind to present him with a gift—a little token of my immense regard," he continued thoughtfully. "I should be vastly interested to hear how he receives it. The nature of your work requires you to be an observant man, Daroga. I shall expect a report containing exact details of his . . . well, what shall we say? . . . his *gratitude.*"

I bowed low to avoid looking at a smile which made me deeply uneasy—the smile of a man whose mother had taught him to appreciate the finer points of torture.

Behind this sudden whim I sensed the khanum's jealous anger.

It seemed that Erik was to be punished after all for those months of willful desertion. . . .

The girl was an odalisque, a slave of the royal harem who had completed her training as a concubine, but not yet been chosen to serve in the royal bed. There was no greater honor for the shah to bestow upon a favored servant than the gift of a harem virgin—the gift of a wife.

When I had stammered my rehearsed piece, there was a deathly silence in Erik's softly lit apartment, a tension that pulled every muscle taut as a bowstring.

He stared at the girl with a ravening hunger that the mask could not disguise, and his sudden, overwhelming desire was like sheet lightning, shocking in its savage intensity. I saw his shoulders hunch against the pain, his hands lock on his knees and claw upward into his flesh in a desperate attempt to contain the screaming tyranny of his own body.

When he looked up at me it was with bitter hatred, as though he understood the exact purpose of my presence here tonight.

"Bring her forward," he said.

Erik's voice had lost all its beauty and become a harsh, metallic rasp which made the girl shrink instinctively against the arm of the eunuch who restrained her. She was dragged across the room and thrown at his feet, in accordance with his curt gesture. Rising slowly, like some great unfurling shadow, he leaned forward and pulled off the girl's veil to reveal huge eyes edged with antimony, staring up at him with undisguised terror.

"How old are you?" he demanded harshly.

"Fifteen, master." Her voice was barely audible.

"Have they told you what is expected of you?"

"Yes," she whispered.

"Very well. I have seen what lies behind your veil, my dear . . . now you shall be accorded a reciprocal honor. Come forward and remove my mask."

The girl did not move; she continued to kneel at his feet, staring up at him in horror.

"To refuse me now is to refuse the shah himself," said Erik steadily. "If you resist I shall take you by force and then return you to execution at his hands. But only come to me willingly for this one night and I swear you shall go free at dawn. One night buys you the rest of your life and the means to spend it in honorable comfort. And perhaps, after all, that night will not be so terrible as you fear. . . ."

As he bent to offer the girl his hand, she shrank away, pressing her hennaed fingers together in a desperate gesture of supplication.

"You would rather die than lie with me?" he demanded with pained disbelief. "You would truly rather die?"

The girl collapsed at his feet in a weeping, hysterical heap and Erik turned from her abruptly, clenching his hands around his arms.

"Take the child away," he said.

The eunuch looked at me in astonishment, expecting guidance, and I went hurriedly across the room to speak in a low urgent tone.

"Apparently you have not understood the custom, Erik," I whispered. "The girl is the shah's gift, a personal token of his esteem. To return her in this fashion would be counted an unforgivable breach of etiquette—an insult that would never be forgiven."

"Take her away," he repeated tonelessly. "Tell the shah I have no desire for nubile girls. Tell him I am . . . *incapable* . . . of using such a gift. Damn you, tell him whatever is necessary to ensure that she receives no punishment."

I made a sign to the eunuch, who promptly dragged the weeping, hysterical girl from the room. I knew it would not be possible to buy his silence; the man would accept whatever money I cared to offer and still run blabbing to the harem with this tale. Malicious gossip is one of the few pleasures left to the frustrated, incomplete male. Whatever

I chose to tell the shah when I gave my report, the khanum would most certainly hear the truth.

When we were alone Erik poured a glass of arrack with trembling fingers.

"You had better go," he said wretchedly.

I shook my head. "I would like to talk to you first."

He passed one hand across the mask.

"Yes," he said, "that is a right I cannot deny you—but I should be grateful for a few minutes of privacy now . . . just a few minutes alone . . . you understand?"

I nodded slowly, turned toward the door, and paused to look back again.

"Erik . . . why did you send her away? You desired her and she was yours to use exactly as you pleased. Why risk offending the shah for the sake of a girl who is only a slave?"

He gave a great cry of rage, lifted the table in front of him, and threw it across the room with a force that splintered the legs asunder from the marble top.

"Only a slave . . . only an animal!" he roared. "You asinine Persian dolt—get out of my way quickly, before I forget all that I owe you!"

I shrank back against the wall as he made for the door, pulling it open with a savage force that tore some of the hinges from the jamb.

As I watched him stride away, with breathless apprehension, I knew that anyone who crossed his path tonight would not live long enough to repent of their folly.

My spies in the harem brought the story to me the next day.

Erik had been required to present himself at a window of the torture chamber normally reserved for the khanum's exclusive use, the lady herself choosing to watch from a balcony above, with her attendants. I am told that from this position it was virtually impossible to see into the torture chamber and that it was already commonly understood that today's amusements would take place outside the famous mirrored room.

The khanum looked down upon her favorite through an intricately woven lattice that reduced her figure to an intriguing silhouette.

"I have chosen to honor you today, Erik, with a little entertainment of my own devising," she said softly. "I think you will agree that I have studied your art with some distinction and I would welcome your opinion on my choice of subject. Draw back the curtain on the window."

He pulled the velvet drapes apart and stood for a moment grimly contemplating the sight that met his gaze before turning back to the balcony. The eunuchs say that, when he spoke, the chill of his voice would have frozen the Caspian Sea.

"I see you have learned nothing under my tuition, madame. I find your choice of subject vulgar and tedious, the work of an amateur who has failed to understand her artistic limitations."

There was an awesome silence in the gallery. Those who were watching the khanum closely say that she flinched and flushed crimson beneath the aperture of her veil.

"Vulgar and tedious as my entertainment may be," she spat venomously, "it will still take place entirely as planned."

"Then, madame, I regret it will take place in my absence."

And turning his back upon her rudely, Erik walked out of the harem without waiting to be dismissed.

They say that the entertainment eventually continued in the absence of all spectators, but I knew the death of the little slave girl would not be the end of the matter.

No one else had ever dared to treat the khanum with such contemptuous insolence.

I knew that she would take a terrible revenge upon the author of her public humiliation.

I waited for the order to arrest him, but it did not come, and the only logical reason I could find for this extraordinary forbearance was the shah's reluctance to be parted from a man who was still of use to him. Whatever fate the khanum was brewing for Erik would have to wait until the new palace was completed to the shah's satisfaction.

With the coming of the hot weather Tehran became deserted, as all who were able to took themselves off to their tasteful summer residences in the cooler regions of the Shimran Hills. It was by tradition a quiet and somnolent period in the court year, the last moment imaginable for an attempt on the shah's life; but in August he was attacked while mounting his horse by four Babi dissidents, who had approached him under the pretense of presenting a petition. I can only think that these men were determined to achieve martyrdom, for though the shah was wounded by a pistol shot and thrown from his horse in the confusion, the assassins were quickly overcome by the royal guard, one of them dying in the ensuing scuffle.

Panic ensued. Although there was still a month left of the country season, everyone rushed back to the walls of Tehran, fearing the outbreak of revolution. The Russian mission fled, the British lay low, vast numbers of so-called conspirators were promptly seized, and everyone remotely connected with the Babi sect went in daily fear of his life.

Swift and bloody were the reprisals that followed in the wake of the young shah's grim and merciless mood, and I was obliged to show my loyalty in a manner which filled me with loathing. It was not the hunting down of the conspirators that made me balk—I was well accustomed to such activities—but the horrible fate that awaited these ill-advised extremists. Even Erik showed no enthusiasm for his task when asked to devise a suitable torture to precede the execution of Suleiman Khan, the principal instigator of the conspirator.

The night before the execution Erik came to my apartment and sat fingering the strings of his violin with a restless unease that filled me with foreboding. I knew that the shah had been dissatisfied with his original suggestions—not *enough*, he had snapped angrily, not *sufficient* to teach the people the fate of traitors.

"You disappoint me, sir. I had expected better of your imagination. Perhaps you are losing some of your famous talent for death. I advise you to think again with some speed. . . ."

You disappoint me . . . dangerous words in the ears of any imperial servant! Erik had been given twenty-four hours to rectify his failure and I knew now, as I looked upon his quiet despair, that he had succeeded.

"You have satisfied the shah at last?" I prompted nervously.

"Yes"—Erik plucked a string absently—"he is well pleased with the final . . . design."

Morbid fascination obliged me to ask for details. Quietly, without emotion, he told me that the body of Suleiman Khan was to be pierced in various parts, the holes to be of sufficient width to accommodate lighted camp candles which would be permitted to burn down to the flesh. The traitor would then be dragged through the streets to the place of execution, where his body would be cleft into two neat halves by a hatchet.

We were both silent for a while; I utterly appalled, and he himself finally sickened by the ugly excesses that he had been forced to dredge up from the black vaults of his mind.

I watched him draw his hand caressingly over the polished wood of his violin.

"I am weary of manufacturing these living nightmares," he said slowly, "very weary. Do you have any opium, Nadir?"

I frowned. "You're taking too much opium these days—far too much!"

"Yes, I know," he said grimly. "If I take enough over a sufficient length of time it will kill me—and what a great loss to the world *that* would be!"

"Erik—"

"Don't preach at me"—he sighed—"my mind is like the floor of an abattoir, slimed with blood and filth. Opium draws a beautiful veil across my eyes . . . it lets me forget, for a little while. Now, do you have any or not?"

The laws of hospitality forbidding me to deny the need of any guest, I went silently to a cupboard and returned with the accoutrements of our national vice. There cannot be a man in Persia who is not well acquainted with an opium addict. The rich indulge themselves in comfort while the poor starve and sell the clothes off their backs to support the deadly habit. Opium quiets a troubled soul, bathing its anguish with a soft, insidious balm, and I knew of no man who stood in greater need of its soothing poison than Erik.

I gave him the pipe with its decorated porcelain bowl, the size of an egg, and its slender stem of cherry wood; I gave him the tongs and the glowing coals that would make the precious weed bubble and fume.

"If you want to retain any sanity at all, you have to get out of Persia soon," I said. "You know that, don't you?"

He shrugged. "When the palace is finished, I'll think about it."

"You may not have the leisure to think about it," I warned him.

"The moment the last stone is in place you had better be prepared to take good care of your health. You have more enemies than any other man in the country, and you will not have the shah's protection for much longer. The woman wants your blood, Erik. I tell you, you've burned your boats now, make no mistake of that."

He sucked the sweet smoke deep into his lungs and exhaled slowly on a long sigh.

"Ah, well," he mused with a sort of dreamy, distant sadness, "hell is full of burning boats, did you know that, Nadir? I daresay that's what makes it so bloody hot."

I smiled faintly. Even in the darkest mood he retained that odd, engaging little quirk of humor, an unexpected sense of fun which made him seem strangely human even in the most bizarre of circumstances. Since Reza's death he had been the only person who regularly made me surprise myself with laughter at a time when I had thought I would never learn to laugh again.

Perhaps I did wrong to give him opium and fuel another deadly vice, but I would have had to be a hard man indeed to deny him those fumes of peace.

When the bell in the minaret summoned me to prayer, I left him alone in a familiar cloud of sickly fragrance. Presently my prayers were disturbed by the melancholy playing of his violin, and in spite of my religious obligations I found myself listening transfixed.

All the grief in the world seemed to be distilled through those soft, vibrant notes.

It was as though the devil himself wept teardrops of pure sound.

he rest of the conspirators died in a horrific public spectacle which shocked all the resident European missions.

The thirty executions were personally carried out by the ministers of state, the offenders being variously bayoneted, gouged, and generally cut to pieces before the watching court; but the spectacle was sufficiently unoriginal to exonerate Erik from any part of its devising. Clumsy, disorganized, and entirely lacking in finesse, it bore the stamp of our new prime minister's healthy respect for his own preservation. It was difficult to pinpoint a victim for revenge when the entire government had been obliged to take responsibility for this mass execution. The shah's French physician, when invited to show his loyalty by wielding a knife at the event, excused himself by remarking humorously that he was already professionally responsible for too many deaths to voluntarily increase that number now. The shah had laughed heartily and appeared to accept the excuse with good grace, but shortly afterward the good doctor was served with a glass of poison and died in great agony.

I, fortunately, was considered of too mean a rank to be honored with an invitation to take part. I was relieved of my duties as spy and bodyguard and sent back to Mazanderan to ensure that no Babi activity in the region would disturb the shah in his winter retreat. Consequently I did not see Erik for many months, and the first I knew of the new palace's completion was a command to attend the shah at the Garden of Echoes.

When I arrived I found the vast audience chamber quite empty. The mass of the court was still at Ashraf, the Shah's presence here today being in the nature of a passing visit for the purpose of inspection. For all its palatial exterior the building was really only an elaborate hunting box, a play pavilion designed to amuse and entertain its royal master. Right from the beginning there had never been any intention of housing the entire court. Only the favored few would ever be invited to attend the king of kings in this whimsical folly, and those who were invited to do so would do well to avoid unguarded words in private conversation. Erik had warned me that the place was not called the Garden of Echoes for nothing.

When the shah appeared abruptly at my side, I was so startled that I dropped the dossier containing details of my loyal activities during the preceding months. He had not entered the room through any of the doors upon which I had been keeping a wary eye, and it seemed to me that he must have walked straight through the wall behind me.

Nothing could have delighted him more than my very genuine stupefaction.

"Ah, Daroga!" he said with the gloating glee of a schoolboy, "I see that I have startled you. An amusing little device, is it not?"

"Most amusing, Imperial Majesty."

I rose from my knees in accordance with his gesture and stared in dismay at my documents, which were now hopelessly muddled. I knew that the entire palace had been riddled with secret passages and trapdoors for the shah's exclusive use. Personally I considered the whole thing very childish, a devilish game of hide-and-seek which would inevitably result in many wonderful tragedies. It was a sad waste of Erik's talent. All he had wanted to do was build something beautiful, but at every step of construction he had been dogged by his patron's insatiable demand for novelty and diversion. I knew that the trapdoors and secret passages had formed no part of Erik's original design; his wonder of architecture had been reduced, at the end of the day, to an elaborate toy designed to please a vicious little boy. Its very real beauty was entirely lost upon the shah.

"How do you care for my new house of pleasure?" continued His Majesty. "Would you say that it was unique of its kind—*truly* unique?"

I hastened to assure him that it was. In spite of his glee there was something querulous and even petulant about his mood which alarmed me. He was like a spoiled child who had been forced to wait overlong for a promised gift, determined to find fault because reality could not quite compare to his dream.

"The secret passages are very cramped and airless," he complained suddenly, "quite uncomfortable in fact. I was obliged to remove my hat."

I did my best to look sympathetic. Personally I considered the greatest miracle of this building was the fact that Erik had somehow managed to keep his hands off his master's neck during the course of its construction.

"There cannot be another monarch in the world who possesses a palace such as this," I assured him fatuously. "You have a great jewel of architecture and a servant who is truly without equal in this world."

The shah frowned and flicked a speck of masonry dust from his voluminous skirts.

"As he has served me, so may he serve others. They say his fame has already spread to Constantinople and that the sultan seeks to lure him from my service."

I felt my mouth turn dry with apprehension.

"I'm sure Your Majesty may quite safely ignore such malicious rumors. Erik's loyalty—"

The shah laughed abruptly.

"Do you think me foolish enough to believe in that man's loyalty? He owes allegiance to no one, as I believe you know very well. Erik is entirely without scruple of any kind. He is a murderer—and worse than that, he is a thief."

"A thief?" I echoed uneasily. "Surely a man of such honestly acquired wealth need not stoop to theft."

"I believe that he steals purely for amusement, Daroga—to test his own powers of legerdemain. That matter of the cat's collar was never resolved, as you know. And cut glass has been found in the Peacock Throne—*glass!* There was a time when such shameless arrogance amused me, but the khanum advises me of his insolence and I find I am increasingly inclined to agree with her judgment of him. A man such as he is not to be trusted with state secrets."

The shah turned away and began to stride restlessly up and down the room. I did not dare to argue with him, and after a moment he turned to look at me thoughtfully.

"I am relieved to find you do not speak in his defense. There have been moments in this past year, Daroga, when I have been afraid your own loyalty was not above reproach."

I prostrated myself at his feet, in the proscribed act of self-abasement, my forehead coming to rest against the tip of his riding boot.

"Get up, get up!" he said testily. "I have devised the perfect means for you to demonstrate your loyalty to me now."

I raised my head fearfully. Allah, what was this?

"It may interest you to know that the khanum suggests I should have his eyes put out."

Yes, I thought . . . a fitting punishment for his crime against her. What use are eyes to a man who willfully refuses to see a woman's wretched lust?

"But on reflection," continued the shah coolly, "I am not convinced that such an act would necessarily extinguish his gifts and render him useless to another monarch. I wish to preserve the unique quality of this palace . . . he shall build for no other king. Every man who worked upon this site is to be put to death—including its creator. You will arrest Erik tomorrow night when he returns to Ashraf."

"Tomorrow?" I echoed dimly.

Again the shah frowned.

"Tonight he completes a minor alteration that I have required to my private chamber, and I do not wish him to be disturbed. Tomorrow I have no further use for him."

Seating himself on the dais he glanced critically around the audience chamber, but evidently found no further cause for complaint that would have gained Erik another night's reprieve.

"I shall leave the means of execution in your capable hands, Daroga . . . but be quite sure that no damage is inflicted upon the skull. It is my wish that his head should be preserved with embalming fluids and mounted on a pillar in the Gulistan. The sultan and the emir will both be sick with jealousy to hear of my new ornament."

I looked at the floor, terrified that my expression would betray my disgust.

"Well," demanded the shah brusquely, "are my instructions not sufficiently clear?"

"They are perfectly clear, O Shadow of God." I made an elaborate obeisance and backed away to the door.

"Daroga!"

"Your Majesty?"

"Instruct your men to search his apartments very carefully after the arrest. I fully expect that collar to be found hidden among his possessions."

Once more I bowed my head in acknowledgment.

I had twenty-four hours to make my arrangements.

Shortly before dawn my men surrounded Erik's apartment at Ashraf and I entered his room alone.

He was startled.

"It is customary to knock first before entering," he said rather shortly. "What the devil are you doing here at this hour? I did not invite you."

"This is not a social visit," I said loudly, allowing my voice to carry into the corridor beyond. "I come here in my official capacity, as chief of police in this region, to arrest you for treason. You must prepare to leave at once."

He began to laugh, but when I made a violent sign for him to be silent, he was suddenly quiet, watching me curiously.

"We don't have much time," I whispered. "Find whatever you have of portable value and give it to me quickly."

He leaned over to touch a hidden spring in the wall and immediately a stone moved to one side, revealing a small cavity from which he took a casket.

"I have been working all night on the shah's personal commission, you find me about to bathe." His voice carried effortlessly out to the ears of my waiting men and I saw with relief that he had accepted the rules of this desperate game.

"You will be permitted a few minutes in which to dress," I said.

He handed me the casket, and when I opened it I found a veritable dragon's hoard of treasures within. There were precious gems of every description, some official rewards for his services, but many others quite plainly appropriated. I recognized a great diamond that had once belonged to Mirza Taqui Khan and, lying on the bottom of the box, the missing cat's collar with a fortune in jewels winking in the torchlight.

I looked at him accusingly and he gave me a graceful, almost humorous little shrug.

"You know my weakness for beautiful things."

I sighed as I tipped the contents of the casket into a leather bag and fastened it safely beneath my coat. He wished always to surround himself with beauty and I knew that a diamond or a butterfly was of equal value in his eyes. I had to go back to the cavity in the wall to find the money that he had stuffed carelessly at the back and forgotten. When I had emptied the secret compartment I gestured for him to close it.

"Give me your hands," I muttered. "They will expect to see you bound."

For a moment, as he stiffened in anger, I thought his insane pride would ruin everything, that he would sooner die than suffer himself to be tied and constrained like an animal.

"Give me your hands," I repeated, with authority. "Erik—it is the only way."

He looked at the rope with a fear and loathing that showed me a grim shadow of his past, and as I passed the rough, fibrous binding around his wrists, his fists clenched, as though in an effort to restrain some primitive instinct to resist. I felt that I was binding some wild, mythological beast; only the trust which had slowly grown up between us prevented him from turning on me now and rending me to pieces with savage claws.

His wrists were so incredibly thin that I bound them cautiously, fearing their deceptively fragile appearance, and as I did so I noticed that the flesh was covered with old scar tissue.

"How did you come by such injuries?" I asked curiously. "Was it that window in Tehran?"

He shook his head briefly, still staring at his bindings as though he could not quite believe he had permitted this thing to be done.

"I broke a mirror once," he said. "A well-meaning and very misguided lady bound up my wrists and saved my life."

"Your mother?"

He looked up at me, and something in his expression made me shiver.

"My mother would have let me bleed to death," he said stonily. "And who is to say she would not have been right in that?"

I fastened the rope in silence, once more struck dumb by the bleak tragedy of his existence, and when I had finished I went to the door and called my men into the room.

"Search the apartment and make an inventory of all you find." I turned back to Erik, who stood with his head bent, staring at the floor. "You, sir, will come with me now."

We rode away from the palace in the light of the rising sun, I leading Erik's horse, and my deliberately depleted escort riding on ahead to inform the prison of our imminent arrival. When the last horse was out of sight, I leaned over, cut the ropes that bound him, and handed him the two leather bags that I had secreted on my person.

"Go," I said simply. "Follow the coastal road and get out of Persia while you still can. All I can give you is a few hours' start before the shah's men begin to search for you."

He sat very still on the horse, staring at me.

"How will you explain this?"

I shrugged. "I shall say that you used your magical skills to free yourself and attacked me when I was unprepared."

"You will be punished," he persisted gravely, "even if the shah believes your tale. And if he does not believe it—"

"That is my concern"

"Why are you doing this?" he demanded suddenly.

I looked away down the empty road.

"My son would have wished you to live. . . . All that I do tonight, I do in memory of him."

"Oh, God," he whispered brokenly. "You will never be reconciled, will you? You will never forgive."

I turned in the saddle and looked at him squarely.

"There is nothing to forgive," I said. "You gave him a beautiful, painless death. . . . I am reconciled and my soul is at peace. It is time to consider your soul now, Erik."

He made an impatient gesture. "Your faith teaches that infidels have no souls, no appointed place in paradise."

"Your conscience, then," I countered. "I think you have a conscience, whatever you may like to believe—and tonight I appoint myself as its keeper. Wherever you go and whatever you do in the future, you may consider yourself answerable to me. That is the price you must pay in return for your life. There must be no more wanton murders."

"Oh, really," he scoffed, "and what is to stop me breaking this ridiculous bargain of yours whenever I choose?"

"I do not believe you would break your word to me, Erik."

"What makes you think I'm going to *give* my word, let alone keep it? Killing is like opium, Nadir . . . a bad habit . . . an addiction."

"Any addiction can be overcome when there is a will for conquest," I said steadily. "Besides, I'm not offering you a choice—this is an ultimatum. If I don't hear from you now what I wish to hear, I shall simply deliver you for execution after all, you have *my* word on that! And remember, my men are not yet too far away to hear a pistol shot."

"What exactly are you asking me to swear!" he asked warily.

"I'm not a sentimental fool." I sighed. "I know what your life has been—and I know there will inevitably be occasions when you have no alternative but to strike first to save yourself. But there is a world of difference between killing in self-defense and killing for perverted pleasure. All I am asking is that you acknowledge that difference and abide by my request. Now—will you give me your word?"

He did not speak, but after a moment's hesitation he held out his hand to me and I met it unhesitatingly with my own. His grip was cool and strong and I had no desire to shy away from it with revulsion and dread. I let my hand lie in his until he chose to break that moment of contact, the symbol of our simple, sterile friendship.

"Follow the coastline and keep to the undergrowth. It's a dangerous path—you must beware of quicksand and countless other hazards— but you dare not take an inland road. By tomorrow the shah's men will be searching all known routes that lead out of the country."

He sighed. "And you, my poor fool, will be in prison awaiting execution in my stead. Do you honestly think me so devoid of human feeling that I will simply leave you to that fate?"

"You need have no fear for my life," I said. "I'm not quite the innocent at intrigue, you know, I have made my plans. The body of a Babi dissident will be left upon the Caspian shore, dressed in your cloak and mask. By the time it is found, scavengers will have rendered it identifiable by no other means. I am convinced the shah will be sufficiently satisfied to spare my life. And should my estate be forfeited for negligence—well, you have taught me to grow weary of Persian ways. Perhaps I shall go to Europe and settle in a country where queens no longer amuse themselves with torture chambers."

"Even in Europe you will need to eat," he said grimly.

From within his bag of treasures he produced a handful of precious gems and held them out to me, pausing for a moment, on reflection, to remove the huge diamond from his palm.

"I suppose I should not burden your squeamish conscience with that," he sighed. "I can't pretend it was very honestly acquired. But the rest you may quite safely take—there is nothing there that need cost you any sleep."

"Erik," I protested, "this is not—"

"Take them!" he said sharply. "I have already agreed to your damned eccentric terms, have I not? At least permit me to make one gesture of myself toward my keeper . . . and my friend."

We were both silent then, stunned by the harsh simplicity of those last two words. I knew that friendship was an alien emotion to him, as frightening, perhaps, as it was unfamiliar. Friendship intruded uneasily on his existence, demanding responsibility, accountability, and loyalty. But I did not believe he would lightly cast aside the pledge he had made to me.

Removing the mask and cloak, he handed them to me and I suddenly saw that there were tears glistening unshed in his mismatched eyes.

"Take care of yourself, Nadir," he said softly. "Take very great care. . . . Your tiresome health has become very dear to me."

I think I smiled; it was suddenly impossible to speak.

I sat and watched him ride away until he was only a dim shadow. And then I spoke to the empty expanse that lay between us, in the faultless French he had so painstakingly taught me over the years of our association.

"*Au revoir, mon ami,*" I said sadly.

And tucking the mask and cloak safely out of sight in a saddlebag, I turned my horse's head toward Sari and rode on alone.

Erik
1856-1881

y mind has touched the farthest horizons of mortal imagination and reaches ever outward to embrace infinity. There is no knowledge beyond my comprehension, no art or skill upon this entire planet that lies beyond the mastery of my hand. And yet, like Faust, I look in vain, I learn in vain. . . . For as long as I live, no woman will ever look on me in love.

Now at last I have found the courage to turn away from the foolish echoes of human gladness. Optimism, blind hope, pathetic yearnings . . . I have let them all go, one by one, and I am as content as I shall ever be on this earth, in my peaceful solitude.

My kingdom lies in eternal darkness, many feet below the level of the Parisian streets outside, shrouded in the chill silence of the grave. Darkness and silence have been my companions since the day I chose to turn my back upon the world of men and create an empire that was solely mine.

From the moment of my birth my destiny was to be alone.

But it took me more than forty years to accept that harsh and unrelenting fact—to understand where peace and resignation lay. . . .

I was not at peace when I arrived in Belgium in the spring of 1856.

For three years I had traveled aimlessly once more through Europe, retracing old steps and old haunts like some curious pilgrim, seeking out whatever architectural monuments I had missed as a wandering boy. I would sketch at dawn in the deserted streets and return to my lodgings before the early-morning vendors began to sell their wares. And there I would stay, shunning the light of day, until the sun sank beyond the horizon and it was once more possible to step out into the poorly lit thoroughfares without exciting instant attention.

I was no longer obliged to prostitute my talents in order to eat. The years in Persia had made me wealthy, rich enough to indulge my interests and my increasing aversion to the human race; there was no longer any grim necessity to entertain gawking crowds with the skill of my fingers and the horror of my face.

My taste for death, already severely jaded by those grievous excesses in Persia, had been abruptly curtailed by an oath which I could not ignore. Nadir's voice haunted me all across Asia, making me restless and uneasy in the Orient, where the political assassin is much in demand and the ending of a life all too easily accomplished, with no questions asked.

I had learned to control my black and violent moods, first with opium and later, in Belgium, with morphine. I abandoned an opium pipe for fear of damaging my voice, and in that surge of star-spangled euphoria, the result of my first experiment with a needle, I began work upon the opera that I conceived as my maximum opus.

I called it: *Don Juan Triumphant.*

I was beginning to grow very cynical. . . .

For months I drifted through Belgium, just as I had drifted through the rest of Europe, never staying anywhere long for fear of hostility and reprisal. Antwerp, Ghent, Brussels . . . and finally—lured by the soft, familiar lilt of my native language—to Mons. How good it was to hear French spoken everywhere. I had learned many tongues, but nothing compared in my ears with the seductive vowels and lovely, rolling consonants of the most beautiful language in the world. I felt a sudden longing to settle in this eminently civilized land and build myself a house.

The back streets of Mons revealed a man entirely suited to my rather singular needs; susceptible to my voice and willing to do my bidding without asking tiresome questions—a man I could control entirely, simply by exercising my larynx. I had learned by now that such men were to be found in most crowds—men who turned at my first words to stare with an odd, glazed intensity that appeared to exclude the mask. I have no idea what freak arrangement of my vocal cords enabled me to reduce certain people to a state of trancelike obedience—regrettably, it is not possible to perform dissections upon oneself! But I regarded my voice as a weapon, as lethal, in its way, as the Punjab lasso, and I never scrupled to use it whenever the opportunity was offered.

Jules Bernard had completed his apprenticeship as a rough-mason, and as soon as I was certain that he would be of use to me, he became my well-paid slave, handling transactions that had become distasteful to me as I increasingly embraced reclusive habits.

Had I been satisfied with my house, our relationship would no doubt have terminated with the placing of the last stone; but long before we reached roof level I was disillusioned with my design. Jules, instructed to handle the sale on completion of the building, was immediately besieged with half a dozen truly ridiculous offers.

"Perhaps you might think of contracting, sir," he suggested tentatively.

My first impulse was to laugh . . . and then I paused.

Why not?

I was still young. . . . I badly needed occupation, even if I no longer needed money, something to take my mind from a composition which was consuming me steadily, from within, like a cancer. *Don Juan Triumphant* was eating me alive. I needed to lock the score away in a chest now and forget all the dangerous and unthinkable things it represented to me.

Five years later Jules—then a married man with three small children tumbling around his modest rented quarters—was running a thriving business for me. The service I offered was unique in many ways. It was customary for an architect to arrange contracts, not to build himself. It was also customary for an architect to meet his clients, but this I steadfastly refused to do. My terms were so eccentric, it is a wonder the business survived at all, but Jules revealed an unexpected capacity for smoothing the feathers of ruffled customers. It became fashionable to have a house designed and built by the mysterious, elusive architect who merely signed his plans *Erik;* who had been known to refuse a commission rather than grant a personal consultation. In short, I was, yet again, a very successful novelty, for which the wealthy were prepared to pay quite handsomely.

After five years of this existence I discovered that I was bored to tears building glorified boxes to house fat, complacent businessman and their even fatter and more complacent wives. A terrible restlessness was growing steadily upon me, a restlessness that seemed to be compounded partly by frustration and partly by an emotion I simply could not fathom . . . an urge to return to the land of my birth, which was as primitive and inexplicable as the instinct which drives a salmon to return to its native stream.

"I'm going away for a while," I told Jules abruptly one morning. "There is nothing here you can't handle, is there?"

"No, monsieur," he said nervously—even after all this time he was not at ease in my presence. "Will you be away for long?"

"I cannot say."

I would have left the mason's yard without another word, but he suddenly ran after me, almost with panic.

"Monsieur . . . at least tell me where you may be reached—I may need you!"

No one in this world needs me . . . no one ever will. . . .

"You will manage," I said quietly. "I trust your competence, and it's in your interest to keep this business solvent in my absence. Tell me . . . have you engaged a tutor for your eldest son yet?"

"Monsieur," he protested, "it is beyond my means."

"You have access to the accounts," I said irritably. "Why haven't you taken what you needed? The child is intelligent and deserves to be educated. He should be old enough now to learn to read and write. See to it without delay!"

He stared at me in bewilderment.

"I—I would never steal from you," he stammered.

"Then you are a fool," I said. "You have a fine family. Take whatever you require for their welfare and there will be no questions asked of you."

He was silent for a moment, his long, thin, rather anxious features set into puzzled lines. Again I made to leave and a second time he prevented me.

"Where are you going?" he demanded with a sudden touch of fear.

I stared past him into the dark street, with unseeing eyes.

"I'm going to Boscherville," I said.

I stood at last outside the garden gate of the old house, staring . . . remembering. . . .

So many times, in my imagination, had I razed this building to the ground, that I was shocked to find it still standing.

How dare it stand there in all its quaint, old-worldly charm, housing a family who lived happily unaware of the grief I had suffered behind those ivy-covered walls. The tears I had shed in that attic bedroom! The lonely terror and fear of being shut away from the world forever! *I hated this house!* I wanted to blow it and all its attendant memories from the face of the earth!

I knew now why I had come back to Boscherville—it was to remove this abominable desecration from the landscape of Normandy forever.

There was a light burning in an upstairs window, annoying evidence of peaceful occupation. I could not simply set fire to this building without rousing the wretched inhabitants from their beds. No more murders, I had promised Nadir; and even had I not promised, it would still have seemed a mean and shameful wickedness to kill innocent children sleeping in their beds.

As I thought of the children, my hand closed around a wad of thousand-franc notes. These people would be homeless once I had gratified my morbid urge for destruction—and no one knew better than I the fate that awaited the destitute and the homeless. I would drive no French child down the dark paths of decadence which had swallowed my own youth. I was willing to pay generously for this satisfaction. Let them go away and talk for the rest of their lives of the madman who had paid for the privilege of burning their house to the ground. . . .

I tethered my white mare to a tree on the opposite side of the road, and she whickered her indignation at finding herself bound. She had carried me across the plains of Asia without a single night spent under such restraint, and for me to deny her freedom now was to abuse the perfect trust that lay between us. Her eyes reproached me for the insult, but I dared not leave her to wander free this time. Fire is the greatest terror in the world to a horse, and a bolt of panic from her now would almost certainly cost me my life.

Taking a pistol from my cloak, I hammered three times on the front door and waited beneath the wooden canopy, secure in the knowledge that I could not be seen from the bedroom windows above. Anyone wishing to satisfy his curiosity would be obliged to open the door. And since there was not a man on this earth that I could not overpower with my freak strength and my singular knowledge of armed combat, I waited with a calm that was almost indifference. There was a tub of flowers growing by the front door and I reached down absently to remove a few strangling weeds that had gained a hold. It always annoyed me to see a fragile bloom struggling for space. . . .

A light showed suddenly beneath the door and I heard the familiar sound of the old bolt sliding back. A rash and foolhardy householder this, who really deserved to die for his stupidity. . . . I stood back in the shadows as the door opened, curious to see how far this incredible recklessness was going to extend. Small wonder the world is full of rogues such as myself when idiots like this invite villainy every day!

A candle wavered out over the step and I froze in horror to find that this careless, ill-advised occupant was a woman I would have recognized anywhere, in spite of the gulf of years that lay between us.

And when she turned to look at me with wide, staring eyes and one hand stealing defensively to her throat, her look of aghast recognition was also unmistakable.

"Holy Virgin!" she gasped. *"Erik!"*

It is strange how the deeply etched habits of childhood emerge from the mind in moments of shock. I found myself automatically giving a stiff little bow, and saying with cool formality, just as I had been taught to say all those years ago: "Good evening, Mademoiselle Perrault, I hope I find you well."

Both hands flew to her mouth now. She gave a strangled little sob and burst into tears as she gestured wildly for me to follow her into the house.

I went with slow, leaden-hearted dread into the drawing room, but was spared the meeting I now feared above all else. Apart from ourselves the room was empty. The relief was so immense, the disappointment so acute, that I had to sink into the fireside chair for fear of falling. My heart was pounding so wildly, I was afraid she must hear it, and I glanced at the brandy decanter on the chiffonier with intense longing. But she was too harassed to see my need and I could not bring myself to commit the gross incivility of asking a lady for spirits. It was bad enough to have sat without invitation in her presence. I gripped my hands on the wooden arms of my chair and struggled for composure.

"Where is my mother?" I asked uneasily.

She began to cry harder than ever.

"You must know where she lives now," I persisted. "You need not be afraid, I shall not go there . . . but I should like to know."

Again the wildly fluttering hands brushing ineffectually at the graying, carroty hair, the familiar quivering lips set in a face that always reminded me of a startled rabbit's.

"Oh, God," she whispered, "I thought you knew. . . . I thought that was why you had come back. Erik . . . your mother died three days ago."

Still I sat there gripping the chair and willing away the threatening veil of darkness. Months I had spent trying to suppress that inexplicably fierce impulse to return here! Drawn by the need to set fire to this house, had I come home, driven by a primitive intuition, merely to put a torch to my mother's funeral pyre?

She was here in this house and she was dead.

And all I could think of was the fact that I should now be able to kiss her cold cheek at last . . . that she would never be able to shrink from my touch again.

"Perhaps you would like to see her," Marie suggested nervously.

I ignored a suggestion which rocked the foundations of my questionable sanity and continued to stare into the fire.

"Why did she come back?" I demanded. "She hated this house as much as I did. . . . Why did she come back here, of all places? Did he die . . . was that it . . . did he die?"

Marie looked at me with confusion.

"Erik . . . your mother never left this house."

I clenched my fists on the chair.

"Are you telling me that they lived here openly together—that they dared to raise more children beneath this godforsaken roof? They were to go away, I heard him say that! After the marriage they were to go away where no one knew her. . . ."

I was shouting now and Marie's face puckered into folds of extreme distress, but I could not be calm. The thought that I might have half brothers or sisters here in the very village which had driven me away all those years ago hurt more than I could ever have imagined possible. I could not bear to think what cruel children would have told them of their monstrous sibling; I could not bear to think of their shame and anger . . . brothers and sisters, who had never seen me, and yet must have wished me unborn every day of their taunted lives.

How dared they stay here!

"How dared they!" The roar of my voice seemed to rattle the old oak beams in the ceiling, and Marie shrank back in terror.

"There was no marriage, Erik," she stammered. "Dr. Barye went back to Paris a few weeks after you disappeared and your mother never saw him again. She never remarried. She lived here in this house alone, until the last few months of her life, when I came to nurse her."

I was silenced, numbed and made utterly hopeless by this terrible revelation.

I suddenly saw it had all been for nothing—my flight from this house and all the horrors that followed, as I floundered deeper and deeper into a quagmire of unending, self-perpetuating wickedness. God wanted nothing from the abomination he had created in some careless moment of aberration . . . even that childish act of sacrifice was now reduced to a bitter mockery. There was nothing left to separate my soul from those of the eternally damned.

And the siblings I had conjured up in panic were just illusions . . . just illusions. I had no brother after all; I was quite alone in this empty, echoing world now . . . there was no remembered tie of blood . . . nothing! Nothing!

In silence I rose and went upstairs to my mother's room.

Candles burned on either side of the old beeswaxed mahogany bedstead, the flames leaping and flickering in the draft from the open window. This, then, was the light I had seen from the road outside . . . a light shining in the darkness to lead me home at last.

Slowly, very slowly, I turned back the sheet that covered her and stared incredulously, for the waxen face revealed on the pillow was the face of a stranger, old and altered beyond belief.

Time ravages beauty and preserves plainness. I would have known Marie Perrault in any crowd, but this withered woman on the bed I would have passed in the street without any recognition.

Death had made her ugly, shriveled the flesh from her cheekbones and sunk her eyes so deeply beneath her brow that there was now, by some last, bitter twist of fate, a real physical resemblance between us.

And as I looked at her, I suddenly understood her revulsion at last—because now I shared it!

I felt no anger or grief as I looked down upon her . . . nothing except a disgust which enabled me to forgive every act of cruelty that she had ever shown me.

Yes . . . I forgave her everything in that moment; but I turned away without touching the hands that lay stiffly folded on her breast.

I did not kiss her, now that I had the opportunity.

I knew that she would not have wished it.

And I no longer felt any desire to do so.

eturning to the drawing room, I found Mademoiselle Perrault sitting by the fire with a little sewing lying unattended on her lap. I had made the cruel assumption that *mademoiselle* was the still the correct form of address and nothing in her sad, dowdy form suggested that I had been mistaken. She got up hurriedly when I entered the room, clutching the material against her withered breast, as though it were some kind of shield against my presence; I found I could only admire the noble effort she was making to control her old instinctive terror of me.

Even as a small child I had been aware that she was afraid of me—it used to amuse me to see her twitch with nervousness whenever I came near. And yet in spite of her timidity she had always shown me kind-

ness. I remembered her picking slivers of glass from my fingers on the
evening of my fifth birthday . . . and once a long time before that, I
remembered her arguing with my mother, on my behalf. . . .

They didn't often argue; no one won arguments with my mother,
certainly not Mademoiselle Perrault, who always looked as though she
wouldn't know how to say boo to a goose. But that night she was angry
enough to have raised her voice above my mother's, and I, like the
obnoxious child that I was, had crept down from the attic to listen
outside the closed door.

"I don't know how you can begin to think of doing such a thing,
Madeleine! He won't be four until the summer!"

"Oh, for heaven's sake!" my mother had retorted irritably. "I'll be
back from Rouen by nightfall. I'll lock him safely in his room with the
dog, he'll be all right. He knows how to use a chamber pot, and I'll
leave him food and drink—not that he'll eat it! I don't know why
you're making all this fuss, no one's likely to run off with him, for
God's sake!"

"Well, I don't think it's right, Madeleine, I really don't . . . a
child of that age to be left alone for so many hours. . . ."

The upshot of this curious conversation was that Mademoiselle Perrault came to look after me for the day while my Mother was in
Rouen.

I remember it very well. With my mother's iron hand removed I
proceeded to behave like a perfect little beast. I swung on the curtain
rails and frightened her half to death by hanging upside down from
the top of the banister. It's a good job we didn't have a chandelier. . . .

"Don't do that, Erik, dear!" she said with a helplessness that only
made me swing with more vigor and daring. She always called me *Erik
dear*, as though it were my given name. I used to think it was very
funny and mimic her behind her back, until my mother grew angry
and beat me for the impertinence.

"Please don't do that, Erik, you know your mama would be very
cross if she saw you."

But Mama wasn't there, that was the whole point; Mama wasn't
there and under the timid supervision of this mouse-faced lady I was
suddenly free to do exactly what I wanted.

While she was washing dishes in the kitchen, I went into the drawing room and climbed up to the top of the glass-windowed cabinet. There was a box of chocolates there, a very big box, left over from Christmas; I took off the pink ribbon and Sasha and I ate the lot between us.

A little later Sasha was sick. I was feeling decidedly odd myself by that point and before I knew what was going to happen, there were two horrid brown messes on the beautiful carpet that my mother prized so highly.

Sasha at once slunk under the table, with her tail between her legs, and I hastily followed her example. I began to cry then, for I knew that when my mother came home I would be beaten for this most heinous crime while Sasha—poor, poor Sasha—would be put out in the snow, in disgrace, for the rest of the night.

We were still huddled together under the table when Mademoiselle Perrault found us.

"Don't cry," she said kindly, when I was finally persuaded to crawl out from my hiding place. "I shall clean everything up and your mama need know nothing about it."

I remember staring at her dumbfounded.

"Aren't you going to tell her?" I whispered in disbelief. "Aren't you going to tell her how naughty I've been?"

"No, dear," she said, getting down on her hands and knees with a bucket of soapy water. "That can be our little secret, can't it? Now, why don't you be a good boy and find me some old newspapers?"

I never put another spider on her shawl after that. . . .

This nervous, anxious, well-meaning lady had taught me to respect all members of the weaker sex. She had dropped one pearl of purity into my soul, and even now, after all these years, it was still there, displacing a little of the dank, disgusting sludge of depravity. I had done many terrible things, but I had never harmed a helpless woman.

Not all women were helpless, of course. There was the khanum. . . . God knows she came closer to Allah in my presence than she ever guessed on more than one occasion! I suppose my senses were deceiving me, but there were times when I honestly began to wonder what that bitch really wanted from me. Times when I almost believed . . . but that is absurd, I flatter myself! And yet . . . perhaps there really are women like Javert, with a taste for the bizarre and the obscene. I often wondered what it would have been like to bury myself in all that warm pulsating wickedness, prior to killing her. . . .

But by and large they were unworthy prey, women, fragile creatures who already seemed created to endure too much suffering; cruel husbands, childbirth, and early death. . . . And it's really very difficult to kill someone when all your inner instincts would oblige you to take off your hat first!

"Are you still afraid of spiders, mademoiselle?" I demanded suddenly.

"Oh . . . yes!" She gave a nervous little laugh and edged away from me nearer the hearth. "Such a silly, childish thing, was it not—your mother never had any patience with me over it. Oh, dear . . . I should have been prepared for this. After all, I placed an advertisement in the *Presse* as soon as I realized that—that she did not have every long. I hoped against hope that you would see it, but it seemed such a unlikely chance, after all these years, even allowing for the circulation of the *Presse*. . . . After all, we did not even know if you were still in France, let alone Paris. She often spoke of you, Erik. . . ."

I turned away abruptly. Did she think me a child still to be comforted by tinsel fantasies and pretty lies? My mother had hated and feared me. Why pretend now that it had been otherwise?

"When is the funeral?" I asked harshly.

"Tomorrow," Marie whispered. "There won't be many mourners . . . just a few acquaintances that she made after . . . well . . . *after*. . . ." She spread her hands helplessly and I nodded curtly to signify my understanding. "I think perhaps it would not be wise—"

"I have no intention of attending the event," I assured her, and hardened though I was, her palpable relief hurt me. I did not need to be told what scandalized horror would attend my presence in the graveyard. The last service I could render to my mother was to allow her to be laid to rest with the dignity that had been so dear to her.

But at least I could play my requiem for her. . . .

Sitting down at the old piano, I quickly lost myself in the music, my fingers caressing the keyboard with ecstasy. Music was the secret sanctuary of my soul; music was my god, the only master I would ever serve again. I wished I could build a monument to its glory, a shrine where I could worship and revere. It would be a fitting act of homage to raise a mausoleum dedicated to the splendors of harmony and lyric, a wonderful fusion of my deepest creative urges. Something vast and resplendent . . . something on a scale never before conceived . . . an opera house perhaps. . . .

My mother had often spoken of the need for a definitive Parisian Opera House. Like most people who have failed to realize a childhood's ambition she had considered herself something of an authority on the subject; and certainly public interest in a permanent Opera House for the capital dated back over a hundred years. More people than my mother had felt heatedly on the subject and Professor Guizot's strong opinions on optimum location and auditorium shape had informed much of my studies under his guidance. Delighted by my natural interest in his pet obsession—I had learned to love opera at a very early age—he had consequently directed me from the works of Blondel to those of de Chaumont, Damun, Patte, and Dumont. Those last months before I ran away I was so deluged by contradictory material that I am sure that even then I could have put together a reasonably lucid exposition on the need for a topologically expressive exterior. I had never been to Paris, but the professor had shown me extensive street plans and once amused me by entering a furious dispute with my mother over the relative site merits of the Place de la Concorde over the Butte des Moulins. I remember that he was well and truly routed by my mother's passionate indignation.

"Ladies," he told me later, polishing his steamy glasses when we were alone once more in the dining room, "are regrettably incapable of arguing a point without resorting to emotion. You may take it from me, Erik, that the Butte des Moulins offers a far superior situation."

"Arrogant man!" snapped my mother when the professor had gone. "The Butte des Moulins will never in a thousand years be considered an elegant quarter of Paris. It would be an utter social travesty to build there. The Place de la Concorde is the *obvious* solution!"

Personally I had considered they were both wrong, but I was far too well brought up to say so at the time. I would have placed the Opera in the very center of Paris, as befitted a great monument which would inevitably become the social hub of the city. The Boulevard des

Capucines seemed to me the obvious place—but no doubt the arguments would go on for another fifty years before a decision was finally made. . . .

I became aware of Marie hovering uneasily at my side, and I stopped playing abruptly.

"Don't stop," she said quietly. "That requiem is your own composition, is it not? Your mother—"

"Would have dearly loved to hear it played?" I sneered. "Mademoiselle, I outgrew my need for fairy tales many years ago."

Suddenly Marie rushed to the cabinet in the corner of the room and began to pull out sheets of my old childish designs.

"There was never a day when she did not think of you, Erik. Look, do you see? She kept everything—everything that reminded her of you."

I stared at the papers tumbling out on the floor. They proved nothing to me except that my mother was a notorious hoarder who could throw nothing away. We had lived entirely surrounded by relics of the past: Grandfather's architectural library . . . Grandmother's English jewelry . . . looking at the hearth now I could see a stack of newspapers that must be many weeks old.

Marie was ferreting in the drawers, bringing out a wad of legal-looking documents which she thrust into my hands.

"The deeds of the house, details of your grandfather's stock investments," she explained feverishly. "They were all to be left for you in a bank vault in Rouen. It's there in her will if you don't believe me."

Guilt, I thought, with a flicker of remorse for my heartlessness . . . guilt is surely the saddest of all human emotions. But guilt is not love; it is a fire that consumes without giving warmth to those embraced in its tangled coils. Poor Mother. . . .

Wordlessly I gathered up my old musical scores and designs and threw them on the fire. Then, while Marie stood with her handkerchief pressed against her mouth, I bent mechanically to gather up the newspapers and send them the same way.

I never read newspapers. I had no interest in the present; only the past and the future excited my imagination these days. The antics of the Empress Eugénie were no concern of mine. . . .

My God, some of these papers were six months old and turning yellow. But one was recent enough . . . thirtieth of May, 1861. My eyes were drawn inexorably to the leading story:

Garnier Wins Commission for Paris Opera House.

I stood up with the paper in my hand, devouring the article with numbed outrage. Charles Garnier, aged thirty-six, winner of the public competition held for the design of the new Paris Opera. . . .

Public competition?

I wheeled around on Marie.

"What do you know of this?" I demanded, taking an aggressive step toward her. "What do you know of it?"

She didn't know much, but it was sufficient to supplement the article and fuel my uncontainable fury. Architects, both professional and amateur, had been required to submit their designs anonymously in that competition, their names and addresses in a sealed envelope. . . .

I crumpled the newspaper in my hand and walked away from her quickly before my hands fastened around her neck in sheer ungovernable frustration. The initial round of the competition had opened in December . . . and it had been December when I was first struck with that devastating feeling of restless unease. Lacking the means to interpret my premonition . . . intuition . . . whatever it was . . . I had let precious months slide by. Because my own supreme indifference to the affairs of men prevented me from purchasing something as simple as a newspaper, I had lost my only chance of circumventing the strict, hierarchical system that normally governed public architectural appointments in France. I had lost by default to a young, barely known architect, a previous winner of the Grand Prix de Rome. . . .

It was too late to design that shrine to my one pure and unsullied love. I had betrayed my music—and betrayed it by the worst of all human crimes: uninformed ignorance!

The urge to kill became so strong that I thought I should die of it.

Garnier . . . Charles Garnier . . . be very glad of the miles that separate us tonight!

The terrible silence in the room was punctuated by my ragged breathing and Marie's gasping terror. She was white with fear when I turned to look at her, and immediately I was ashamed. This poor, pitiful little woman deserved only kindness at my hands. I must be calm; I must channel this fury and turn my unseemly thoughts away from murder in this house of death; I must remember my promise. . . .

An hour passed according to the clock on the mantelpiece, an hour in which I did nothing except sit staring into the dying fire. Calmness returned to me at length in the wake of resignation and new resolve. I accepted that it was too late to create the original design. But it was not too late to stand on the site and watch this great mausoleum rise beneath the guidance of my own hands.

It was not too late to build!

I left the old house in Boscherville shortly before dawn, leaving my mother's body in the care of her faithful friend. Marie would keep the keys to the house and await my instructions; I trusted her discretion implicitly.

I left without returning to look one last time upon my mother's dead and unlovely face. The beautiful features, delicate as a butterfly's wing, were buried safely in the mists of my memory. I could not wipe them from my mind, but there was a certain comfort in knowing that I would never see that face resurrected.

She had never existed for me outside an illusion.

She had never existed; and now at last I could forget her forever.

aris was another shock for which I was totally unprepared.

The romantic old city which I had once explored as a wide-eyed, fugitive boy—the variegated Paris of Voltaire and Desmoulins—was being swept into oblivion beneath the hands of the emperor and his grand prefect, Baron Haussmann. As I made my way back from the demolished site of the new Opera in the grayish first light of day, it seemed to me that everything eccentric, artistic, and historic was being relentlessly destroyed beneath the imperial drive for wide-open spaces and uniformity. When I looked at the impersonal apartment blocks that were beginning to line the wide boulevards—a monument to the emperor's vulgarity, materialism, and rampant bad taste—there was a moment when I considered death too kind a fate for these tyrannical authors of destruction.

There had been much at fault in the old Paris, but it had never deserved to be gutted so mercilessly—beautiful buildings torn down for no better reason than that they simply stood in the way of progress. This was murder, rape, and wholesale pillage on a scale beyond imagination; the soul of the city had been bled white by a heartless and insensitive decimation.

I rode to the edge of the city, to the new slums where the impoverished had been driven by high rents in the wake of Haussmann's ruthless sweep of rebuilding. Many of the Parisian poor were homeless now, wandering the streets, like Arab nomads, in search of property within their means. I saw children sleeping in the gutters, wrapped in old newspapers, and my blood boiled at the sight of such cruel injustice.

It was here among the poor that I found lodgings. I had the means to stay in the finest hotel suites in Paris, but I instinctively shied away from the rejection of the well bred and the wealthy, the looks of suspicious distaste which always preceded the information that a particular hotel room or tasteful apartment was not available. Not available to *me*, was what they meant of course . . . a man in a mask must inevitably have some social stigma to hide. The poor were less particular as long as one could pay, but even so three landlords shut their doors hurriedly in my face before I found a man greedy enough to overcome his instinctive fear of me.

I paid the extortionate amount he required for hot water, and when I had bathed, I sat down and wrote the letter that would bring Jules Bernard from Belgium. His honest, well-dressed person, coupled with my money, would acquire me lodgings in a more salubrious area for a time, until the inevitable hounding and extortion forced me to move on. For the past five years he had acquired all my lodgings for me, and I was galled by my increasing dependence upon him, my growing inability to outface the stares of tailors and shoemakers. Whatever I required now, Jules obtained for me—everything from shirts to morphine. In Russia and the Orient it had been possible to go about my business with some degree of freedom, but here in the Mecca of the civilized world, where everything was so respectable, I felt increasingly like a hunted spider, hiding in a web. I was rapidly losing the buoyancy and optimism of youth; I knew that I would starve now, rather than sing or display myself in any way before a crowd; I preferred to work in the dark these days, unseen and unheard. And for that I needed Jules.

I knew that he would come immediately upon receipt of my letter, simply because he dared not refuse.

And as soon as he came, I would set him to work.

Six weeks later I had everything I needed.

For a respectable man Jules had turned out to be the most accomplished spy. I knew all that I needed to know about Garnier and his designs, and I had in my employ some of the best stonemasons in the region. Once Jules had passed the word in the right quarters, human greed brought the men one by one to my door to face my harsh and exacting scrutiny. I was prepared to pay for the best and I rejected ruthlessly until I found it.

On first sight of Garnier's plans my instinct had been to abandon the whole project and return to Belgium at once, for the exterior design filled me with despair. I saw at once that the Paris Opera would be ugly and unoriginal, as squat and unlovely as a huge toad planted on the bleak new Parisian landscape. I particularly disliked the colonnaded loggia across the face of the building. The whole concept was vulgar, not to say profane—and yet . . .

And yet it was grandiose, conceived on a scale of breathtaking ambition that brought me back to the plans again and again. It would dwarf the palace at Mazanderan with its three-acre site, seventeen floors, and five cellars below street level. This building, with its fireproof girders and many modern refinements, was reaching out to the future and represented a truly monstrous feat of engineering. Since it seemed that Garnier's gross and forbidding child must indeed come into the world, then I intended to preside over a birth which would inevitably prove difficult and protracted. It is possible to love an ugly child if you have tended it for long enough, nursed it through danger, and buried yourself in its future. In time that loggia would seem no worse to me than an unfortunate birthmark, a sad blemish that would fill me with loving pity and make me long to protect the unfortunate building from the comments of its cruel critics. It would be beautiful inside, with its magnificent grand escalier, its marbled columns, mirrored foyers, and chandeliers. . . .

It would be beautiful inside. . . .

When I had completed the estimate for the stonework, I wrote directly to Garnier. I knew a lot about him by now. Born in the notorious Rue Mouffetard, one of the worst slums in Paris, son of a blacksmith with social aspirations, he had only escaped his appointed place in his father's business because he proved physically incapable of working the huge bellows. A nervous, delicate, gifted man, he had clawed his way into the middle classes through his own restless industry and determination and now resided with his young wife in the Boulevard St. Germain. Excitable and eccentric, the man possessed the imagination of a true artistic genius, and I knew he would see me, if nothing else.

No true artist could have resisted the provocative flattery of my outrageous proposal.

Garnier indicated a chair on the opposite side of his untidy desk and turned down the gas lamp in accordance with my request. If he was surprised by the mask he gave no sign of it as he sat back and studied me calmly in the half light, pressing the tips of his fingers together, like a church steeple.

"Let me make one thing perfectly clear from the outset, monsieur," he said with an aggression that rather amused me. "I have asked you here tonight purely out of interest. Your proposals were so utterly *unorthodox* that I confess I could not resist the opportunity of meeting the author of such colossal impertinence. May I ask what makes you think I would accede to bribery?"

I raised my shoulders in a careless shrug.

"Every man has his price. You are, if I may say so without giving offense, relatively unknown in your chosen field and the government has naturally taken advantage of that fact in the matter of your remuneration."

He sat upright in his chair suddenly.

"Meaning?" he challenged softly.

"Meaning that while it is usual for a public architect to have his fees set at three percent of expenditure, I understand yours have been fixed at two. Why should you feel morally beholden to a government which intends to cheat you from the very outset? And you must know what will inevitably happen. Every time you run over budget you will face accusations of artificially inflating expenditure in order to increase your architectural fees. You will be comfortable, of course—very much more comfortable than you have been up till now on your annual eight thousand francs as a city architect. But you may rest assured, monsieur, that the government of this land has absolutely no intention of making you a millionaire in return for the work of a lifetime. And you will be an old man by the time this building is completed."

He laughed suddenly.

"I'm only thirty-six, my friend. How long do you think it's going to take me to complete this work? If it took ten years—which God forbid!—I should hardly be in my dotage."

I smiled unseen behind the mask.

"If you finish it in ten—which you won't!—you will still be broken in spirit and health from doing battle every waking hour of every day with cheeseparing bureaucracy and thieving contractors. You'll be a physical wreck before they're done with you, Garnier—you're just too naive yet to know it! So be sensible and accept my compensation. I offer you the opportunity to feather a comfortable little nest of your own. Is there nothing you want to build for yourself and your wife?"

He frowned, pushed back his chair with an irritable gesture, and got to his feet restlessly. A small fellow, physically unimposing, he carried himself with a certain arrogance that began to trouble me. This man was proud of his humble origins, proud enough to have defiantly settled within fifteen minutes' walk of the slum in which he had been born.

Was it really true that everyone had a price?

"Suppose my moral objections forbid me to take this money for my own use?" he said suddenly.

I shrugged and prepared to alter tack a little.

"When you receive demands ad nauseam to use fewer men and cheaper materials at every stage of construction, you may find it useful to have a little extra funding that the government knows nothing about."

He nodded, as though that was something he could better accept.

"You have submitted two estimates, with widely differing figures," he continued. "Perhaps you would care to explain your purpose in that."

I sighed; it was tedious to be obliged to spell out every last little detail, and I did not for one moment believe he was as simple as he was trying to make out.

"The higher estimate is for the ministry. The lower represents the true fee that I would expect to receive."

He looked at me in some astonishment.

"Those figures are quite untenable," he protested. "You would have to be operating at a loss to keep to them. Do you usually work for nothing, monsieur?"

"Only when it amuses me to do so. I am a wealthy man, Garnier—you need have no doubt of my ability to finance this little indulgence of mine . . . or to purchase your goodwill in the matter."

"This is a government project," he pointed out sternly. "You must realize that there are correct channels of procedure that will bind me hand and foot."

I laughed.

"There are few things on this planet more open to corrupt practice than a government project. I could hide for many years in the paperwork generated for the Ministry of Fine Arts. The final choice of contractors will be yours."

He came out from behind the desk and stood over me.

"I don't think contracting is your normal line of business. You are an architect, aren't you?"

Again I smiled grimly behind the mask. This man was no fool. What had he guessed?

"My competence extends to many fields," I said coolly. "For the moment I choose to contract. There is no question of professional rivalry between us."

"But there could have been," he persisted shrewdly. "I think I am correct in assuming that, am I not?"

I declined to answer him, and my hands clenched automatically on the arms of the chair. The old claustrophobic sensation of caged bars closed in around me and I suddenly knew I had been a fool to come here tonight. I had been terribly mistaken. This man was as honest as the day was long. What in God's name had made me think I could get away with such outrageous madness?

"I am sorry to have wasted your time," I said grimly, getting to my feet. "Forget this happened—forget you ever saw me. I shall not trouble you again."

"One moment." He was staring at the mask with a sudden intense interest that made me deeply uneasy. "Please sit down again," he continued with a new cordiality in his voice. "I would like you to see something."

I sank into the chair with a terrible feeling of foreboding. Not since the day I woke in that Gypsy cage had I ever felt quite so deeply trapped. I realized with horror that it might be necessary to kill him now in order to escape from my own arrogant stupidity. And his wife was in the apartment. She had opened the door to me and I had seen her suck in a startled breath before she collected herself sufficiently to direct me to her husband's study. What on earth should I do if she started to scream?

I was a fool, an unspeakable fool! When would I ever learn to keep away from people?

From a file in the bottom drawer of his desk Garnier extracted a handful of papers and passed them to me.

"I think you will recognize these designs," he said.

I stared at the papers in my hand with disbelief.

"How did you get hold of them?" I demanded passionately. *"How?"*

He did not answer for a moment. I watched him cross the room and return with two glasses of brandy. Giving me one, he sat upon the edge of the desk and took a sip from his own glass, his curiously arranged features betraying a certain repressed excitement.

"I had a tutor at the School of Fine Arts," he began conversationally, "an elderly, rather eccentric fellow who took an interest in promising students. He was a good-natured old man, very interesting in his own way—had a stock of good stories to tell, if you had the patience to bear with his rambling. Before he died he entrusted me with these papers, asked me to keep them safe . . . told me that if I ever had the good fortune to come across the man who drew them I would have the honor of knowing the greatest architect in the history of the world. I always thought it a pretty tale, an old man's fantasy. . . . How old were you when you designed these buildings, Erik . . . seven . . . eight?"

I let the papers fall in my lap. For a moment all I could see was my cheerful, pompous, opinionated tutor lying silenced forever. His visits had been the light of my childhood; before it was boarded up, I had stood at the attic window for hours on end, waiting for that first glimpse of his carriage which would send me running down the stairs in wild excitement to the front door. . . .

"What else did he tell you besides my name?" I muttered at last.

"Sufficient for me to understand why you wear that mask," said Garnier slowly, with the air of a man choosing his words now with some care. "Sufficient to make me thankful that you never entered the ministry's competition."

I glanced up at him in resentful surprise.

"What makes you so damned sure I didn't enter?"

He spread his hands in what I later learned was a rare gesture of self-depreciation.

"If you had," he said, "I should still be earning that miserable eight thousand francs a year."

It was too late to acquire the contract for the excavations, but Garnier made surreptitious arrangements for my presence on the site in spite of this.

He had offered me a position in the new *agence*, which would have given me the opportunity to work on the definitive designs, but after a few nights of agonized indecision, common sense obliged me to decline. To be imprisoned in a draftsman's office, surrounded by nineteen well-educated young men, most of whom had been students at the School of Fine Arts, was an ordeal I simply lacked the courage to face. Awkward silences, furtive whispers, staring eyes . . . there would be no escape from my terrible difference in such a closely confined environment. And I knew that as soon as I got my hands on those designs I would inevitably cause friction and ill feeling. I would be unable to stay silent, and the result of my outburst would be an uncontrollable violence that could only end in murder. It was better to stay away from temptation rather than let my evil temper put an end to my dream. Garnier did not press me to accept. I'd like to think that perhaps he understood.

I don't know what he said to the excavating contractor, but that man always treated me with wary respect, as though he believed my ubiquitous presence on the site to have some official capacity. Whether he thought me an *inspecteur*, a *sous-inspecteur*, or a *des-*

sinateur was never entirely clear, but he never argued with any of my suggestions and he was always careful to call me sir.

And so I was there when things started to go drastically wrong. . . .

Excavating in the area of the *cuve*, the substage section of the building which descended twelve meters belowground, they hit water.

"What the devil is it?" muttered Garnier.

My abrupt message had brought him rushing to the site and he was now peering down into the collapsing footings in undisguised dismay, his collar parting company with his shirt in evidence of his hasty toilette.

"A subterranean tributary of the Seine, by the look of it," I said grimly. "I'd say it cuts through this entire area."

Garnier raked one hand through his untidy black curls.

"Christ! Of all things . . . of all *places!*"

I nodded. "They can do no more unless the water table is lowered."

He let out a colorful expletive which common decency forbids me to record.

"Have you any idea what that would entail?" he said furiously.

"I'm afraid I know exactly what it's going to entail."

Pulling a paper from my sleeve, I handed it to him. He studied it for a while and then looked up incredulously.

"You are actually suggesting that I create an artificial lake beneath the stage?"

"You really don't have very much choice," I explained patiently. "You can evacuate the water during the course of construction with the steam pumps as described, but that double casing is the only means of controlling the river's flow and permanently protecting the foundations from erosion. Of course you'll have to seal with bitumen to resist seepage, but that shouldn't present a problem."

"And the cost?" he said warily.

I shrugged. "Submit the figures you think you can get out of the ministry. I will take care of any shortcoming."

"You must be utterly mad." He sighed.

I didn't contest that remark, merely spread my hands in a philosophical gesture.

"My only concern is that the work should go ahead without delay. I can't lay a single stone until these excavations are completed. And I'm not by nature a patient man, as you will learn."

Folding the paper, he placed it carefully in the pocket of his over-coat.

"Nothing stands in your way for long, does it?" he mused, looking back at me thoughtfully over his shoulder. "Why do I have this strange feeling that opposing your wishes could prove very prejudicial to a man's health?"

I smiled faintly.

"I would never advise any man to ignore his deepest instincts, Gar-nier."

"That sounds uncommonly like a threat." He frowned.

"I rarely waste time making threats," I said calmly.

And before he could reply to that, I walked away across the quag-mire of mud to signify that our conversation was at an end.

Eight giant steam pumps worked night and day for eight months to drain the saturated subsoil, and Parisians were driven insane by the incessant pounding. I had a certain grim sympathy with their discom-fort, for I suffered as much as anyone else from the rhythmic thump-ing, which seemed to echo in my head long after I left the site at night. I had no need to be there of course—this was not my contract —and yet I found I could not keep away.

In January 1862 the concrete foundations were poured, and as soon as the first section was cast I began work on the masonry substructure.

The outer world ceased to exist for me at that point; time no longer had any meaning. I was only vaguely aware of Garnier's trials, his bitter and protracted struggle with the government against demands for more stringent economy; but each time I saw him he looked paler and more harassed. I listened to his furious complaints with guarded sympathy and counted myself well out of that particular arena. God knows how he refrained from shedding blood at some point in those first nine years.

Nine years!

Is it really possible to let nine years slide away, almost without noticing the change of the seasons? I had never been so utterly ab-sorbed, so blissfully unaware of frustration. On a site the size of this it was possible to largely avoid association with the other contractors, but I had already taken the precaution of creating my own secret place deep in the vaults of the foundations. A device set into the double case wall beneath the substage area afforded me a place of darkness and privacy to which I might retire whenever I was angered to the point of violence by idleness, corruption, or pure stupidity. It served me well on many occasions; in the whole course of those nine years not a single workman died by my hand and I began to wonder if I had conquered the need to kill after all.

I drove my men hard—hard enough, I daresay, to have earned a dagger in the back more than once. The distinction of receiving the highest wages on the site was doubtless the only incentive they had to bear with my tyranny. It had to be fear that made them obey my instructions with such prompt alacrity—fear and sheer financial dependence. I wasn't stupid enough to believe it could ever be anything else. . . .

The Opera House swallowed my life whole. I arrived at the site before dawn, seldom leaving before midnight, and as the years passed, I found it increasingly difficult to leave at all. When harsh winters forced a halt in masonry work during January and February, for fear of freezing temperatures, I continued to haunt the rising building like a lost soul, often disappearing into the vaults of the theater to make strange alterations whose purpose I could hardly explain even to myself. Secret ways which no one need ever know about . . . invisible trapdoors . . . there was an intense satisfaction in leaving my unseen mark upon this building, which I could only suppose was a fixation of my disordered mind. There seemed to be no other explanation for what, even in my own eyes, was exceedingly odd behavior.

My life was measured out in meters and each meter was a mental milestone, a little thrill of achievement, as I watched this awesome mausoleum reach up toward the sky. Monolithic Ravière limestone shafts for the main façade; sixteen columns of red Jura stone; twelve of rose granite; thirty of Sarrancolin marble. . . . There was no end to the wonder of touch that now lay beneath my fingers, and I wandered through the edifice each night, like the shah in his harem, bestowing my caresses with wary impartiality, lest one lovely column should feel jealous or neglected. I was glutted with beauty . . . satiated and contented by excesses beyond my wildest dreams. The sight of the giant Corinthian columns that supported the arches of the auditorium dome made me feel like a Druid priest at Stonehenge. . . .

Garnier, on the other hand, must by now have felt like the sacrificial sheep on the block. Year by year my pity for the man grew stronger as he battled through personal tragedy—the death of his only child being swiftly followed by the death of his father—and fought like a stag at bay to preserve the integrity of his dream. Twice in succession the government axed a million francs from the opera's credit budget; by March '67 the project was five hundred thousand francs in debt and Garnier was at his wit's end!

"You were right," he told me in despair one evening, "right in all you predicted. I should have trained as a gladiator, not an architect. . . . I don't suppose you have two million francs about you, do you, Erik?"

I laughed and accepted the hip flask of brandy which he offered to me, not the first he had downed this evening by the look of him, poor devil—not by a long way.

"If I had, you should have it gladly," I said.

"Yes, I know." He sighed, screwing the top back on his flask with unsteady fingers. "Why aren't you the emperor, Erik. Why the hell aren't you the emperor?"

I can only assume that he was too drunk to know what he was doing, for as I assisted him out of the dark and silent building, before he broke his neck on the dangerous construction debris, he suddenly flung one arm around my shoulder with rough camaraderie.

"If they ever make you the emperor," he said aggressively, "I'll be the first one out in the street throwing my bloody cap in the air."

I got him a cab, since he was clearly too far gone to get home alone in any safety, and he wrung my hand hard for a moment before getting in and slumping back on the seat.

"You'd have made a damned good emperor," he said in maudlin tones, "do you know that, Erik . . . a damned good emperor!"

Yes . . . he did not normally indulge, but he was very, very drunk that night. I very much doubt that he ever remembered what he said that evening, let alone who it was who had put him in that cab. . . .

A guarded respect had grown up between us over the years, preventing the clash of our volatile personalities which on first glance might have seemed inevitable. Garnier had a truly spectacular temper when roused, and the restraint he managed to employ when dealing with government idiots never ceased to amaze me. He didn't care what he did to keep life blood flowing into the Opera coffers; he would thump a war drum or grovel like a spaniel, whatever was required, and I admired that more than I could say. I, too, would have fought like a tiger, but I would not have begged; my stiff-necked pride would have been the cord which strangled the Opera in its birth canal.

We were astonishingly patient with each other, as though we both understood what it was to own minds that were ceaselessly and painfully awake. We shared a rage for perfection and an imagination that was in constant ferment. And so that third evening in September 1870, when he came to the Opera and found me working alone, without the mask, I felt curiously calm and indifferent toward a discovery which would normally have filled me with mortified fury.

He looked at me with shocked surprise, but he had the grace not to stare and I felt I could forgive him that first moment of paralyzed wonder. To be perfectly honest he was no oil painting himself. I had seen his singular features rather unkindly caricatured in the popular press, more than once—the angular face ravaged with lines of worry and intermittent ill-health, the eyes deep set beneath a curiously flattened skull. Perhaps it helped that he was ugly; perhaps I was simply too exhausted for violence, but at any rate I felt no inclination to kill him for this outrage.

He came calmly across the scaffolding that surrounded the inner auditorium cupola structure and examined the area on which I was working with approval.

"I don't know how you can see in this abysmal light," he remarked pleasantly. "You must have the eyes of a cat."

I said nothing. He was dressed for dinner and no doubt his wife, Louise, was fuming in their carriage at this very moment, waiting to go home. Surely he would not linger now. . . .

"I'm building an opera house," he said quietly. "You, on the other hand, my friend, seem quite determined to turn it into a tomb."

I turned to look at him in surprise and he spread his hands in an expressive Gallic gesture.

"Your men say that you are killing yourself."

I laughed harshly. "You mean they *hope* I'm killing myself."

He shook his head slowly.

"That little Bernard fellow is very anxious; he begged me this morning to speak to you because he dared not do so himself."

Jules? I frowned as I considered this unexpected information. The man had seven children now to feed and educate—Madame Bernard seemed to conceive every time her husband hung up his trousers! On reflection I supposed it was perfectly natural that the man should be anxious about the source of his livelihood. Surely he hadn't dared to tell Garnier about the morphine!

"Twenty hours a day," continued Garnier slowly. "Have you no home to go to, Erik?"

Still I was silent, thinking of the dozen apartments Jules had rented for me since I began work on the Opera. Each time the pattern had been similar. First the anonymous, abusive letters, then the wanton unprovoked damage, and finally the aggressive blow or nervous tap of the proprietor upon my door.

"Please try to understand, monsieur . . . the other tenants have begun to complain. . . ."

I never argued or protested, simply left with weary resignation before the violence began. I already saw there was no point in purchasing a property at Haussmann's wildly inflated prices; it would not solve my predicament, and besides I needed to husband my resources; my financial commitments were considerable and my capital was dwindling rapidly. I was no longer the enormously wealthy man that I had been ten years ago; the Opera and Jules's rapidly increasing family of hungry, ignorant little rabbits had seen to that.

Each time I was hounded from a flat, my next residence was in an area a little less elegant, a little less respectable, until I found myself once more on the edge of the city among the very poor. In consequence I had began to work longer and longer hours at the Opera, dreading the moment when I should have to return to those dingy and dangerous streets.

"The Opera is my home," I observed with a flippancy that did not quite conceal the grim truth of my statement.

Garnier looked at me steadily and there was an odd sort of pity in his dark eyes.

"Not for much longer, I'm afraid," he said.

Nine years of self-restraint exploded in my head like a barrel of gunpowder; in a moment I had him by the throat and we had lurched dangerously close to the edge of the scaffolding.

"What are you talking about?" I snarled. "You gave me your word I should finish this work—you won't go back on it now and live, I promise you!"

I flung him to the plank flooring and there he remained a moment, tenderly fingering his neck.

"There's no need for such violent anger," he said quietly. "I assure you this has nothing whatsoever to do with me."

"What then?" I demanded rudely. "Explain yourself!"

He sighed and sat back upon his heels, brushing the white dust from his immaculate black trousers.

"I suppose you are *aware* that we're at war with Prussia?"

"Of course I'm aware of it, you idiot, who isn't?"

He gave a little shrug. "Sometimes I feel you are not quite in the same world as the rest of us. The talk is all over Paris that the emperor surrendered at Sudan yesterday. The public fury at his failure is almost uncontainable. The boulevards are full of crowds shouting, 'Down with the Empire!' Can't you hear the roar outside? They say there will be another revolution in the next twenty-four hours."

"The emperor was a very sick man," I said grimly. "They had no business to send him out to war as they did when he could barely sit a horse."

Garnier glanced at me in surprise.

"You must be the only man in France who remembers that now. There's no compassion in the streets today."

"There never is," I said, and turned back to my work.

"Erik . . . there's something more."

"Yes?" I did not bother to look around.

"They say the German army is preparing to march on Paris. Do you know what a siege will mean?"

"A lot of children will starve," I said darkly. It was always the children who suffered—the children and the animals.

"Yes, yes," said Garnier with a touch of impatience, "but have you thought of what it will mean for us—for the Opera?"

I swung around in horror and again he spread his hands helplessly.

"It's a government building and will be requisitioned for the war effort. All work will automatically be suspended for an indefinite period. God knows when we will be able to work again or even if the building will survive the German shells. Erik, do you understand what I am saying?"

I understood.

I understood that men, rash, stupid, mindless men were about to take my sacred trust away from me. Paris would be shelled by Bismarck's great German war machine and nine years of ceaseless labor might be ruined in as many seconds.

I picked up the mask and swung down from the scaffold in stony silence.

"Erik!" Garnier shouted in alarm, peering after me in the poor light of my lanterns. "Where are you going?"

"As far away from *men* as I can get!" I spat viciously.

There was only one way for me to go now, and that was down . . . down, down, down, into the bottomless dark reaches where no one went now, down the endless flights of stone stairs to the fifth basement and my secret place beyond the lake.

When the great stone closed behind me, shutting me in the cavernous expanse of the foundation's double casing, my single candle lit a moment of stunning revelation. I suddenly realized that I had spent my entire life searching for one place where I would feel at peace, somewhere to rest in safety from prying eyes.

Once I had known such a place. That first year I had spent in Giovanni's cellar, nestled snugly like a young animal in its nest, I had touched a security and happiness that I had been unable to find again, no matter where I wandered. As long as Giovanni was there above me, like God in his heaven, I knew that I was safe. Boys all over the world learn to call their fathers sir; it is a mark of respect which in no way denies affection. But in my heart he was always father, always . . . until the day that Luciana came and broke my life in little pieces. . . .

I closed my mind against them. The pain was more than twenty-five years old, it was weak and contemptible to be unmanned by it yet again. They were both dead and gone, forget them . . . let them go!

And yet I found now that I was remembering that cellar with desperate yearning. Surely it would be possible to recapture that sense of well-being and contentment if only I could re-create the environment in which I had first experienced those alien and elusive feelings. If I made a nest of my own deep beneath the Parisian streets, no one need ever find me again; there would be no sniggering, no ugly shouts, no stones thrown and no knives drawn.

There would be . . . *no one!*

Yes . . . that was the true revelation! The sudden understanding that I no longer wanted anyone, that I was weary of struggling to exist in a world where I could never belong. I had spent the best part of forty years banging my head against the walls of reality till I was bloody and bemused by my failure. What a fool I had been, when the answer was here all the time.

A quiet dark place waited to embrace me. All I had to do was what any sensible spider would have done many years ago—scuttle inside to safety and stay there.

As I lit more candles and began to explore like an excited child, fantasies unwound in my head like a spool of golden thread.

My house would be of irregular shape, but it could spread as far as I wished in either direction, one room leading off another. In that moment of far-reaching vision I saw everything, every last tiny detail from the glorious pipe organ that would line the wall of my bedchamber, to the canopied open coffin where I intended to sleep.

There had to be a coffin, you see, because Garnier had been quite right—this place was my chosen tomb, a monument to my own insane genius. The Paris Opera was a pyramid in opulent disguise and I the pharaoh who would lie deep in its heart in the secret glory of my afterlife.

The dream faded, like a wilted candle, leaving me once more in nothing more than a dark, damp hole. But I had seen the ultimate vision. It was months, years, away from my grasp, and yet nothing, not even the might of the Prussian army, should stand in the way of its fulfillment.

The most fantastic house on this earth would be guarded by every device my magician's mind could conjure.

I would never sleep above the surface of the ground again.

I f I had not made that decision when I did, I would have been arrested in the first week of the siege, when spy mania swept the city. Anyone who, in dress or manner, betrayed even the slightest difference from their fellowmen was denounced to the new republican authorities as a suspected traitor. The deaf and the dumb were hounded without mercy, and even a stammer was sufficient to justify the spiteful persecution of an angry mob. A score of infantrymen who had fled from the enemy at Courbevoie were paraded through the city with their hands tied behind their backs, bearing placards that invited honest folk to spit in their faces.

The hysteria passed, spirits lifted, and Paris settled back to enjoy the novelty of a siege that no one expected to last for long. Viewing the fortifications became a pleasant family outing on Sunday afternoons, and while the regiments drilled, the benches in the Champs-Elysées were full of gossiping citizens lolling in the sun. Guitars twanged, organs were ground, and merry-go-rounds were in full swing. People took opera glasses to study the Prussian batteries at Meudon, and the occasional puff of smoke from the gunboats was dismissed with lighthearted derision.

Everyone knew that Paris was invincible. With her enceinte wall, her ten-foot moat, and her lines of forts stretching over a circumference of forty miles, she presented a formidable front to any investing army. And the new government had not been idle. The catacombs had been sealed, elaborate barricades placed across the Seine, electrically fired land-mines laid in weak spots. Paris was ready to face the worst that Moltke's vast army was prepared to offer, and the papers predicted that the Prussians would soon be slinking home in humiliated defeat. . . .

Four months later, when the shelling of civilian areas finally began, the city had already been crippled by a harsh winter of increasing deprivation. The temperature had plummeted twelve degrees below zero. Men froze to death on duty at the outposts, and with the city's stocks of firewood virtually exhausted, desperate men and women fought over trees, felled telegraph poles, and threatened to flay the National Guard which stood on duty outside a wood depot in the Rue des Belles-Feuilles.

With the Prussians installed at Versailles, Paris starved beneath a merciless iron-gray sky. The Left Bank of the city shuddered each night beneath a rain of shells which set the streets on fire. From the roof of the Opera House I saw columns of smoke rising in the still, cold air beyond the Seine. The Prussians were deliberately directing their fire at churches and hospitals, and as the batteries closed in around the city, any building flying the red cross of the Geneva Convention was automatically singled out as a target. The institute for the insane, the asylum for the blind, the hospital for young children . . . nothing was sacred anymore. I found it hard to believe that men could sink so low. . . .

The Opera House had been requisitioned as an arsenal and a warehouse for vital food supplies, and I lived in perpetual terror of fire breaking out through someone's carelessness. One million liters of wine stood on the premises, and more than once I heard drunken carousing echoing through the building. The Prussian batteries were not yet close enough to shell the Right Bank, but a single carelessly dropped cigarette was all it would take to blow the Opera's powder magazine sky high. All the time that I worked alone on my secret house my heart was full of dread. I never left the premises unguarded except for the few hours it took me, once a fortnight, to make my way to Jules's rented house on the Left Bank, and there, in a dark, curtained room, pay the wages of men who would otherwise have starved for want of employment. All over the city builders had been turned off government sites for the duration of the siege; the Opera, the new Hôtel-Dieu, the two thousand unfinished houses in the area of Haussmann's redevelopment. . . .

I continued to pay the men in my employ without begrudging the few francs they might manage to earn elsewhere in the meantime. Food was rapidly becoming a prerogative of the rich, but no one who had worked for me at the Opera was permitted to starve. When prices soared beyond their means, I simply raised their due to the level of a living wage. I never looked at the men when they came into the room. I stood with my arms folded beneath my cloak and my face to the wall while they collected their envelopes in terrified silence and crept away. For the duration of my presence in the house, Madame Bernard and her little ones cowered out of sight in a bedroom. It was still possible to obtain morphine in return for an exorbitant sum and a great deal of patience; I always took care to pay Jules rather more than I owed him for this singular service and then leave without further delay. The ritual depressed me—made me long to get away from that atmosphere of suppressed fear. It was better to be alone.

By the seventeenth week of the siege Paris was on its knees. The butcher's stalls in the great central market were selling slaughtered cats decorated with paper frills and colored ribbons, and the rat market on the Place de l'Hôtel de Ville was besieged with desperate customers. The animals in the zoo at the Bois had been slaughtered so that the restaurants might serve elephant to those with the means to pay for the delicacy.

Someone would most certainly have eaten Ayesha if I had not found her first. . . .

I was wandering the streets aimlessly that night, listening with indifference to the shells whining overhead like the howling of a high wind in autumn. There was no one around. Everyone with any sense in this area was lying low in a cellar out of harm's way, but I no longer cared whether I was blown to pieces by a Prussian bomb. A telling little incident at the Bernard house had virtually dulled the last of my fading appetite for life.

All the men had gone. I had been settling up with Jules when there was a scream in the hallway and the sound of something tumbling heavily down the stairs.

Without thinking I ran out into the narrow, ill-lit passage just as Madame Bernard reached the bottom step and snatched up the small child who whimpered at my feet. Clutching the little girl against her breast, she began to back away up the stairs.

"Madame, that child is injured. Let me look at her."

"No . . ." she stammered, still edging backward up the stairs. "No, monsieur, you are mistaken. . . . It was nothing, just a little tumble . . . two or three steps, that's all . . . that's all."

She was lying. The child had fallen down the full flight and now lay white and unprotesting in her arms. I started up the stairs and was frozen by the woman's shriek of fear.

"Stay away from her! Don't touch her!"

"Madame—"

"Why do you have to come here?" she spat, suddenly veering from terror to aggression. "Frightening the children—frightening everyone? Why don't you keep away?"

"Annette!" gasped Jules in horror. "Annette, for God's sake, be silent!"

"We don't need your cold charity," she continued doggedly from the landing, "we don't need your money. You won't buy my children as you have bought my husband! Go away, monsieur, go right away and don't come back. Do you hear me? Don't ever come back here again!"

She turned and ran onto the landing and almost at once a door slammed behind her on a roomful of crying children.

I came slowly back down the stairs to where Jules was waiting with both hands clutched against his thin chest.

"Monsieur," he whispered helplessly, "monsieur—I beg you to forgive my wife's outburst. She is not in her right senses. She meant no offense. She—"

I silenced him with a look and tossed two hundred francs onto the shabby hall table.

"Get that child to a doctor quickly," I said coldly, and walked out of his house.

My heart was like a lump of lead dragging heavy in my breast as I made my way back through the squalid, snow-laden streets. On the bank of the Seine, as I paused to study the ice floes that were blocking the river, I heard a prostitute hail a passing soldier.

"Monsieur . . . I will take you to my room in exchange for a piece of bread."

The man paused and spoke, but I could not hear his reply; presently they moved on together in the direction of the Rue de Grenelle.

Staring out across the frozen river, I wondered briefly just how hungry a woman would have to be to accept bread from my hand in return for her services. I'd never dared to approach a prostitute; I'd never been able to face the humiliation of having my money refused. The memory of that little slave girl in Persia still burned in my mind.

Something pulled at the hem of my cloak; and as I turned, thinking to find the elegant cashmere snagged on the remains of a paling, I found that I, too, had been accosted by a lady desperate for food.

A very little lady. . . .

There, on the pavement, almost indistinguishable against the dirty snow, a cream kitten sat with the claws of her chocolate-colored paws entangled in the material.

With a cry of disbelieving delight I swept her up off the snow and examined her beneath the yellowish light of a gas lamp. She was caked with filth but her breed was as unmistakable as it was inconceivable. There were no Siamese cats in Europe, and yet I held one in my hands, a rare and precious jewel dropped from heaven into the landscape of hell.

Of course I knew she could not possibly have dropped from heaven. Some enterprising French traveler had evidently succeeded in smuggling a breeding female from the palace at Bangkok, knowing that the Empress Eugénie would be prepared to pay handsomely for such a unique animal. Everywhere rich ladies would be clamoring for a similar novelty; no doubt the man had expected to make a fortune.

But the empress had fled and the rich were now eating their fine-blooded racehorses. No one was interested in acquiring another mouth —only in that little extra something for the cooking pot. Dead cats had become a fashionable substitute for flowers and sweets as a gift for a sick friend; boiled cat, served with pistachio nuts and olives, had become a delicacy for connoisseurs. I could well imagine the horrible end which had overtaken the mother and the rest of her litter.

But this little creature was born to survive; I could see it in the irrepressible impishness of her crossed blue eyes. Fate, which favors some against the longest odds, had brought her soliciting to a man who would have died of hunger before he separated her from her lovely pelt. Tucking her safely beneath my cloak, I hurried through the streets with fresh purpose in my step.

Ayesha changed my life. Over fifteen thousand kilos of salted horse-meat had been stored at the Opera, and supplies were not yet entirely exhausted. I could not bring myself to consume horseflesh, but I stole for Ayesha and stayed out of the room while she ate to control my revulsion. There were plenty of rats in the cellars, and within a few weeks she had lost the scragginess of starvation and grown sleek and contented. She followed me around the secret house like a puppy and sat beside me while I worked. I could not wait for the day when she would be big enough to wear that Persian collar. To see her strutting in its stolen magnificence would be a pleasure beyond imagination. She was my amusement, my joy, the chosen companion of my soli-tude. If there had been no horsemeat and rats, she would have eaten human flesh; I would have killed, if necessary, to feed my precious, precious little lady. . . .

Nineteen weeks into the siege the beleaguered government capitu-lated and an awesome, resentful silence descended like a shroud around the city. The German troops marched down the Champs-Elysées, and in their wake the poor, who had borne the brunt of all the hardships, were summarily required by a reactionary assembly to pay all debts and rents, postponed for the duration of the siege, within forty-eight hours. Plunged into bankruptcy, incensed by the immedi-ate suppression of six newspapers, the lower classes rose in fury and a new revolution rocked the city. The government fled to Versailles, the Commune of Paris was declared, and as the screaming mobs took to the streets the real horrors began.

No longer was the madness of destruction confined to the Left Bank. The Opera was seized by the National Guard and the red flag of the Commune, which now flew from the roof, made the building a perfect target for the Republican forces. More bombs screamed down on the battered city, but now they were French shells, the shells of civil war. Soldiers swarmed all over the barricaded Opera House and there was vicious fighting in the streets outside. I had become a pris-oner in my own home; to all intents and purposes I was under house arrest, for I knew that if I showed myself, I would be shot on sight as a spy.

Down into the cellars came the citizen generals with their pistols and their ridiculous red sashes, their cigarettes glowing in the darkness like tiny embers as they supervised the incarceration of political prisoners. The perfect silence was punctuated by their crude oaths and raucous laughter. . . . I hated these cruel intruders shepherding their victims down to the Communard dungeon below the fifth cellar. I hated them all, National Guardsmen and Republicans alike—fools . . . ignorant fools! How dared they violate my sanctuary with their filthy, destructive war! How dared they imprison me like this!

Five weeks it lasted, but it seemed like five years, before the Communards fell to the Republican forces in a savage barrage of hell's flames, massacring hostages and setting fire to state monuments as they abandoned their positions. In their wake the Hôtel de Ville and the Palace of the Tuileries were left in black smoldering ruins. Once more the streets of Paris were burning.

Since the Opera had been used as a field hospital for Communard troops, it had so far escaped this relentless arson; but one evening, at the height of the crisis, I was driven from the house on the lake by a terrible presentiment of doom. Careless of discovery, I began to comb the vaults like a demented bloodhound, and there in the third cellar I found a member of the National Guard laying the fuses that would connect with a dozen barrels of gunpowder.

"Are you acting upon orders from your commanding officer?" I demanded stonily.

The man spun round in alarm, drew his pistol upon me, and took aim.

"Are you acting upon orders?" I repeated with grim insistence. "Have you been told to do this?"

"No." He laughed suddenly, his eyes wide and staring with a blind lust that was immediately recognizable to me. "This place has been forgotten by the generals, but not by me—not by me. I'm going to blow the filthy imperialist abomination off the face of the earth . . . but I'll settle with you first, my interfering friend—"

The Punjab lasso silenced him before he got the chance to pull the trigger, and I dragged his body out into the street when darkness fell, leaving it with others likewise abandoned.

Then I went back for the gunpowder.

Patiently I ferried the barrels across the lake and stored them in my own cellar with a strange, secret pleasure.

I had sunk my life and my livelihood in this splendid monument; nursed it from puling infancy and caressed its beautiful stone and marble body like a fond lover. The National Academy of Music was mine, and I reserved exclusive rights to its destruction. If the day ever came when this precious edifice should be razed to a pile of dust and rubble, it would be my hand that lit the fuse. Mine alone.

Those tense uneasy weeks of intrusion and unforgivable violation showed me the ruthless measures I must now take to secure my retreat from the rest of mankind. To my original design I added a torture chamber, an exact replica of the hexagonal mirrored chamber I had once built for the khanum. It was nothing more or less than a simple mantrap; no interfering busybody who found his way in would ever find his way out again except through suicide. Sited beneath the sub-stage area, with a trapdoor affording access to the third cellar, it was also a useful shortcut back to my house. There were more than six thousand steps in the Opera and most of them led down; a shortcut would not come amiss under such conditions.

Beneath the subterranean waters I laid the cable which permitted a simple electric bell to give ample warning of intruders on the lake.

And so my labyrinth was wired for death, a vast web encircling the minotaur's secret lair.

Let foolish, unsuspecting men step with care in the maze of my creation.

All roads did not lead to Rome!

ithin a month of the Communards' surrender omnibuses and fiacres were plying the streets again and prostitutes were soliciting once more on the Boulevard des Italiens; it was as though the horrors had never been. And yet Paris was altered forever, hardened and embittered beyond measure by the taste of defeat. The death throes of a proud city would never be forgiven and hatred of the Germans was buried deep.

Work continued on the Opera amid all the inevitable delays and hostilities that were the aftermath of war and revolution, with Garnier desperately fighting to complete a building which was now viewed with the utmost suspicion by the new government as an imperialist monument. By the time he had struggled through to reach the theater's inaugural night, I had already been many years snugly installed in the bowels of the fifth cellar.

The house in Boscherville had been sold, and at dead of night Jules and I had ferried my mother's furniture across the subterranean lake. He had asked no questions of me, as usual, merely obeyed my instructions implicitly; but I saw the fear on his face when he found himself inside my unique apartment; I saw the sick, terrified certainty dawning in his eyes that he would never be permitted to leave this place alive.

When the last stick of furniture was in place, he stood in my bedchamber staring hopelessly at the magnificent open coffin on its raised dais, the black mourning candles, and the funereal tapestries.

"You're going to kill me now, aren't you, monsieur?" he said dully. "You're going to kill me because I know too much."

I turned to look at his craven figure with sudden pity. He had been a man when I first met him, young and eager, ready to go out and leave his mark upon the world. Twenty years of being worked like a marionette by the strings of my vocal cords had sapped all his initiative away and reduced him to the mindless cipher I saw then. I had deprived him of independence and initiative to the point where he was quite incapable of surviving alone in a hard world. In many ways it would have been a kindness to have finished him that night . . . but I knew I could not do it.

"Come here," I said.

He came slowly, with a dragging step . . . head bent, resigned and unresisting; my throat tightened at the sight of his painful apathy.

"If you ever speak of this place to anyone I shall kill you," I continued calmly. "Betray my secret and I will hunt you down wherever you may flee. There is no place on this earth where you will be safe from my hand. But swear to keep silent and I will raise your family in all the comfort you could ever have wished."

He lifted his head uncertainly.

"I—I don't understand, monsieur," he stammered. "What are you asking of me?"

"If I am to live here in perfect peace I shall require an agent in the outside world. You know my habits and my requirements by now. An hour before dawn on the first Sunday of every month you will take a cab to the Rue Scribe and wait for me there. Whatever I need in my solitude you shall bring to me. In return for that service I shall pay you a salary of ten thousand francs a month."

His mouth dropped open beneath its straggling moustache.

"Ten thousand!" he gasped. "Ten *thousand?*"

I shrugged. "It is admittedly an exorbitant amount to pay in return for a little shopping. But you have nine children to educate, and if one of them doesn't take the Grand Prix de Rome I shall want to know the reason why. Of course, that does not mean you are to discourage any scientific interests they may display—medicine, for instance, is a very worthy calling. And surely," I continued softly, looking past him to the beautiful pipe organ which now filled one entire wall, "surely *one* of them will prove musical. . . ."

He was stunned, entirely incapable of making any coherent reply.

That ludicrous sum finally convinced him, as no empty threat could have done, that he was dealing with a dangerous madman whose whims could never safely be ignored. The fact that I had no idea how I was going to honor this pledge indefinitely was quite immaterial. I would find a way.

Before we parted on the bank of the lake, he hesitated for a moment, looking at me with an odd expression that I could not quite place.

"What will you do in this terrible solitude?" he demanded suddenly. "How will you fill the bleak and empty days?"

I gazed into the darkness of the great vaulted chamber, unaccountably disturbed by the question.

"I shall fill my days with music and scientific research," I murmured.

"But you will be alone, monsieur," he persisted, "quite alone down here."

"I have always been alone," I said.

And leaving him standing on the bank with his lantern, I stepped once more into the little boat and rowed back across the lake.

On the second of January, 1875, I was examining the eight counterweights of the auditorium chandelier for safety when Garnier appeared at my side. He looked both furious and deeply upset as he handed me a letter.

"Look at this!" he muttered. "Tell me if it's not the final straw!"

The letter was from de Cumont, of the Ministry of Fine Arts, informing Garnier that six seats had been reserved for his party on the inaugural evening in the *deuxième loge*, "against the sum of one hundred and twenty francs."

"What a bloody impertinence!" I exclaimed.

"I knew I could rely on you to think so." He was obviously a little mollified by my open anger. "It's an unforgivable insult, is it not? They want to make me look a fool, stuck away out of sight in such inferior seating. They mean to humiliate me in public. Well, they can go to the devil and take their miserable offer with them. I wouldn't dream of attending now! I shall stay at home and read a book instead."

"Oh, Charles, don't be a fool." I sighed. "Don't you see that's exactly what they want you to do?"

There was a little silence between us. It wasn't until the words were out that I realized I had used his Christian name. He looked taken aback, even a little bemused, but his expression was not one of displeasure—oddly enough, rather the contrary.

"You have to agree this is a calculated political attack," he said uncertainly.

"Of course it is. But you must brazen it out—shame them all by attending and you will be vindicated by your own achievement, I promise you. This is your moment, the culmination of fifteen years' enslavement to a dream. No one can take it from you now except yourself. Even if they choose to seat you in the cellars, you are still the foremost architect in France. You have to attend . . . if you don't, you'll spend the rest of your life regretting it. And regret is a very poisonous emotion, it warps and distorts every aspect of a man's life until there's nothing left but bitterness and despair. Don't let them make you bitter."

He looked at the counterweights of the chandelier.

"Sometimes your compassion shames me," he said quietly. "Of course I shall attend. Will you be there, Erik?"

"Yes. You won't see me, but I shall be there, watching, as your great triumph is unveiled."

"Our triumph," he corrected firmly. "Our triumph, Erik."

And to my great astonishment he insisted on shaking hands with me.

It was a night to remember, the fifth of January, 1875. From my hidden vantage point high above the Grand Escalier I watched the crowds arrive. A host of preening, posturing members of society lined the stairs of cantilevered marble, some of them the poorer for a thousand francs, the cost of a ticket obtained through the unofficial channels of the the open market. I, who had paid nothing for the privilege of seeing kings and queens pass beneath my contemptuous gaze, was amused by the blatant bowing and scraping I saw taking place down there. However many monarchs and emperors she may dispense with, France retains a sneaking admiration for blue blood. The instinctive urge to crawl and curry favor with one's superiors is as ingrained as the stench of onion in a peasant's hands. King, emperor, president . . . it doesn't matter what they choose to call them, the undignified groveling continues in spite of Communes and revolution. Equality, liberty, fraternity—they are simply illusions of the deluded poor.

We were treated to Meyerbeer that night, Meyerbeer, Rossini, and Delibes. I could see the audience scanning the *première loge* with their opera glasses, searching in vain for a sight of Garnier. At the end of the performance he was spotted as he descended the Grand Escalier and there was a great burst of impromptu cheering and clapping.

"Bravo, Garnier! Bravo, bravo. . . ."

He glanced up once toward the ceiling, as though searching for something, then, overcome by the tremendous ovation, he bent his head and hurried out to his carriage, clutching his wife's arm. I was too far away to see clearly, but I know he was in tears. Recognition is sweet, and no one deserved it more than he, a great architect . . . a noble man. I was very glad the public had chosen to vindicate him in this spontaneous and exuberant manner. I felt neither jealousy nor resentment. The acclaim of men meant little to me now; I had outgrown my childish need for applause.

At last the evening ended and they all went to their homes, those stuffed tailor's dummies and their mincing, overdressed wives. I was left alone in the silent splendor of the the great double-horseshoe staircase, lit by the huge candelabra on either side. King, emperor, god . . . I was now free to walk through my domain unhindered by the vulgar crowds.

I walked all night, visiting every area of my kingdom, using my skeleton key to open and shut two thousand five hundred doors. But when I crossed the huge main foyer with its ten crystal chandeliers, I instinctively averted my eyes from the mirrors. These cruel instruments of suffering abounded everywhere in the glorious upper reaches of my palace, and a single careless sideways glance was all it took to give me a sword thrust of pain. But all beauty must have its imperfection, all happiness its share of sorrow. The mirrors reminded me why I was here, why I could never bear to leave this place and build again, as Garnier would.

The urge to create had been burned out of me during those fifteen years of ceaseless labor, and in its place there was only the need to possess.

To have and to hold, from this day forward . . . till death us do part. . . .

I knew that night that I had relinquished the outer world for good.

There remained one little problem to vex my splendid isolation.

Ten thousand francs a month I had promised Jules in an insane moment of arrogance. I didn't need to keep that ridiculously extravagant agreement, of course; I had the power to hold that unfortunate little man in fear for the rest of his natural life. But I hated broken promises and dishonored pledges; I hated going back on my word. Disappointment is such an *exhausting* emotion—all that energy dissipated first in painful hoping and then in futile, hopeless resentment. It's like waiting for a birthday present that never materializes. . . . *Horrible!*

So, ten thousand francs a month must be found with some alacrity or within twelve months I would be a pauper once more. And that really would rather annoy me! One grows accustomed to a comfortable income, you see, money pads the edges of so many unpleasant situations in life; it makes one wonderfully independent. And quite apart from Jules I had some expensive habits to finance. I liked to be tastefully dressed by exclusive tailors; I liked my cloaks and dress suits and shirts to be made exactly to my requirements from the very best materials. I wanted all the beautiful books in the world to line the walls of my library; I wanted the most advanced scientific materials available for my researches. I needed morphine and occasionally a little food; Ayesha liked smoked salmon and caviar. . . . Really, I could not possibly think of managing on less than twenty thousand francs a month.

Absurd! That sort of money was not to be had for the asking!

Or was it?

Suddenly I had the most wonderfully outrageous idea.

The idea itself was not exactly new; only the application of it.

Years ago, as I worked alone upon my secret passages, it occurred to me that what a mausoleum the size of this badly needed was a ghost.

Ghosts are a testimony to the past; they give a building character, a sense of mystery and hidden allure.

"There really ought to be a ghost," I had said to Garnier with mock severity, when we began work on the Opera once more; and he just laughed heartily, said the budget wouldn't run to one, that the minister would have an apoplectic fit at the suggestion, and how did one order them anyway?

"Put an advertisement in the *Revue théâtrale,*" I suggested innocently.

"Oh, yes?" he inquired with delight, losing for once those harassed furrows which had aged him twenty years since our first meeting. "And how do I word it? 'Wanted, one ghost, experience and good character required. Ability to sing tenor would be considered an advantage.' "

"That ought to do," I said seriously. "I'm sure you'll be besieged with offers."

"Yes," he said, wiping the tears from his eyes. "I'm sure I will be. A ghost indeed. . . . Erik, I should be out of my mind by now without your droll little comments to keep me sane. A ghost . . . yes, that's very good. . . . I must tell that one to Louise."

And he went off laughing.

That was all I had intended at the time—to make the poor hounded wretch laugh. He'd been seriously ill for months during the occupation by the Commune and he didn't look nearly strong enough to face the struggle that lay ahead with the Third Republic—the threats of the minister, the personal accusations of fraudulent malpractice and mismanagement that would continually be leveled at him as the cost of the Opera spiraled upward. . . . Yes, the ghost was no more than a joke at first, intended to amuse a sick man with many worries. It was only later that I began to see certain possibilities for myself.

Wanted, one ghost, experience and good character required. . . .

It might be amusing to apply for the post. After all, I did have experience. I'd been a ghost before, and a damned good ghost too. I'd driven my mother half out of her mind before I was ten and then I hadn't even been trying. I'd had a vocational training, as it were; surely this was a role which lay well within my range.

It was just a game to begin with, permitting myself to be glimpsed occasionally as I stalked the upper corridors, appearing and disappearing at will via my carefully concealed trapdoors and hidden passageways. A series of little tricks and illusions added mightily to my awesome reputation among the corps de ballet, silly children for the most part, who dearly loved to be frightened half to death by a shadow and a disembodied voice. Soon they could talk of nothing in the dressing rooms but "the ghost." Those who had actually seen me were privileged beings, entitled to respectful silence whenever they began to embroider their tales. Dreadful little liars, of course, all of them, but who cared? Certainly not me! There is no legend without artistic license, no tale that will not benefit from the fertile imagination of the storyteller. And what imagination those girls had! Better than mine at times; sometimes I took notes for future reference!

So the game was already well established when I began to see how it might gain me rather more than a good laugh. The Opera Ghost was growing weary of his role as an unpaid amusement. Perhaps it was time he applied to the management for a salary.

The more I thought about it, the better I liked the idea. The corps de ballet were already calling me "the Phantom of the Opera," an intriguing soubriquet which appealed to me very strongly, until I realized that it would mean signing my ransom notes *P.T.O.* One did not wish to descend to the ridiculous!

O.G. I became and *O.G.* I have remained.

But I still liked to think of myself as the Phantom. . . .

Looking back, the whole thing was quite criminally easy to arrange.

I was blessed with two managers, neither of them mental giants and one of them surely the biggest fool in the history of theater. Poligny! Ah, dear, credulous Poligny, your interesting little personal vices served me as well as your simple mind. I frightened you out of your wits that night in box five when you first heard my voice. For after all, a ghost who knew so much about one's dubious private affairs had better be humored, had he not? Particularly when his terms were so reasonable.

Twenty thousand francs a month and box five on the grand tier to be reserved exclusively for my personal use.

Extortionate?

Hardly! A really efficient ghost is hard to come by these days; and no one could say I didn't give value for money in my own way.

Poligny left box five as white as a sheet, with instructions to write my terms into the lease of the Opera House.

I expected a prolonged period of struggle, particularly from his partner, Debienne, but one swift manifestation of my displeasure was sufficient to bring capitulation from them both. My reputation, swelling out of all proportion among the corps de ballet, had done most of the work for me. Everyone already believed in the ghost. It was unbelievable how quickly I obtained my power over them and how seldom I was obliged to crack the whip in order to remind them who was the master here. A little magic, a little clever ventriloquism, and they were mine for the taking.

Through similar means I obtained the worthy services of Madame Giry, the box keeper; and with this old lady acting as go-between, I established an entirely foolproof system of receiving my unorthodox allowance. Oh, they tried to track me down, of course they did; but their consistent failure only increased their fear of me, and Poligny would not hear of involving the police—he had far too much to hide.

Once the pattern of my life was set, my existence proceeded with ceaseless regularity along a bleak and empty continuum entirely untroubled by emotion. I listened to endless operas and studied voice with cool composure. I wrote notes to the management whenever I had cause to raise some matter of grievance; a little missive from O.G., arriving mysteriously on a desk through the locked doors of the manager's office was guaranteed to put Poligny out of humor for the rest of the day! Sometimes I complained just for the pleasure of winding him up like a clockwork toy. Occasionally I even interfered with casting. I made sure that Madame Giry's little daughter, Meg, was promoted to be leader of a row—the child could dance as well as any of the others and it cost me very little effort to make her widowed mother smile with pride. But by and large I remained aloof and totally indifferent to the insularity and mediocrity of the performances. Very few people went to the Paris Opera for the quality of its music; they went to see and be seen.

I was indifferent to most things by that time, anyway—middle aged,

well past the angry frustrations of youth, a tall mourning candle burning steadily down into a pool of black wax.

All emotion and regret was behind me now that I had willingly
embraced the existence of the living dead.

I never expected to feel anything again. . . .

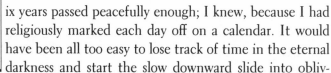 ix years passed peacefully enough; I knew, because I had
religiously marked each day off on a calendar. It would
have been all too easy to lose track of time in the eternal
darkness and start the slow downward slide into oblivion; to sink into the complacent carelessness that would inevitably
result in capture. I daresay I grew more eccentric with each passing
year, but I was determined not to lose my faculties or my fastidious
social standards. Jules saw to it that my dress suits were kept immaculate and that I never needed to wear a shirt more than once. The first
room I had completed in the house had been my glorious bathroom
with its exotic green marbled bath. Later I added a guest bathroom
beyond the second bedroom. God knows why, I certainly had no intention of entertaining anyone! It just seemed the done thing at the
time.

Yes, a full six years of reclusive, self-indulgent solitude passed before
I had the first of a devastating series of shocks.

I remember the evening very well. It was January 1881 and a cold,
cheerless Paris mist had shrouded the city, bringing an early dusk.
Seized by a sudden desire for fresh air and exercise, I ventured out into
the dark streets some considerable time before theater hour. The hood
of my opera cloak hid the mask, and thus attired I safely escaped
notice from passersby. To anyone who saw me I was simply another
frozen Parisian, hurrying home out of the cold and the threat of approaching rain.

I had reached the Rue de Rivoli and was brooding resentfully on the sad, blackened remains of the Tuileries palace when a rising wind whipped away the last of the mist and began to drive storm clouds overhead. As I turned to retrace my steps, the heavens opened; rain lashed down in torrents from the leaden sky and within minutes the street was awash with water. When you can no longer bear to get wet with total indifference, you know you are getting old. I raised my hand imperiously to a passing brougham cab.

The cab drew into the curb some distance ahead and waited for me. Almost immediately a man coming out of an apartment block on the same side of the road saw the cab and began to hurry toward it with an exclamation of delight. I saw nothing of him except his back, but he was wearing an opera cloak, like myself, and at this hour I could guess his destination with very little trouble.

"*My* cab, I think, monsieur," I hissed with a hostility that made him step aside in surprise.

Instinctively averting my face from his gaze, I swung into the carriage, slammed the door shut, and rapped my gold-topped walking stick on the dividing wall.

"To the Opera!" I said curtly, and sat back waiting to be obeyed.

To my astonished fury the door opened and the carriage rocked gently beneath the weight of the man who climbed inside.

I looked up, but the oath on my lips never took breath.

"Drive on, fellow," said this impertinent intruder calmly. "It so happens that I, too, am bound for the Opera. This gentleman and I are very well acquainted and I know he will be very happy to share the journey with me. . . . Is that not so, Erik?"

I could not reply. All I could do was stare at Nadir Khan with numbed disbelief.

"Will that be all right, monsieur?" shouted the driver uncertainly.

"Yes," I snapped. "Drive on!"

As the brougham lurched out into the open road, Nadir took off his opera hat and his gloves and laid them on the seat at his side. The first thing I noticed about him was his hair. Once black and luxuriant, it was now thin and very gray, making him look at least sixty. I was shocked at the change in him, shocked and horrified.

"Well, Erik," he said, "this is indeed a pleasant surprise."

"That is entirely a matter of opinion," I retorted, trying to hide my conflicting emotions behind a fine veneer of sarcasm. "What the devil brings you to Paris after all this time?"

"Oh"—he shrugged—"I have been here for many years now, ever since I was released from Mazanderan."

"Released?" I echoed, with grim foreboding. "How long were you held?"

"Five years," he said with indifference.

I looked out the window at the rain-lashed streets and my hand tightened on the walking stick with a mixture of rage and grief. My God! Five years in a Mazanderan jail! No wonder he looked more than sixty. . . . It was a miracle he had come out alive!

And what on earth was I going to do now, faced with the one person in this world that I could not simply remove from the dark paths of my solitude?

Invite him home?

I couldn't! It was impossible! *Unthinkable!* We no longer existed in the same world. There was no plane on which we could meet now, after more than twenty-five years.

"Did you leave Mazanderan of your own accord?" I demanded warily.

Nadir laughed.

"Let us say I was not invited to stay. My estates were forfeited, but I have been permitted to draw a modest pension from the imperial treasury in recognition of my royal descent. It has been sufficient for me to cultivate a taste for the opera. I hold a season ticket and attend as often as I am able to."

"You don't have a box?" I asked indignantly.

"But of course not, I am hardly—"

"You shall have one without delay. I shall speak to the management at once."

He looked bewildered.

"The management?"

Damn! What had possessed me to say that?

"I have some influence at the Opera," I continued guardedly.

"Influence?" I saw his expression change dramatically.

"I was one of the original contractors," I explained hastily. "I built the place."

"Oh, I see." He relaxed and sat back on his seat, a look of delight replacing the quiver of anxiety. "Then such a magnificent feat of engineering must have won you many further commissions."

"It was not a feat of engineering," I retorted coldly. "It was an act of love. I had no interest in further futile contracts on the surface of this earth once the building was completed."

I could not think why I was talking like this. Had I taken leave of my senses? Why didn't I just draw him a bloody map and have done with it?

Mercifully the carriage stopped in the rank on the rotunda and I opened the door, gesturing for him to get out.

On the pavement he paused to look back in surprise when I made no effort to follow him.

"Are you not attending tonight after all?" he inquired, looking puzzled.

"I never attend the Opera, except in my official capacity."

"Surely your official duties terminated with the completion of the building."

"Some duties can never be relinquished," I said.

I saw his gloved hand tighten on the carriage door. The suspicion in his dark eyes was now quite unmistakable.

"Erik, I don't like the way you talk of this, it gives me a very bad feeling."

"You had better hurry," I said, ignoring him. "The curtain rises in fifteen minutes and I am impatient to be home."

"Where do you live?" he demanded suddenly.

"That is no concern of yours or any other living creature."

"But it is nearby," he persisted. "You directed the cab to the Opera before you recognized me, so it must be nearby."

I shrugged contemptuously.

"Still the policeman, Nadir? Still tracking down a scent like the perennial bloodhound? Old habits die hard, don't they?"

"Don't think you can confuse me with your sarcasm," he retorted. "Why should you hide your home from me in this mysterious manner? Have I not deserved your trust?"

Beneath the mask I bit my lip until I tasted blood.

"I never entertain visitors," I said.

"Erik," he muttered with undisguised alarm, "What are you hiding from me? What have you done?"

I leaned forward in my seat to fix him with an icy stare.

"This is not Mazanderan," I told him coldly. "You have no jurisdiction in this country. Now, listen to me and listen very carefully. *Do not follow me.* I warn you very seriously that anyone who tries to gain access to my house without my knowledge will have bitter cause to regret it. And you ought to know by now that my warnings are not to be treated with contempt. Remember the scorpion . . . remember the scorpion and keep well away from my house. . . . Do you understand, Nadir? *Keep away!*"

His hand slid from the carriage door and he stood back with trancelike obedience. He made no effort to prevent the brougham moving away, but although I knew my secret was safe for tonight, I felt no complacency.

Once before he had broken free of my control, torn down the swaddling cocoon of sound with which I had bound him. Unlike Jules he was not a natural subject; his will was too strong, his sense of identity and purpose too well developed.

Whenever he chose to fight my voice, I knew I would be unable to hold him.

I saw him so many times at the Opera after that evening that I wondered how I could possibly have overlooked his presence all these years. I must have been going around with my eyes closed!

He prowled around the building outside theater hours, questioning the hundreds of people who worked on the premises, making notes in a little black book and generally making an absolute nuisance of himself. Persistent and efficient as he was, I knew it was only a question of time before he unearthed some very interesting answers, and my sense of unease increased steadily.

One evening, roughly two months after Nadir first appeared on the scene, I returned to my house to find the alarm bell ringing. I knew there was no one on the lake . . . so it had to be the torture chamber. There was someone in the torture chamber!

My heart gave a sickening lurch of fear as I considered who it must be.

Turning off the electrical supply, I rushed into the chamber in a breathless panic. The room was still as hot as a furnace, but it was in pitch darkness now and I could only dimly see the blacker outline of the body which swung from the iron tree in the corner.

I stood absolutely still, paralyzed with horror, too shocked even to cry out. A great pressure seemed to have gathered behind my rib cage and there was a curious numbness in my left arm.

Why? Why must the only victim of this virtually obsolete mantrap be my honest, stubborn, foolhardy friend? It was my fault . . . all my fault . . . I had known what he was like, I should have dismantled the whole device as soon as I knew he was on the premises.

Nadir, I warned you. . . . I warned you to keep away!

It was a long time before I could conquer my revulsion and horror sufficiently to cut the body down and switch on the lights.

The blackened, distorted face and the bulging eyes were almost unrecognizable; it was a full minute before I suddenly realized that I was not looking at Nadir after all, and my relief was so great that I began to laugh hysterically.

Returning to the drawing room I sat down at the piano and played Chopin's Prelude in B minor, sotto voce, until I was calm enough to go back and examine the body with indifference and rationality.

The clothing alone was sufficient to place it now. I knew this man. His name was Joseph Buquet and he was one of the chief scene shifters. We had once had the misfortune to meet on the little staircase by the footlights which leads down to the cellars, and since I had not been wearing the mask, the fellow had had a damned good look at me. He had been responsible for one of the few authentic descriptions which now circulated around the dressing rooms of the corps de ballet.

How he had stumbled upon my secret lair I could not tell. Perhaps in the course of his work he had leaned against the mechanism that released the stone in the third cellar. I would have to alter the setting if that was so, make it more difficult to open. I really couldn't have people dropping in like this!

I looked down on him with a little regret and a great deal of annoyance. Did I ask people to come here and kill themselves? Did I lure them deliberately to their end? Well, then, I was not responsible for this death, I would *not* be held responsible. I was no more at fault than any householder who sleeps with a loaded shotgun in the house for fear of intruders.

Besides, this wasn't murder, it was suicide. And if a man wants to commit suicide, who am I to stop him?

I did not like to throw the body in the lake. Even weighted down, dead bodies have an unpleasant habit of finding their way back to the surface when filled with the noxious gases of putrefaction.

It occurred to me at length that if Buquet had taken his life here in my house, he might just as easily have chosen to take it in the third cellar. And so a few hours before curtain time I took the poor fellow back there and hung him up neatly like a coat on a peg. He was old and no doubt had had a sad, hard life. I'd probably done him a favor. . . .

He was found at the end of the performance, but his demise excited little excitement. A policeman came, asked a few routine questions, yawned, and went away again. One more suicide for an unhallowed grave, that was all; hardly a case that required the attention of the Paris Sûreté!

I resolved to put the unpleasant incident out of my mind, but at the end of the week, when I went to box five on the grand tier I found an envelope addressed *For the attention of O.G.* sitting on the ledge.

I hardly needed to open it; I knew exactly what I was going to find inside.

Promptly at eight o'clock that evening I rapped once on the door of Nadir's flat in the Rue de Rivoli.

Darius showed me inside. . . .

"So you are the Opera Ghost!" said Nadir grimly. "You can have no idea how much I hoped I was mistaken!"

I took off my cloak and sat down uninvited in the fireside chair, taking in the paucity of my surroundings with appalled eyes. It was perfectly evident that he did not live in any great luxury on his imperial pension, and I remembered his beautiful estate in Persia with hot shame. I would never willingly have brought him to exile and sadly reduced circumstances . . . never!

"You're not even going to bother to deny it, are you?" continued Nadir, outraged at my silence.

I peeled off my gloves slowly and laid them in my hat.

"What is the point in my denying anything? You've already tried and condemned me, haven't you? But I don't see why you're so angry. I'm a very harmless ghost, as a rule."

"That's not what I hear, Erik. The whole establishment goes in fear of you!"

"Oh, really?" I sighed. "A few silly girls and credulous old ladies?"

"And a management that meets your every demand!"

I frowned. "The world is full of victims and predators. Survival of the fittest is only the process of natural selection. Good Lord, you lived in Persia long enough to know that. And my terms are modest enough, all things considered."

"Twenty thousand francs a month is hardly modest!"

"I have expensive tastes," I said.

He made a gesture of angry despair and sank into the chair opposite.

"I risked my life to save you," he said slowly. "I risked everything I possessed!"

I tried to laugh.

"You really mustn't take that to heart. We all make errors of judgment from time to time."

"I wanted to preserve your unique genius," he continued inexorably, exactly as though I had not spoken, "your brilliance . . . your enormous capacity for good."

"I beg your pardon," I said ironically. "I'm afraid you've really lost me there. I think you must have a wire crossed somewhere."

Still he ignored my desperate banter, staring at me with a saddened disbelief I could scarcely bear.

"And this is how you repay my sacrifice," he said dully. "You become a ghost!"

He looked about to weep, and suddenly I wanted to die of shame.

"You promised me." He sounded as though he were choking on the words. "You *promised* me you would not kill again except in self-defense."

I looked away into the fire. The sound of the clock ticking steadily on the mantelpiece seemed to mock us both with its cozy domesticity.

"I've tried to keep that promise," I said softly.

His thin hands clenched on the arms of his chair.

"Well, you obviously didn't try hard enough, did you?"

"What do you mean by that?"

"Joseph Buquet is what I mean."

I raised my shoulders in a noncommittal gesture.

"The man committed suicide. The police are satisfied of that, are they not?"

"Yes," he admitted grudgingly.

"Well, then, what has that to do with me?"

Nadir got up and came to stand over my chair.

"Do you think I don't recognize your trademark when I see it? How many suicides were there in Persia, Erik—can you even remember? Can you? Or have you wiped it all out, lost it in the mists of some opium-induced fog?"

Suddenly he paused, bending forward to seize my right arm and jerk back the sleeves of my shirt and dress coat. He stared for a moment at the mass of bruises which followed the lines of my collapsed veins.

"May Allah forgive me!" he muttered. "This is my fault. You were ready to die that night when I came to arrest you. I should not have interfered. I see now that in condemning you to live I did no service to you or to the world."

I pulled down my sleeves, retrieved and refastened the gold cuff link which his violence had sent spinning into the hearth.

"Do you mean to betray me to the police?" I inquired with indifference.

He laughed shortly.

"Would I live long enough to do it?"

I stared at him. It was a shock to find that even after all this time words still had the power to hurt me.

"You honestly think I'm capable of that?"

"I don't know what you're capable of, Erik, not anymore—not with your veins full of morphine."

"What are you going to do?" I asked dully.

"What can I do?" he demanded, with resentment. "What can I do that isn't going to haunt me with guilt all the rest of my life?"

"Nadir—"

He turned his back on me abruptly.

"Go back to the Opera," he said coldly. "Continue to haunt the premises if it gives you satisfaction to squander your talents in this extraordinary fashion. Blackmail Poligny as you will—from what I've seen of the man I daresay he deserves it. But if there is one more mysterious death in that building—just one—I promise you I shall tell the authorities everything I know. And they'll find you, if they have to take the Opera apart brick by brick. They'll find you wherever you have gone to ground. I mean to watch over you very carefully from now on, Erik. This is the last chance I shall give you. Next time there will be no reprieve—for either of us."

I rose slowly and, collecting my stick, hat, and gloves, signified my intention of leaving. Nadir stood back and let me pass unhindered to the door.

"Erik."

I turned to look back at him, wondering if he saw past my cold dignity to the flayed remnants of my pride.

"You could have been such a very great man," he said sadly, "distinguished beyond all other members of the human race. It's such a waste —such a tragic waste!"

I went slowly down the shabby stairs and out into the street beyond. He had destroyed my complacency and my peace of mind, insulted, threatened, and humiliated me. Men had died at my hand for far less than I had meekly accepted from Nadir tonight.

I should have felt angry, but I only felt sad—sad and degraded beyond measure by the bitterness of his terrible disappointment.

I wished I could hate him, but I couldn't.

He was still my conscience.

rom that day he became my shadow and I knew that every move I made beyond the lake would eventually find its way into that wretched little notebook of his. I found his persistence utterly infuriating and yet in its own way curiously flattering—almost . . . *endearing*. And eventually, to spare us both an intolerable amount of inconvenience, I agreed to meet him once a week on the banks of the lake, so that he might satisfy himself as to my continued good behavior.

I'm not convinced that either of us was acknowledging his true motives for this regular ritual. Ostensibly he was keeping me under surveillance and I was jealously guarding my territory, but we smiled automatically when we met and there was a vague feeling of mutual regret on parting that I was reluctant to analyze.

I was beginning to understand that he was very lonely. He had acquaintances here in Paris, even some arrangement with a lady of doubtful reputation—to be honest, I was quite amazed at what he confided to me at times! But there seemed to be a great void in his life that he had been unable or unwilling to fill. After all these years I don't think he had ever really got over losing his wife . . . losing Reza.

"So there you are!" he would say brusquely, whenever I chose to materialize out of the darkness beside him. "You're late again. Don't you know I've better things to do than hang around here waiting for you to show up?"

Actually the truth was that he didn't have anything better to do, and I found that rather tragic. Christ, how could a man so innately good and kind as Nadir be reduced to voluntarily spending time in the company of a half-crazed monster? Why didn't he just have me arrested and put his misplaced guilt behind him? It was no fault of his that I was a murderer, an extortionist, and a morphine addict.

The still waters of resignation that had surrounded me now for more than six years were being relentlessly stirred by his presence. I'd finally come to terms with reality and succeeded in constructing an ideal existence in which to live out what remained of my life in numbed indifference. I had my music, my inventions, a regular income, and I was contented. . . . I was bloody contented!

Now suddenly I was afraid.

I didn't want Nadir back in my life; I didn't want anyone. But I was glad to see him waiting for me on the far bank of the lake each week and that gladness was a deep inward terror. Because it meant I hadn't really learned to do without people after all; I'd started to need his stern criticism, his serious conversation, and the occasional outraged laughter that I discovered I could still light in him. I was groping out once more in the darkness, but sooner or later I knew that I was going to touch cold metal bars and draw back in horror at the sight of my prison. Once I admitted to myself that I could still feel emotion I became vulnerable, I exposed all that painful scar tissue to the knife again. And I wasn't young and resilient anymore, I no longer had those remarkable powers of healing. I couldn't bear the thought of any more pain.

My old interest in divination had never left me, and from time to time I still consulted the tarot cards in a desultory fashion. It was a long while since they had revealed anything significant, but now of late, each time I picked a card at random I seemed to turn up *Death*.

Death . . . or *the Lovers.*

I could not interpret this cryptic message, but it seemed to be irredeemably bound up with a feeling of doom that was beginning to weigh ever more heavily upon me. I felt very strongly that somewhere beyond the lake a knife was being sharpened, honed to a gleaming point in readiness for me to run upon it in the blinding light of day.

I was afraid . . . but I did not know what I feared.

And so, even as I walked with Nadir, talked with him, rejoiced in the warmth of communicating directly once more with a human soul, there was a part of me that looked at him with wary suspicion and wondered what part fate had assigned him in this new unrehearsed opera.

Not the lover, that was for certain. I'd seen enough girls leaving his apartments in Persia to be reassured that all his instincts were purely heterosexual.

Death, then. . . .

Oh, God, surely not his! I could think of no conceivable situation in which I would be prepared to do him harm—nothing in this world that would make me commit such an unthinkable horror.

But if it was not his death I saw, then it must be mine.

Well, I was not afraid of death. I'd spent the best part of fifty years waiting patiently for its release.

No, it wasn't death I feared now.

It was that other inexplicable symbol.

Twenty-two face cards in a Tarot pack.

Why was I suddenly so sure I should have turned up *the Fool?*

"You're very preoccupied today," said Nadir with severity. "I don't like the way you keep staring into space and forgetting to answer me. And flexing your left hand all the time . . . you're not trying to make me nervous, by any chance, are you? It won't work, you know."

"Don't be stupid," I said absently. "My hand's gone numb, that's all."

"I'm not surprised," he muttered. "This place is a cold as a tomb. I really don't see why we can't take coffee at your house in a civilized manner. I consider it most uncivil of you."

He was right, of course. It was very inhospitable of me, appalling bad manners in fact; but my house was my barricade against the world and I could not bring myself to breach its defenses. Once he knew its secrets I would be entirely at the mercy of his good intentions. It would be total surrender—a sort of captivity which I was simply not prepared to tolerate.

"I have to go now," I said. It was always time to go when the conversation turned, as it inevitably did, to the location of my secret lair. "Don't wait for me here next week," I added.

"Why?" he demanded instantly. "What are you up to now, Erik?"

"The present management is retiring from office." I sighed. "I expect to be rather busy for a week or so in consequence."

He frowned. "I should like to know just exactly what you are planning."

"Oh, nothing more than a little letter of welcome. You know, I consider it very poor spirited of Poligny and Debienne simply to give up the ghost like this."

Nadir's lips twitched on the verge of a smile and then, as I watched, down came all that schoolmaster dignity, like a shutter, just as it had done that night in Persia when I offered to teach him how to pick pockets.

"Surely you're not going to continue to play these iniquitous tricks on Messieurs Richard and Moncharmin." He sighed.

"Why not? It's been a very profitable arrangement up till now."

"I had hoped—"

"For what?" I laughed. "A change of heart in some maudlin access of remorse? *Confession*, perhaps?"

He turned away abruptly. "You make me very glad I'm not a Catholic," he said rather bitterly. "Just remember, whatever you decide to do now . . . I shall be watching you."

"You're always watching," I retorted amiably. "What a pity you never *quite* manage to see."

And handing him his pocket watch once more, I left him alone in the darkness.

I had made light of the matter to Nadir, but in point of fact this change of management was a damnable inconvenience to me. I could not be sure that Poligny's successors would prove one half as gullible and malleable as he; and should they prove obstinate, my allowance could very quickly come to an untimely end. For myself it hardly mattered—I had sufficient now to see myself out in comfort. But Jules had two sons at the School of Fine Arts, one at the School of Medicine, and six more children whose futures must be considered.

I had no intention of abandoning my commitment to a man I had quite unwittingly destroyed.

So, I would have to tackle Poligny—make sure he passed on the terms of the Opera lease before he cut his losses and ran. I needed to put the fear of worse than God in him one last time.

A curt note deposited on his desk would bring him quaking in his shoes to watch the evening's performance from box five; my voice would do the rest.

We had been through this little farce of mine many times now. Nothing amused me more than the deferential way in which Poligny approached the armchair in which he perceived my voice to be sitting, the earnest, anxious expression on his fat face as he conversed nervously with thin air. Hidden inside the enormous column of hollowed marble, which I raised and lowered exactly as I pleased, it was all I could do sometimes not to laugh out loud as I watched the absurd obsequiousness of his gestures. Short of getting down on his hands and knees he could hardly have shown me much more respect! He was indeed my very favorite victim, riddled with theatrical superstition and credulous beyond belief. It honestly amazed me that anyone so naive could possibly have any habits that would not bear public scrutiny, but there he was—a fat, stupid fish dangling helplessly on the end of my line. He had made my existence quite criminally comfortable, and I was going to miss him sadly.

We should have one last, cozy little chat before I said au revoir. . . .

I reached box five early in the morning, well before anyone was around. There was a long uncomfortable wait ahead of me inside that hollow pillar, and since I was not eager to take up my position there a moment before it was necessary, I sat back among the shadows and read *Madame Bovary* and *Salammbô*. They say that Flaubert became a recluse in order to write; I found that interesting. . . .

Two hours later, having finished both novels, I turned in boredom to study last night's program, which had been dutifully left on the little shelf for my perusal by my worthy Madame Giry.

Meyerbeer! Thank God I hadn't bothered to attend for weeks. There is a very commonplace talent if I ever saw one, a man who thought spectacular stage effects would compensate for the mediocrity of his music. The only things worth remembering in *Le Prophète* were the roller skaters and the horse! At least Mozart knew that music must speak for itself. *Don Giovanni*, now, that was truly memorable; and

The Magic Flute—charmingly whimsical—amusing! Although of course we didn't have anyone at the moment who could do justice to the Queen of the Night. I had yet to hear a soprano *acuto sfogato* who didn't sound like the whistle of a demented peanut vendor. Mercifully, it was a role that lay well outside the range of La Carlotta. Really, that woman's voice left me stone cold. What a great pity our current leading lady never felt the urge to go back to her native Spain. . . .

I tossed the program aside with a gesture of contempt and studied my pocket watch with a sigh. Seven o'clock in the morning—time I was no longer visible on the premises.

As I stood up, the newly installed electric lights in the auditorium were lit unexpectedly and I shrank back against the hangings in fury. Damn them, *damn them!* Who was it now? Not scene shifters by the sound of the high-pitched laughter.

Silly, giggling chorus girls no doubt, ballet dancers escaped from the unending regime of rehearsals in the dance salon behind the stage. Normally I would have had a little good-natured fun at their expense, given them a new tale with which to terrify their wide-eyed colleagues, but today I wasn't in the mood for foolish pranks. I felt strangely tired and out of sorts; that peculiar sensation of constricting pressure was back in my chest. I simply wished they would go away and leave me in peace.

A chord was struck in the orchestra pit.

"Meg!" said a girl's nervous voice. "For pity's sake, you'll be heard and then there'll be trouble. You know we shouldn't be here."

"Oh, don't be so spineless, Christine Daae, no one's going to hear us . . . except perhaps the Phantom."

"The *what?*"

"The Phantom. Don't tell me you've never heard about the Opera Ghost! My dear child, what sort of dream do you live in? Everyone knows about the Opera Ghost. No . . . don't laugh! It's true. Look . . . you see box five up there on the grand tier . . . that's his. Always has been as far back as anyone remembers. It's never sold at the box office, even on a gala night. They say it would bring terrible bad luck on the whole theater if it was."

"How do you know all this, Meg Giry?"

"Never you mind how I know, I just do that's all. We know a lot about the Opera Ghost, Ma and I, but it isn't safe to talk about it here. And you'd better believe me for your own good—he doesn't like people who don't know how to show a proper respect, and when he's angry terrible things happen."

"What sort of things?" I heard real alarm enter the other voice now.

"Awful things!" said Meg cheerfully, "truly *awful*. The floor in our dressing room starts to run with blood . . ."

Up in box five I blinked in surprised amusement. That was a new one! Little Giry should be writing Gothic novels, not prancing around the stage dressed as a water nymph!

". . . disembodied hands come out of the wall and crawl across the stage," continued Meg with glee, "and people just disappear and are never seen again alive. Like Joseph Buquet."

"I thought that poor old man hanged himself."

"Oh, that's just the story that was put around by the management to prevent a panic. Everyone who knows *anything* agrees it was the Opera Ghost who did it."

I frowned. This I did not like so well. Little Meg had better watch her wagging tongue. I had engineered her promotion to leader of the row; I could just as easily reverse that arrangement when I spoke to Poligny tonight.

"Of course he's not always angry," Meg added absently. "Sometimes he's quite kind. . . . Look, I shouldn't say this, it's a secret, but he's been very generous to Ma and me—he gave me a chance, you know, got Monsieur Poligny to notice me."

Silent and resigned in my hiding place, I abandoned all thought of humiliating Meg. She was only a child, only a silly chattering, harmless child who had no idea that she was annoying a cantankerous, aging monster. . . .

"It isn't the first time he's made changes to the cast, you know, Christine. Ma says the Opera Ghost knows everything about music and that Monsieur Poligny relies on his judgment entirely. Why don't you sing for him? Wherever he is he'll hear and perhaps he'll make changes for you too."

"Don't be silly, Meg!" The girl sounded suddenly very uneasy.

"Are you afraid of him?"

"No, of course not! As a matter of fact I don't believe a single word you've told me about him!"

"Yes, you do! You've gone as white as a sheet!"

"I think we ought to go now."

"Oh, Christine, you're always so serious, you never have any fun! Listen, Ma says that *Faust* is the Opera Ghost's favorite production. you know the role of Margarita, don't you?"

"Yes, but I haven't—"

"Oh, don't be such a wretched little coward! Sing for the Phantom, Christine. Let him hear you! Who knows what may come of it."

The girl sounded frightened to death, and I suddenly felt rather sorry for her. If she couldn't stand up to little Giry's bullying, she had no future on the stage as a prima donna—probably couldn't sing anyway. But I might as well listen, I really had nothing better to do at the moment, and I could always put my hands over my ears if it was too painful.

I sat back in my chair indulgently and, as Meg's inept fingers fumbled for the right chords, prepared to be quietly disappointed.

When the girl began to sing, I leapt from the chair as though I had put my hand upon live wires and received a fatal voltage.

Oh, how strange!
Like a spell does the evening bind me!
And a deep languid charm
I feel without alarm
With its melody enwind me
And all my heart subdue. . . .

Oh, it was certainly painful, quite unbearably painful . . . but I had no desire to put my hands over my ears!

Perfect pitch, a crystal clarity of tone, no weakness in either register . . . this girl possessed a near perfect instrument!

And lacked the inner will to play it!

I had never heard a voice so sweet and true, nor one as utterly *negative*. Her boundless potential lay almost wholly untapped, like a rich vein of gold buried beneath the dead weight of strangling indifference. There was nothing there except faultless technique. She sang without soul—no expression, no joy, no sorrow . . . *nothing!* It was like listening to an extraordinarily talented zombie!

There was something terribly wrong with this girl, a near extinction of spirit that made her voice affect me like a cry in the dark. She was dying slowly on that stage, drowning in my ears. . . . I couldn't bear to listen a moment longer. I must not think what I might have made of that lovely, lifeless voice had it only been entrusted to my care.

But first I must see what she looked like; I must know so that I could take great care never to listen to her again by some monstrous mischance. A second time would surely drive me right out of my mind!

Forgetting my normal caution, I moved from the shadows to the velvet-hung ledge of the box and looked down. I looked out into the bright light of the auditorium's new electric globes.

And the knife that I had dimly feared all these months buried itself to the hilt in my throat.

Her name was a stranger's, unfamiliar and foreign.

But she was not a stranger to me.

I knew this girl. . . .

Beneath me now the horseshoe auditorium lay dark and silent once more, its lights long since extinguished.

For a long time I remained slumped in that armchair in box five, risking discovery with dull indifference. I felt as though I had been disemboweled; I was shaking from head to foot and I could not get my breath.

It had to be a hallucination, an optical illusion created by the lights and my troubled mind. The morphine was slowly rotting my brain, dragging me down into a morass of incoherent, impossible dreams.

And yet I knew what I had seen!

I couldn't wait for Poligny now, I'd have to deal with him another day when I had my wits about me. I had to get away from this place quickly, crawl back to the safety of my lair, and hide like a mortally wounded animal.

At no time during my entire residence at the Opera had I been so vulnerable to discovery as I was on that desperate flight below. I blundered through the corridors, taking no heed to move with stealth, neither knowing nor caring who might observe my progress. My left hand was so numbed that the pivots of the stone in the third cellar refused to yield to me at first. I clawed at the mechanism with a cry of rage and my fingers were bleeding before the stone finally responded to my clumsy touch and admitted me to the sanctuary that lay behind it.

I vowed that I would never go back above the ground again. I would stay here, like a hermit crab in its shell and drown myself in my music. Somewhere in the labyrinth of my mind I would find a grave deep enough to bury this shameful longing; if I burrowed fast enough, like a demented mole, it would be possible to escape from the pain . . . the unimaginable pain!

Yet everything that met my gaze here in my precious home now filled me with bewildered horror. I saw, as though for the first time, that my room was a mortuary chamber and my bed was a coffin.

A coffin!

Everywhere I looked my eyes recoiled in shock from the evidence of my chosen existence; I stared in cold disbelief at the residence of a corpse.

What was I doing here in this tomb? I was alive! I was *alive!*

I was alive and I had never lived.

Ayesha leapt from the pipe organ to welcome me, but now there was no comfort in the warmth of that soft, sleek little body. The touch of her fur was just a horrible mockery and I turned from her fawning affection with revolted despair.

Like a house with no foundations, unable to resist the first tremor of an earthquake, my existence had tumbled all around me in ruins.

I suddenly saw that there was nothing left for me here.

No refuge.

No place to hide.

Hell is not a place, it's a state of mind and body; hell is obsession with a voice, a face, a name. . . .

I was obsessed with Christine Daae, irretrievably and disgustingly fixated with the desire to possess what I knew I could never have. It

was as though I had lain nearly half a century in suspended animation
and now awoke to the ravages of sheer animal hunger.

I tried to stand back and mock at my weakness with sneering detachment, to tell myself it was utterly *indecent* to feel the lovesick
yearnings of a callow boy at my age. My lust was an obscenity which
must be scourged out of my hateful body.

I punished myself without mercy for the wickedness of wanting. I
set up a mirror and forced myself to look into it, without the mask; I
withheld my morphine until I was a shaking wreck. . . .

But still I wanted her. . . .

I began to lie to myself, to cheat and deceive that other half which
cried out that this could not be, this must not be.

Oh, yes, said this newly awakened side of me with masterful cunning, *I know all about* that, *I accepted* that *ages ago, I'm only going
back up there now to amuse myself, truly. . . . Look, you can rely on
me to be sensible. Have I ever not been sensible? Have I ever shown you
up, made you ashamed of me? I think you might trust me to behave
now.*

He was very strong, this other side of me, ungovernable as a wild
stallion and terribly clever. I began to listen helplessly to his insidious
whispering.

*You only want to see her, that's all, just to see her. What's wrong
with that, you gutless fool? Listen. . . . I'll tell you what you ought to
do now. . . .*

And so it began—the shameless plotting and scheming to establish
communication between Christine and myself.

A series of minor misfortunes befell her succeeding dressing rooms,
so that eventually she was resettled exactly where I wanted her, in a
long-disused room at the end of an unfrequented corridor. Here in this
room many years ago I had taken the precaution of installing a system
of pivots behind the huge mirror to conceal the old Communard road
which led down to the lake. The poky, inconveniently placed chamber
was highly unpopular with artistes and said to be haunted; I had
driven out more than one hapless occupant with a little subtly applied
ventriloquism.

But I was glad of this room now, glad of the glass which showed
itself to Christine as a mirror and to me as a window. Night after night

I stood behind the wall and worshiped her in silence while her dresser combed out her lovely dark hair. I saw her face gazing sightlessly into the little mirror on the dressing table. Her eyes were always distant and preoccupied, ineffably sad as they searched the mirror in a hopeless quest for something that was never revealed. Often, just before the curtain rose, she would sit very still with her hands pressed against her temples, as though listening intently for a voice she could not hear. I knew by now that her father had died some time back, that they had been inseparably close, that she still mourned his passing with an unnatural and unhealthy intensity. Such quiet, controlled, and yet infinitely destructive sadness made me ache to comfort her even as my eyes devoured her.

I knew this child was not a natural survivor. The world would crush her under its cruel heel without compunction, never seeing the delicate petals that lay bruised and trampled in the mud. Spiteful rivals, unkind critics, ruthless managers, and dubious patrons . . . I cringed at the pain that inevitably lay ahead of her. Without the protection of a strong man she would be destroyed body and soul by the brutal demands of a notoriously callous profession.

The cruel familiarity of her features still stunned me with grief. She was a lovely, wilting flower that I longed to rescue from the strangling creep of weeds. I wanted to plant her safely in the labyrinth beneath the Opera House, to hide her from the world so that no one else should ever find her, hurt her . . . take her away from me. I could make her grow—I *knew* I could make her grow—if only I dared to reach out and lift her from the barren, acrid soil that was stifling her natural talent.

To steal her . . . to spirit her away. . . .

What madness!

"Go away!" she said rudely to her dresser one evening.

"*Mademoiselle!*"

"Go away, go away, go *away!*"

Behind the mirror I stiffened in alarm as Christine flung into the room and threw herself down on the little stool at her dressing table. In all the weeks I had been watching her I had never guessed she could summon sufficient energy and emotion to have a prima donna's tantrum. Something had happened, something had roused her from her customary apathy and brought a flush to her pale face.

"Beast!" she exclaimed, when the dresser had left, obviously just as startled as I was. "That fat cow . . . that *mean* fat cow. . . . I don't sing like a limping sparrow. . . . I *don't!* I hope you get nodules on your cords, Carlotta. . . . I hope that every time you open your mouth you croak like the horrid toad that you are!"

I was almost smiling at this splendid animation, governing an absurd impulse to cheer, when Christine suddenly put her head down on the dressing table and began to cry like a lost child.

"No, I don't wish that," she whispered brokenly. "I don't wish anything so wicked, God forgive me. I know it's true—I can't sing, I never could. Oh, Papa, why did you make promises you knew you couldn't keep? There's no Angel of Music waiting for me. There never was an Angel of Music. Why did you lie . . . why didn't you just *tell* me I'd never be any good?"

Behind the mirror my blood had begun to throb hotly, drumming intense excitement through my veins.

She wanted an Angel of Music—an angel who would make her believe in herself at last.

I'd been the Angel of Doom for the khanum. There was no reason in the world why I could not be the Angel of Music for Christine. I couldn't hope to be a man to her, I couldn't ever be a real, breathing, living man waking at her side and reaching out for her. . . .

But I could be her angel.

My voice was my one beauty, my only power, my only hope; my voice would open a magic pathway into her life. I could not steal her body—but I could steal her voice and weld it irretrievably with mine; I could take it and mold it and make it mine forever, one little part of her that no other man should ever possess. All I had to do was break the silence that stood like a wall between us.

Softly at first, infinitely softly, I began to sing an old heathen, Romany song. The hollowed bricks carried the haunting melody relentlessly to her, permitted my voice to envelop her gently like a poisonous mist, seeping inexorably into her mind and staining her soul with darkness.

I watched the dawning awareness of her body. Like a snake responding instinctively to its charmer, she rose slowly and lifted her hand to my unseen presence. In her eyes I saw tremulous joy and bewildered recognition; it was as though she had been waiting all her life for this moment of revelation.

Before the huge mirror she knelt with a humility and reverence that stunned me momentarily into silence.

I knew then that there could be no turning back.

Wherever this shadowed path might lead, we were both irrevocably committed to follow it to the end.

Counterpoint: Erik and Christine 1881

From the journal of Christine Daae, 1881

This isn't a diary, not in the accepted sense of the term.

I've no intention of sitting down dutifully each day to record tedious details of what I had for breakfast, which gown I ordered from my seamstress, and who said what to whom in the course of rehearsals. It's surely the height of vanity to assume anyone will want to read about your petty, unimportant little life a hundred years from now. I don't want anyone to read this document ever, for if they do I'll surely be locked up somewhere out of harm's way and people will go around shaking their heads and saying: "Poor Christine, such a shame, but of course I always had the suspicion she wasn't quite right in the head— never had her feet on the ground, you know, even as a young girl."

No, this isn't a diary.

It's simply an attempt to prove to myself that I still retain my hold on sanity, that what has happened to me is real and not the product of an unstable mind and a wildly overactive imagination. The events of the last three months have been so strange, so bizarre, so wonderful, that I dare not speak of them except here on this paper.

I have heard the Angel of Music.

Oh, God . . . somehow I hoped it would look better neatly written down in my orderly copperplate hand; but it doesn't. It just looks what it is—mad!

I am not mad. I do not suffer from hallucinations, nor do I dream. I hear his voice inside my head as plainly as I hear anything else, but it is not a voice that belongs to this world; it is far, far too beautiful to be human.

Papa often spoke of the Angel of Music, but though I continued to listen to his stories with delight, I only really believed in the Angel when I was very young. It was just one of Papa's whimsical fancies, a bedtime tale that I hugged throughout my childhood and relinquished sadly when I reached the age of reason and disillusionment. I daresay I reached that age far later than most girls. Papa had a horror of my growing up and leaving him; he kept me a child until the day he died . . . and then suddenly I had to grow up overnight.

I entered the Conservatoire to study voice, just as he had wished, but I knew at the end of the first week that I was never going to be able to fulfill his dreams. I was never going to be a great prima donna. Either I'd forgotten how to sing or I never knew how to do it in the first place; increasingly I came to believe the latter case was true. Papa was a wonderful musician, but he'd allowed fond parental bias to sway his judgment where I was concerned. He'd built me a castle of dreams and abandoned me there; and day after day I wandered farther from the beautiful rooms we had inhabited together, until I found myself locked in the dungeon of despair. That was a place Papa had never told me about. I didn't know it existed until I heard the heavy door clang shut behind me; but I knew I'd never get out again because I didn't have the key. And the Angel of Music would never find me now, even if he bothered to come looking. I had lost the will to strive for perfection and the ability to dream; sometimes I felt I was only half alive.

And then, on the very night when I had finally decided to abandon my hopeless career altogether, suddenly the Angel of Music was there with me.

I can hardly describe what I felt when I first heard his voice. There was an enormous exultation, but also a terrible fear of my own unworthiness, an utter terror that he would leave me as suddenly and as mysteriously as he had come. Even now after three months' tuition and a progress that is astonishing in my own ears, I am still riddled by the fear that one day I shall fail to please him. He's so stern and exacting in his demand for perfection; he never praises me, even when I know I have done well. He remains aloof and cold in his timeless, imperishable wisdom and I know that the worship of a mortal heart can mean nothing to him.

But his voice is my inspiration and my reward. It lifts me from my earthly shell and carries me to the very edge of the universe, a wondrous flight of body and soul that leaves me utterly exhausted.

When he is gone I only wish to sleep, for I know that in my dreams I shall hear that voice again.

I am living in a dream.

There is no reality, no existence, beyond those fleeting hours in which I teach her. The time between her lessons is a meaningless void, and the nights when she does not come to the theater are one long, unending fever of anguished waiting. It seems to me that I do nothing now but sit staring at the clock, willing time away, so that once more I may be close to her. So near, so near . . . and yet so far away.

The calendar tells me three months have passed, but they could be three seconds or three centuries for all the difference it makes. I am intoxicated by my power over her voice. I have broken the chains of mediocrity with which the Conservatoire had bound her and set her free to explore the outer reaches of her own genius. Again and again I toss her to the sky like a young gerfalcon and each time she soars with greater confidence and strength before returning to the safety of her master's gloved hand. All she needed was belief and will and inspiration, and these things she has found in my voice.

She's ready now to face the world's acclaim, and nothing on this earth will prevent me from masterminding her career here at the Opera.

When I have drunk her success and gorged on her triumph, like a glutted spider, I shall surely appease the ravening hunger that consumes me from within.

In time the pain will lessen.

I have to believe that.

*   *   *

Before he left me tonight the Angel of Music told me the strangest thing. He said I must be prepared to sing Carlotta's role in the gala performance on Friday night. I asked him how that could be, for even if Carlotta should not appear, I'm not her understudy, no one's going to think of me.

"You will not ask questions," he said coldly. "Everything will be arranged according to my will, that is all you need to know."

I was frightened. I begged him not to do this to me, I said I was not ready to face such a challenge alone.

"You will not be alone," he said more gently now. "I shall be with you all the time. As long as you believe in me, you will hear my voice in your mind and you will not be afraid to sing like an angel yourself. Trust me, child. Give me your soul and in return I will give you the heart of Paris."

La Carlotta has been taken ill and so has her understudy. What a shame! Could it possibly be something they've eaten?

No one suspects the Opera Ghost this time, of course. Why should they? After all, these little things are sent to try us!

Desperation has seized the management, for they're new to this game and don't know how to handle last-minute alterations—and these alterations are extremely last minute, I've made quite sure of that. There's a full house tonight and both Richard and Moncharmin have an instinctive aversion to losing money that I suppose I really ought to commend. They're out of their minds at the thought of having to cancel. The answer is there on their desk, of course—all they have to do is listen to O.G.

"How the hell do these wretched notes keep getting in here, Moncharmin? We've already had the locks changed twice! This black-mail is really getting quite beyond a joke. What does the damned lunatic want now?"

He doesn't appear to want anything for once. He merely informs us —as a passing courtesy, so he says—"

"Hah!"

". . . that Christine Daae knows all Carlotta's roles."

"Daae . . . *Daae?* Isn't that the little Scandinavian girl? Good

Lord, she's very young, barely out of the Conservatoire, if I remember rightly. Do you really think she's up to it?"

"I haven't a clue, dear fellow, I leave all that side to you. At least you know a top C when you hear it. I don't pretend to know the first thing about music, I'm only here because the minister likes my after-dinner conversation. Still, if Daae knows the roles, you'd better get her in here quickly. The curtain goes up in half an hour and I hardly think Carlotta or Mademoiselle What's-her-name will have their heads out of a bowl by then. We'll just have to make do for tonight and be prepared for a few refunds."

Refunds?

In the deep cavity beneath the floorboards of the manager's office I smile at their pathetic ignorance. . . .

Five minutes to curtain time and though I am sick with nervousness I am deeply aware that I am not alone.

He is with me.

I feel his presence at the very core of my being; I am filled with his strength and glory. His music swells within my body like a beautiful, burgeoning child, and suddenly I'm not afraid anymore. The pen shakes in my hand even as I write these words, but I'm not afraid.

He has given me the wings of an angel and taught me how to fly.

I shall not disappoint him tonight!

What a triumph!

She has brought the entire auditorium to its feet. The full standing ovation has lasted almost ten minutes now and still their rapturous applause is ringing in my ears.

I can scarcely believe in the perfection of my creation. The sense of power and elation it gives me to see her standing out there on the stage, almost buried in flowers, is overwhelming . . . but there's something else, an emotion so utterly unfamiliar that I can hardly classify it.

Happiness? Is this how it feels, this tremendous surge of warmth and breathless euphoria?

They are helping her from the stage now. Poor child, she can hardly walk, she doesn't understand what's happened to her, it's all too much. She's looking desperately around her, as though somehow she expects to see me in this moment of glory, to be rewarded by an angel's smile. But she sees nothing, nothing, and she knows in her heart that she never will.

Oh, Christine! If there were indeed a loving God in heaven it should be my arm around your waist now, my shoulder upon which you lean in your utter exhaustion.

But there is no God to hear my desperate prayer.

I turn from the sight of my triumph and slip away into the darkness whence I came. Beneath the mask my face is wet with tears.

Happiness is like the first blissful intoxication of morphine.

It doesn't last very long.

I saw the Vicomte de Chagny tonight in his brother's private box.

I had made the inexcusable error of looking up and I was so startled when he raised his hand to his lips, in acknowledgment, that I almost forgot to make my bow. Carlotta glared at me when I came off the stage; I had kept her waiting a second or two longer than normal before permitting her to take her final ovation, and she was furious.

"Stop courting the public, you scheming little minx!" she snapped as she swept past me. "You needn't think you're ever going to get the chance to sing in my place again!"

She's never forgiven me for that gala night. I think she's made trouble for the management, because neither Monsieur Richard nor Monsieur Moncharmin has so much as looked at me since. They seem to want to forget it ever happened. In spite of my triumph I haven't been offered any better role. The Angel of Music has continued to teach me without comment and I dare not ask any questions. I can only think that I must have disappointed him after all, that he has decided I'm not ready for the world yet, for he never even said "Well done!" He wasn't there in my dressing room after the gala performance when I so badly needed to hear his praise. . . . I went home and cried myself to sleep that night.

I was walking back to my dressing room when the Vicomte caught up with me. He was very breathless, as though he had run all the way down from the grand tier, and I felt myself blush as he caught my arm.

"Don't run away, Christine. You never used to be this shy when we were children. Why do you look at me these days as if you don't even recognize me?"

"Oh, Raoul." I sighed. "That's all in the past. We can't pretend to be equals anymore. If I'm seen with you in public now, people will say I'm a light woman."

"Not in my hearing they won't!" he said fiercely.

The old, stubborn cleft was there in his chin still. He had the same look of undaunted determination that had once made him run fully dressed into the sea to rescue my new silk scarf, regardless of his governess's furious protest. Dear Raoul—he never cared what anyone thought even then. But now he was twenty, one of the most handsome and eligible young men in France, and his family would want to marry him to some rich and titled lady. It was no use my clinging to an old childhood romance.

"We can't go back," I said sadly. "We can't ever go back, Raoul. Those days are gone for good."

"Who wants to go back?" he demanded cheerfully. "I'm not asking you to play hide-and-seek anymore. I'm asking you to come to supper with me."

"I can't!"

I was horrified. The Angel of Music had sternly forbidden all earthly distractions. No late nights, no admirers; I must be prepared to show my total dedication by renouncing all girlish pleasures. "Perfection de-

mands sacrifice, you must be prepared to suffer self-denial," he had once told me coldly.

Well, it had never been a sacrifice to obey him implicitly—until now.

The cleft in Raoul's chin deepened as he frowned.

"You have another engagement?"

"Yes . . ." I said hastily, "yes. . . . I'm afraid so. It's very awkward, Raoul, I really can't back out at the last minute."

He smiled nonchalantly, but I could see he was hurt. That famous Chagny pride was stung by my inexplicable attitude.

"Perhaps another evening, then. I'll remember to make an appointment first, shall I?"

"Raoul—"

"Oh, please, don't apologize. It was highly presumptuous of me to assume you would have nothing better to do at a moment's notice."

He raised my hand to his lips in a cool gesture of civility and walked away without looking back. I longed to call after him, but I knew that I must not. The barriers between us were insurmountable now and no longer simply those of social class. I had taken vows before the Angel of Music, vows that were as sacred and binding as those of a nun. I was no longer a girl; I was a high priestess serving a chosen master. Raoul and I must forget each other; we had no future in either world.

I went to my room, powdered my flushed cheeks, and tried to regain my composure. I would go home and take a little laudanum, make sure I slept so that I would come to my lesson in the morning fresh and alert, betraying no sign of my spiritual treachery.

As I replaced the powder puff on my dressing table the air around me was splintered by the awesome resonance of a voice that seemed to come straight from a tomb.

"I will not tolerate disobedience!" said the Angel of Music.

She has an admirer! How could I have supposed it would be otherwise?

The Vicomte de Chagny.

Raoul!

He's disgustingly young, good looking, fashionable, comes of ancient and distinguished lineage. Oh, I know all about him. . . . I've made it my business to know, and regrettably I've no reason to suppose he's either a fool or a knave. He doesn't come to the Opera, like so many of our noble patrons, simply to run after every pretty chorus girl in sight. Apparently he doesn't run after anyone—except Christine! The sincerity of his admiration shines out of honest eyes that are nicely set in smooth and regular features. He watches her avidly through his opera glasses and stands to applaud whenever she comes forward to take her bow. He gives every evidence of being wildly in love and I can't think why his family haven't put a stop to it, as they surely should. Such ancient lineage ought to be my protection, but when I look at him I see a naive determination that fills me with dread. I remember that there are no parents alive to sternly remind him of his duty to their house, only a lax, indulgent elder brother whose authority might well be defied. If he sets his eyes on marriage I shall be utterly defeated.

More than once I've seen him come backstage pestering her, presuming on an old childhood friendship. Impudent, self-assured boy! The way she shyly smiles at him in an absent, unguarded moment makes me sick with rage. She knows my instructions, she fears my anger; and yet that involuntary smile, refusing to be repressed, betrays her time and time again.

I've tried to govern my unreasonable jealousy, but I can't. I know he's going to spoil everything, blunder into the delicate fabric of my dream and rip it to shreds. If he doesn't stop hanging around her soon, he's going to meet with a fatal accident, in spite of Nadir's vigilance.

Raoul de Chagny! I hate him!

I hate him for interfering like this, for making it necessary for me to show harshness to her.

I can't bear to hurt her, but I'm going to have to punish her now and it's all his fault, all his fault. . . .

Raoul de Chagny, respect the fury of the Opera Ghost and take great care how you walk alone in his kingdom at night!

*   *   *

It's becoming harder and harder to deal with Raoul. I've tried to be cold with him, but he refuses to take my coldness seriously; and it's so difficult to keep saying no when I really want to say yes.

Tonight he was waiting in the wings with an armful of flowers when I came off the stage. There have been flowers from him in my dressing room every night this week, but I haven't dared to acknowledge them, even with a note of thanks. It was impossible now to ignore him or refuse to accept his token with everyone watching, but as soon as I could get away I ran to my room, tossed the flowers fearfully onto a chair, and laid my hot cheek against the cold mirror, like a guilty child awaiting punishment.

"You are late!" said the Angel's voice inside my head.

"Forgive me," I whispered, "I was unavoidably detained—"

"So . . . the Vicomte de Chagny is unavoidable?"

There was ice in the voice now, a controlled and deadly anger that filled me with terror. The Angel knew everything . . . everything . . . it was impossible to keep secrets from him.

"He was waiting for me when I came off the stage, I did not ask him to be there."

"You encourage him to pursue you."

"No," I stammered feverishly, "that isn't true. I sent him away and told him never to send me flowers again. Oh, please—please don't be angry. You know I cannot bear your anger."

"The time for anger has passed," announced the voice implacably. "You have ignored my warnings and now you will be punished. Until you cast this mortal weakness from your soul you will not hear my voice again."

I fell to my knees before the mirror.

"He means nothing to me, I swear to you he means nothing. I will do anything you ask, I will never see him again if that is what you command . . . but don't leave me now . . . please don't leave me!"

The sudden silence was awesome.

I crumpled to the floor and began to weep. Again and again I begged for his forgiveness, but he did not answer me and my grief became wild and uncontrollable panic. The mirror showed me my demented reflection as I began to beat my hands frenziedly on the thick glass.

"Christine!"

His voice took hold of me like two mighty hands, no longer cold and remote, but gentle and strangely sad.

"Calm yourself, child. . . . Be still now and I shall give you one last chance to prove that you are worthy of my guidance."

"Anything." I sobbed, only wanting to crawl inside that voice and hide forever. "Anything you ask."

"You may continue to see him here at the Opera as long as you treat him with cruel indifference. Speak to him coldly, reject his tokens, and make him the most miserable young man on this earth. When I see you make him suffer, I shall know that you have not betrayed your vows to me, that your heart is pure and entirely unsullied by earthly bondage."

I bowed my head in acknowledgment and his voice rewarded me with such ecstasy that, although I was aware of pain, there was no room in my head for bitterness or resentment.

If this was mindless enslavement and submission to a cruel master, I was beyond caring. I could not renounce my immortal guardian for the sake of a young man's smile.

I had been chosen by the Angel of Music.

I would serve and worship him until the last star was extinguished in the heavens.

I've won, for now, it seems; yet my conquest is a hollow victory that fills me with nothing but shamed despair.

I've taken her innocent, childish heart and cruelly twisted it into submission; and for every tear that has fallen down her pale cheeks I have shed a hundred in remorse.

This has to be the most wicked thing I've ever done in my life, but I can't stop. . . . I can't let her go, I can't let him take her from me.

Oh, God, what a grim farce this has become!

Even if all things were equal, I'm still old enough to be her father! But all things aren't equal. I know I haven't got a chance in a fair fight, so I'll fight the only way I know how, and I'll fight to the death if I must.

He's only twenty, only a boy, a harmless, charming young fellow with the whole of his life in front of him.

But I'll kill him if I have to . . . if there's no other way to keep her.

Yes . . . in spite of Nadir, in spite of my promise, I'm quite sure that I'll have to kill him in the end.

I once heard it said that troubles never come singly, and as far as I can see a truer word was never spoken.

It's all just as I feared. The new management is flexing the muscles of independence and quite flagrantly disregarding my wishes; my allowance has not been paid and box five has been sold for the first time since I amended the Opera lease. It's quite insupportable! I have made my displeasure known to them by letter, but it's beginning to look as if they're going to require tangible proof of my wrath before they give in. I'd give a great deal to have Poligny back, especially now that I wish to further Christine's cause.

Pure jealousy on behalf of our leading lady is preventing the management from realizing Christine's potential; Carlotta is a famous name and they're terrified of losing her.

Well, if they don't start listening to me, they could lose her for good! I've never killed a woman yet, but I don't mind making an exception for that spiteful creature; she's made Christine cry more than once and I won't have it. . . . *I won't have it!*

Last night I caused the entire performance to be disturbed by maniacal laughter issuing incessantly from box five. The hapless occupants of the box were eventually ejected by a municipal guard, loudly protesting their innocence; and in their absence the terrible laughter continued to disrupt the proceedings.

I consider that the management has received fair warning and consequently I have delivered my instructions with every expectation of being obeyed.

The part of Margarita shall go to Christine this evening.

If she doesn't sing that role tonight, someone's going to be extremely sorry!

A truly unbelievable thing occurred tonight!

Halfway through one of her most triumphant arias Carlotta began to croak like a toad. By that I don't mean to imply that her voice cracked—a dreaded fate that can overtake any one of us—it was simply transformed! I was utterly amazed—it was as though the fate that I had wished upon her had been meted out by a vengeful angel.

The most awful silence descended on the auditorium; people were too shocked even to hiss, and Carlotta eventually ran from the stage in hysterics. Hardly surprising—no one, even her worst enemy, could have expected her to continue under such dreadful circumstances. And when Monsieur Richard came to me in great agitation, begging me to sing Margarita in her place, I repeated my triumph of the gala night.

I feel terribly uneasy about it all now, though. This is the second time I've taken over the lead because some unpleasant fate has befallen Carlotta. There's a dark side to the Angel of Music that has begun to frighten me. When I asked him if he was responsible for Carlotta's strange malady he laughed and said it was his pleasure to make even my smallest wish come true.

He laughed!

Surely an angel should not laugh!

It was some time before he recovered from his terrible mirth, and when he had done so he did not seem inclined to teach me. Instead for the first time he began to talk to me like a real person; he spoke of his hopes for my career and for once permitted me to ask a few questions. He said such outrageously amusing things about the management that I could not help laughing, too, and I suddenly realized that we were talking like old friends, easily and without restraint.

Even his voice had changed. No longer inside my head, it seemed to issue directly from the mirror, and though still of unearthly beauty, it had lost that awesome, godlike resonance.

Almost without knowing what I was doing I began to drift closer and closer to the mirror. I found myself imagining his face as that of a real living man, and I felt a deep need to reach out and touch solid flesh. I began to explore the surface of the mirror with restless caressing fingers. All these months I have heard his voice in my sleep and woken with my hands reaching out hopelessly into the darkness. Again and again he has passed through my restless dreams like a winged shadow, and though I have clutched with desperation at his fleeting image I have never, never been able to see his face.

Now I had the crazy sensation that this pane of glass was all that separated us, and in a foolish, off-guarded moment I confided my desperate wish to see him. I begged him to appear to me here in this very room, just as the Angel Gabriel once appeared to the Holy Virgin.

His anger was swift and terrible; it seemed to leap at me through the mirror like an electrical shock and made me recoil with bewildered pain.

"It is enough that you hear me!" Hard and cold as hail, his voice was abruptly back inside my head. "I tire of your mortal greed. Remember that what has been granted to you can also be withdrawn."

And then he was gone.

Neither tears nor hours of desperate penitence succeeded in winning his forgiveness, and I am terrified that this time he has gone for good.

I only wanted to see him . . . just to look once upon his beautiful face.

Why did that make him so angry?

Tonight she asked to see me, begged me to appear to her in a vision or a dream. I had just enough command of myself to show cold displeasure and then I fled from her innocent request before my grief betrayed me.

Memories crowded in on me as I rowed across the lake, memories of that other lovely girl who had died of her wish to see me.

"I want you to take off the mask, Erik, do you hear me? I want you to take it off right now."

It all came back so vividly, the sound of her scream and the land-slide of falling masonry; it might have been yesterday.

I've never felt such abject despair. This whole insane travesty is spinning out of my control, and if I don't put a stop to it now I dare not think how it will end.

I must not go back to her.

I will not go back!

There is only silence in my dressing room. There's nothing I can do, there's no way to reach him now that he has chosen to leave me; our separation is as final as death.

He's never going to come back.

I've lost him, just as I lost my father . . . but this time it's my fault, I've brought it all on myself. I've destroyed everything with my own hand and there are no words in existence that can express my grief at the loss.

In the depth of my despair I finally confided my secret to Raoul, willing myself to believe he was the one person in the world who would understand. Ten years ago we had both believed in angels, in ghosts and demons and things that go bump in the night. Bravely sitting alone in a dark room, we'd told each other horror stories that made us cling to each other in delighted terror. Two against an adult world, we'd shared childish dreams and confided our most foolish thoughts without fear of being laughed at.

Raoul did not laugh at me now, but even before I had finished speaking I knew what a terrible mistake I had made. In the slight stiffening of the arms that held me, I felt the involuntary withdrawal of belief, an instinctive response of pure common sense which told me, more plainly than words could ever do, that Raoul had grown up and left me playing quite alone on some solitary, nonexistent seashore.

He looked extremely worried, made me sit down, and proceeded to ask a lot of questions that left me in absolutely no doubt as to what he was thinking. Was I having headaches and dizzy spells? Had I seen a doctor? Perhaps I was working too hard; perhaps I ought to see a specialist.

"In what?" I demanded coldly. "Psychiatry?"

He looked terribly embarrassed as he got down on his knees and took both my hands in his.

"Now, don't put words into my mouth," he said uneasily. "All I'm saying is that perhaps you ought to think of leaving the stage for a while and have a complete rest."

"You think I should be locked up, don't you? You think I belong in a lunatic asylum!"

He groaned and pressed my hand against his lips.

"I don't think anything of the sort. But I really am very worried about you, Christine, and I do think you should take medical advice."

In silence I withdrew my hands from his, and after a moment he got off his knees and went to fetch his hat and gloves.

"I have my carriage outside. Will you let me take you home?"

"No. Thank you, but no—I would prefer to walk."

He nodded, sighed, drew on his gloves, and reluctantly prepared to leave. In the doorway he turned to look back at me.

"You'll think about what I've said, though . . . consider taking a holiday at least?"

"I shan't need to consider it. I have no part after tomorrow night until we give Faust again next month. I shall have all the time in the world to rest."

"Oh . . . well, in that case, perhaps . . ."

I stared at him so stonily that he lapsed abruptly into uncomfortable silence.

"I'll say good-night, then," he continued awkwardly after a moment, and at length, receiving no response from me, he closed the door.

When he had gone I turned to look at the huge, ominously silent mirror.

Had it really happened or was it only a dream?

Perhaps I should seriously think about seeing that psychiatrist after all. . . .

Before I saw Christine I thought I already knew all there was for a man to know about the bitterness of love.

But now I understood why the manuscript of *Don Juan Triumphant* had always defeated me. What had I ever known of love . . . childish fantasies . . . schoolboy worship . . . simple, earthy lust? I'd grasped only the counterpoint, never the theme, but now there was no shield of ignorance to spare my senses. I looked directly at the sun and was knifed by its pitiless, searing light.

I was a prisoner inside the cage of my own body, shut up day and night with a hot, hard, throbbing agony from which there was no respite or relief except in morphine. The dosage was rapidly escalating to a suicidal level, and from the white hell of this drugged intoxication there began to emerge a music almost beyond human comprehension. Music that no one would ever dare to play in public; music that raped the auditory senses, violated the listener's body, and threatened the equilibrium of the brain.

All the tenderness and all the hatred ever generated in the world from man's most basic instinct was captured between the staves of that manuscript.

And still it was not enough to grant the final release that would let me forget, let me rest.

Tonight I went back to the mirror and waited for her, walled up against reality, suddenly facing a truth that I had spent my entire life denying.

I was not set apart from the rest of mankind, hermetically sealed by my disfigurement from its most turbulent and treacherous emotion. I was no longer a cold, contented genius, a reigning king or even a ghost.

I was just a man . . . just a very desperate man, finally prepared to commit the ultimate theft.

I left the stage this evening in low spirits, reluctant to forsake the theater and enter that unwelcome state which is euphemistically known in our profession as "resting." A lonely flat and a yawning maid were all that waited for me now, and the prospect of the silent weeks stretching out ahead filled me with growing despondency.

But as soon as I walked into my dressing room I was aware that the very air around me pulsed as though it were electrically charged, and I was suddenly filled with a powerful foreknowledge of joy.

He is here, I'm sure of it. In spite of his anger, in spite of his silence, I know now that I am forgiven; and surely such forgiveness can only mean one thing.

Mortal, immortal, it no longer matters, for love transcends all barriers and I am confident now that he is as helpless against its brutal grip as I am.

Tonight I shall beg him to take me with him, away from this world where I don't belong, which is so full of mocking strangers. Tonight I am ready to relinquish the earth and everything upon it in exchange for my Guardian's beloved presence. Death is a price I no longer question or fear to pay. This past week has been enough to teach me that without him there simply is no life for me at all.

There is nothing left for me to do now except lay down my pen and wait. . . .

usic and the swift turn of a mirror on its pivot permitted me to take her hand and draw her down through the labyrinthine passages to the lake that divided our two worlds. Wrapped in the shroud of my voice, blind and slavishly obedient, she came with wordless joy, following me over an unending bridge of song until at last we stood in the house beyond the lake.

Now was the time to stop and let silence betray my wicked deception, but my voice was drunk on its own power and refused to let the dream end yet. I rocked her on the sweet tide of my music until she slept in my embrace and then for a long time I simply held her, cherishing the weight of her body in my arms and the slight pressure of her head against my shoulder. So light and fragile! She seemed no more than a child . . . a dead child lying in my arms.

I wanted to hold her like that for all eternity, but with the passage of time her slight weight became an intolerable, leaden burden that made every muscle in my body scream out in protest. At length I carried her through to the second bedroom and laid her down upon my mother's bed, covering her tenderly with a shawl and watching the pale material slowly settle and cling to the outline of her form, enveloping her with a warmth and intimacy that I could never share. If it's possible to be jealous of a shawl, then I was wickedly jealous.

As I stood looking down on her I was overwhelmed by the dismal futility of my insane impulse. Why had I brought her here? I couldn't keep her in a state of trance for the rest of her days; I didn't want a mindless, mechanical doll, an automaton without choice.

I wanted Christine, all of Christine.

And I could not have her.

Simple! Accept it! When she wakes you have to confess this miserable sham. You've had your dream, you've held her in your arms and tomorrow you have to take her back. Tomorrow it will all be over.

But I didn't want to think about tomorrow now.

I went to my room and tried to occupy myself with the little mundane rituals that persuade us all that life will continue normally. I changed from my dress suit into a full-length kimono of black silk, with satin lapels, and sat down at the organ to stare at the manuscript of *Don Juan Triumphant.*

"Don't you know people pay good money to see freaks? Don Juan himself could not have drawn more skirts in one afternoon. . . ."

Don Juan Triumphant! What a bitter irony this opera was; what refinement of self-mockery! And yet what incredible music flowed there. It was far and away the best thing that I had ever composed . . . all the notes in red ink . . . it really ought to have been written in blood.

I glanced at the most recently completed section and turned the pages hurriedly. Not that, not tonight; I dared not play that with Christine in the house. Turn back to the beginning, to the tenderness that precedes the terrible violence of lust; turn back and remember only the beauty tonight.

I sank into the music as though it were a warm pool of soothing water and let myself drift and float along the staves, improvising subtly and building new melodies. I ceased to be aware of my surroundings and the relentless passage of time that brought morning to this world of eternal darkness; I ceased to think . . . and to hear . . . never even seeing the merciless little hand which came up behind me and stripped the mask away.

I spun around on the organ stool with a cry of demented anguish and the look on her face as she backed away with the mask in her nerveless hand—the horror and the utter *disbelief!*—severed my last link with sanity.

Cursing and screaming like a crazy, wounded wild animal I cornered her against the wall, fastened my hands in a murderous grip around her little white neck.

I never got the chance to find out if I truly meant to kill her. The pain struck like a bolt of lightning, exploding in my chest and spreading out down my left arm with paralyzing intensity. With a choking groan I let go of her and staggered back a step, willing the spasm to subside, but it only seemed to increase in severity until it forced me to my knees at her feet.

The world narrowed to a pain beyond tears, a panting fight for breath, and Christine sobbing just beyond the reach of my hand.

Dimly I became aware that she, too, was now on her knees beside me, her fingers clutching tremulously at my sleeve.

"Tell me what to do," she whispered. "Please . . . tell me what to do?"

I could not speak. My lips moved, but no sound emerged; all I could do was claw out in desperation toward the mask.

Let me cover myself. Let me die with some vestige of human dignity!

She seemed to understand my frantic gesture and slowly pushed the mask across the floor to me. Now that she was free to run from me she made no attempt to do so. She continued to kneel on the floor beside me, and the rhythm of my ragged breathing seemed to match her quiet sobbing in a wicked mockery of harmony.

Ayesha had leapt down from the pipe organ and was now circling around me, spitting and hissing at Christine, swishing her tail with primitive, animal fear. Like a little guard dog she was trying to protect me from this unknown intruder who had caused me harm, and the low, wicked groaning that gathered in her throat warned me that she was about to attack.

I knew I had to get Ayesha away from Christine before the animal ripped her face to pieces in sheer terror.

With a mighty effort I gathered the angry cat into my arms and staggered the half-dozen paces to the black leather couch.

"Don't come any nearer," I gasped.

Then there was silence for a time—silence and blackness.

When Christine swam into my gaze once more she was standing in the middle of the room, staring at the canopied coffin on its dais. Her eyes were fixed and glazed, the eyes of a child waking from a beautiful dream to find herself in a living nightmare; it was as though that final inanimate horror had pushed her right over the edge of sanity.

I realized then that if I died, Christine would die too—slowly, painfully, of starvation and terror, beating her little hands against the unyielding stone walls of her prison. No one would ever hear her screams, no one would ever find her. A poor, demented, foaming wreckage, she would sink down at last upon the floor and share with me in death what she could never share in life. Already I could see madness gathering momentum in that unnatural, gelid stare.

"Christine . . ."

She turned very slowly in the direction of my voice, but she did not seem to see me.

"I want to go home now," she said hopelessly. "I want to go home to Papa. It's nice at home . . . not like this . . . it's not like this at all."

She sounded as though she were eight years old, and I dared not think how much further she would regress if I did not halt this deadly downward spiral into panic. I knew that I must occupy her quickly, give her some simple task on which to fasten her attention.

"Do you know how to make tea?" I asked faintly.

A puzzled frown hovered now on the face which had been so terrifyingly empty of expression.

"Tea?" she echoed vaguely, groping toward reality with slow uncertainty. "You mean English tea . . . with milk?"

"No, no . . . Russian tea, with lemon. It's really very easy. . . . All you have to do is . . . light the samovar."

"The samovar," she repeated, like a dull-witted child trying very hard to master a foreign language. "Where is that?"

"Over there." I managed to make a feeble gesture in the direction I wished her to look. "That big brass urn . . . beside . . ." We were both staring directly at the coffin now. "Beside . . . the cat's basket. You see the cat's basket, don't you, under that red canopy. . . ."

Again that black, blank stare born of reeling senses.

"It's a coffin," she said with dull horror.

"No," I insisted steadily, "it's a Persian cat basket. . . . The shah has one just like that . . . for the royal cats. . . . The high sides keep out the drafts, you see? . . . Cats don't like to be in a draft. Do you like cats, Christine?"

"It looks like a coffin," she persisted, with all the stubbornness of the feebleminded.

"You must learn not to judge everything by appearances." I sighed. "There is nothing in this room for you to fear, child—nothing at all. Do you believe me?"

She looked back at me and nodded slowly.

"It's not really a Persian cat basket, is it?" she said after a moment.

"No . . . but after all, it's just a wooden box, isn't it? To a flea it would be a palace . . . a beautiful silk-lined palace. Can you imagine how big the world must seem to a flea?"

She laughed and then put her hand over her mouth, as though she could not quite believe the sound had issued from her lips.

"Don't be afraid to laugh here in my house, Christine . . . your father used to make you laugh, didn't he?"

"My father is dead," she said quietly, "but, yes . . . he used to tell me silly stories too . . . especially if I was afraid."

She came closer to my couch and gazed down at me steadily; at my side Ayesha stirred aggressively, but the pressure of my hand held her still.

"You're very ill, aren't you?" Christine said sadly. "What shall I do if you die?"

I closed my eyes for a moment. I had never guessed that speech could be such terrible physical toil, never dreamed that one day I should be laboring to quarry words while an awesome block of travertine lay in a crushing weight upon my chest. But she was clinging to my voice as though it were a reassuring hand, trusting it to guide her past the yawning void which had gaped at her feet.

"What shall I do if you die?" she repeated, her voice rising once more on a note of growing fear. *"What shall I do?"*

I opened my eyes and smiled up at her calmly.

"I suppose you would have to put me in the cat basket eventually," I said. "But first I really would be far more grateful if you simply went and made that tea."

There is no Angel of Music.

There is only Erik!

Here in his house upon the lake, five levels below the surface of the earth, I am a prisoner, not of lock and key, but of wrenching pity and strangely lingering fascination.

His face! Dear God . . . shall I ever forget the moment that he swung around upon me, the awesome grief and rage which almost cost him his life?

What can I say about that face? It alters everything and yet . . . changes nothing. I can't explain that contradiction; it's not possible for me to stand back and make neat, rational judgments. This is an entirely different world from the one in which I normally exist; there are no judgments here. Only . . . feelings!

In a curious way his illness has saved us from utter ruin, made it possible to make a transition from fantasy to reality that would have been unthinkable to me only days before. In many ways it seems the most natural thing in the world for me to be here with him now, to think of him as Erik and not as some nameless, faceless angel. He's so real! No longer an illusion or a vision, but someone I could reach out and embrace, if only I dared. Somehow, in spite of the shock of discovery, it's a tremendous relief to be able to do something so utterly normal as make him a drink. Though, to be honest, I don't think I've quite mastered that samovar yet; he accepts my efforts with a quiet ironical patience that makes me feel he would laugh if he did not fear to hurt my feelings.

My existence here is curiously cozy. In my room I have found all that I need, a wardrobe full of clothes, shoes, hats, and cloaks—even a little writing desk with an ample supply of expensive notepaper. Tears sting at the back of my eyes when I consider the effort and thought he has evidently put into preparing for my comfort. I am filled with the strangest sense of homecoming, of suddenly belonging; and yet whenever I remember what lies behind that mask I think of Raoul with sudden, shameful yearning. The comparison is quite unavoidable, the contrast so cruel, so very nearly unbearable, that it seems the only way to retain my sanity is not to dwell on Raoul at all.

I know that this state of affairs can't continue indefinitely, and yet I don't want it to end. I don't want to think about the world above, think about Raoul, face all the conflicts and terrible decisions that are going to be inevitable in the end.

I just want to stay here with Erik and pretend that nothing's ever going to change, that he's always going to lie wearily on that couch and never ask for anything more terrifying than a glass of my truly abysmal tea.

There is no Angel of Music.

And yet he continues to live in my mind . . . in my voice . . . and in my soul.

I appear to have acquired a nurse!

Not the lover I craved beyond all reason but a gentle, attentive little nurse! Frankly I'm not convinced that being cared for as though I were her sick father is better than nothing. I'd like to take my heart out of my body and beat it to pulp for betraying me in this truly undignified manner. Rude health is one thing I've always been blessed with . . . infernal irony that it should desert me now!

I'm perfectly well aware that she likes me here on this couch, that it makes her feel safe. As long as she thinks I'm too ill to get up she can tell herself she has nothing to worry about. I'm beginning to realize just how much of a child she really is, how terrifyingly immature and vulnerable—even unstable. There's a fatal flaw running through her, like a hairline crack in a Ming dynasty vase, but that very imperfection makes me love her with even greater tenderness. I don't suppose for one moment that that boy is aware of the never-ending care she'll need. Whoever marries Christine is going to have to be prepared to play the father as well as the lover; if she lives to be eighty, she may never be more than a child at heart, a lost and frightened little girl bewildered by the demands of reality.

I haven't the least idea where to go from here, but I can't lie on this wretched couch for the rest of my natural existence, which happily begins to look as if it won't too long. It's two weeks now since I saw Nadir and if I don't meet him soon I know the suspicious devil is going to start looking for me with serious determination.

That is a complication I could very well do without at the moment! So I really don't have any choice.

Tomorrow I shall have to leave her alone while I row across the lake to face his inevitable questions.

I've just had a shock!

When I carried a tray into Erik's room this morning I found him standing by the pipe organ in full evening dress, wearing the mask, a wide brimmed felt hat, and the most beautiful black cloak. He looked suddenly so strong, so incredibly powerful, that I felt my hands begin to tremble against the tray. I've never seen him on his feet before, I didn't realize he was so tall . . . and yet I seemed to recognize the inherent authority—the awesome mystery!—with which he was now invested. It was like a half-forgotten dream returning to me, and I suddenly understood that this was how he must have looked the evening that he brought me down here. I had no conscious recollection of that strange journey, but some deep-buried memory stirred now, sufficient to make me clutch the tray against my breast in an effort to still the sudden trembling in my heart.

"I've brought your breakfast," I said stupidly.

He turned to look at me, and the movement caused the cloak to swirl gracefully around him.

"You must forgive me, my dear," he said with the quiet indulgent civility with which he always addresses me. "I'm afraid I have to go out for a little while."

"Out?" I echoed. "Out of the house?"

"I'm not a total recluse, child . . . and I have an important appointment to keep. You're not afraid to stay here alone, are you?"

"I don't know," I said. "Can't I come with you?"

"I regret that is not possible."

Gentle still, there was an edge of unquestionable command about his voice now that made me bow my head in humble acceptance.

"You will . . . take care?" I whispered.

"If you wish," he said gravely. He was looking at me steadily beneath the wide-brimmed hat and there was something in his glance that made me take an unexpectedly deep breath. As he began to walk toward me I found that I could not take my eyes off him. He moved with slow majesty, as though his whole body was informed by the rhythm of a music he alone could hear, and I was stunned by the breathless terror which seized me as he approached. As he put out one hand to trace the outline of my hair, my heart beat so rapidly in my throat that I thought I would suffocate.

But his fingers merely brushed the air against my cheek, then fell away, without touching.

"Wait for me here," he said abruptly, and a moment later the door closed behind him.

When I was alone, I sank down on the organ stool and tried to regain my breath; I was shaking all over with emotions I could not identify.

He had meant to touch me, I was quite sure of it. He had meant to touch me and then, at the very last moment, he had changed his mind.

I wasn't sure whether I was trembling now from sheer relief or unacknowledged disappointment.

I wasn't sure of anything anymore.

Here in his house there were only questions without answers.

adir was waiting for me on the far bank, and long before I disembarked I could see that his face was very grim. He waited only for me to set foot on the bank beside him before launching into his attack.

"Christine Daae!" he said severely and without civilized preamble. "Christine Daae, Erik?"

Hell! I had been afraid of this!

"What are you accusing me of now, Daroga?" I demanded guardedly. "Surely not murder!"

"I know that the girl has not been seen for the last two weeks. I also know that if anyone disappears unexpectedly around here, you're usually to blame for it."

"This is a theater." I shrugged. "Girls run off with their lovers all the time."

"Well, in this case it appears the lover has been left behind! You must know that the child is virtually engaged to the Vicomte de Chagny. Are you intending to send him a ransom note too?"

I caught hold of Nadir's arm with a grip that made him gasp.

"She is *not* engaged to him!" I spat furiously. "Who is spreading such filthy, inaccurate lies about her? Is it the chorus . . . the press . . . the damned boy? Tell me!"

Nadir said nothing for a moment. He looked at me so oddly that I released him and stood back uncomfortably.

After a moment he said, very quietly:

"Let her go, Erik. This whole farce is quite unworthy of you."

"I don't know what you are talking about," I said coldly. "Are you actually trying to imply that I am keeping that young girl a prisoner in my house?"

"Let her go," he repeated patiently.

"Damn you!" I cried, suddenly aware once more of that warning pressure in my chest. "You know me better than that."

"Erik, you can't deceive me, I know that she is with you."

"Yes . . . all right. . . . She's with me," I admitted with fierce resentment, "but I swear to you it's of her own accord. That's not inconceivable, is it, not utterly beyond all human belief?"

Nadir made a gesture of frustrated despair and turned away from me.

"Just let her go and we'll say no more about it. I don't suppose for a single moment that you would harm the girl. But this isn't Persia. You must know that by the standards of your own country this is not the way . . ."

He hesitated, as though wondering whether he dared to continue.

"Well?" I said in a strangled voice. "Go on—*say it!*"

He looked at me with undisguised pity.

"This is not the way for a gentleman to win a lady," he said with difficulty, "and whatever else you may have been in your time, Erik, you've always been a gentleman . . . haven't you?"

I stared at him.

And suddenly, without any warning, I began to cry.

Where is he? Why doesn't he come back?

Oh, God, I'm so frightened here without him! I can't bear the sight of this room now that it's empty, the gaping, silk-lined coffin on its carved platform, the tall black mourning candles, and the menacing pipe organ which seems to glare threateningly at me from the wall. It's like a room out of some horribly twisted nightmare.

I don't understand why I feel like this when for two weeks now I've walked calmly in and out of this chamber without blinking—God knows, I've even dusted it! And all the time he's been here I haven't dwelt on the terribly abnormal decor. The coffin is a cat basket because he says it is; if he told me the world was flat I think I should believe him. But now that he's not here it's a coffin once more. . . . I'm shut up all alone in a house that was designed as a tomb, waiting frantically for a madman to return to me.

It's a relief to write everything down; it calms me somehow, stops me flying into a hysterical panic now that I've discovered I can't find the outer door. It's very odd. For two weeks I haven't even thought of looking for the door and now suddenly I can't think of anything else. There has to be a door somewhere!

I feel a little calmer now that I've left his room and returned to my own. The strange pale-colored cat is sitting on my bed watching me with a sort of quiet contempt, as though she wonders why I don't simply curl up and go to sleep in his absence.

My dear, it's the only thing to do, surely you realize by now that you and I exist only in his presence!

Perhaps it is because Erik speaks to her as though she were a woman that I imagine I hear her thoughts now. She's not quite so hostile as she was at first; occasionally now, when we are alone together, she permits me to stroke her, although she studiously ignores me if Erik is in the room. She's really very beautiful, very unusual, I've never seen a Siamese cat before. It seems fitting somehow that something so unique and lovely should belong to Erik. Apparently her collar was once the property of the shah of Persia. It's studded with huge diamonds, just like a necklace— it must be worth a fortune. . . .

I envy her that calm, blissful animal ignorance, the inability to understand that Erik could die of a second seizure at any moment. Cats don't look ahead and contemplate the future, don't complicate their lives with doubt and uncertainty. They live only for the present; they know exactly what they want and they aren't afraid to take it.

I wish . . .

I wish I were that cat!

"Christine."

She came obediently across the drawing room and knelt beside my chair in silence, with her head bowed.

"I have to take you back above the ground tonight," I said slowly. "There is someone who knows that you are here."

"Raoul?" Her head jerked up and her voice came alive with an eagerness that made my wretchedness complete. "Is it Raoul?"

"No." It was suddenly very difficult to continue, almost impossible to maintain my ironical calm in the face of that instinctive response. "No . . . someone else. Someone who knows me and has promised to make difficulties if he is not satisfied that you stay here of your own free will."

"I see." She looked grave and rather troubled.

"You've never asked me to take you back, Christine. Do you want to go?"

"I don't know." She sighed. Her head drooped lower and lower until it almost rested on my knee . . . almost, but not quite. She's never touched me of her own accord and I knew she was quite unaware that her hair was brushing my hands now. Intolerable sensation, that soft, unconscious caress! I sat back in my chair to be free of it, aware that fear was gathering like a knot in my throat.

"You're very unhappy. Is it because you don't want to be here with me?"

She shook her head.

"I'm so confused!" she whispered. "I want to go back—but I want to be here too. And I don't understand why, Erik. . . . I don't understand what I feel for you."

The vague fear became sickening dread, but I knew I could not hide from this moment any longer.

"Perhaps it is only pity you feel," I suggested, "pity . . . and fear."

She looked up in surprise.

"I'm not afraid of you, not now."

"Oh, Christine"—I sighed—"you should be. You should be very afraid indeed."

And I proceeded, with calm and dispassion, to tell her why.

I did not spare myself and I did not spare her; she had to know— she had the right to know before she made her choice.

When I had finished my grim confession she sat very still, staring into the hearth. No tears, no hysteria, just . . . acceptance; perhaps in her heart she had always known.

"If I don't come back you will kill Raoul."

It wasn't a question, it was a statement. I knew from her tone that she did not expect an answer and so I did not trouble to give one. Instead I got up and went to fetch the small casket that I kept on the mantelpiece.

"Tonight we shall attend the masked ball at the Opera together. In your room you will find a selection of theatrical costumes. Choose the black domino. . . . It is what they will expect you to wear."

"*They?*"

"You will write a note to the Vicomte de Chagny asking him to meet you at the door that leads to the rotunda. During the course of the evening you will explain that you can never be his wife and tell him that you wish to devote your life to furthering your career under my guidance. I shall wait for you behind the mirror in your dressing room, and if you choose to come back to me it will be apparent to all concerned that you return of your own free will."

I offered her the casket and she took it from me with obvious hesitance.

"Inside this box," I continued, "you will find the key to the gate that leads from the underground passages out into the Rue Scribe. The other object—which you will not recognize—is also a key . . . my front-door key, if you will. Before we leave here tonight you will understand exactly how to operate the mechanism."

"Why do you give me these things?" she demanded uncertainly.

"I have given you the means to betray me to your young man, Christine. If I return to this house alone tonight I shall expect to find him waiting for me—and I shall expect him to be well armed."

So now I know what lies beneath the mantle of gentle courtesy and almost fatherly affection. Those graceful, sensitive hands, which are so beautiful to watch, are the hands of a man who is capable of killing without a qualm of conscience when provoked.

I'm not shocked. Merely surprised that I should have been too naive to perceive this for myself. For somehow this veiled undercurrent of threat is the final missing piece in the jigsaw of his alluring mystery; it is part of an awesome power that excites as much as it terrifies.

I think in a strange way I'm deeply relieved to know just how dangerous he really is.

It gives me an acceptable motive for coming back to him; and it spares me the agony of examining my hopelessly muddled feelings.

Heaven knows, it wasn't easy telling Raoul about Erik. We met, as arranged, at the masked ball, and when I'd stumbled through my feeble explanations he was as pale as his white domino costume. I was relieved I had chosen a deserted private box on the pit tier in which to talk to him.

"The man is obviously quite insane," he said ominously. "I think this is a matter for the police."

"No!" I breathed in horror. "Raoul, if you involve anyone else in this I shall have to deny everything. Why can't you just try to understand?"

"Understand what—that you're in the hands of some unscrupulous hypnotist who has determined to take advantage of your innocence for his own ends? I tell you this, if I knew where to find him I'd damned well call him out and put an end to this miserable farce once and for all."

I shivered and clutched his sleeve urgently.

"Don't even think about challenging him, you wouldn't stand a chance."

"Oh? Good at duels, is he? I thought he was supposed to be old enough to be your father and likely to drop dead with any undue physical exertion!"

I turned away miserably.

"I haven't lied to you, Raoul."

"Oh, well, I'm truly privileged tonight, aren't I? You're in the hands of some unprincipled maniac and I've been honored with the truth! Where is he, Christine? I demand to be told!"

I backed away from him.

"I won't tell you, it wouldn't be safe. I swear if you ever approach him, Raoul, you'll be dead before you can take aim to fire. For God's sake promise me you'll never try to find your way down there alone!"

"Now, look here—"

"Promise me!" I screamed. "Promise!"

He stood back in alarm at my raised voice; he suddenly looked so young and frightened that I wanted to cry.

"All right," he said, in a low, strained tone, "there's no need to shout like that. I know I don't have any right to ask questions. . . . I don't have any rights at all, do I?"

A moment more we stared at each other, like two children who had fallen out and had no idea of how to go about making up; and then, in an excess of hopelessness, I replaced my mask and fled out into the crowded public rooms.

For an hour or so I wandered up and down the grand escalier *searching for the spectacular Red Death costume in which Erik was disguised.*

But I could see no sign of him and at length, glancing at my watch, I returned to my dressing room and began to write while I waited for him to take me back through the mirror.

Two hours!

It is two hours since I left her among the crowds on the *grand escalier* and came back here to learn my fate. I'm still dressed as Red Death, high plumed hat and striking red cloak that trails behind me like a king's train. No mask necessary to complete this costume, though! Everyone else is masquerading, but I—I have come as myself!

The silence in the passage is like a closed coffin, claustrophobic and stifling; and relentlessly it shows me my own folly. I should not have confessed to my black past. Even if she comes back to me tonight, I'll never be sure now that it isn't out of fear for that boy's life. Two weeks of building up her trust, and I destroyed it in as many minutes. What a fool I am! Why did I tell her? She didn't have to know!

I'm so tired! Everything's such an effort now, all those hundreds of stairs stretching up into infinity . . . hard to believe that only six months ago I never even used to notice them.

This whole sorry business is like some nightmare contract that I despair of completing on time and to budget. Well . . . Giovanni told me long ago that there's only one thing to do when you grossly underestimate on a costing—you have to be prepared to withstand the loss.

But instead of accepting that sound advice I continue to behave like a crazy gambler in a casino, recklessly raising the stakes at every round, irrespective of my ability to pay up at the end of the day. I'm actually laying lives on the table now, digging a grave that's big enough to swallow us all.

The sound of the door opening makes me look up eagerly and then sink back in weary disappointment as a figure in a white domino enters stealthily.

Chagny! What's he doing here, skulking about like a criminal behind the curtains of the inner room? He looks as pale as his costume, and if I'm not mistaken he's lost weight this last fortnight—it certainly doesn't look as though he's arranged some secret lover's tryst!

Have they quarreled, I wonder? Have I reduced him to spying on her? Well, if he feels only a tenth of what I feel for her I daresay the poor lad is in agony, but I'm not going to pity him. It's a terrible mistake to start pitying the enemy!

So . . . no quarter on either side, Chagny! And to each man his own choice of weapons! Youth, beauty, and right are in your corner. But you don't have my voice. And when she comes, you shall see its power demonstrated here in this very room.

A long wait before the door opens again and Christine enters. We both remain utterly still in our respective hiding places while she sits and scribbles furiously before laying down her pen and locking the paper away in a drawer.

I hope you're watching and listening very closely, young man, I'd hate you to miss this particular performance.

There. Do you see?

Does the sound of your voice make her smile like that?

Can your unseen presence lift her from her chair and make her turn with slavish joy?

Can you spirit her away from beneath the very eyes of a stupefied rival . . . *like this?*

Oh, please! Examine the mirror to your heart's content, monsieur! You won't discover its secret, I can assure you! Yes! That's shaken you rather badly, hasn't it? You're beginning to wonder if you may indeed be dealing with a ghost!

If I were you, I'd go home now and have a few stiff brandies. Think about taking a trip somewhere far away where you can forget the evidence of your credulous eyes and your feeble human senses. They say the North Pole can be very pleasant at this time of year. . . .

Believe me, my friend, I've sent a great many people a lot farther than that in my time!

Killing is like riding, you see, one never really loses the knack.

This is the last warning I shall give you, Chagny.

Don't tempt me to clear the stage!

eyond the lake lies a hidden world of magic, a temple of dreams which I explore with ever-deepening wonder.

Day by day I sink a little deeper into the quicksand of Erik's influence. He draws me effortlessly through a succession of brightly colored and constantly changing dimensions until my mind spins like a whirling kaleidoscope, a soaring kite on an infinite length of string.

My awareness of the world is utterly changed now and I look back on my old self with fierce contempt. What a poor, ignorant caged creature I was before I knew Erik, imprisoned within my limited perceptions, no thought in my head beyond the next performance, the next new gown. Now I see and hear and understand in a way that would have been completely beyond me six months ago.

I do not languish in his power like a pale prisoner denied the light of day, but grow ever upward beneath the benevolent sun of his genius. Where once I was content to be a wilting marigold, I now aspire to the glorious height of a sunflower. He has captured all the wonders of the universe, enchanting baubles that reflect shafts of incandescent light.

And like a child starved of toys, I reach out eagerly with both hands, turning my back gladly on the world I have left behind.

I often sit on a cushion at his feet, with my back resting against his chair, and beg him to read to me, gazing into the flickering fire while his voice paints pictures in my mind. Sometimes he reads to me from the Rubaiyat, *weaving the delicate, melancholy rhymes of Omar Khayyam into a rich tapestry, that I may touch the ancient poet's regret for the fleeting swiftness of life and love. Shakespeare . . . ancient legends . . . and then, tonight, an old minstrel song that made me close my eyes on tears . . . the story of the white rose who loved a nightingale against the will of Allah.*

"Night after night the nightingale came to beg for divine love, but though the rose trembled at the sound of his voice, her petals remained closed to him. . . ."

Flower and bird, two species never meant to mate. Yet at length the rose overcame her fear and from that single, forbidden union was born the red rose that Allah never intended the world to know.

The thought of that white rose filled me with such bitter shame, made me hate my ignoble cowardice, my unworthy physical shrinking, the childish, lingering revulsion for that face. Yearning to turn and reach out to him, I remained unable to conquer that inner fear. It was a chasm I dared not cross. And so instead I sat there, like the little mouse in Aesop's fable, not daring to look upon the lion bound by cruel ropes. Chained by fate and shackled by pride, he starved in silent pain; and because I lacked the courage of a rose, I could not set him free.

When the story ended we sat in silence for a long time until at last he leaned forward with a sigh.

"It's very late, my dear," he said gravely. "I think it's time you went to bed."

Drifting into my bedroom, my mind still revolving ceaselessly around that lovely Arabic tale, I caught a movement from the corner of my eye and turned to find upon the counterpane the biggest spider I had ever seen in my life. It was easily the size of my fist, and at the sight of its black malevolence I let out an unlovely shriek which brought Erik to my door.

"What is it?" he demanded in alarm.

Unable to speak, I simply pointed and he laughed as he went over to my bed.

"I'm afraid we get a lot of these down here. He is a big fellow, isn't he? I suppose his mate is in here somewhere too."

"Oh, God!" I said with feeling, glancing nervously across the floor. "Do you really think so?"

"They're usually found in twos," he said absently, bending to catch the hideous thing gently in his hands. "When I've put this one out I'll come back and look, if you wish."

I stared at him in horror.

"You're only going to put it out? Won't it just come back?"

"That's not very likely, my dear."

"But it might," I persisted stubbornly. "Erik, I would die of fright if one crept over me while I was asleep. I've always been terrified of spiders. I'd feel so much happier if you just . . . well, just got rid of it permanently."

He stiffened, and when he turned to look at me there was something in his eyes which made me shiver.

"You want me to kill it?" he said expressionlessly.

"If—if you don't mind," I stammered, suddenly unnerved by the pulsing venom of his gaze.

"Oh, I don't mind at all," he said with an anger that was now unmistakable. "I rather think the spider might have one or two objections to make—but then, after all, it's only a spider, isn't it? Just a mindless, soulless, ugly thing that has no right to live and frighten people!"

Without another word he clenched his fist tightly, dropped the crushed insect on the carpet, and walked out of the room.

"Erik!" I cried after him, in alarm. "What about the other one?"

"Kill it yourself, if you can find it!" he said coldly, and shut the door on me with a savage bang.

I covered the spider with my shawl, so that I should not have to look at it, and when I had glanced warily beneath the sheets, I sat miserably on the bed with my legs tucked up beneath my chin.

It was the first time he had ever spoken to me like that—as though he hated me!

Slowly I slipped into the lace-trimmed nightgown and ventured at last beneath the sheets, exploring each fresh cool expanse with tentative toes. I lay awake for a long time, brooding on his anger, but I must have fallen asleep at last, for the sensation of something brushing my cheek made me wake with a scream.

I leapt out of the bed in a mindless panic and rushed into the adjoining room.

"Christine!" Erik laid his book aside and came toward me in concern. "Oh, my precious child, don't cry like that!"

I covered my face with my hands; I was shaking from head to foot like a perfect fool.

"Erik . . . I know you're very angry with me . . . but please, please, go in and find that other spider. I know there's one still in there. . . . I know it!"

"You really are very frightened, aren't you?" he said quietly.

"Yes. . . ." My teeth were chattering with cold and terror. "Yes! I'm sorry, but I can't help it. I know it's cruel, I know they have the right to live like any other creature, but I just can't bear them! If one touched me, I think my heart would stop."

He gestured for me to take his seat by the fire, the same slow, rather elegant unfurling of hand and wrist with which he often drew me toward him when he sang. There was something infinitely powerful and irresistible in that movement; something that made me feel I would follow that hand even if it led me over the edge of the world.

He guided me into the chair, as though I were a marionette incapable of moving without his aid, and yet still he did not touch me.

I sat and stared into the hearth while I listened to him moving furniture in the next room. Presently he came back and threw a crumpled piece of paper onto the fire.

*"It's gone now," he said sadly. "Go back to bed and I will bring you
something to make you sleep without nightmares."*

*I got up in silence, like an obedient child, and returned to my room.
In the doorway I glanced back and saw him staring at the paper, which
was shriveling and turning black against the coals.*

He made no movement and no sound.

And yet I am almost sure he had begun to cry.

If you touched me I think my heart would stop.

She doesn't know it, but she's answered the question I dare not ask.
This is a love that Allah never meant to be. These are petals which will
never willingly open, even for the song of a nightingale.

Once more I stand and watch her sleep. I did not need to give her
so much laudanum. She'll sleep the clock around now, in a deep
drugged, dreamless slumber that will admit no conscious memories.

If I took her now, comatose and unresisting, in this very bed where
I was born, she wouldn't even remember in the morning. . . .

I want her!

But I will not sink to the level of a mindless beast. Murderer, thief,
unscrupulous extortionist, contemptible drug addict . . . this is one
crime I cannot commit. I can take nothing from her that is not given
of her free and conscious will.

So I will close the door and return to my music and my morphine.
Peace waits for me now in that sweet, familiar needle. The price of the
oblivion that drowns all thought and desire is a simple pinprick and a
single, welling drop of blood—the only blood-red rose I shall ever sire
in this world!

Good night, Christine! Look with tolerance, if you can, on the pale
ashes of my indulgence tomorrow.

Morphine is a vice that delivers me from greater sin.

*I woke in the early afternoon from a dream I have had several times
before.*

*It's always the same. I'm standing on a high cliff staring down into
the still, dark waters of an uncharted and seemingly bottomless pool.
The landscape of surrounding rocks is chill and forbidding, evil looking*

and inherently ugly, exuding an ever-present sense of menace which makes me want to turn and run.

And yet I linger, shivering in the cold wind and staring down with futile longing. The pool is guarded by a huge sea spider who lurks unseen just below the surface; and yet I know that beyond this hideous guardian of the depths, Neptune waits for me upon a golden throne, waits to crown me as his queen with a tiara of flawless black pearls. I know that if I can only kneel before his throne at last I shall be lifted up into his mighty embrace and these two clumsy appendages on which I walk will be transformed into a mermaid's graceful tail. A thousand sea horses will form the litter that carries us through the wonderful splendors of his world to the palace of white coral where I shall live forever and ever.

All I have to do is make that fatal plunge. . . .

The dream makes me sad and terribly angry, for what's the use of aspiring to a mermaid's tail?

Even if the spider wasn't there, I don't know how to swim!

I got up at length to bathe and dress in my beautiful private bathroom of pink marble. Such opulence! It's like a Turkish bath, designed to please a favored lady of the harem. I might be the sultan's favorite, with one exception: There are no demands made of me in return for my spoiled indulgence.

Chopin's Mazurka in F minor drew me out into the drawing room at last, to take my silent position upon the sofa. Chopin had less than a year to live when he wrote this piece, and there was something sadly significant to me in hearing Erik play it now. He has not told me so, but I know that he, too, is nearing the end of his life. Nothing he does or says marks him as an invalid, but I'm not a complete fool, I have always understood that he is far more seriously ill than he will ever admit.

He didn't notice my presence—he never notices anything when he plays!—but the cat did. I saw her sit upright on the piano and look at me with hostility.

Go away, *she seemed to be saying,* we don't need you here!

At other times I had permitted her slit-eyed enmity to drive me back into my room, but today I was determined not to give ground; I wished to hear Erik play and I would not be intimidated by a jealous feline. I stayed on the couch and watched the animal prepare for war.

She leapt down onto the center of the keyboard, fracturing his beautiful music into jarring discord. Only an animal would have dared to disturb him like that and only an animal would have received such indulgence in return.

"My darling!" he protested laughingly. The depth of love in those two words caused all the muscles in my stomach to tighten with sudden rage, but still I did not move to betray my presence.

Twice he replaced her on top of the piano and twice she promptly jumped down again, nudging against him with insistent demand, refusing to be ignored, pushing her head beneath his hand. I watched his hand trace the line of her body from her nose to her tail, a swooping, sensual caress that made the creature arch with unashamed ecstasy. Even in silence there was always music in those hands, a cadence which seemed to flow irresistibly through his fingertips. When he bent and kissed the delicate little skull, I found my fists were clenched against the pain.

Willful and insatiable, the cat continued to seek his attention until at last he capitulated to her demand and lifted her into his arms. With the ease of long familiarity she came to rest with her head and front paws stretched over his shoulder, and there she remained, smug and sleek with contentment, working her claws rhythmically into the dark fabric of his tailcoat.

The blue eyes, half closed with pleasure, seemed to regard me with the superiority of unquestioned possession, as though suddenly she understood that she had nothing to fear from me.

No need for jealousy, no need to flaunt her little powers of seduction. I could not hope to take him from her.

I did not dare!

hen Christine and I parted on the banks of the lake this morning I told her we must not meet again for a week.

This arbitrary decision to place time and distance between us—born of a disturbing sense of ill omen which refused to be satisfactorily placed—was a difficult resolution to keep when the moment of parting came. It becomes harder, not easier, each time I have to let her go. The temptation to keep her shut away down here with me is almost irresistible.

I tried to convince myself that I was simply being practical. She had her theater commitments to consider and I knew that if I wasn't very careful my selfishness would end in ruining the career I desired to further. No one had contested her absence up till now, during a period when her presence was not required onstage—no one except Nadir, who of course missed nothing and was now inclined, since Buquet's death, to view even the most innocuous event with intense suspicion. The death of her father seemed to have left her entirely isolated. She kept a little maid, a sad, simpleminded creature from what I gathered, who had evidently too little curiosity or too little courage to report her mistress missing. It had become grimly apparent to me that, apart from young Chagny, there was no one in the world to care what became of Christine—no friends, no relations. She might have lain drowned in the Seine these last few weeks for all the difference her absence had made to her colleagues at the Opera.

But they were due begin a run of *Faust* again on Saturday and I knew I could not permit her to miss a single rehearsal or performance on my account. She belonged to the upper world of daylight and applause; I had to accept that there would always be young men to admire her; I had to condition myself to her absence, learn to hold a loose rein, when all my instincts were to clutch and hold and smother.

I had to tear down some of the walls I had built to preserve myself from hurt and learn to trust her. . . .

Of course, I did not tell her that. I said instead that I wished to have some time alone to complete my opera. Expecting to see relief betray itself in her eyes, I saw instead a flicker of resentment and puzzled hurt. She looked like a child who has been told to keep out of the way.

"I'm very sorry if I disturb you," she said, not looking at me as she spoke. "I always try to be very quiet when you're working."

"Oh, Christine, it isn't that! It's simply that your very presence in the house is distracting."

Her head flew up and there was a look in her eyes that I could not comprehend.

"Perhaps you'd find me less distracting if I possessed a tail and a diamond collar!" she said shortly.

And taking the key to the gates in the Rue Scribe from her pocket, she pulled up the hood of her cloak and hurried away.

I can't begin to imagine what she meant by that remark; it isn't like her to snap cryptic comments.

Why is she suddenly so angry?

Does it mean she won't come back?

"A week?" said Raoul warily. "You are not to go back for a whole week? Why?"

"Because he's busy!"

I sat glaring down at my gown. Run along and play now, Christine, I have more important things to do. *All these weeks Erik's led me to believe that I'm the center of his universe, and now he's just going to put me out of his mind as easily as he might shut a book! I can't believe it! If I didn't know better I'd think that cat was behind this!*

They're so incredibly, inhumanly close that it seems perfectly within the bounds of possibility!

Is he bored with me? Tired of wasting his genius on a miserable shrinking violet? Will he really be waiting for me on the lake a week from now?

Raoul had placed his opera hat and gloves upon the dressing table.

"Well," he began uncertainly, "since it seems that for once we are not governed by the crazy whims of your mad professor, perhaps you would do me the honor of coming to supper tonight."

I glanced at the silent mirror angrily.

"I'd be delighted to," I said.

When am I going to learn to interpret my premonitions with accuracy?

I know perfectly well now why I sent her away; I'd hardly been back in the house an hour when I had a second attack. Oh, not serious, not like the first, but enough to make it clear that I obviously have less time than I thought, that perhaps it would be more accurate to start thinking in terms of months, rather than years.

I'm so glad she wasn't here to see!

If I'm careful for a week she'll never need to know it happened.

When Raoul came to my dressing room tonight after the performance, he found me hastily fastening my cloak, and checked himself with sudden unmistakable disappointment. We'd had a wild and wonderful seven days. We'd driven out to the Bois, thrown buns to the elephants in the zoological gardens, patronized a different restaurant and theater every night; we'd laughed at the comedies, pulled faces at the tragedies, argued gaily over menus, and sipped from the same champagne glass. And I could see in his eyes now how hard it was for him to accept that this pleasant state of affairs wasn't going to continue.

"You're going back to Erik, aren't you?" he said unhappily. "I rather hoped that after this week you would find the strength to change your mind."

I didn't answer for a moment. I was already deeply aware how unwise I had been to spend so much time with him these last few days, how terribly disloyal to Erik.

"I have to go back, Raoul, you know that."

"Why do you have to go back? I simply don't understand this hold he seems to have upon you. You behave as though you had no mind of your own. Christine, if you're frightened of him—"

"I'm not frightened of him . . . not for myself, anyway. You need have no concern for my safety. Erik would die rather than hurt me."

Raoul came across the room and took hold of my arms. His fair, boyish face was flushed and the piercing blue eyes suspiciously bright.

"Are you in love with him?" he demanded simply.

"I don't know," I said.

He nodded and stood back, taking his hands off my arms.

"Is there any chance that you may know sometime in the near future? Or shall I just go away for good and stop pestering you? I daresay that would suit Erik nicely, wouldn't it? I expect you might find he'd make a miraculous recovery once I was off the scene!"

Tears pricked my eyes and I turned away to pick up my gloves.

"If you had seen him, you would never say anything so cruel and heartless."

"Tell me about him!"

"I've already told you,"

"Well, tell me again. I want to hear it again!"

"What do want to hear about?" I cried furiously. "The murders . . . the thefts . . . the morphine?"

"I want to know what he looks like."

I stared up at him with sudden contempt.

"He looks like you, Raoul! He looks exactly as you will look—when you've been dead for a few months! Now, are you satisfied, have you heard enough?"

Raoul sank down on the stool beside my dressing table and leaned his head against his hand for a moment.

"You're really not lying about that, are you?" he muttered at last.

"No," I said coldly, "everything that I have told you about him is the truth. Including what I feel for him."

"I see."

He got up slowly, brought a little jeweler's box out of his coat pocket, and set it on the table.

"I bought this today. I was hoping you might accept it, but since there doesn't seem to be much chance of that, I may as well leave it anyway. I hardly think they'll want to take it back."

I opened the box with trembling fingers and the light of the gas jets showed me a huge ruby, surrounded by diamonds.

"Oh, Raoul!" I sighed. "I can't possibly wear this for you while Erik lives."

"It was you who said he may not live much longer."

"Raoul . . . please!"

Again he took hold of me.

"All you have to do is tell me you don't love me, that you don't want to marry me. That's all you have to say to make me go away."

He waited in tense silence for me to speak, and when my eyes dropped helplessly away from his, he pulled the ring from its red velvet bed and slipped it determinedly onto my finger.

"I don't mind if you feel you have to hide it for now," he said. "You and I have kept secrets since we were ten years old."

When he kissed me, I made no effort to stop him, and the feeling of guilt became almost unbearable.

As soon as I was alone once more, I took the ring off my finger and hung it out of sight upon the chain that held my crucifix. As long as I wore it there it was simply a bauble, and I could persuade myself that, in my own way, I remained true to them both. I was not yet able to accept that I must make a choice between them; I still believed that as long as I confined them both to their separate worlds, I could stave off a tragedy worse than any Shakespeare ever set upon the stage.

When the Opera House had emptied, I slipped out into the streets, holding my hood tightly in place to protect myself from the cold wind. My throat was sore with the onset of a heavy cold and I had had to force *my voice tonight in order to sing. That was a direct contradiction of Erik's sternest instructions, but what could I have done? I could hardly have played the prima donna and refused to go on at the last minute. Monsieur Richard would probably have canceled my contract on the spot if I gave myself such airs. He's been in a terrible humor since all this business with the Opera Ghost began, they say he would tear a contract up as soon as look at you these days.*

As I approached the gates that led to the underground passages, I was accosted by a man.

Well, not exactly accosted! The man who stepped out of the shadows shrank back against the wall when he saw me, with an exclamation of horrified apology.

"Mademoiselle! Please forgive me, I didn't mean to startle you like that! In the darkness I thought for a moment . . ."

He trailed into a silence that seemed to indicate both confusion and distress, and immediately I felt a curious concern.

"Who were you expecting to find here at this hour of night, monsieur?" I demanded, detaining him when he would have slipped away.

"No one!" he said with unmistakable terror. "I wasn't waiting for anyone, mademoiselle, I assure you!"

"Is it Erik?" I persisted gently. "Were you looking for Erik?"

The man grew very still and in the darkness I saw his eyes widen with disbelief.

"You know Erik?" he whispered in awe.

"I am going to meet him now, on the banks of the underground lake."

The man stared at me for a moment, then slowly crossed himself. As he fumbled inside his pocket and brought out a small packet, I was able to see that his eyes had filled with tears.

"God bless you and keep you, mademoiselle," he said emotionally, "God make his face to shine upon you all the days of your life. So you are his little angel. When he asked me to order all those ladies' garments, I was so afraid that the solitude and—and this,"—he tapped the packet significantly—"must have turned his mind."

Reaching out impulsively the man lifted my gloved hand to his lips.

"So it was for you, the wedding dress and the ring. Mademoiselle, I can't tell you how happy I am to make the acquaintance of such a very great lady. I can't tell you how glad—"

He halted abruptly, as though embarrassed by his own indiscretion.

"Give him this for me," he continued, making an effort to speak with calm detachment. "Erik was to have met me here a week ago, and when he did not come I was afraid that—that . . . but I can see I was wrong, quite wrong." The man handed me the packet with a sigh. "I daresay you know what this is, but you must not despair, mademoiselle, truly you must not. For your sake he will find the strength to stop. I think he would cut out his heart to please you . . . but of course, you know that. I hope you will not think me presumptuous if I say that God has surely chosen you in his wisdom, just as he once chose Our Lady. Mademoiselle . . . I shall remember you both in my prayers to-night. . . ."

Once more he clutched my hand and then, overcome with emotion, he suddenly hurried away down the Rue Scribe, got into the brougham that was waiting there, and drove off.

I was left staring down at the packet of morphine that lay in my gloved hand.

Erik had the wedding dress and the ring. All he needed was the bride. . . . I stiffened in sudden fear as the significance of the man's words bore down upon me.

Erik should have met him here a week ago.

Why hadn't he kept so important an appointment?

Unfastening the gates I ran down the black passages to the lake. The air was dank and chill beside the water, and the candle I had lit barely penetrated the thick gloom along the bank.

There was no one waiting for me and no sign of a lantern bobbing on the lake.

"Erik?"

My voice echoed eerily in the blackness, seeming unnaturally loud in the vaulted cavern. And when there was no response, terror descended upon me, the raw disbelieving fear of a child abandoned in the dark.

"Erik . . . are you there?"

The silence mocked me, leered at me from the leaden waters; the candle wavered and went out, leaving me trembling with fear, frustration, and mounting panic.

"Erik, where are you?" I screamed. "Erik!"

"Hush . . . I am here."

His hand fell lightly on my shoulder, and my breath seemed to stop as he turned me slowly round to face him. The yellow light of his magic lantern now showed me his powerful, shadowed figure enveloped in the familiar swirling cloak, made the mask and the frills of his dress shirt seem luminously white. Darkness framed him so magnificently, showed only what he wanted me to see. One sob of relief from me in that moment and I believe he would have taken me in his arms; but, though my eyes were full of tears, I was suddenly consumed with anger at his willful deception.

"You were here all the time, weren't you? Why didn't you answer me?"

He sighed and stood back from me and immediately the moment was gone.

"A little scientific experiment, child . . . a study of that curiosity known as human behavior."

"A very cruel experiment, don't you think?" I retorted with some bitterness.

"Science is never as cruel as love," he said simply. "Come with me now. The boat is moored nearby."

I followed his outstretched hand . . . followed the man who was my dark angel, my guardian, friend, and father; followed him deeper into a kingdom where there was neither dawn nor sunset, into a timeless world of endless night.

The house on the lake was very warm. The contrast of atmospheres made me cough, and instantly Erik turned to me with an intense concern that should have warned me.

"What's wrong with your throat?" he demanded with anxiety.

"It's only a cold," I hastened to reassure him. "I sang over it quite easily, and no one noticed anything was wrong. There was a full standing ovation. Oh, I wish you had been there to hear it—"

"You think it would have given me pleasure to hear you ruining your voice?" he demanded ominously.

"Erik, I couldn't possibly have refused to go on—"

He brought his fist down on the keyboard of the piano with uncontrollable fury.

"How dare you perform in defiance of my known instructions! You vain and stupid child, have you learned nothing?"

I crept to the sofa and sank down in terror.

"I'm sorry," I whimpered, "I didn't think it would matter just this once."

"You have no discipline," he said furiously, "no self restraint! I suppose the Vicomte de Chagny was in the audience tonight. I suppose he sent flowers to your room and invited you to supper. You sang to please him tonight, not me. For the sake of that damned boy you would risk your pitch and flexibility and high pianissimo?"

I burrowed into the cushions of the sofa in a vain attempt to distance myself from his demented rage. This was not the cold, controlled anger he had shown over the spider, but an irrational, aggressive fury that I suddenly understood might boil into violence at a single wrong word. I had been so sure he would never hurt me, but now as I saw those hands clenched into ugly fists upon the piano, I remembered how they had once fastened in a murderous grip around my neck. I remembered, and in remembering, wondered how I could ever have forgotten.

Silent tears rolled down my cheeks as I bowed my head and let him rain curses on my infantile folly without a word of protest. I dared not move or speak.

At last he was silent; the rage was gone and he looked down on me with sudden remorse and familiar tenderness.

"Forgive me," he said gently. "I forget how young you are, how susceptible to the temptations that surround you. But you must not

*abuse my most precious possession and expect me to say 'well done.' Now
. . . please dry your tears and blow your nose, my dear. You know I
can't bear to see you cry."*

*"I c-can't," I stammered, hunting nervously through my pockets, "I
can't seem to find my handkerchief. I m-m-must have dropped it when
we came across the lake. Do you have any h-h-handkerchiefs, Erik?"*

*He looked at me so sadly that I could have bitten my clumsy, stutter-
ing tongue.*

*"I don't have much call for handkerchiefs, my dear. . . . There are
certain advantages, you see, in being without a nose."*

My hand flew to my mouth.

*"Oh, Erik! I didn't think, I'm so sorry! Please don't give it another
thought, I can quite easily sniff."*

*"There are few things more objectionable than a sniffing child," he
said ruefully. "Wait here and I'll see what I can find."*

*He was gone some considerable time, but when he returned at length
he brought with him some half-a-dozen lace-trimmed ladies' handkerchiefs. I saw at once that they were not new, like the other items in my
room. Each one had been carefully folded on a sprig of lavender and
bore the initial M in one corner.*

*"I see you're looking at the initial," he observed rather wearily. "I
can assure you they didn't belong to a former admirer! If you look
carefully you will see the lace is quite yellow with age and disuse. The
owner has been dead for twenty years."*

*He walked away to the fireplace, and as I studied his stiff, unbend-
ing figure I suddenly understood who that owner must have been.*

"What was your mother's name?" I asked softly.

There was a long silence before he turned to look at me.

"Madeleine," he said.

*He spoke the word as though it were a prayer, with an extraordinary
resonance which seemed to make each of the three syllables tremble on the
air for a moment, like an echo.*

*"What a lovely name!" I exclaimed with involuntary envy. I wanted
to hear him say it again, but something about the way he looked at me*

made me change my mind hurriedly. There was an ambivalence in his eyes that rather frightened me, and yet I was gripped by a deep and primitive curiosity that would not be denied, even by vague fear. If his mother had been dead for twenty years, then she must have died in 1861, the same year that I had been born in Sweden.

A dull buzzing seemed to throb through my veins, as though my entire body was echoing the frantic rhythm of my pounding heart.

"Do you have a likeness of her?" I demanded suddenly.

He stood so still and tensely that he might have been carved out of black granite. Then from a second casket on the mantelpiece he drew a small hinged double picture frame, containing two faded line portraits, and gave it to me.

One portrait was of a dark-haired man, approaching early middle age, but enormously good looking, with gentle, humorous eyes. And the other . . .

The other was me!

Old-fashioned hairstyle and a certain hardness about the lips and eyes, but unquestionably me.

Erik leaned forward, took the picture frame from my quivering hand, and replaced it in the casket.

"How is this possible?" I whispered. "How can it have happened?"

He shrugged. "From time to time certain bone structures are repeated without a blood tie. No human face is entirely unique, my dear. I daresay somewhere in the world there may be another poor devil who looks like me."

"Tell me about her, Erik."

"I would rather not," he said coldly.

"Please!" I persisted with urgency. "I must know something."

"She was very young and very beautiful," he began with reluctance, speaking in sharp bursts, as though clipped sentences might minimize his pain, "She hated me and I hated her. I ran away from her when I was about nine. . . . I'm sorry! Do you mind? I can't talk about this!"

He turned his back on me and spread his hands against the mantel-

piece, the cloak unfurling from his arms like the wings of a bat. After a moment he told me rather harshly that he would be very much obliged if I simply took my cold off to bed.

Taking the packet of morphine from my pocket, I looked at it sadly before laying it on the manuscript of Don Juan Triumphant, *where I knew he was sure to find it.*

Then I did what any sensible person surely does when Erik gives her a direct command.

I obeyed him without question.

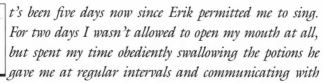

t's been five days now since Erik permitted me to sing. For two days I wasn't allowed to open my mouth at all, but spent my time obediently swallowing the potions he gave me at regular intervals and communicating with him when necessary by note. In this matter of my voice his regime remains as stern and unbending as it was in those days when I knew him only as the Angel of Music. Absolute dedication to my vocation, absolute submission to his will.

"If you don't keep silent, I shall be obliged to gag you," he said, and in spite of the gentle humor of his tone I knew instinctively that he was prepared to carry out that threat if necessary.

He wrote a letter to the management, instructing them to call upon the services of the understudy during the period of my indisposition, then proceeded to cosset and care for me as though I were no more than four years old. I spent a good deal of time lying on the sofa beneath a blanket, staring surreptitiously at the casket on the mantelpiece. I wanted to look at that portrait of his mother again, for its very presence in the room seemed to obsess me, but I knew that for his sake I must make no reference to what was rapidly becoming an idée fixe. *This* strange, cruel twist to our curious relationship would not bear the weight of examination. But I thought endlessly about the woman I resembled, wondering what she must have done to make him hate her and remember that hatred with such terrible pain. Sometimes I wonder if he's ever known a single moment of true happiness here on this earth. . . .

Yesterday, announcing my vocal cords to be free of infection, he permitted me to try a few scales, listening with terrifying intensity to the quality of my pitch. Evidently what he heard caused him satisfaction, for he said I might continue my lessons today and resume my role of Margarita at the Opera the following night.

". . . and this evening, if the air continues mild enough for your throat, we might take a carriage out to the Bois. Would you like that, Christine?"

"Yes," I said, with slight surprise. We had occasionally rowed on the lake or walked along the bank, but this was the first time he had ever suggested taking me out into the real world above.

The day passed as quickly as all the other days I had spent in his company. In the afternoon he permitted me to explore his laboratory, which was a truly wondrous place, answering my questions with a simplicity that neither patronized nor bored, encouraging me to experiment with his many devices just as I wished.

"Are you really sure you want me to meddle, Erik? I might break something that you can't mend."

"Yes," he agreed gravely, "yes . . . I think that is a thing you might well do eventually. Still, no matter. It's a risk that must be taken."

I knew, as I walked from one bench to the other, touching the vast complexity of instruments that lay between us, that he was not talking about the laboratory.

"I've never known anyone who seems to belong so much to the future as you do."

He shrugged. "Well . . . I've never been much at ease in the present. I'm afraid it has simply become the habit of a lifetime to escape from it in any way I can—magic, music . . . science."

He let the sentence drift and turned away to adjust the flow of a pipette. I sensed that he had said rather more than he intended to and now regretted a confidence that revealed the grim despair lurking beneath his proud and cynical reserve.

Later that evening we emerged from the underground passages to find a brougham waiting for us at the end of the Rue Scribe. I had seen enough of his magic by now to half believe him capable of producing a carriage from thin air whenever he chose, but he only laughed when I questioned him and told me that his traveling arrangements were really as mundane as anyone else's now that he had put the dragon out to grass.

"Dragon?" I wondered for a moment if I had misheard him.

"Yes . . . poor fellow! Very old and deaf now, of course, never hears the thunder brewing in the caldron anymore. Naturally, I had to let him go. . . ."

Once more I was aware of the sudden blurring of our two worlds, the falling of that soft gauze curtain which obscured the dividing line between fact and fantasy. It frightened me a little to discover that his power was just as strong here in the gray Parisian street as it was in that mysterious shrine belowground. I was twenty years old, in full possession of my faculties, and I knew there were no such things as dragons.

And yet I had only to listen and they would exist in his voice; the dream would become reality the moment I abandoned my disbelief, and I would not return to this world until he chose to bring me back.

But what if one night he should choose not to bring me back at all?

This prospect, suddenly seen clearly for the first time, made me cling to the dull, familiar sight of the street with stubborn alarm; and accepting my unexpected resistance, Erik fell silent, releasing me. I had never resisted the lure of his voice before, and I knew he was disturbed by his failure to draw me with him into that other land. Doubt and *sadness passed in fleeting succession through his eyes; it was almost as though—as though, somehow, my refusing to follow had aged him.*

We traveled to the gates of Paris, where the Bois de Boulogne stretched out its formal emerald acres in proud testimony to the late emperor's dislike of chaos. For some time we explored those quiet, deserted paths that would be crowded by visitors in the light of the sun. Even the coldest winter day attracted hundreds of skaters to the frozen lake and the chalet that stood on the center island. Gentlemen, their faces swathed with mufflers, pushed fine ladies in sledges, while liveried servants exercised lithe greyhounds swathed in overcoats. In summer there were gondolas on that lake, lit with colored lights, an endless procession of happy Parisians passing through the delights of the zoological gardens. All simple, human pleasures that I knew Erik could never have shared, even in those days when he had still lived in the world. If he had been here before, it would unquestionably have been after dark, when the park was cold and empty, entirely devoid of laughter and gaiety.

"This place is a perfect triumph of elegance and artifice," he remarked thoughtfully, as we returned in the direction of our carriage an hour or so later. "There would be mechanical ducks on that lake if the emperor had only had the foresight to order them!"

I glanced at him warily, uncertain how he would take a direct contradiction.

"I think it's rather beautiful," I said.

He seemed surprised, but not displeased.

"It's all a sham, Christine, nothing more than a clever trick of engineering. This entire park wears a mask. What you see is not real nature."

"Well, perhaps—perhaps it's not reality that I want to see."

"You're not opposed to deception of the senses, then?" he asked with guarded optimism. "You could, perhaps, under certain circumstances, find some illusions . . . acceptable?"

We had come to the brougham and turned quite instinctively to face each other. Slowly, hesitantly, as though fighting against the warning instincts of a lifetime, he offered his gloved hand to help me ascend the carriage step. It was the first time he had ever directly invited physical contact from me and the moment was fraught with tense significance for us both. My fingers had only to close that little distance between us and I would be a child to him no longer.

And in the moonlight his gloved hand was elusively normal; it looked warm and strong and quite curiously reassuring, the hand not of a monster and a murderer, but of a gentle, loving man, who waited with infinite patience for one little sign of hope. . . .

A coach lumbered toward us at that moment, bearing a number of young gentlemen who were quite obviously much the worse for drink, and Erik automatically drew away from me at the sound of the first crude shout.

"Now, then, what luck we've found here! A lady of the night! Lovely lady . . . won't you join our brave company instead?"

"That's right, dear mademoiselle. Spare your favors for a more deserving customer. There's titled blood here waiting to be comforted—a pining young nobleman jilted by his cruel diva!"

"Damn you, Edouard!" A familiar voice was suddenly raised furiously in the dark interior of the coach. "You drunken, disgusting pigs, I should never have agreed to come with you! Drive on, for God's sake!"

"My dear Raoul, why all this fuss? So your pretty little cock-tease dropped you—they're all the same, those stage girls! The least a friend can do is treat you to a good honest whore—and who else but a whore do you find in the Bois at this hour? Driver . . . driver, pull up over there like a good fellow."

"Get into the carriage quickly!"

Erik's voice was like ice, and I obeyed it without hesitation, tearing the hem of my gown in my haste to follow his curt command. The other brougham was now swaying dangerously as it unloaded its occupants on the opposite side of the road. Three young men were laughing as they dragged Raoul out of the cab between them and sent him sprawling unceremoniously in the mud.

Erik leapt into our carriage, slammed the door, and ordered our driver on.

And in that same moment Raoul looked up at my window and recognized me.

Oh, God! The look on his face when he saw me! I could not help twisting my head to look back at him with despair and I saw him run after our carriage, until the sheer hopeless futility of the effort defeated him.

When I turned back in my seat, I found Erik watching me with all the dangerous stillness of a jungle predator.

"I must deplore your young man's taste in company, my dear," he said chillingly.

After that he ignored me for the remainder of the journey, staring out the window in a brooding silence that seemed to crush me against the carriage seat.

When we returned to the house on the lake he went straight to the piano in the drawing room and began to punch the keys in a series of savage chords. He was sliding rapidly into the blackest mood I had ever seen, and I cast around desperately for something to take his mind from that disastrous encounter.

"Shall I sing for you?"

He stopped playing and sat back for a moment, making a deliberate effort to halt the insidious downward spiral before he spoke.

"Of course . . . your lesson." He sighed. "I promised, did I not? Come, then, you shall choose the piece yourself tonight, a reward for your days of patient obedience."

I chose the duet from Rigoletto. *Let him sing out his rage and purge himself of the dark emotions that were festering inside. Only when he was rid of that savage anger would it be safe to sing the soft Breton melodies that might restore his shattered peace.*

Our voices met in a fierce, almost elemental clash, soared and swooped and fell at length into the startled silence that greets a truly unique achievement. But stunned as I was by my success, I was totally

*unprepared for the rare and astonishing tribute which he chose to pay
me as he looked up from the keyboard.*

*"You would triumph now on any stage in the world, my dear. I
wonder if you know what happiness your voice has given me these past
six months, what pride I take in your remarkable attainment."*

*I bowed my head to hide my sudden emotion. Too much, this praise!
It took my breath away and made me feel weak and tremulous. I knew
now why he so seldom indulged in praise—it obviously wasn't good for
me, I couldn't cope with it. Somehow it was far easier to bear his gentle
yet relentless criticism.*

"You are weary," he said kindly. "Perhaps we should stop now."

*"No . . . I'm not tired, Erik, not in the least. I'm just . . . I'd
like to continue, please."*

*"Very well." He turned away and began looking through scores,
allowing me time to regain my composure. "We'll try the final scene
from* Aïda. *I always think this scene should be played in a wedding
dress, don't you?—a young girl choosing to be entombed with her lover,
preferring to die in his arms below the ground rather than face life
without him. Terrible melodrama, of course, but one can get away with
almost anything on the stage providing the music has the strength to
carry the scene. There's a wedding dress in the costume closet. Perhaps
you'd like to put it on."*

I didn't move.

"A wedding dress?" I echoed uneasily.

He glanced up at me and then quickly away.

*"It's only a costume," he said coldly, "only a prop to help you feel the
character better . . . but of course, if you'd rather not, we'll forget I
mentioned it." He began to close up the score. "Perhaps it would be as
well to leave this scene after all. You're obviously not ready to face the
emotional demands of the 'Terra, addio.' "*

*"I am!" I declared indignantly. "I'm perfectly capable! Oh, please,
Erik, let me try! It's such a wonderful part, such a beautiful story!"*

*"Yes," he murmured faintly, staring down at his hands where they
rested soundlessly against the keys, "it's a very beautiful story."*

He said no more and after a moment I hurried away to change.

Unlike the rest of the outfits that hung in the costume closet, the wedding dress was bandbox new, cut to the extreme dictates of fashion from shimmering white satin. It fitted me perfectly, just as though it had been tailored to my measurements, and as I fastened the hooks the words of that little man in the underground passage came back to me.

So it was for you, the wedding dress and the ring. . . . God has surely chosen you in His wisdom, just as he once chose Our Lady. . . .

Adjusting the veil, severely hampered by the lack of a mirror, I closed my eyes against a memory which threatened fresh tears. If I had a franc for every tear I've shed these last six months, I'd be a wealthy woman now!

The dress spread out around me like the stiff petals of a flower, and I needed no mirror in truth to know how it became me. Erik had exquisite taste and a wonderfully acute eye for detail. I wondered how many designs he had discarded before deciding on this particular gown. Perfection, always perfection . . . nothing less would ever do in anything to which he set his mind.

Making a mighty effort to compose myself, I returned to the drawing room.

"Erik . . ."

He turned slowly, and as he stared at me the score slid from his grasp and dispersed itself in loose sheets across the floor.

"Leave them!" he said curtly when I made a movement to retrieve the scattered papers. "We'll work without accompaniment. Begin from your recitative 'My heart foreseeing . . .'"

I hesitated uncertainly. He knew that Radames should begin this scene, it wasn't fair to throw me in like this without so much as a guiding chord.

"Begin!" he repeated, and the ominous note of rising anger in his voice acted on me like a spur on a highly strung mare, made me plunge into the recitative without a further thought.

" 'My heart foreseeing your condemnation, into this tomb I made my way by stealth, and here, far from every human gaze, in your arms I wished to die.' "

I waited for him to reply with the answering recitative, but abruptly he turned away from me.

"This was a mistake . . . a terrible mistake! Christine, please go back to your room and take that gown off quickly."

He wrapped both arms around his chest in a fierce strangling hold that frightened me, made me take a step toward him in alarm.

"Are you ill?" I whispered in horror. "Are you ill again?"

"No!" His voice was a strangled breath that somehow, at the last moment, managed to become a bitter laugh. "Yes . . . perhaps it is a kind of sickness, in a way. Go to your room and leave me alone for a while, would you, my dear?"

"But if you're ill I ought to stay—"

"Damn you!" he cried, slamming his clenched fist against the piano. "Damn your infernal innocence! You bloody ignorant child . . . get out of this room quickly and bolt your door! Do you hear me? Bolt your door!"

Picking up the skirts of the wedding dress, I fled to my room. I had never noticed before that the door was fitted with bolts, but now I slid them into place with feverish, clumsy fingers, stripped off the gown, and threw myself onto the bed, shaking with terror and rage. Suddenly I felt a desperate longing for Raoul, dear, safe Raoul, the playmate of my childhood who would never, never frighten me like this. Oh, God, how could I ever have thought I wasn't afraid of Erik? Surely he was the most terrifying person ever set upon this earth! That insane temper, the overt, barely controlled physical aggression that increasingly seemed to threaten imminent violence!

"I won't come here again!" I vowed into the suffocating pillow. "I'll never, never come back here again!"

At first when I heard the organ begin to play, I burrowed deeper into the pillows with my hands over my ears. I didn't want to hear his hateful music, I didn't want any more to do with him. But it was impossible to shut out the swelling power of the organ, and slowly, reluctantly, I took my hands away and started to listen intently. I had never heard this music before, but I could guess what it was—Don Juan Triumphant. He had never permitted me to look at the manuscript. He said it was dangerous, and that assertion had always puzzled me, for I could not begin to understand how music could present any danger.

As the notes drifted through me, strangely urgent and compelling, I found that I had begun to rock gently to the primitive, pulsating rhythm. I became aware of answering pulses all over my body, pulses in my wrists and neck and groin, of which I was normally quite insensible. The rhythm of my heart was rapidly gathering a frenetic pace, accelerating with the escalating beat of this truly extraordinary music, and almost involuntarily I began to let my hands wander over my body. There was a swelling heaviness in my breasts that caused my nipples to stand erect against my exploring fingers; but now the irresistible pulse was beating harder and more insistently below my stomach and my hand traveled farther and farther until it reached a place I had never known existed.

Neither innocence or ignorance was a shield against that music which was deep inside me now, gathering a throbbing momentum that made me twist and writhe, reach out instinctively into the shadows as though to pull some unseen presence down upon me.

My arms had wrapped around the pillow and I rode each thrusting note until the crescendo burst inside my head, flooding my entire body with extraordinary sensation.

When the organ stopped I lay still in the darkness listening to the slowing drum of my heart in the awesome silence.

Was this what he had meant by danger?

What a strange array of twisted emotions bound us together, and in comparison how terribly inadequate the simplicity of my love for Raoul appeared. First love, shallow and insubstantial, entirely devoid of the unplumbed shadows and incandescent light of my bondage to Erik.

Oh, Raoul! We could have been so artlessly happy together, you and I, if all this had never happened, if I had never known Erik and glimpsed into a world beyond all human imagination. It's so cruel, so unfair, that our love has been cast into this acid bath of doubt when we were young and should have made our life together. A simple, cheerful, normal love would have been ours, a love that had no power to char and destroy with its own fire.

But I've been changed, Raoul . . . changed beyond all recognition by a man who fills me with such fear that I have locked him from my room and from my bed.

And even though I flee from him, I am not free of his control, his music reaches through the very walls, consuming, possessing, tossing me like a piece of driftwood on a stormy sea . . . drowning me. My thoughts are no longer those of an innocent ingenue, and I fear the knowledge I have begun to crave is not yours to give.

I can't go back, I dare not go on. The sea is rising to my lonely rock and soon there will be no way to escape from the flood tide.

And I can't swim! I can't swim! Oh, Raoul . . . I'm so afraid!

Disgust and shame at length drove me up into the dark streets, where I might walk alone with my grief. If it had not been for that doomed encounter in the Bois I would never have given in to my absurd need to see her in that wedding gown. The dress would have remained, like the ring that I had bought for her, just another safely hidden secret, a beautiful waterfall of white satin to be fingered sadly in a private moment of indulgence and then firmly shut away out of sight . . . out of temptation.

I dared not think how near I had been to losing control, how terrifyingly easy it would have been in that moment to rape her. I'd raped her with music instead, and perhaps that crime was almost as bad as the one it had so narrowly prevented. Either way I'd violated her trust and destroyed a rare and precious innocence—soiled the delicate ambience that had lain between us all these weeks. The silence in her room, the bolts which remained drawn, were mute testimony to the magnitude of her horror and revulsion.

I walked along the wet pavements, safely shrouded in the cloak and mask, blindly following a path I had trodden many times before, until at last I stood once more outside the Chagny house.

The boy obsessed me. I was so mired in jealous fear that I had to come here repeatedly, under cover of darkness, just to torture myself by looking at him. I knew his habits of an evening, the general hours of his coming and going. I had watched him step in and out of his carriage many times, sometimes with friends, sometimes alone; I had observed his pleasant demeanor with servants and listened to his easy laughter, an open-natured, confident, well-bred boy, so secure in his youth and beauty.

I climbed now onto the balcony of his first-floor room, and there, hidden by the partially drawn curtains, I watched him undress and toss his mud-stained garments to his waiting valet. No good-humored banter tonight, I noticed. The boy was grim and unsmiling and, judging by the late hour of his retirement, must have abandoned his drunken companions in the Bois and walked until he found another carriage.

I studied him with bitter envy. The gaslight was kind to a face and body that had no need of kindness, that would have braved the cruelest light of day. A golden youth, fair haired and smooth skinned, well proportioned, powerfully built. If I wanted to be critical, I might remark a certain lack of height, but he was taller than Christine, so I could hardly deceive myself that it mattered.

Against my will I pictured him slowly divesting her of that wedding dress. I saw her shy modesty yielding first to wondering exploration, then finally to ecstasy; and I knew that afterward they would continue to lie together in the darkness . . . peaceful, satiated, their bodies still entwined, her beautiful hair covering them both like a cloak of gossamer. . . .

Did I cry out aloud at the cruel clarity of that intolerable vignette, or was it merely some involuntary movement of anguish that suddenly alerted him to my presence? I cannot say. But whatever it was that betrayed me resulted in the curtains being abruptly flung back and I found myself looking down the barrel of his revolver.

For a long moment we simply stared at each other, both too

shocked to react to this unthinkable confrontation. Then, as his free hand began to rattle at a stiff catch on the full-length windows, I turned and dropped neatly into the garden below.

As I walked away slowly I heard him burst out onto the balcony above.

"Stop!" he shouted furiously. "Stand where you are, Erik, or I give you my word I'll shoot!"

Pausing to look back, I saw that the light was behind him, making a truly magnificent target of his barely clad figure. I was unarmed, but he could not possibly know that, and against my will I found myself impressed by the courage of an overimpetuous boy, angry enough to face an experienced killer in the dark. Incongruous, perhaps even a little absurd, but it was not to be sneered at, that courage.

And yet a sneer was all the defense that was left to me.

"Firearms have no place in the hands of children," I said with grim sarcasm. "I advise you to put that thing away, boy, before you hurt yourself."

Turning my back on him with deliberate contempt, I continued my unhurried progress toward the screening trees and had taken some half-dozen steps in that direction when his first bullet grazed my shoulder. The second and third were wider of the mark, but not, I knew, by intention. If he'd possessed only a slightly better aim, that boy would have shot me down in cold blood—shot me in the back!

I thought of the many nights I'd watched him, the innumerable occasions when I could have been rid of him for good, and yet had found myself constrained by some spurious notion of fair play. Tonight he'd shown me exactly where I stood. A gentleman is accorded honorable acquittal in a duel, but a monster—*a thing!*—may be shot in the back without a moment's compunction.

Trembling with anger, I walked the streets until the first reddish light of dawn began to threaten and made me instinctively retrace my steps to the Opera.

But I returned to my house with the quiet purpose of decision, an unshakable decision that owed much to that angry gunshot.

Perhaps I couldn't have the dream, perhaps her voice, her smile, and her gentle companionship were all I could ever hope for.

But I wouldn't live with that boy's shadow any longer, I wouldn't tolerate his rivalry.

It was time to ask Christine to make a clear and legal choice.

I stayed in my room today until the continuing, crushing silence drove me out.

Erik looked up when I entered his chamber, but he did not speak, even when I knelt at his feet. When the minutes continued to tick away in deadly stillness, I realized that his voice had become, for me, a drug as powerful as morphine, necessary to my senses, vital to my existence. His silence was a punishment beyond my strength to bear.

"Erik, if you don't speak to me soon I shall go quite mad!" I said at last. "I can't bear to be locked up here with only my own thoughts for company."

His hands tightened on the arms of his chair.

"Locked up?" He echoed, with horror. "Is that what this house has come to mean to you—a prison?"

"It's not a prison," I said slowly, "until you make it so. But you've frightened me so badly this last week, Erik, I feel I hardly know you."

"No"—he sighed—"you are just beginning to know me, that's all. There's so much darkness here inside my head, sometimes it frightens me too. But it need not be like this, Christine. If I could just live like other men, walk through the Bois in daylight and feel the sun and the wind upon my naked face . . . Oh, Christine, I would dare to do so many things if you were there beside me as my wife."

I remained silent, grief stricken and appalled, unable to reply, and he got up abruptly and walked away from me.

"I see you do not care for my voice half so well when it speaks of things you do not wish to hear. Simple words can be reduced to obscenities by my tongue, can they not? Wife . . . husband . . . love."

I knelt on the floor with my head bent, feeling like a criminal who deserved to be guillotined.

"What happened yesterday will never be repeated," he continued

quietly. *"If you married me I would accept any condition you cared to name, anything . . . you understand?"*

"Erik . . ."

"You don't believe me! You think because I look like a monster it is inevitable that I should behave like one."

"No," I whispered, *"I believe you."*

He grew very still, staring down at me with utter wretchedness.

"It's that boy, isn't it?"

Terror knifed through me and I shook my head wildly, instantly denying the accusation. I dared not think what he would do to Raoul if I admitted that I already wore his ring next to my heart.

"It wouldn't be for very long," I heard him say softly. *"Six months perhaps and you would be a young widow . . . free to make a true marriage."*

When I covered my mouth with my hands he turned away in despair.

"I won't beg!" he said with sudden coldness, *"not even for your love. I have asked you to marry me, but I don't want your answer now. I would like you to come back tomorrow evening, after the performance, and tell me what you have decided. Will you promise to do that, Christine? Will you promise to come back and tell me . . . even if the answer is no?"*

Staring at the floor, unable to look up into his eyes, filled with more misery than I had ever thought it possible for a human heart to hold, I heard myself accede to his request.

eep away from the edge!

I couldn't remember who had said that to me, or on what occasion it was said, but oddly enough I remembered my reply with startling clarity.

Why?

Why must I always keep away from the edge?

I'd found the wedding gown crumpled on the chair where she must have thrown it last night, and as I bent to shake out the creases and hang it back in the closet, the snapped chain fell out from the folds of satin where it had been nestling unseen. The chain and the crucifix . . . and the ring!

I sat down on the bed and examined it with dull horror. The diamonds were of the highest quality, embedded in a setting which betrayed its newness by an absolute absence of scratches and accumulated tarnishing. This was no keepsake worn to remember a deceased relative. I knew who had given it to her and I knew why she had chosen to wear it secretly out of my sight.

Twenty-four hours I had given her because I did not yet have the courage to face her answer without making a disgusting spectacle of my grief.

But, as I looked at the ring, I knew without question that I was going to have to find that courage and let her go with dignity. She did not love me, but she respected me enough as a man—*a human being* —to honor me with the decency of a considered reply. And I, in my turn, must honor her decision. I would keep my pride this time, no tears, no degrading groveling to make me burn with shame at the memory. Pride was all I would have left to sustain me through the ordeal of her refusal, pride would make me wish her well and let us part with civilized courtesy. . . .

I could not stay in the house now, there seemed to be no air. I was overcome with a fierce urge to climb up and up into the cool evening breeze, somewhere very high where I might feel closer to the God in Whom I had so constantly denied belief.

It's all been a lie, you see, one long sorry lie, designed to save my pride from further hurt, to say there is no God.

In my heart I still believe in miracles. God is the greatest magician of all. He Who turns an ugly caterpillar into a beautiful butterfly is surely capable of changing distaste and fear into love.

Tonight I'm prepared to go down on my knees, just as I used to do as a very small child, and offer up one last purely infantile bargain.

"Please, God, let her love me and I promise to be good forever. . . ."

I could pray here, but I know it's no use, I might as well be in the lowest pit of hell. I'll never be heard down here. I have to get to the rooftops of Paris, close enough to touch the stars.

The statue of Apollo on the roof of the Opera House, ten stories above the level of the streets, is about as close as I can get to heaven now.

Surely He will hear me from there!

I was so lost in panic-ridden thought as I made my way toward my dressing room that I hardly recognized the little page who ran up to me and touched his cap.

"Mademoiselle . . . I was asked to give you this as soon as you returned to work."

Glancing at the envelope he held out toward me, I immediately recognized Raoul's sprawling, untidy hand and my heart gave a painful jerk.

"When was this given to you?"

"This morning, mademoiselle, by the Vicomte de Chagny's driver.

. . . I can take a reply if you like," the boy added cheekily. "Only cost you a franc for my trouble."

Instead of reprimanding him for his impertinence, I hurried the boy into my room and made him wait while I hastily scribbled one line on a piece of paper. I had no envelopes to hand, but I doubted he had the education to read what I had written.

"You know the Chagny house?"

"Yes, mademoiselle. Everyone knows it."

"If I give you five francs will you run all the way there?"

The boy's pasty, freckled face split into a wide grin as he pocketed my money.

"Mademoiselle, for five francs I'll fly!"

I was too distracted to return his smile. When he had gone I began to walk up and down my room like a mad thing. I did not want to open Raoul's letter; I was certain that, after the debacle in the Bois, it would be full of cold, correct sentiments and nothing else—a formal severing of our engagement.

Would he come now in answer to my desperate plea? Or, offended and hurt as he must surely be by my conduct, would he simply tear the paper to pieces and ignore it?

An hour passed, taking the remains of daylight with it, and driven by increasing desperation, I went to the grand escalier, *where I could see everyone who came and went both through the main entrance and the subscriber's rotunda.*

My watch ticked away another leaden ten minutes.

He wasn't going to come! He'd deserted me . . . and who could blame him after the way I had treated him all these weeks . . . who could blame him!

Fifteen minutes later Raoul finally strode through the rotunda toward the staircase. If there had been any coolness or reserve in his manner, it did not long survive the sight of my face as I ran to him.

"Christine! My God! What's the matter? Whatever has happened to make you look like this?"

"Hush! Not here! I can't tell you here, Raoul, there are too many

people around. We must go somewhere very quiet where we can be quite
alone. You don't mind lots of stairs, do you?"

"Of course not . . . but I don't understand—"

"Oh, Raoul, I'm so frightened!"

"If he's hurt you . . . !"

"No . . . oh, no, it isn't like that! But I can't explain here. Let's
go up to the roof. No one ever goes there after dark, it's the one place in
the whole theater where you'll be quite safe from him. No . . . wait!
Who is that foreign-looking man on the stairs? He's been watching me,
I'm sure of it. . . . And he appears to know you, he bowed. . . ."

"I'm not sure who he is. Odd fellow, he's approached me once or
twice now and asked some very curious questions about you. People say
he's Persian."

"Well, ignore him! Don't catch his eye, pretend you haven't seen
him! Listen . . . I know another way up to the roof. . . ."

The last thing I expected to hear, in this windswept oasis high above
the streets, was the sound of her voice in harmony with his.

Is this how You answer the prayers of the penitent, God?

Is this how You reward repentance and welcome home the prodigal
son?

I came to hear Your voice and instead You choose to mock me with
theirs, to show me that there is to be no divine intercession on my
behalf, no mercy, no last little miracle. My infamous crimes have set
me quite beyond the pale of Your forgiveness . . . all You wanted was
vengeance upon me for those years of iniquitous blasphemy!

Well, now that You've had Your vengeance in full measure, are You
satisfied? Are You satisfied, God?

Oh, yes, I believe in You. . . . I've always believed in You! You're
so infinitely cold and cruel, You simply have to exist. I've seen enough
of Your handiwork in my time, and it knocks my malice into palest
insignificance by comparison. Floods and earthquakes, sickness and
famine, crippled adults, mutilated children . . . and still we come
like ingenuous fools to pray for Your help in time of need! It's laugh-
able, really . . . quite pathetic! God is love! Hysterically funny! Say

rather that God is an idle itinerant, too feckless to care what happens on an earth created for the sole purpose of providing amusement on a rainy day!

What were You doing, for instance, all those months that I lay festering in my mother's womb? Were You perhaps in divine hibernation . . . taking a holiday . . . experimenting?

Well, whatever it was, You had a nasty shock when I appeared, didn't You? You didn't have the grace to admit You'd lost grip of things, nodded off for a moment and made a damned botch of it in consequence! We're not permitted to say that God makes mistakes, are we?—merely that He works in mysterious ways! Oh, God, what a charlatan You are! You're an amateur. . . . You never had any training, did You, never submitted Your master's piece for inspection . . . never had any competition!

You couldn't bestir Yourself to help Your own Son when He cried out to You on the cross! So why should You care now about the crucifixion of a monster?

When I had finished raving at the stars like a lunatic, there was silence once more across the zinc- and lead-lined roof; Christine and Chagny had long since gone back below, absorbed in their young love and totally unaware of how they had betrayed themselves in my silent presence.

I knew everything now. The shells had fallen with relentless accuracy and blown my last feeble hope into oblivion.

I'd listened to his desperate plans for flight, heard her tired acceptance, watched him bend to claim her lovely, upturned mouth as though it was his God-given right. They'd clung together like two frightened children abandoned in a dark wood, shoring up each other's confidence with protestations of loving trust.

Tonight, when the performance is over, he is to take her away—far away to a place where I can never find her, where she can begin to forget what he calls her terrible ordeal, her intolerable burden.

An intolerable burden. . . .

You've brought me full circle, haven't You, God? Right back to that moment all those years ago when I knew I had to run away.

Only, this time it's she who will run—run away from me as though I were some loathsome, slavering beast, an animal who can't be trusted to behave like a gentleman and do the decent thing. Oh, it wasn't the kiss that hurt beyond bearing . . . strangely there was a painful beauty in watching her in his embrace. If I really were her father, it would surely be a joy to see a worthy young man so passionately in love with my dearest child.

No, it wasn't that kiss which betrayed me, but the cruel and careless trick with which she intends to win her freedom. She promised to come back. She promised! And she lied! That is the final anguish . . . the knowledge that she doesn't care enough to put me out of my misery, that she's not even going to tell me. She's just going to run away with him and never give me another thought. She must hate me very much to do that. Strange—I never guessed that she really hated me; I must have made a damned good actress of her in the course of her tuition!

I'd like to die now. Right now, this very minute! I'd welcome the last convulsion of this tired and sluggish muscle in my chest, but by some incredible irony my heart is beating with curious serenity, as though it's never known a single moment's transgression.

So what are You up to, God? What cruel perverse little jest have You left to play? Surely You're not going to inflict a miracle cure and deny me the right to be struck down after this!

You denied me life—will You deny me death too? Is that to be the punishment for my unspeakable crimes against humanity—another twenty years of penal solitude upon this earth?

Beneath my towering pinnacle Paris spreads out in all its splendor, a multitude of lights flickering along Haussmann's neatly regimented boulevards. Nothing could survive that dizzying drop. All they'd find would be a smashed red pulp in dress clothes, unrecognizable . . . unidentifiable. . . .

I have only to let go. . . .

Suicide . . . the ultimate sin, the one crime we are never given the opportunity to confess. Thieves and murderers may enter heaven, but the suicide, never receiving absolution, is unable to die in a state of grace and must burn forever.

So that's why You brought me up here, God! You thought I'd be stupid enough to fall into Your trap! One rash act of folly on my part and You would have been spared the loathsome necessity of gazing upon Your ugly miscreation throughout eternity!

Well . . . I don't need You. I never needed You! There is a greater Master yet, one who remains loyal, even to a backsliding apprentice . . . a Master who reminds me even now that my indentures to him were never broken . . . merely postponed.

I am not forsaken! I'm no longer alone in the darkness! Before my eyes I see a thousand little devils lighting black candles along the path which leads toward the edge . . . the blindingly beautiful edge.

Love is a scorpion's paralyzing poison, but now a thousand little mouths are sucking it steadily from my veins, emptying my mind and preparing a black void to receive the Master's presence. I feel the grief receding, dispersing beneath the rage which is mushrooming out inside me like some monstrous fungus. All the evil in the world has been let loose tonight, whipped up into a mighty cyclone and irresistibly directed toward the high peak of Apollo's lyre . . . drawn to my brain like lightning to a conductor.

A cold breeze stirs my cloak, sends it billowing out around me like the wings of the Angel of Death, as I lift my head slowly to look upon my Master's awesome power and hear his solemn promise.

Beyond the edge there is no pain.

Beyond the edge you will be reborn in the glory of darkness.

Rise up and follow me. . . .

Feeding on the putrefied remains of love, I have completed the final process of metamorphosis, swollen and blossomed uncontrollably into a mighty, all-powerful shade of hell.

All that remains to be done is for me to tear through the chrysalis of mortality and reveal the ravening black-winged creature that lusts to live.

A dark and towering shadow, rising like the phoenix from the ashes . . . malevolent . . . omnipotent. . . .

The Phantom of the Opera!

"There are a good three hours before the performance—why don't we just go now, straightaway, no hanging around?"

"I can't do that! What if Erik should attend tonight and not hear me sing one last time! Oh, God, why have I let him talk me into this?"

"Christine! For God's sake! You're not changing your mind, are you?"

"I—I think I ought to sing. The management—"

"Damn the management! I'll soon settle with their nonsense! They needn't think they can hold you to any stupid contract!"

"Please . . . no scenes, Raoul, not for the sake of three hours. Have you got a box for tonight?"

"No. I didn't know you'd be appearing, so I didn't bother to book one."

"Run around to the Salt Boxes, then, and see what they can do for you. There's bound to be an odd seat left somewhere."

Raoul pushed the hood of my cloak back from my face and studied me for a moment with unnerving intensity.

"I'll ask them for box five, shall I?" he demanded coolly.

I bit my lip and looked away.

"Is he going to be there?" Raoul persisted stubbornly. "Is that why you're so determined to sing?"

"I honestly don't know what he intends to do tonight. But as long as there is the smallest chance that he may attend this performance, I have to sing. Can you understand that? It's the only way I know to say good-bye to him."

Raoul looked as though he intended to argue, then all of a sudden he gave in with unexpected weariness.

"All right," he agreed unhappily, "if that's what you really want, then we'll wait. Perhaps it's for the best after all—perhaps I ought to hear you say good-bye to him. It might stop me wondering for the rest of my life whether you really only meant to say au revoir."

If ever there was a time to put my arms around Raoul and tell him how much I loved him it was now—now, as I watched that fretwork of pained doubt settle over his handsome face like a fine cobweb. I'd clung to him in despair up on the roof, burying my fears in the warmth of his youth and undoubted affection. I'd wanted him to hold me forever,

wanted always to see his dear, familiar face looking down on me, prom-
ising a life lived out in light, free of shadowed, unknown terrors.

I've loved Raoul since I was fifteen years old, shyly and uncertainly
for the most part, hardly daring to hope that he would ever look beyond
our childhood friendship and brave the hostility of his family for my
sake. And yet, now that I have all the proof any girl could ask of a
young man's love, I find my tongue is chained and fettered in cruel
silence.

Up there beneath Apollo's lyre, with only the wind and the stars to
witness my betrayal, I was able to say that I loved Raoul and mean it
with all my heart. But here—here in the presence of this omniscient
mirror . . . the words dry in my throat and refuse to be spoken again.

Suddenly I'm rendered utterly dumb with horror by the knowledge
that I can kill Erik with three simple syllables.

I can't speak those words which Raoul so badly needs for reassurance;
and even as we cling together, I feel we have been torn apart, each of us
holding nothing but the shadow of our own lonely doubts.

The luck of the Devil is with me tonight, the planets themselves realign themselves in my favor at the Master's behest!

The Persian is watching, and just for once that suits me uncommonly well.

Nadir?

Nadir no longer exists. I have washed friendship from my heart, just as I have purged myself of love. For the first time in my life I am unfettered by weak and contemptible emotions. I am filled with the power of hate, and hate gives me the strength to cut free from the shackles of humanity at last.

He's following me even now, thinks I haven't seen him—the fool! I could have killed him half a dozen times on this journey back down from the roof of the Opera, but I don't choose to do it . . . not yet! The daroga of Mazanderan will render me one last professional service before I send him to the mercy of Allah.

You see, I could kill anyone tonight, Daroga. If the Holy Virgin herself was to appear before me I could put a dagger through her heart without a moment's compunction! I no longer have a foot in either camp; I have made my choice. Like Lucifer, I prefer to reign in hell.

I must move more slowly—once or twice he's almost lost me. Damn you, Daroga, must I light your way like a paid guide? You walk like a tired old man, keep closer can't you? yes . . . that's better! We're in the third cellar now, we're nearly there!

And here is the stone. . . .

Are you watching, Daroga? Are you watching very carefully and congratulating yourself on your great skills of detection?

Of course you are! You've waited a long time for this, have you not, and at last your long persistence has been rewarded. Now you know the secret of the Phantom's lair. And when the chandelier crashes down in the auditorium tonight, when Christine Daae disappears from the stage in the ensuing pandemonium, you will know exactly what to do with that knowledge. You will know where to find me and you will know exactly who to bring with you on your final manhunt.

I know you so well, you see. You have all the instincts of a highly efficient policeman. . . . Really, you were always far more competent than you ever gave yourself credit for! You won't waste valuable time approaching the cynical Paris Sûreté with wild moonshine about an opera ghost. You'll simply get on with the job yourself. Your stern integrity will compel you to complete the mission that was entrusted to you all those years ago in Persia. You, too, Daroga, will pluck the weakness of old friendship from your heart tonight and remember only the righteousness of your cause. As I have betrayed your trust, so will you betray mine.

When the curtain falls on the final act, I want that boy in the house on the lake, helpless and entirely at my mercy.

I want the Vicomte de Chagny, Daroga!

And I know that I can trust you to bring him to me!

*   *   *

In half an hour the curtain rises on Faust *and I will sing one last time for Erik, without even knowing if he will hear me. At the end of the performance Raoul's carriage will be waiting at the door. I shall not come back here to the dressing room even for my cloak, lest the sight of the mirror sway my wavering resolution to flee.*

I know I'm not doing the right thing and yet there doesn't seem to be anything else left to do. How can I go back to Erik too frightened to say yes and yet unable to say no? How can I look upon his grief and still stay sane? Oh, Erik, why did it have to be me? You chose a timorous, shrinking mouse on which to lavish your passionate devotion when, if God was loving, you should by rights have had a splendid young lioness!

How can I marry you now and willfully withhold your rights as my husband, how can I punish you on our wedding night by turning away and denying you physical love? No woman in this world has been ever been loved as you have loved me. Why isn't it enough, why can't I span the awesome void that lies between us?

I love you, Erik, I love you in so many different ways . . . but my love is the love of a child afraid to grow up. Children run away and hide when they meet a situation they can't face, when they see the dream is over and a terrifying reality beckons instead. My love is just a shoddy, broken little toy that I'm too ashamed to own. Don't cry for my loss, Erik. . . . I've never been worthy of your tears.

What I'm doing to Raoul is almost as wicked as what I've done to you, but I'm too tired to fight his determination any longer. I just want the decision taken out of my hands. He's so eager to pluck me from the ruins of my disastrous enslavement and suddenly it's the only way out that I can see, to go away with him. God knows I'd never find the courage to go away by myself.

I'm quite sure that Raoul has no concept of the price of victory. All those years ago when he rushed into the sea to fetch my scarf, he seemed honestly astonished to find himself soaked to the skin.

I think he might now be equally surprised to find that no one who walks through fire can hope to emerge unscathed.

You told me so many beautiful stories, Erik, you taught me that even fairy tales can have a tragic ending.

The white rose and the nightingale were punished by Allah for stealing a forbidden love.

Somehow I don't think any of us are destined to live happily ever after. . . .

The arrangements were quite simple to make—simple, that is, for me.

One hour in my laboratory yielded all the materials I needed, and well before curtain time an explosive device was in place beneath each of the eight steel hawsers that held the counterweights of Garnier's chandelier in place. All eight were connected to a timing mechanism, and the quantity of explosives had been carefully calculated to blow through steel coils as thick as a man's wrist.

Entirely devoid of emotion, I worked with cool efficiency, and when I had finished I concealed myself behind scenery on the stage, dressed in a red hooded cloak that was an exact replica of the one Mephistopheles would wear tonight. It seemed fitting somehow to be dressed as the Prince of Evil, a nice touch of which my Master would approve. A good apprentice always pays close attention to detail, you see. If a job's worth doing, it's worth doing well. . . .

When the charges detonated, I had roughly a second to admire the spectacular effect of seven tons of glass and metalwork plummeting from the gilded ceiling, before an equally finely timed interruption to the hydrogen supply plunged the stage into darkness. The ensuing panic was so great that no one saw me hurry Christine along the deserted corridors to her dressing room.

She made no sound during our flight through the mirror. There was no screaming or struggling. She had entered that state of passive indifference which descends on a victim just before execution, surrendering to my silent insistence with the unquestioning resignation of total hopelessness.

The wedding gown was laid out upon her bed, and only when I had told her to put it on did she show the first sign of horrified protest.

"Erik . . . please . . ."

"Put it on! I insist! You must be properly dressed to receive my guests."

"Guests!" She stared at me without comprehension.

"Wedding guests, my dear—witnesses to the crime, if you prefer. Now, do as I say. I shall give you half an hour to prepare for the reception."

I locked the door upon her as calmly as if I had done it many times before, astonished to find how easy it was to lock a living thing inside a cage. No guilt, no remorse, no vicarious claustrophobia . . . I was no longer capable of suffering on her behalf.

I went to my room, stripped off my costume, and for the first time donned evening dress with the aid of a full-length mirror. Mirrors, too, had lost their power to knife me. Protected by the Master's shield, I was insensible to all earthly pain. As long as I served him I knew that nothing in this world would be capable of hurting me again.

Music was flowing through my head like a tidal wave, driving me toward the organ with irresistible force. The final act of *Don Juan Triumphant* was writing itself, I was merely the medium, the midwife who would bring this thunderous cacophony of sound into the world.

Madness welled out beneath my fingertips, swirled up like a loathsome living thing into a maelstrom of ugly, passionate notes. I had never played like this before, never rained such savage torture upon my own auditory senses. Music filled with hate, music that lusted to kill . . . on and on I played until the keyboard itself seemed on fire and my fingers leapt back as from a powerful charge of static electricity.

The sudden silence in the house was deafening.

The music had been nothing less than a violent physical assault, and suddenly I remembered Christine with terrible fear.

She was kneeling on the floor by the wall when I entered her room and her forehead was covered with blood. I did not need to ask how she had come by such injuries. I was neither surprised nor shocked, merely annoyed that I had been stupid enough to leave her alone while my wicked music mercilessly clubbed her senses.

I carried her back to my room and laid her on the couch, attending to her cuts with professional indifference. How incredible that hate can cure love so completely; I might have been handling a corpse, I was so calm, so detached and utterly devoid of tenderness.

"Why are you laughing?" she asked fearfully.

"I'm laughing at you, my dear . . . at your truly remarkable *incompetence*. You don't even know how to go about killing yourself with any efficiency, do you? What have you succeeded in doing except give yourself a headache and ruin your dress? You're really not very practical, are you? Why didn't you consult me first? I would have been quite happy to give you the benefit of my considerable experience in death."

"Don't talk like this," she whispered. "Please, Erik. Don't talk about death and laugh like that—it frightens me."

I shrugged with indifference as I looked down on her white face.

"Yes . . . I seem to remember how very little it takes to frighten you, Christine. But you really shouldn't be frightened of Death. He's very approachable, really, not at all aloof, never passes by on the other side of the road simply because he's not been introduced. He makes no distinctions of class . . . a flea-bitten rat or a beautiful princess, it's all the same to Death. But of course, like anyone else he enjoys a little novelty in his work. It helps to pass the time. So I expect he was quite amused by the chandelier. I never cared much for that chandelier, did you? I remember telling Garnier that it was quite overdone, but of course he wouldn't listen. He had this streak of pure vulgarity and he hated criticism. Most artists do. . . ."

She lay as still as a statue on the couch, her hands clenched around the smooth satin folds of the wedding dress.

"The chandelier . . ." she echoed dully. "Oh, God . . . Erik . . . are you telling me that the chandelier was not an accident?"

"Surely you didn't think it was obliging enough to hop down off the ceiling of its own accord, did you?"

"But—but people must have been killed!"

"Oh, yes. I daresay that's quite likely! It's really very difficult to be a murderer without killing people from time to time, you know. By the way, you left this behind . . . have you missed it?"

I dropped the chain with its crucifix and engagement ring into her trembling hand and sat back to watch her reaction. If it were really possible, I would have said she went a little whiter.

"If you're going to be sick, my dear," I said coldly, "I hope you'll tell me in good time for me to fetch you a bowl. This was a very expensive carpet."

"*Why?*" she whispered. "Why are you doing this . . . why are you being so *cruel?*"

"Any cruelty I show tonight I learned from you, my dear, on the roof of the Opera. Oh, yes, I heard it all—everything . . . that boy has a very penetrating voice, you know. Of course, you can't help loving him, I know that, none of us can choose where we will love. I'm perfectly willing to be reasonable and accept that it's all his fault. Yes, it's him I blame . . . and it's him I'm going to punish when he comes here to take you back."

She sat up against the black cushions in alarm.

"How can he come here?" she stammered. "He doesn't know the way?"

"Oh, Christine! How gravely you underestimate the determination of the importunate lover! Do you honestly doubt that he would slay dragons and hack his way through a forest of thorns to fight his way to your side? That's really not very noble of you, child, not very romantic at all."

"He doesn't know the way," she repeated stubbornly, clinging to the phrase as though it were a magic talisman to keep him safe, *"he doesn't know the way."*

"That won't matter. I've arranged for him to have a personal guide, you see. I can quite safely rely on Nadir to bring him. Isn't it nice to have people about you that you can really trust, Christine? Nadir was a good friend to me once upon time. *Once upon a time.* . . . That's how the best fairy tales begin, isn't it? Now . . . what shall I tell you about Nadir? Shall I tell you how he wept when his son died in my arms? Shall I tell you how he nursed me through Persian poison and risked his life to save me from the shah's malice? No . . . I don't think I'll tell you any of it. Why should I? You don't deserve to understand about Nadir. All you need to know is that he dies with your lover tonight because of you—because of your treachery! Because of you I'm going to lose my only friend! Unless . . . Of course! How could I have forgotten that? There is a way. . . . There is a way it could be done. . . ."

"Erik, please, please don't be so angry—"

"Angry . . . *angry?* Why should I be angry? You have a perfect right to run off with whomever you please, do you not?"

"I never meant to hurt you—never!"

I leapt off the couch and walked away from her. This was too much! I was honestly afraid I might do her a very serious injury if she continued to treat me like a poor idiot.

"Really?" I sneered. "You were going to let me wait here all alone tomorrow night, walking up and down, up and down, staring at the clock? You were going to let me drag up all those hundreds of stairs to your dressing room to find you gone—no word of regret, no letter, nothing—*and you didn't mean to hurt me?* You'll forgive me, my dear, if I have to say I find that rather difficult to believe."

"I didn't want—"

Control was slipping rapidly from my grasp as I swung round upon her.

"I *trusted* you! I trusted you to treat me like a civilized human being and come back with your answer. All these months I've worshiped you as though you were some sacred vestal virgin. I've never even *touched* you! And you wouldn't come back . . . you wouldn't even come back and say good-bye. There was nothing I would not have done to make you happy, nothing at all. My God, I even killed to please you! I don't suppose you remember the spiders, do you? Poor creatures! There they were, doing no harm, minding their own business and hoping to be left in peace. Spiders are useful, don't you know that, you ignorant child? But it wasn't enough simply to have them shut away out of your sight, was it? No, you wanted them killed, crushed out of existence, because you hated the sight of them, they were ugly and they frightened you! Well, there's someone I hate, too, someone I've been afraid of for a long, long time, and tonight I'm going to kill him so that I won't ever have to be frightened again. It's all right to kill if you're frightened, isn't it, Christine? You showed me that! Yes . . . on the roof of the world you showed me the way. God helps those who help themselves, you know . . . and if God can't be bothered, there's always Someone else who will. But generally speaking I've got rather used to shifting for myself. It was something my mother drummed into me very early. . . . I couldn't have been two when she began to refuse to fasten my buttons and tie the mask in place. I remember her throwing a pile of clothes at me one day in a temper—she had a terrible temper, Christine, I daresay that's where I get mine from— 'Do it yourself!' she snapped. 'You're simply going to have to learn to do things for yourself!' I sat in my room all day because I couldn't fasten that bloody mask and I didn't dare to go downstairs without it. Sasha would have helped me, if she could, but poor Sasha didn't know how to do it either. All she could do was lick the tears off my face. Dogs like tears, did you know that? I suppose it must be the salt. You'd think I wouldn't remember it, but I remember everything, *everything*. I was cursed with these extraordinary powers of recall, you see. . . . Sometimes I would have given anything simply to be able to forget, as other people do. Anyway . . . I soon learned to do what was necessary—and that, my dear, is precisely what I intend to do tonight. I don't want to remember how he took you away from me, Christine, so I'm simply going to take him away instead. I'm going to make him disappear from your life. I'm a wonderful magician, you see, I can make anything disappear, if I really want to."

I lapsed into a silence which Christine seemed unable or unwilling to break. Her eyes were half closed, as though she was slowly losing consciousness, and I wondered detachedly if she was suffering from concussion. Beating her head against a stone wall couldn't have done her any good at all. . . . Perhaps I ought not to let her go to sleep.

Just as I was leaning over to shake her, an electric bell rang jarringly in the silence and her eyelids snapped open in terror.

"Don't be alarmed, my dear, it's only our guests ringing the doorbell. They're late, I expected them before this . . . but better late than never, I suppose. Oh, now, please, don't get up. If I draw back the curtains you will have a perfectly good view from the couch."

The touch of my finger on the master control was sufficient to cause the wall paneling to slide back, and when I drew the full-length black velvet curtains aside, the torture chamber revealed beyond was immediately flooded with brilliant light.

"A word of explanation, child, to spare you confusion. This panel is a two-way mirror—we can see them, but they cannot see us. They can, however, hear us, as you will observe. . . . Good evening, Monsieur de Chagny . . . Daroga. You come here tonight to my private theater without invitation, but there, I let it pass, I'm not one to stand on undue ceremony. I would point out that all valuables—including your lives, incidentally—are deposited here at your own risk. The management cannot be held responsible for any damage that may be incurred during the entertainment. Ah, monsieur, I beg you, do not mouth at us like a ridiculous codfish. I'm sure your passionate entreaties are very moving, but I have taken the precaution of ensuring they cannot be heard on this side of the wall. Daroga . . . a word with you, if you please. Step away from the young man, right away, and approach the mirror nearest to you. . . .Yes, that's better, you've learned, haven't you, you've learned that it's always best to do as I say with some alacrity. I'm sorry. . . . I appear to have startled you. You never saw this particular little trick, did you? I have to confess that the idea was the khanum's. So easily bored that woman was, so insatiable for novelty! She thought it would be amusing to separate two victims within the same illusion, allowing one to die first while the other watched the fate that lay in store. You will find that the caging is entirely resistant to heat and permits you to observe the entertainment without suffering the least inconvenience. When it's over you will be free to do exactly as you will. I see you've brought a pistol with you. I hope you'll be considerate enough to use it when the time comes, rather than send for the police. It would save a great deal of trouble all around, wouldn't it? But for now let us concentrate on the diversion in hand. . . . I'm sure the young man will prove a fascinating subject for study. These aristocrats always know how to die with dignity. It's all those years of practice, you see. . . .What is it, three revolutions in a hundred years? . . . something like that . . . we're in the Third Republic now, aren't we? England made do with one civil war, of course, but then the English have so much more self-control. Now . . . Monsieur de Chagny . . . Raoul—you don't mind if I call you Raoul, do you?—I trust you're not going to disappoint me. No, of course you're not. . . . I'm sure you're going to die very beautifully! You have that look about you which promises a tasteful death. I wonder if you'll look quite so handsome when you've hung yourself from that tree in the corner. Ridiculous suggestion, isn't it, you can't begin to believe you would do it, but you'll be surprised what a difference a few hours in a high temperature will make. By the way, you might be interested to know that I have your little bride here watching. Speak to him, Christine, give the young man a little encouragement. Oh, my dear, you'll really have to cry harder than that, or he'll never hear you —and you have such a special *talent* for crying, it would be a dreadful shame to waste it!"

I turned away from the window and sat down, breathing heavily. I was beginning to feel very odd, as though it were me and not Chagny who had been locked many hours in that furnace of illusions; me who was beginning to hallucinate, slipping involuntarily out of my appointed time and wandering hazily through spinning memories. Past and present seemed to have merged indistinguishably together, showing me all at the same time a mirror smashing, a knife plunging up into vast expanse of gut, a girl tumbling soundlessly from a parapet, a child lying limp in my arms . . .

And suddenly . . . the Master's awesome frown of displeasure!

Something was wrong, something was going badly wrong, but I didn't know what it was, I didn't understand why it wasn't working. Mortar's very difficult to mix that first time, it's not easy to attain the perfect consistency required to cement the stones of pure evil in place. This was a very advanced art and suddenly I was a clumsy, uncertain apprentice, blundering with hopeless ineptitude beneath the Master's stony eye; suddenly I was terribly afraid that I'd set my hand at last to the one skill I couldn't acquire.

Panic and fear began to eddy around my brain.

I did the chandelier . . . the chandelier, that was good, wasn't it, that showed promise . . . ?

But it was no use making excuses, trying to bolster my failing courage and sense of imminent failure. The chandelier was just for practice. *This* was my Master's piece . . . and if I failed tonight I'd never be a master, I'd never be a master after all . . . immortal, invulnerable to human pain.

I felt His anger beating against my skull, and suddenly I could see that He, too, had lied. It wasn't beautiful here beyond the edge, it wasn't beautiful at all. . . . It was full of ugly, leering shapes that filled me with sudden terror. . . .

You lied to me, Sir. . . . Why did you lie?

"Let him go, Erik . . . please!"

I opened my eyes to find Christine kneeling on the floor at my feet. Had I fallen asleep for a moment so that I never saw her leave the couch? But suddenly her voice was all I needed to anchor myself once more to the present, to raise anger enough to overcome that moment of spineless self-doubt.

"I'll marry you," she continued feverishly, when I remained silent and unyielding. "Erik, if you let him go I swear I'll marry you in any church in France."

I started to laugh quietly.

"Oh, I see—you've determined to be the noble martyr! And he's going to agree to that, is he, this nice young man of yours . . . he's going to come out here, shake my hand, and say 'Congratulations, Erik, the best man won'? Oh, no, my dear, I don't think that will do somehow. Even an opera has to have a more convincing plot than that!"

"We'll go away," she said urgently. "Just turn everything off and I'll go away with you. You don't have to let them out now—all it will take to free them is a letter to the management."

"You're really thinking this out very carefully, aren't you?" I said bitterly. "I honestly think you'd be quite prepared to go through with this horrible farce. Are you listening in there, Chagny . . . are you overcome by the astonishing nobility of her suggestion? My God, boy, you *should* be!"

"Erik—"

"Forgive me for interrupting you so rudely, my dear . . . please continue. Do tell me how this wonderful little opera of yours resolves itself. . . . I really don't think I can be bothered to wait for the opening night. What happens when we've had this very civilized wedding? Do you throw yourself under the wheels of a cab as we leave the Madeleine? Or are you going to make the truly grand romantic gesture and stab yourself in the bridal suite? I've got one or two excellent knives that would be admirably suited to the purpose, not too heavy for a lady's hand. You might like to have a look at them while we're waiting."

"I don't understand." she sobbed. "Why are you mocking me like this? Only a few hours ago you promised it would be enough simply to call me your wife."

"Well, I've changed my mind!" I shouted suddenly, throwing the organ stool across the room with a savage force that brought the red hangings down upon the coffin. "Perhaps I don't want a Druid sacrifice after all, a petrified little girl who shrinks from my touch and tries to commit suicide the moment I leave her alone. Perhaps I don't want a dead wife lying in a glass coffin. I don't want you, Christine, are you so vain, so stupid that you can't comprehend that? I don't want your pity or your fear—I don't want you!"

Silence fell upon the room as the last echo of my demented rage died away, leaving us staring at each other with disbelief.

Christine had stopped crying; her eyes were suddenly wide and glazed with shock.

"What do you want?" she demanded uncertainly. "Erik, please . . . tell me what you want."

If you don't tell me what you want straightaway, you will have nothing at all.

I felt myself shrinking and shriveling before her clear, candid gaze. I was once more that small boy, twisting a napkin around my finger in absolute terror that my request would be denied. Such a little thing really, a kiss . . . most people don't give it a moment's consideration. They kiss on meeting, they kiss on parting, that simple touching of flesh is taken entirely for granted as a basic human right.

I've lived on this earth half a century without knowing what it is to be kissed . . . and I'll never know now.

It's not my birthday . . . and I haven't been good. . . .

I drifted toward the hearth and ran my fingers absently across the mantelpiece. Somewhere along here was the location of the switch that would connect an electrical current to the old Communard powder kegs stored in the cellar.

It would be very quick, and very merciful. They wouldn't even know what hit them . . . if I could just remember where I sited that switch. . . .

A movement behind me made me turn sharply, a reflex born of a lifetime's wariness.

Christine stood there.

She had shrouded her face in the wedding veil, and seeing this I suddenly knew a moment of intense remorse. I'd totally dismantled this child . . . taken her to pieces in my crazed determination to make her heart tick in harmony with my own. I'd taught her to sing like one of God's own angels, I'd loved her more than anything else upon this earth . . . but my love had destroyed her, reduced her to a pitiful creature barely aware of her own actions . . . made her as mad as I was myself.

As I watched, she slowly lifted the veil back from her face, just as a bride does, and I was able to see the black shadows beneath eyes that brimmed and overflowed with tears. With trembling hands she removed my mask and let it flutter to the floor between us; then her fingers crept hesitantly to the smooth lapels of my dress coat.

A moment longer she stood, like a terrified swimmer on the top of a dizzying cliff, contemplating a plunge that was utterly beyond her courage.

"Take me!" she whispered. *"Teach me. . . ."*

Stunned, incredulous, scarcely able to believe in what I heard and saw, I lifted her face with trembling hands and kissed her bruised and bleeding forehead with all the uncertain timidity of a terrified boy.

And then suddenly I was no longer the teacher, but the pupil . . . for her arms were around my neck, her caressing hands an insistent pressure against my skull, drawing me forward with unbelievable strength into her embrace.

When her lips closed over mine I tasted the salt of tears, but it was impossible to say whether they were mine or hers.

Deeper and deeper she swam down into that embrace, pulling me like a lost pearl from the sucking mud of the ocean bed, dragging me relentlessly back up with her into the searing light of day. She kicked away the crutches of hate that had sustained me so long and made me stand with helpless wonder while her hands once more sought my face and drew it down to hers.

A long long time she held me, as though she could not bear to let me go, and when at last we drew apart, we stared at each other with silent awe, dazed by the intensity of what we had shared.

It was finished then, of course . . . that kiss ended everything.

The moment I knew that she was mine—truly mine—I knew I could not kill that wretched boy.

Raoul
1897

I had no trouble when I came to book box five for this evening's performance. No one looked up in horror, one hand to his mouth, no one rushed off to consult an anxious management over my heinous request. In the seventeen intervening years since I last attended this theater, staff have died, moved on, and been replaced; no one remembers the Opera Ghost now, except as a vague legend, and I daresay that no one remembers me either. I'm thirty-eight this year, but if I'm honest with myself I have to admit that I look at least ten years older. Grief and bitterness have aged me to a point where no one in Paris would now recognize me as the Vicomte de Chagny. Not that I mind that. I haven't come here tonight to be recognized. . . . I've come to remember and to pay tribute to my memories.

Drawing my watch from my pocket, I frown as the minutes tick away inexorably to curtain time. It looks as if Charles isn't going to make it in time for the overture! Damnable ill luck, our carriage running over that stray dog. . . . Of course Charles was out of the door like a shot, picking the poor creature out of the gutter, never minding that his dress suit was covered in mud and blood, insisting we find a veterinary surgeon immediately. No mean feat on a Friday night in Paris!

"Look, Dad, you go on to the restaurant without me. I'll sort this out and meet you at the Opera later."

"Charles, I'm not very happy about this! Your mother would never have forgiven me if she thought I'd left you running around Paris alone in the dark. . . ."

That smile! The irrepressibly sunny smile with which he's always resisted my tiresome authority, the smile which makes it quite impossible to protest against his quiet determination.

"Dad! I'm sixteen and I speak French as well as you do! I promised Mother I'd look after you, make sure you ate. Now, go and have your dinner, like a good fellow. I'll meet you later."

It's quite impossible to argue with Charles when he's made up his mind. Ever since Christine died he's been organizing me, providing a nonstop whirlwind of activity to stop me brooding, and I haven't had the strength or the heart to resist his well-meant efforts. It was his idea to come back to France on this visit, to make this pilgrimage to the Opera and see the famous horseshoe auditorium in which Christine knew her great triumph.

But it was my idea to book box five . . . and even now I'm not entirely sure what streak of perversity has brought me back to a place that was once Erik's private domain. There's nothing to distinguish this box from any other on the grand tier—same carpet, same armchairs, same red hangings and red velvet ledge. And yet I like to fancy it has a unique atmosphere, an aura of repressed memories. I like to fancy that if I spoke he would hear me. Odd, really . . . since Christine died I've often felt a great need to speak to Erik. It's as though I've come to believe that he has the right to know—to see at last how it all ended.

A hand on my shoulder.

"Hallo, Dad! Just made it in time after all."

I turn to look up and my heart is squeezed at the sight of this lovely boy who bears no resemblance to me or to Christine. If I ever doubted my own fears, if I ever tried to persuade myself that I was mistaken, I can't do it tonight, can't fool myself any longer. With every year that passes his features conform more closely to that portrait which I keep safely locked in a private drawer. Even Christine never knew it lay in my possession; I never confronted her with it. We kept our secrets from each other to the very end. . . .

Charles slides into the chair beside me with the unhurried grace that sets him entirely apart from other boys of his age, and turns to give me a smile of encouragement.

"I know this won't be easy for you, Dad, but afterward you'll be glad you came and laid the ghost to rest."

My God! Sometimes I swear this boy has psychic powers, he has such an uncanny knack of touching a raw nerve with healing fingers. But of course, he only thinks of Christine . . . he can't possibly imagine the sheer magnitude of conflicting emotions that surge through my weary brain tonight.

The lights dim slowly in the great auditorium and Charles lifts his opera glasses from their case, leaning forward a little in his seat with taut anticipation. In a few minutes he will be quite lost in the music, forgetting me, forgetting his dead mother, forgetting everything except his need to commune with a force that's always been beyond my understanding. Music is in his soul, extends to every fiber of his being, and already in England they are hailing him as the most outstanding young concert pianist to emerge this century. Women crowd to his recitals, embarrassing him afterward with their fulsome praise and overt admiration of his good looks.

"As if it matters what I look like!" he once burst out indignantly. "It shouldn't come into it, should it, Dad? Why can't they just listen to the music instead of making cow's eyes over my face?"

Yes, Charles, at thirteen, had considered it an absolute imposition to look like a young god.

"You don't suppose they only come just to look at me, do you?" he'd asked in horror. Strange how he always insisted on coming to me with all his anxieties—always to me rather than Christine, even when he was very young and I did absolutely nothing to encourage his confidence . . . or thought I didn't. Some sort of poetic justice, I suppose.

Glancing at him now, seeing him safely absorbed in the music, I lay my own opera glasses quietly aside and sit back in my armchair with my eyes closed.

I have no real interest in *Carmen*, you see.

Against the darkness of my lids I have already begun to relive a more personal opera, the one in which I once quite unwittingly found myself playing a leading role.

Seventeen years ago, in the uncharted bowels of this very theater. . . .

*   *   *

The heat in the mirrored chamber had very quickly reached an almost unendurable level, causing me to fling off my jacket and rip open the neck of my dress shirt as I listened in helpless anguish to the conversation in the adjoining room. Sweat was rolling off me in torrents within minutes, soaking the stiff white linen and blinding me with a steady trickle of salty droplets.

I hammered on the thick glass in impotent rage, but it resisted the onslaught of my bare fists and at length I fell back defeated, cursing savagely and gasping for breath. The air seemed to have become very thin and rarefied; I could not suck sufficient quantity into my laboring lungs, and already I was beginning to grow dizzy and disoriented. Slumping down on the floor, where it felt a little cooler, I struggled to concentrate on the terrible scene which was escalating beyond the walls of my prison.

Erik spoke at first with an icy, controlled sarcasm, but as I listened intently I detected increasing signs of insanity in his words and realized with horror that the man was now quite out of his mind. Panic seized me when I heard Christine begin to plead with him and that warning note of impending violence suddenly entered his voice. Dear God, she was making him angry, terribly angry . . . couldn't she see that every word she spoke only increased his rage and bitterness? *Be quiet!* I willed her silently. *Don't say any more or he'll kill you!*

I heard him shouting at her, the sound of some object being hurled across the room; I heard her ask him what he wanted . . . and after that I heard no more. There was a long and terrible silence which seemed to stretch on and on into infinity, and the hollow trembling that came over me sapped the last of my strength and hope. I assumed that the inevitable had happened, that he had strangled her; and if she was dead, I no longer unduly cared what became of me.

When the mirror in front of me opened of itself, I didn't move for a moment; and then with a curious, unhurried calm I paused to pick up my jacket, delaying the awful moment when I would be forced to look upon what he had done. I would not have believed it possible to pass into such state of utter apathy; I felt tired and very, very old as I staggered into the room beyond. My brain appeared to have ceased functioning entirely. Even when I saw them both standing there, I could not at first assimilate the fact that Christine was still alive.

They were standing very close, almost close enough to touch, and Christine was staring up at him with an intensity that entirely excluded me and everything else in the room. She seemed aware of nothing but him: I would have said she was in a state of trance, save for the look in her eyes, that astonishing look which seemed not to be one of fear, but rather one of . . . revelation!

It was he who moved first, turned around and so afforded me a first glimpse of his horrific face. God! She hadn't lied, had she? How was it possible for anything living to look like that?

He walked away from her and approached me slowly, with a heavy sigh.

"Put on your jacket, young man, or you will take a chill," he said with quiet severity.

Incredulously, never taking my eyes off him for a second, I struggled into my tailcoat with difficulty.

"Let me see you walk in a straight line."

"I—I beg your pardon?" I stammered uncertainly.

Again he sighed, with a kind of weary patience, as though I were some particularly dull-witted child committed to his unwilling care.

"It will be necessary for you to row some distance in the dark. I have no intention of allowing you to take her in the boat until I am assured of your strength and sense of balance. Now . . . let me see you walk."

I crossed the chamber and returned in accordance with his gesture. Christine had not moved. She appeared to be frozen to the spot and still she gazed at him transfixedly; but, for the moment, amazement washed all thought of her strange behavior from my mind.

He's going to let us go. . . . I really believe he means to let us go. . . .

"You appear to have taken little harm," continued Erik gravely. "I advise small quantities of fluid at regular intervals during the next twelve hours. Please remember that excessive water will make you ill, as will alcohol. . . ."

I stared at him with wary disbelief. This man who had tried to kill me was now speaking to me as thought he were my father . . . or my doctor! Perhaps I was hallucinating after all. . . .

"I would like you to marry her as soon as possible," he said slowly. "I assume you will be perfectly agreeable to that?"

I nodded at him, utterly stupefied by this turn of the conversation.

"Good. Now, I am going to ask you a very impertinent question and I would appreciate a very honest answer in return. Will you have sufficient income to keep her if your family should cut you off? Now, don't be stiff necked and proud, boy! You're only twenty, you've not entered your majority yet, and I would prefer to give you whatever you need rather than see my child marry a pauperized aristocrat."

I assured him my finances were in an entirely satisfactory condition, convinced now that I was merely taking part in some bizarre dream. Any minute now I was going to wake up limp with relief and swear never to take cheese for supper again!

He returned to Christine and made a curt gesture for me to accompany him. From the corner of my eye I became aware of the Persian standing in the doorway of the torture chamber, watching us without comment.

Erik took hold of Christine's hand, looking down for a moment at her small fingers entwined by his long, skeletal bones. She opened her mouth as though to speak, but he placed a finger on her lips to silence her.

"Hush, my dear, there's nothing more to say now. It has all been arranged. I won't be able to give you away in the church, of course, so I'd like do it now. . . ."

As he joined her hand with mine, I became uncomfortably aware that tears were coursing unheeded down his sunken cheeks.

"I never go to weddings, you see," he murmured dimly. "People keep asking me, but I always say no, weddings make me cry, it's better not to go. I like to keep the invitations, though—I have a whole drawerful of invitations—weddings, christenings, funerals. A whole drawerful—can you believe that, young man?"

I nodded hastily. I would have agreed with him that black was white that night, if he had required it of me—anything, *anything* that would permit me to get her safely away from this temple of doom.

He fell silent for a moment, wiping away the tears which were falling steadily onto our joined hands . . . no longer his alone, I noted, for Christine, too, was now weeping silently.

"I know it's not good manners to ask, but really I should like to have your invitation very badly . . . for my collection, you know. Handwritten and hand delivered. . . . One can't trust to the post, you see . . . not down here. So, will you do that for me, young man . . . will you swear to bring her back the day before the wedding and deliver that invitation to me? I promise that I shan't keep you long . . . but I believe, on such a day, it would be quite permissible to kiss the bride . . . would it not?"

"Yes," I said faintly. The man was mad and dangerous and must be humored, yet it was not easy to remain unmoved in the face of such barely controlled grief. "Yes . . . I will bring her back . . . the day before. Whatever you wish."

I think he smiled—it was difficult to be sure with such severely deformed lips.

"You will find the lantern in the boat," he continued quietly. "Christine knows the way to the other side."

He stood back and gestured for me to take her. Christine made a movement toward him, but I caught her arm and held her in a furious grip as Erik turned his back on us and began to walk unsteadily toward the Persian.

"My dear friend," he said with a sudden, unmistakable affection that astonished me, "I very much hope you'll do me the honor of taking tea in the drawing room before you leave."

The Persian's reply was too soft for me to hear, but it appeared to be assent, for after a moment the two men went through into another room together and shut the door.

Christine stared at the closed door with disbelief, but this time, when I tugged at her arm, she came with me without any further resistance.

I tried not to notice that she was still crying.

or the next three weeks I was very busy, chasing around Paris making arrangements for a hasty marriage and a passage to England with as much secrecy as I could contrive. I knew it would be quite impossible for us to remain in France. My marriage would be considered a terrible mésalliance, frowned upon by friends and family alike and, with so many doors shut against us, it would be infinitely preferable to go where we were not known. Besides, I could not get out of my mind the idea that it would be as well to put as much distance as possible between Christine and the Opera House, and to me the English Channel seemed the ultimate barrier.

She expressed no comment when I suggested that we should go to England for a while, she showed neither pleasure nor interest in my arrangements. I tried to be patient. She had been through a terrible ordeal and she was still in a state of shock; I could hardly expect her to say, "Thank God that's all over!" and behave as though nothing had happened.

But as the days passed, she appeared to grow more agitated and distressed. The shadows under her eyes became so dark that they assumed the appearance of black bruises, and she took to wearing a hat with a little veil whenever we went out . . . which admittedly wasn't often. Left to herself she was inclined to huddle in front of the fire, staring at the flickering coals and moving the beads of her rosary restlessly through her fingers.

Hail Mary, full of grace, the Lord is with thee.
Blessed art thou amongst women. . . .

That seemed to be as far as she could ever get. Her maid told me she repeated those two lines over and over again, and hearing that, a little snake of fear began to twist and writhe at the back of my mind.

The day before the wedding I arrived with an armful of flowers to find her waiting for me, with a little gilt-edged card in one hand. On the table stood a huge brass key and a small, curiously shaped metal object which I could not place.

"It's time for us to go back," she said.

I looked at the invitation, neatly written in her beautiful copper-plate hand, and something inside me snapped. In that moment I ceased to be the high-born hero of our little melodrama, the perfect gentleman and the adoring lover—all those things which had made me into a weak, gullible young man hopelessly manipulated by infatuation. Giving way to the anger and fear that had been festering inside me for many weeks, I caught her by the shoulders and shook her savagely.

"If you think for one moment that I will take you back there, you must be out of your mind!"

"But you promised." She gasped. "You promised him!"

"Of course I promised. I'd have promised to cut off my leg to get you out of his hands. The man is *insane*, Christine, utterly deranged . . . you must be quite mad yourself to think I ever intended to keep that promise!"

She swayed back from me and sank into the chair beside the fire.

"If you won't take me," she said unsteadily, "I shall go by myself."

Leaning forward, I snatched the invitation from her trembling hand and tore it into half-a-dozen pieces.

"If you go back to him you won't be needing to take this with you!" I said furiously. "If you go back now there won't *be* any wedding. . . . Do you understand what I'm saying, Christine?"

She nodded dumbly, staring down at the scraps of white card which had scattered into the tiled grate.

Without another word I slammed out of the building and got into the carriage that waited outside. I waited five minutes, hoping desperately that she would run after me and beg me to stay; but she did not come out, and when I looked up I could see no sign of her at the window.

Reaching home, I shocked my valet by demanding a decanter of brandy in my room, and once immured there in privacy, I proceeded to get very quickly and ingloriously drunk. I wasn't accustomed to hard drinking of spirits; I suppose in many ways I was still remarkably naive and innocent . . . twenty years old and still a virgin! But I'd never wanted anyone except Christine and I couldn't believe that I would ever want anyone else. At some point during the evening I have a vague memory of smashing my glass in the hearth in an excess of outraged self-pity. But the following morning, waking with a pounding headache and a weary resignation, I knew I had to take her back. I would take her back this one last time and then perhaps it would truly be over and we could begin to live our own life together.

When I arrived at her apartment, that half-witted girl of hers informed me that mademoiselle had gone out the previous evening and not yet returned.

No message had been left for me.

"Monsieur," said the little maid timidly, "I am very much afraid for mademoiselle. . . . She is not herself these days."

"I know," I said absently, turning away, with my hat in my hand. "I must have been crazy to leave her alone in that state."

"Do you perhaps know where she can have gone, monsieur?"

I stared at the pedestrians milling carelessly along the streets, the sight of Paris going cheerful and unconcerned about its business.

"Yes," I said, with grim resignation, "I know where she is."

"A sledgehammer?" gasped my driver in astonishment. "Monsieur, forgive me . . . did you say a sledgehammer?"

"I did."

Sitting back in my carriage I glared at the man, and with evident good sense he decided not to pursue the issue any further. It took him almost two hours, but at length he presented me with my odd request and deposited me, in accordance with my instructions, outside the Opera. I told him to wait till I returned; he had been with my family for many years and I trusted both his loyalty and his discretion.

It was shortly after midday and the *grand escalier* was deserted, but I was such a well-known patron that no one would have thought of questioning my presence on the premises, even had they seen me. I carried my coat over my arm and the sledgehammer was carefully hidden beneath.

I knew only one means of entry to Erik's house and made my way unerringly, along the route that the Persian had shown me, to the stone in the third cellar. Knowing that I would find myself once more in the torture chamber, I came armed to smash my way through the toughened glass structure, only to find that my precaution had been quite unnecessary. The mirrored room was in darkness, the door stood open, and I walked into the chamber beyond without the slightest inconvenience.

I was appalled by the scene of devastation which met my eyes. The room had been wrecked almost beyond all recognition; the black tapestries torn down and cut to shreds, the magnificent pipe organ ripped from the wall and smashed to pieces, the dark red carpet littered with shredded sheets of a musical score. All he valued, everything he must have held dear in those years of solitude, had been mutilated and destroyed in some insane ritual of grief.

Staring at the sad remnants of his blighted existence, I knew a moment of shocked pity. My foot crunched on glass and, bending down, I picked up a double picture frame. In one side was a faded line portrait of an astonishingly good-looking man. The other, covered by its fractured pane of glass, I could not see clearly. . . .

A movement in a room beyond made me stuff the picture frame automatically into my pocket, before turning to meet the inevitable challenge.

Expecting Erik, I found myself facing the Persian.

"Good morning, Monsieur de Chagny," he said calmly, in his heavily accented French, ". . . or perhaps, since I perceive it is now past midday, it would be more correct to say good afternoon."

Returning his chained watch to his breast pocket, he glanced around with a look of quiet despair and finally indicated a black leather couch which appeared to have survived the destruction largely intact.

"Perhaps you would care to be seated," he continued with great civility.

I didn't move. "Where are they?" I demanded. "Where has he taken her?"

Silently the Persian waved one hand in the direction of a closed door that I had not noticed before.

"In there?" As I made a movement to step past him, his hand fell heavily on my arm with all the authority of a policeman's.

"Stay here, monsieur. You have no place in that room now."

I glared at him. "I have every right—"

"You have no rights in this matter," he said steadily. "I have no desire to resort to physical force, but if I must, I will. You shall not enter that room while I am here to prevent it."

A tense silence descended between us as we stared at each other—reluctant enemies suddenly, where bare weeks ago we had been ill-assorted allies. The dark olive skin was puckered and swollen around tired eyes, the mouth drawn and thin as though it had been dragged down at the corners by the weight of untold grief. This stern, upright, elderly Oriental, who had once dragged me with him underground with desperate urgency and barely concealed anger, appeared to have been weeping steadily for many hours. He looked like a broken old man who could bear no more. I could easily have overpowered him, with one hand tied behind my back, and yet I found I had no heart to do it. I wanted to cling to the strength and support that anger afforded me, but I found my anger was already deserting me, dwindling rapidly away, leaving nothing behind in its place except emptiness and fear.

I went and sat on the couch, as I had been bidden, gazing dully at the twisted pipes of the organ and the broken black candles strewn among the upturned pewter candelabra.

"Erik did this?"

The Persian nodded gravely.

"Why?"

"He did not expect her to return. He said that he considered you to be a sensible young man and that quite understandably you would forbid it. . . . In your place, he said, he would have done exactly the same. He wished no trace of his presence to be left on this earth after his death. The chamber beyond, which contains Mademoiselle Daae's possessions, was the only room he could not bring himself to destroy. After his last seizure he permitted me to take him there and lay him upon the bed, saying it was only fitting that he should die in the place where he had been born. He would not allow me to remove the mask."

I looked up. "Is he really dying?"

"I cannot think that mercy will be long denied to him now."

"You think he deserves mercy?" I demanded coldly.

"I do not defend what he has done."

"But you forgive him . . . don't you?"

"Yes," said the Persian softly, turning away to pick up a torn sheet of manuscript, "I forgive him."

We were silent for a while. The Persian gathered up several scraps of manuscript and attempted to piece them together before abandoning the futile effort with a weary shake of his head.

"Twenty years he worked upon this piece, monsieur. I begged him to let me take it away with me, but he said he did not wish it ever to be played in public. It is a tragedy . . . so much genius simply to be wiped from the face of the earth without trace."

"How long has she been with him?"

"Since she arrived last night. She asked that I would leave them alone together. Naturally I have respected her wish."

He turned away so hastily that I knew at once he was hiding something.

"Tell me what you saw before you left them."

"Monsieur—"

"*Tell me!*"

The Persian stared at the floor, as though he could no longer bring himself to look into my eyes.

"She removed the mask and gave it to me, asking me to stand as her witness before God."

He stopped for a moment, as though begging silently to be released from this confession, but I merely waited stonily for him to continue.

"She kissed his forehead, many times, moving slowly and carefully as though she feared to leave some small crevice of skin untouched by her mouth. She kissed each closed lid and followed the tracks of his tears with her lips—"

The Persian broke off abruptly and this time he did not continue, nor did I ask him to. The silence in the room grew oppressive, seemed to consume the very air between us.

"What am I to do?" I asked at last. "What am I to do now?"

The Persian sighed heavily.

"Do what Erik trusted you to do, my friend—take the child and cherish her until death parts you. His greatest fear was that she should be left alone in the world. That was why he sent her away with you, even though he knew she was ready to stay at last. Monsieur, if your love for her is truly as great as his, it will survive this revelation unchanged."

I sat very still beneath the Persian's pitying gaze, listening to the huge clock that seemed to be ticking steadily inside my head, ticking away the optimism of youth along with the last hours of Erik's life. I no longer felt young. Here in this house on the lake I had surely aged a hundred years. Erik had judged me strong enough to live the rest of my life with a ghost . . . perhaps he had overestimated my courage.

Time dragged in the artificial light, and when at last the connecting door clicked softly open and shut some hours later, I hardly dared to raise my head. It was the Persian who got up and guided Christine to my side.

Her eyes, which had been so full of torment these last few weeks, were now serene, almost otherworldly, in their newfound peace. A strange pale-colored cat rested in the crook of her arm and she caressed its smooth fur with an absent hand.

Feeling lost and totally inadequate, I stood up and placed an arm uncertainly around her shoulders. The cat stirred and hissed at me with brief hostility, but Christine did not seem to notice.

I looked at the Persian, suddenly desperate for guidance, but he merely shook his head slightly and pressed my hand with renewed sympathy and friendship.

"Take her home," he said quietly. "I will deal with all that remains to be done here."

And so for the last time I rowed across the leaden waters in that cold subterranean vault. The cat came with us, but I did not question its presence. I knew I had forfeited the right to ask questions.

We had no light except for the dim flicker of a single lantern in the prow, so I cannot be sure, not entirely sure, that my senses did not deceive me. But as her hand moved to soothe the agitated animal, I caught no flash of diamonds in the thin gold band which adorned her wedding finger.

It was dark when we reached the streets outside. The day had died into an early dusk without our knowledge, and as we traveled to her apartment in my waiting carriage, her fingers remained hidden from view.

At any time I could have leaned over and snatched her hand from cover, but I did not do it.

If the ring she wore that night was not mine, I did not want to know about it.

We were not married for another month, at her insistence.

She told me that she wished me to have time to reflect, to consider whether I might not prefer to take my freedom instead.

"I want you to be sure, Raoul, quite sure, that you can forgive me first," she said; and to this new Christine, so oddly calm and determined, suddenly quite frighteningly composed and grown up, I made no murmur of protest.

Four weeks later we made our vows to each other in a private ceremony before a priest. There were no guests, only her maid and my driver present to stand as witnesses.

The following day we took the boat to England.

grew to hate the cat!

I'm quite fond of animals as a rule, but I learned to hate that wretched animal as much as it quite obviously hated me.

For a few weeks, before we went to England, I was reasonably certain it was going to die. It cried inconsolably, quite pitiably I suppose, in a horrible, unearthly wail that reminded me uncomfortably of a demented baby. Refusing to eat, it walked endlessly around Christine's little flat, calling for its dead master. I suggested it would be kinder to have it put down, but the look of horror on Christine's face ensured I never made the mistake of mentioning that particular solution again.

By the time we were due to sail, the creature appeared to have reconciled itself to Christine's care and had taken to following her around with a desperation that I might have found sadly touching, under different circumstances. I found it rather hard to accept that the animal was really a cat. In looks and behavior it reminded me more closely of a monkey—willful, destructive, and curiously possessive. It made no secret of its instinctive dislike for me. If I came too near, the fur along its spine rose ominously, the blue eyes narrowed to hostile slits, and the kinked, whippy tail began to wave warningly from side to side. To this day I am unable to look upon a Siamese cat without a shudder of revulsion.

We had been about two months in England when Christine told me we were to have a child, and I swung her up in my arms, ecstatic with relief to know that at last we were to have something, one small area of our life, that *he* could not touch.

I ordered champagne to celebrate the news, and when Christine and I had touched our glasses together, I bent down to lay my hand upon the cat, which as usual lay curled on her knee with a proprietary air. The sense of warmth and well-being that was surging through me made me determine there and then to make peace with the creature I had privately christened "the little white rat."

"Want to be friends, now?" I offered in conciliatory tones, holding my hand palm down beneath the moist black nose to show that I intended no threat.

The cat bit me! Sank its teeth straight into the bone, just as though it were a wretched dog.

"Oh, Raoul." Christine sighed. "Why don't you just leave her alone? You know she doesn't like strangers."

Blood was streaming down my finger, but I was too intrinsically happy that evening to brood on any hidden meaning that might have been attached to those words. I did not even pause to consider the implications of being called a stranger in my own house—by my own wife!

Christine's pregnancy rapidly became the determining factor which governed my decision to remain in England. From the very beginning there seemed to be one complication following hard on another, and toward the end of the confinement she began to suffer from fits and had to be continually sedated.

For weeks on end the house was swathed in silence. Christine was cared for in a darkened room, by a nurse who wore quiet slippers and an unstarched apron; none of my staff were permitted to converse above whispers on the second floor. The cat howled unheard in the servant's kitchen and it was more than anyone's place was worth to let it escape upstairs. I had been warned that any disturbance—noise, bright lights, or a sudden movement—could be sufficient to precipitate a fit, and the longer the fits endured, the greater the chance of heart and renal failure or cerebral hemorrhage. I sat for hours in that heavily curtained room, dreading the moment when the white face on the pillows would begin to jerk in uncontrolled spasms. She was so deeply drugged with chloral that most of the time she was quite insensible of my presence.

I was crushed with guilt and found my thoughts turning involuntarily toward Erik. I knew that he would have killed me for harming "his child," and whenever a breath of air stirred the dark drapes at the window during the evening, I felt a coldness at the nape of my neck and dared not look around.

The doctor struggled for over a month to stabilize Christine's condition, but then there was a sudden, rapid deterioration which caused him to request an immediate interview in my study. He was a forthright, determined man who put matters very plainly. Christine's condition had become so serious that he considered the only means of saving her life would be through immediate surgery.

"Surgery!" The word knocked at my heart like an echo of doom.

"Cesarean section. A very dangerous operation, Mr. de Chagny, I will not deceive you on that point. However, I think I may say, without fear of correction, that there is no more eminent surgeon in the whole of Europe than Professor Lister of King's. You are very fortunate to be in London at this time, sir. Five years ago Lister's teachings were still not widely accepted in this city. Even our best established surgical consultants continued to pour scorn on his antiseptic procedures. . . ."

The doctor's voice buzzed meaninglessly in my ears; I could not concentrate on his discourse on sepsis. To the best of my knowledge this particular operation was only ever performed as a last-ditch attempt to deliver a living child from a dying mother.

"I won't give my consent," I said dimly. "I won't have her butchered for the sake of a child who cannot possibly survive eight weeks before its time."

The doctor glanced at me in surprise.

"The child will be roughly a month premature, certainly no more than that, I can assure you. With care it should have a reasonable chance of survival. But I have to tell you quite plainly, sir, that without this operation both mother and child will unquestionably die."

The world seemed to have stopped turning slowly on its axis; the only sound in the room was the dull thudding of my heart.

If this man was correct—and he could of course be mistaken, for no doctor is entirely infallible on such matters—then it could not possibly be my child that was slowly killing Christine.

"I want you to be sure first, Raoul, quite sure that you forgive me. . . ."

If I refused consent they would both die. If I gave consent Christine might still die, of course . . . but the child could well live—a child who might not be mine.

There was no question of choice now.

"How soon can you operate?" I said with quiet despair.

The reek of carbolic acid is indelibly associated in my memory with the birth of Charles.

They brought him to me, as soon as he was born, and as I looked down with relief on a small, thin, bluish face that was quite recognizably human, tears blurred my vision. He was so tiny and fragile with his little stick arms and legs . . . surely the doctor had been mistaken after all!

I was told it would be as well to have him baptized immediately, and since Christine was deeply unconscious, the final choice of name lay with me.

I called him Charles. It seemed a very ordinary name.

A week later, when we were reasonably certain that Christine, too, would live, Professor Lister advised me seriously to make sure there were no more children.

"It is, of course, entirely a matter for your own conscience, sir, but I would not be true to mine if I withheld my considered opinion. Your wife's case history, coupled with the possibility of a rupture of scar tissue in a subsequent confinement . . . ." He spread his strong hands expressively. "I'm very sorry, Mr. de Chagny, this is not news I would give lightly to a young husband . . . but at least you have your son."

I stared out the window without replying, and at length, no doubt deciding that my hot French blood forbade common decency and consideration toward a wife, Lister frowned and left me to my own thoughts.

I continued to stare out the window for a long time.

There were ways, of course . . . there had been ways since time immemorial . . . ways that were directly against the teaching of our Church and by no means infallible.

But there was only one way to be sure.

And I did not need to ask what choice Erik would have made under such circumstances.

 took a long lease on a house near the Botanical Gardens, hired one of those formidable creatures known as English nannies, and determined to be cheerful with my lot.

On recovery Christine was gentle and affectionate toward me, always ready to put aside whatever she was doing and devote herself to my interests. But there was a distance in her manner, an intrinsic serenity that always seemed to exclude me from her inner thoughts. And somehow the harder she tried to make me happy, the more quietly certain I became that she had loved Erik far more than she ever loved me.

We were not unhappy together, far from it, in spite of the difficult circumstances under which we were obliged to live. Indeed, among those friends we made in England we were generally held to be a marvelous example, with our outwardly perfect marriage and our unquestionably perfect child.

From an early age it was evident that Charles would be exceptionally musical, and as soon as he began to tinker determinedly with a piano I tried to exclude myself from his life, immuring myself in my study, or behind the safe wall of a newspaper, whenever Nanny brought him downstairs for inspection. I suppose I might have succeeded, as so many English fathers seem to do, had it not been for Charles's equal determination not to be shut out. It was difficult to ignore a child who always welcomed my return with such delight, who consistently flung himself off the sixth stair in the blithe expectation of being caught in my arms, who brought me kites and toy soldiers to be mended, and later begged me to attend his recitals "because there will be so many ladies there." He always tiptoed rather cautiously around Christine's fierce devotion, as though her love were a delicate ornament that he feared to break, and he seemed to enter some unspoken conspiracy with me to spare her all worry and pain.

"Don't tell Mother, will you?" he whispered anxiously, as I held him over a sink ten minutes before that first public recital. I promised not to tell, rubbed his white face with a rough towel until some vestige of color returned to his cheeks, and then suffered agonies for him as he walked through the silent, crowded room to seat himself at that awesomely lonely piano. He looked so very young and vulnerable, and when he caught my eye I gave him a nod of encouragement that made him smile.

Christine's hand was in mine throughout that first performance and at the end, when the entire room got to its feet to applaud, I squeezed her fingers very hard while our eyes shared a knowledge that could never be voiced.

Ironically the very thing which should have driven us apart became the link that soldered us together. I thanked God for Charles many times over and not all my reasons for doing so were particularly noble.

The cat—that *damned* cat!—eventually deserted Christine and become positively devoted to him. It took to sleeping on his bed when he was about two years old, a practice I did absolutely nothing to discourage, in spite of Nanny's indignant protests about fleas.

"It's good for a child to have a pet," I said coolly, when called upon to give a ruling in the matter. Nanny subsided into furious silence and no doubt said a lot of hard things about eccentric Frenchmen in the servants' hall later, but I didn't care unduly.

As long as the animal resided in the nursery, it could not be with my wife, insinuating itself between us like some wretched sentinel.

Besides, it seemed oddly fitting that they should form a little menagerie up on the nursery floor.

They belonged together, in a strange way, did they not?

The cat . . . and the cuckoo . . . in one nest!

It lived to a rare old age, that cat, and finally died, with its customary inconsiderate perversity, sometime in the early morning of Charles's twelfth birthday.

You bloody thing! I found myself thinking uncharitably. *He'd have been back at boarding school tomorrow—couldn't you have waited till then?*

I glanced at Charles, who was devastated, yet manfully trying to govern his tears in front of me.

"I'll get a box," I said grimly.

When I returned, I found that he had removed the animal's exotic collar.

"I expect Mother will want to keep this, won't she?"

"I daresay." *Damn! Damn, damn, damn!*

I watched him wrap the stiff animal tenderly in its blanket and lay it reluctantly in the box.

"It seems wrong, somehow," he murmured softly. "Such a plain, rough box—and no ceremony."

"It's only a cat!" I said, rather more shortly than I had intended. "We can hardly have a full requiem Mass, you know!"

He looked so hurt that I was immediately ashamed of giving way to my ugly resentment.

"Look, Charles, they breed them over here now. We can always get another one, if you really want—"

He turned away in silence, revolted no doubt by my clumsy, insensitive suggestion, and began to finger the jewels on the collar with the sort of reverence that is normally reserved for a rosary.

"These are real diamonds, aren't they, Dad?"

"I believe so," I said stiffly.

"There must be enough to make a pendant necklace," he continued thoughtfully. "May I draw some money from my account and have them made up for Mother?"

I swallowed hard as I hammered the lid on the box with grim finality and rather unnecessary vigor.

"It's your money, Charles," I said quietly. "You don't need to ask my permission how to use it."

We went down to breakfast side by side, having agreed not to break the news to Christine until the following day, when the animal would be safely buried and she could not ask to see it.

She was already seated at the table, waiting for us on this special day. Beside her plate was the single red rose that I always placed there on the anniversary of Charles's birth. I had thought it a romantic touch—a single red rose, the symbol of my unchanging love—but she wept so poignantly the first time I presented her with one that I had considered abandoning the idea there and then.

"If it upsets you—"

"No," she had said hastily, "it doesn't upset me at all, it was a lovely thought, Raoul. It just—just reminded me of a sad legend that I once heard."

"Oh, I see. One of your father's old tales, I suppose."

She looked down at the rose.

"That's right," she said softly, pressing the bloom lightly against her cheek, "one of Father's stories. Perhaps one day I'll tell it to you. . . ."

I hadn't pressed her to tell and assumed the incident had slipped from her mind. At any rate, she never wept again when I gave her a red rose and the practice had slowly become a ritual between us over the years. I knew that she kept the petals long after the flower had faded and died. . . .

Now she looked up and the smile that had been hovering on her lips was extinguished at the sight of Charles.

"My dear . . . your eyes!"

He bent down to kiss her cheek with admirable nonchalance.

"It's nothing," he said carelessly, "too much riding in the wind yesterday, that's all. . . . I say, you don't mind if I have kippers, do you, Mother? It's my last day at home . . . and it is my birthday!"

"Oh, Charles!" she exclaimed, with indulgent, halfhearted protest. "What horribly British tastes that school is breeding in you!"

She sat down again at the table, amused, adoring, and skillfully distracted from a line of questioning that might have proved awkward, watching him pick the tiny bones from that objectionable fish, without the faintest suspicion that anything was wrong.

It must have nearly choked him to swallow that kipper for her sake, but he never hesitated; he ate like a starving schoolboy who has nothing but birthday presents on his mind.

Pouring myself a cup of coffee, I watched him with quiet respect and it crossed my mind, not for the first time, that Erik would have been proud of him.

Charles was away at school when Christine died, four years later.

She had been ill for a long time with a gradual wasting sickness that was eventually diagnosed as cancer, but the end came with an unexpected suddenness that found us quite unprepared.

Stunned and numbed with shock, I unlocked the drawer in the table at the side of her bed and removed the contents, which she had made me promise to bury with her.

The drawer was full of pressed rose petals. It seemed to me that for every red bloom that I had ever given her, she herself must have added a white, and the crisp, dried petals were mingled irretrievably together, giving off a faint, lingering perfume as they crumbled to powder in my hand.

Beneath the petals lay the necklace of diamonds which had once been a cat's collar, its gold clasp nestling inside a wedding ring. Lifting the ring out and examining it, I found it to be a simple gold band that looked as new and unworn as it must have done on the day it was purchased in France all those years ago. It was very small, the same size as the ring I had first bought her, which had had to be cut from her hand as her fingers swelled during her pregnancy.

At the bottom of the drawer was a small piece of paper, evidently cut from the score of an opera which I finally recognized as *Aïda*.

My heart foreseeing your condemnation, into this tomb I made my way by stealth, and here, far from every human gaze, in your arms I wished to die. . . .

With the scrap of paper in my hand I went slowly down to the library and took out Charles's well thumbed copy of *Faust*. I was reasonably certain of the quotation for which I searched, but wanted to be quite sure there was no mistake in the wording. When I found it, I copied it neatly down onto a slip of paper and looked at it for a moment.

Holy Angel, in heaven blessed, my spirit longs with thee to rest.

Returning to the drawing room, where the open coffin lay in the semigloom of a single candelabrum, I placed the wedding ring on her little finger, fastened the necklace around her pale, shriveled throat, and tucked the two quotations into the dazzling satin folds of the lining. Then I scattered the remains of the rose petals all around her.

When it was done I had a strange feeling of peace, as though I had completed the final act of some lifelong quest. I had held her in trust for seventeen years until death chose to reunite her with the one to whom she truly belonged. There was an aching sadness which I knew would never leave me . . . and yet there was also a sense of release, a sudden lifting of guilt.

I myself placed the lid upon the coffin, that no undertaker might be tempted by the fortune in stones which would be laid to rest with her.

It rained heavily during the committal, as it always seems to do on such occasions in England. The fresh white roses were bruised and splashed with mud as the coffin was lowered into that gaping maw in the ground.

Beneath a black umbrella Charles held my arm in a fiercely protective grip, as though he feared I might do something very stupid in my grief. His face was white and tragic, but the eyes that rested on mine were full of compassionate understanding.

I remember that when the service was over, he led me very carefully back to our carriage, just as though I were a blind and crippled man. . . .

The final curtains have been taken, the lights have been lit throughout the auditorium, and people are shuffling from their seats, stretching surreptitiously in their stiff dress suits and high-necked evening gowns. The unseemly rush for cloaks and carriages is about to begin, but I, who have nowhere to hurry to now, continue to sit unmoving in the very armchair where Erik must once have sat to look down on Christine.

Charles leans over and lays his hand on mine. He does not speak, for he knows instinctively that there are times when it is better to say nothing, that sympathy can be more easily expressed in touch than in meaningless words. He waits instead, with a quiet patience quite alien to his age, while I collect myself in slow degrees and prepare to leave box five for the last time. I shall not come here again. The memories are too deeply painful, and yet I do not regret this time of reflection, this cauterizing of an old, unhealed wound.

The crowds on the *grand escalier* have begun to disperse, and I can see Charles looking around with undisguised admiration.

"What a magnificent building!" he says with awe, as we step out into the cool evening air. "I wonder if the men who built it are still alive to marvel at their great achievement."

"Erik has been dead for seventeen years," I hear myself murmur softly.

"Erik? Was he a friend of yours, Dad?"

The flicker of eager interest in his voice makes the corners of my lips lift in a sad, ironic smile.

"Your mother knew him rather better than I."

"Was he an architect?"

"Architect, musician, magician, composer—a genius in very many fields . . . so I was once told."

The interest becomes a faintly puzzled frown.

"I wonder why Mother never spoke of him. It's a pity he died, isn't it? I'd have liked to know him."

"Yes . . ." Our cab draws slowly out into the crowded street, and glancing out, I am afforded a receding view of the Opera's imposing baroque façade. "Yes, my dear boy . . . I rather think that you would."

We are silent for a time, and after what he considers to be a decent interval, Charles begins on the subject I've been half expecting. That dog we knocked down earlier is an ownerless stray . . . can't we take it back to England with us and give it a home? I make some feeble protest about the new importation regulations—six months' detention and isolation at a place provided by the owner—but Charles is wearing his mulish look and I know there's no point in arguing. In his eyes I, too, am really another lost dog now, something to be cared for and coaxed back to happiness. . . . So how can I fault such an open heart?

The Opera House dwindles in the distance until it seems no bigger than a doll's house in the shadows . . . a diminutive lost kingdom shrouded by the thick Parisian mist.

Seventeen years, Erik—too long for bitterness, too long for hate. Your genius was not wiped from this earth without trace, and I have brought him here tonight, like a young pilgrim to a shrine, in final payment of a long-outstanding debt.

I, who shared so unwillingly in your tragedy, now find myself, by some ironic twist of fate, left alone to glory in your triumph. This brilliant, loving boy, who calls me father in his innocence, has taught me so many things I might never have grasped about love. I see the world through his eyes now, I glimpse my appointed place in the grand order of things. Like a weary sparrow I can look with fond pride on the giant I have raised as my own. My feathers have grown sparse and shabby in a difficult quest, but I am warmed and comforted by his presence now. I dread the day when I must lose him to the fame and glory that unquestionably await.

His sons will continue the proud Chagny line and I shall take my

Author's Note

It would not be possible to end this book without gratefully acknowledging the various sources which were of inspiration to me during its writing, from the wonderful musical of Andrew Lloyd Webber right back to the original silent film. In the course of my research I discovered many different phantoms—Lon Chaney, Claude Rains, and Michael Crawford all adding their own interpretations to a character who has intrigued audiences for much of this century. Perhaps the most faithful representation of Leroux's original book is the 1967 full-length cartoon. Unexpectedly moving in its final scenes, this adaptation, like the Lloyd Webber musical, allows the Phantom that crucial moment of sacrifice and redemption which other versions have consistently denied him.

When I came to read the Leroux novel, hoping to learn much more about this extraordinary character, I found that the book opened more questions for me than it actually answered. Why, for instance, did Raoul remain so jealous and uncertain of Christine's affection, even after he knew the truth about Erik's hideous disfigurement? Why did Christine insist on returning to Erik, for days at a time, when Raoul was so desperately eager to take her away from danger? Pity and fear hardly seem adequate explanations for her behavior. Was it possible that Raoul was nearer to the truth than he suspected in his angry assertion that Christine's terror of the Phantom was "love of the most secret with me to the grave without resentment . . . almost without regret.

The cuckoo, you see . . .
The cuckoo is a beautiful bird!

exquisite kind, the kind which people do not admit even to themselves"?

One of the most interesting characters I came across in Leroux was
the mysterious Persian, for he, too, posed a number of interesting
questions. Why did he risk his own neck to save the life of a man he
knew to be a shameless murderer? Again, Leroux's explanation, that
"Erik had shown him some slight services and procured him many a
hearty laugh," hardly seems an adequate explanation for putting one's
own life at risk. The pity and tolerance of the Persian seemed to me to
hint at a deep and abiding friendship, a friendship that Leroux, constrained by the genre of his "mystery/thriller," did not have the opportunity to explore.

The little black book began to live on my bedside table and I returned again and again to those passages which intrigued and puzzled
me. Increasingly I found my attention drawn to the final three pages,
to the brief historical outline in which Leroux accounts for the Phantom's earlier existence. The main bulk of his novel—indeed all screen
and stage versions—had dealt only with the last six months or so in
the life of a man who must have been about fifty. I began to feel that
the tale we had come to know as *The Phantom of the Opera* was
perhaps only the magnificent tip of the iceberg, and that somewhere
beneath a huge, human story lay waiting to be told—the story of a
man who was driven to many terrible vices and yet still retained, in
Leroux's own words, "a heart that could have held the empire of the
world." The eventful and exciting past at which Leroux had hinted
must surely have been filled with a number of significant relationships
. . . perhaps even an earlier love affair. This was the story I wanted to
read, and eventually I began to understand that it was also the story I
wanted to write.

I embarked on the project with many deep reservations. No author
can tamper with a well-known classic tale—and particularly one which
has been so successful in different mediums—without an uneasy feeling of presumption. And I was well aware that to set the Phantom in
the historical background which Leroux had envisaged for him would
require research on a very wide scale . . . a knowledge of music,
voice training, ventriloquism, magic, Gypsy lore, architecture, and

stonemasonry, not to mention the historical and cultural background of four different countries.

Eighteen months later the book was finished. It had taken me to Rome and America in the quest for material, but after the early days of initial frustration the research resolved itself in a number of remarkably lucky finds. Munro Butler Johnson's *A Trip up the Volga to the Fair of Nijni-Novgorod* provided valuable details for Erik's life in Russia. Curzon's *Persia and the Persian Question* and Lady Sheil's eyewitness account of Persian court life in the mid-nineteenth century enabled me to slide Erik into the affairs of the existing shah and his grand vazir, Mirza Taqui Khan. Christopher Mead's thesis on Charles Garnier and the building of the Paris Opera was eventually located in America—the only definitive English-language work which presently exists on the architect and his remarkable building.

The Phantom who has emerged in the course of this book owes something to all the many different interpretations of the character that have been made during the last few decades, and a vast amount, of course, to his original creator; but inevitably he has been altered and molded to fit the contours of my own imagination. There is a curious, timeless fascination to this legendary character and I have no doubt that the process of reinterpretation will continue over decades to come.

SUSAN KAY
November 1989